Karen Rose was born in Maryland and was introduced to suspense and horror at the tender age of eight when she accidentally read Poe's *The Pit and the Pendulum*.

After marrying her childhood sweetheart, Karen worked as a chemical engineer (she holds two patents) and a teacher, before taking up a full-time writing career when the characters in her head refused to be silenced. Now Karen is more than happy to share space in her head with her characters and her writing has been rewarded with a series of bestsellers in the UK, the US and beyond.

Karen now lives in sunny Florida with her family.

Praise for *You Belong to Me*:

'[Karen Rose's] glossy blend of romance and crime is completely compelling . . . another enjoyable and page-turning novel from the queen of romantic suspense' *Crime and Publishing*

'Fast and furious' *Sun*

Praise for *Watch Your Back*:

'Tense, compelling and I couldn't put it down until I finished it' *Daily Record (Glasgow)*

'Slash and cut crime at its sharpest' *Northern Echo*

Praise for *Did You Miss Me?*:

'She's up there with James Patterson and Nora Roberts when it comes to sweaty-palm suspense and a twist with a sting in the tail' *Peterborough Telegraph*

'A brilliant book' *Essentials*

Praise for *No One Left to Tell*:

'Rose's rich cast of characters and intricate plot layers give the story real punch. Hang on tight and remember to breathe!' *RT Book Reviews*

'Every page is action-packed' *www.theallureofbooks.com*

Praise for *Silent Scream*:

'A high-octane thrill ride that kept me on the edge of my seat and up far too late at night!' Lisa Jackson

'Rose packs action into every moment . . . Thriller fans will love the high-adrenaline story and robust cast of intriguing supporting characters' *Publishers Weekly*

Praise for *I Can See You*:

'A terrific whodunit' Harriet Klausner

'Rose keeps the action popping' *Publishers Weekly*

Praise for *Kill For Me*:

'Rose has never disappointed with her books and this newest, *Kill For Me*, is her scariest and best book to date' *www.iloveamysterynewsletter.com*

'Rose juggles a large cast, a huge body count and a complex plot with terrifying ease' *Publishers Weekly*

Praise for *Scream For Me*:

'From the first rousing chapter to the last, *Scream For Me* is intense, complex and unforgettable' James Patterson

'Word is spreading about quite how good [Rose] is' *The Bookseller*

Praise for *Die For Me*:

'A blend of hard-edged police procedural and romance – engaging' *Irish Independent*

'Chilling thriller with page-turning passion' *Asda Magazine*

Praise for *Count to Ten*:

'Takes off like a house afire. There's action and chills galore in this nonstop thriller' Tess Gerritsen

'Gripping, chilling and utterly compelling, Karen Rose is a classy storyteller' *Lancashire Evening Post*

Karen ROSE

you belong to me

headline

First published in 2011 by
HEADLINE PUBLISHING GROUP

First published in paperback in 2011 by
HEADLINE PUBLISHING GROUP

This edition first published in paperback in 2015 by
HEADLINE PUBLISHING GROUP

7

Cataloguing in Publication Data is available from the British Library

ISBN 978 0 7553 7392 5

Typeset in Palatino by Avon DataSet Ltd, Bidford-on-Avon, Warwickshire

Printed and bound in Great Britain by Clays Ltd, St Ives plc

Headline's policy is to use papers that are natural, renewable and recyclable
products and made from wood grown in well-managed forests and other
controlled sources. The logging and manufacturing processes are expected to
conform to the environmental regulations of the country of origin.

HEADLINE PUBLISHING GROUP
An Hachette UK Company
Carmelite House
50 Victoria Embankment
London EC4Y 0DZ

www.headline.co.uk
www.hachette.co.uk

In loving memory of A. C. Barrett, who taught me binary when I was seven, gave me my first Poe story when I was eight, and taught me to box using a Hoppity Donald Duck so that I could defend myself against schoolyard bullies when I was nine.

He employed creative means to help me master parallel parking so that I could get my driver's license. He retyped my final university paper from my handwritten draft when my computer crashed the night before it was due, so that I could get a much-needed night's sleep and my degree, and only scolded me a little for not having my files backed up.

He made sure nobody ever told me that I couldn't do anything I set my mind to.

Most of all, he always loved me, every day, every year. I miss you, Dad.

And to Martin, my rock.

Acknowledgments

Marc Conterato, for all things medical. And for everything else.

Danny Agan, for answering all my law enforcement questions.

Frank Ahearn, for the wealth of information on skip tracers and the art of making someone disappear.

Laura Cifelli, Vicki Mellor, and Robin Rue, for your constant support.

Kay Conterato, Terri Bolyard, Sonie Lasker, and Cheryl Wilson – I love you guys.

As always, all mistakes are my own.

Prologue

'Excuse me, sir, you can't go up there.'

Malcolm Edwards ignored the marina manager's deep voice, his eyes fixed on his destination, his weakened body already aching. The *Carrie On* beckoned, rocking as the Chesapeake Bay churned. A storm was coming. It was a perfect day to die.

Just a few more steps, then I can rest. Then the dock began to rumble beneath his feet as Daryl charged up from behind.

'Hey! Stop right there. This is private property. Hey, buddy! I said—'

Malcolm winced as a beefy hand grabbed his upper arm and spun him around. For a moment he looked into Daryl's face, waiting silently as recognition flickered and the man's mouth dropped open in shock.

'Mr Edwards.' Daryl took a step back, his ruddy cheeks gone pale. 'I'm sorry, sir.'

'It's all right,' Malcolm said gently. 'I know I don't look like myself.'

He knew what he looked like. He was surprised Daryl had recognized him at all, despite the years they'd known each other. Malcolm doubted many of his so-called friends would recognize him, not that they'd given themselves the opportunity. Only Carrie had stood by him, and there were times Malcolm wished she had not. In sickness and in health. This was definitely the former.

1

She thought he couldn't hear her sobs in the shower, but he did. He'd give all he owned not to put her through such hell. But man didn't get to make those calls. That was God's territory. Carrie had cursed God as she'd watched Malcolm waste away, but Malcolm didn't have that luxury. He already had enough black marks on his soul.

Daryl swallowed hard. 'Can I get you anything? Help you in any way?'

'No. I'll be fine. I'm going fishing.' He held up a bucket of bait he'd bought for appearances. 'I just want to feel the wind in my face.' *One last time*, he added to himself. He turned toward his boat, determinedly putting one foot in front of the other. The dock rumbled again as Daryl walked beside him, clearly hesitant to speak his mind.

'Sir, there's a squall comin' in. Maybe you should wait.'

'I don't have time to wait.' Truer words were never spoken.

Daryl winced. 'I can get a crew to take you out. My grandson is a fine sailor.'

'I appreciate it, I truly do, but sometimes a man just wants to be alone. You take care, and thank you.' He made it on board, his body sagging as his hands closed over the wheel. It had been far too long since he'd spent a day on the Bay. But he'd been busy. There'd been doctors and treatments and . . . He looked up at the forbidding sky.

And making things right. He'd had too many things to make right, especially the one thing that had burdened his mind for twenty-one years.

He thought about the letter he'd sent and hoped it wasn't too late. He hoped he could handle the wheel long enough to get far enough out to do what needed to be done. He hoped drowning really was just like going to sleep.

The water grew choppier, the wind more brutal the farther out he got. Finally he killed the throttle and listened to the waves, his eyes closed. He drew the salty air deep into his lungs, savoring this, his final day. Carrie would be sad, but part of her would be relieved. She'd put on a brave face that morning when he kissed her good-bye. He'd told her he was going fishing after his doctor's appointment.

When the authorities knocked on her door to give her the bad news, she'd swear that her husband could never have taken his own life, but deep down she'd know the truth.

He stepped onto the deck, setting up his fishing poles. There were appearances to be kept up in case someone found his boat intact after he was 'swept overboard' by a rogue wave. He was baiting a hook when a harsh voice broke into his thoughts.

'Who are the others?'

Malcolm spun around, the bait sliding through his fingers. A man stood a yard behind him, feet planted firmly, arms crossed over his chest. There was hate in his narrowed eyes and Malcolm felt fear shiver down his spine. 'Who are you?'

The man took a steady step forward despite the rocking. 'Who are the others?'

The others. 'I don't know what you're talking about,' he lied.

The man pulled a letter from his pocket and Malcolm's stomach roiled, recognizing both the letter and the handwriting as his own. Malcolm thought back twenty-one years and thought he knew who the man was. He definitely knew what the man wanted.

'Who are the others?' the man asked once again, carefully spacing each word.

Malcolm shook his head. 'No. I'm not going to tell you.'

The man reached into his other pocket and pulled out a long filleting knife. He held it up, examining the sharp edge. 'I'll kill you,' he said, with little emotion.

'I don't care. I'm going to die anyway. Or had you not noticed?'

The boat pitched and Malcolm stumbled, but the man stood firm. *He's got sea legs.* If he was who Malcolm thought he was, that made sense. The man's father had been a fisherman back then.

In the years since, businesses had been lost, lives splintered. Ruined. *Because of what we did. What I did. He'll kill me. And I'd deserve it.* But he had no intention of divulging the others' identities, nor a wish to die horribly. He lunged toward the side.

But the man was fast, grabbing Malcolm's arm and shoving him into a deckchair, binding his hands and feet with a length of twine he pulled from his back pocket. He'd come prepared.

3

I'm going to die.

The man rose, threateningly. 'Who are the others?'

His heart pounding, Malcolm stared up at the man he'd wronged. And said nothing.

The man shrugged. 'You'll tell. If I had more time, I'd do everything to you that you did to her.' He met Malcolm's eyes. 'Everything.'

Malcolm swallowed as he remembered everything that had been done that night, so long ago. 'I'm sorry. I said I was sorry. But *I* didn't do anything to her. I swear it.'

'Yeah,' the man said bitterly. 'I got that from your letter. And when you finally confessed, you were too much of a coward to sign your name.'

It was true. He'd been a coward then, and now. 'How did you know it was me?'

'I figured it was one of you. You all ran together then. You all signed that team picture.'

Malcolm closed his eyes, seeing it. They'd been young and so damn arrogant. They thought they had the world by the tail. 'The one in the trophy case at the high school.'

He sneered. 'The very one. Your handwriting hasn't changed much in twenty-one years. You still make your M's the same way. It didn't take a genius to track that letter to you. Which brings me back to the reason for my dropping by. You will tell me what I want to know.'

'I won't. Like I said in the letter, that's between them and God. So no. I'm sorry.'

The man's sneer became a sinister smile. 'We'll see about that.'

He disappeared below deck, and Malcolm pulled at his bonds, knowing it was futile. His mind was flashing pictures, all the sick, disgusting things that had been done to the girl that night so long ago, as he'd stood and watched. And done nothing.

I should have done something. I should have made it stop. But he had not, and neither had the others. Now he'd pay the price. *Finally.*

He heard the thumping of something being dragged up from the hold. It was a woman. Malcolm's gut turned to water. She was wearing a sweater exactly like the one he'd committed to memory

4

just hours ago. When he'd kissed his wife good-bye.

'*Carrie*.' Malcolm tried to stand, but could not. She'd been bound, blindfolded and gagged, and the man was dragging her by her arm. 'Let her go. She did nothing.'

'Neither did you,' he said mockingly. 'You said so yourself.' He shoved Carrie into a chair and held the knife to her throat. 'Now tell me, Malcolm. Who. Are. The. Others?'

Desperately Malcolm glanced at the man's narrowed eyes before returning his own to the knife at his wife's neck. He couldn't breathe. Couldn't think. 'I don't remember.'

A drop of blood ran down Carrie's throat as the knife nicked. 'Don't you dare lie to me,' the man said quietly. 'If you know who I am, you know I have nothing to lose.'

Malcolm closed his eyes. He couldn't think when he was looking at her. He was too scared. 'Okay. But take her back to shore, first. Otherwise, I won't tell you.'

Carrie's scream of pain was muffled by the gag in her mouth. Malcolm's eyes opened and he stared, horrified. Then he retched, violently. He couldn't look back, couldn't look at the finger the man held out for his inspection.

Severed. *He'd cut off her finger*. 'I'll tell you,' he rasped. 'Dammit, I'll tell you.'

'I thought you might.' The man stepped away from Carrie and she tucked herself into as small a space as her bonds would allow, whimpering. From his front pocket the man pulled a notepad and pen. 'I'm ready when you are.'

Quickly Malcolm spat the names, hating himself for it. For all of it. For staying that night, for watching. For writing the letter and endangering his wife. The man showed no emotion as he wrote the names, then pocketed his notepad.

'I've told you,' Malcolm said, his voice cracking. 'Now take her back. Let me get her a doctor. Please, put her finger in some ice. Please. I beg you.'

The man studied the knife, red with Carrie's blood. 'Did she say that?'

'*Who?*'

The man's jaw cocked. 'My *sister*. Did she beg?' He grabbed Carrie's hair and yanked her head back. He held the knife to her exposed throat. 'Did she?'

'Yes.' Malcolm's body shook with sobs. 'Please. I'm begging you. My wife did nothing. Please. I gave you what you wanted. Please don't hurt her any more.'

The man's arm jerked, the knife sliced, and Malcolm screamed as blood spurted from her body. *No. No. No. Please God, no.* She was dead. Carrie was dead.

Callously, the man cut through the twine with which he'd bound her and her body landed at Malcolm's feet. 'I should leave you here to watch the birds eat her flesh,' the man muttered. 'But someone might find you before you died, then you'd tell on me. I could cut your tongue out, but you'd still find a way to tell. So you have to die too.' He lifted Malcolm's chin, forcing him to look up. 'I'll cut your tongue out anyway. Any last words?'

Standing naked on deck, he watched as the last of his clothes sank below the gray water, following the path Malcolm and his wife had taken. They'd be chum by nightfall.

The worst of the storm had passed as he'd dealt with the disposal of the bodies. There had been a lot of blood. Luckily he'd brought a change of clothes. He'd shower off the Edwards' blood before sailing the *Carrie On* to a private marina whose owner would be asking no questions. There he could hose the blood off the deck and remove any markers identifying the boat as Malcolm Edwards'.

Going below, he paused at the galley counter, where he'd put the notepad for safekeeping. He couldn't risk getting it covered in blood. Not like he needed the list anyway. The names were already etched in his mind.

Some he'd expected. A few were surprises.

All would wish they'd done the right thing twenty-one years ago.

One

Zz Top growling in her ears, Lucy Trask sang along as she jogged the path that cut through the park behind her apartment, not caring that she was hopelessly off key. Gwyn was their singer, after all. Nobody cared what Lucy's voice sounded like, only how her bow sang. Besides, nobody was around to hear her this morning except other runners, and they had earphones just like she did.

This time of the morning there was no one she needed to impress, nobody whose opinion she needed to worry about. It was one of the many reasons she loved the hour before dawn.

She rounded the curve at the end of the path and slowed to a stop, her serenity suddenly gone. 'Oh, no,' she murmured sadly. 'Not again.' It was Mr Pugh, sitting at one of the chess tables, his tweed hat illuminated by the street lamp behind him.

She detoured off the path, jogging to the green where her old friend had spent so many hours checkmating all challengers. Those days were long gone. Now he sat alone in the night, his head down, the collar of his coat pulled up around his face.

She sighed. He'd wandered out of his apartment, again. She slowed her pace as she drew close, approaching quietly. 'Mr Pugh?' She touched his shoulder gently, taking care not to startle him. He didn't like to be startled. 'It's time to go home.'

Then she frowned. Normally he'd look up, that lost expression in his eyes, and she'd take him back to Barb who was so weary from caring for him all the time. Tonight he didn't look up. He was

7

still. So very still. Her heart sank. *Oh no. No, no, no.*

She reached to press her fingers to his neck, then covered her mouth to muffle a scream when his body slumped over the table, his hat tumbling off his head. For a moment she could only stare in horror. His head was misshapen, caked with dried blood. And his face . . . She stumbled backward. Bile burned her throat.

Oh God. Oh God. His face was gone. So were his eyes.

She took another step back, blindly. 'No.' She vaguely heard a whimper, realized it was her own. Her breath hitched in her lungs and she forced herself to breathe.

Do something. Her hands shaking, she found her cell in the pocket of her shorts and managed to dial 911, flinching when a crisp voice answered.

'This is 911. What is the nature of your emergency?'

'This is . . .' Lucy's voice broke as she stared at the remains. She closed her eyes. *Not remains. It's Mr Pugh. Somebody killed him. Oh God. Oh God.*

'This is . . .' She couldn't speak. Couldn't breathe.

'Miss?' the operator repeated urgently. 'What is the nature of your emergency?'

Sternly Lucy cleared her throat. Called on years of training. Forced her voice to steady. 'This is Dr Trask from the Medical Examiner's office. I need to report a murder.'

Monday, May 3, 6.00 A.M.

Detective JD Fitzpatrick studied the small crowd gathered behind the yellow tape. Neighbors, he thought. Some still wore bathrobes and slippers. Some were old, some middle-aged. Some cried. Some swore. Some did both.

He ventured close enough to listen in as he approached the crime scene. This was the time to listen, when shock had their tongues loose.

'What kind of animal could do that to a helpless old man?' one of the younger women was demanding furiously, her hands clenched into fists.

'He never hurt anyone,' the man next to her said in a bewildered tone.

'Goddamn gangs,' an old man muttered to no one at all. 'Not safe to leave your house any more.'

JD noted the well-maintained grass of the small community park. There was no evidence of gang presence here, but he'd seen it clearly enough on the drive in. This had been a pocket of safety for these residents. A sanctuary that the ugliness outside hadn't yet touched. An illusion, he knew. Ugliness was everywhere.

Now the dead man's neighbors knew it too. It didn't take a gang to do a murder. One perp was enough, especially if the victim was elderly and vulnerable.

'This is going to kill Barb,' an old woman cried brokenly, leaning against another old man. 'How many times did I tell her to put him in a home? How many times?'

'I know, honey,' the man murmured. He cradled her gray head against his shoulder, shielding her eyes from the scene. 'At least Lucy's here.'

The old woman nodded, sniffling. 'She'll know what to do.'

Barb was probably the wife or daughter of the dead man, but JD wondered who Lucy was and what it was that she'd know to do.

Two uniformed officers stood inside the yellow crime-scene tape, shoulder to shoulder. One faced the neighbors, the other the crime scene. Together they were a barrier, blocking the view of the victim as best they could.

CSU was already here, snapping photographs and processing the scene. Between the cops and CSU, nobody in the waiting crowd could see much of anything now, but JD knew that many of them had seen enough before the scene had been secured.

The two uniforms pointed to a third cop standing next to Drew Peterson, the leader of the CSU team. The cop was Hopper, JD was informed. The first responder.

'Thanks.' JD stepped around the two uniforms, steeled for what he'd see. Still he fought a grimace. The victim sat in a chair fixed to the pavement, his body sprawled over a park chess table, his head and face beaten so severely that he was unrecognizable. *Who would do that to an old man? Why?*

The victim wore a beige trench coat, buttoned to his neck, belted around the waist. His hands were shoved in his pockets. There didn't appear to be any blood on his coat or around the chair. The only blood visible was dried on the victim's face and scalp.

Officer Hopper approached, a grim determination in his steps. 'I'm Hopper.'

'Fitzpatrick, Homicide.' After three weeks on the unit, the words still felt strange in JD's mouth. 'You were first on?' he asked and the officer nodded.

'This is my beat. The victim is Jerry Pugh. Sixty-eight-year-old Caucasian male.'

'So you knew him. I'm sorry,' JD murmured.

Hopper nodded again. 'Me too. Jerry was harmless. Sick.'

'He had dementia?' JD asked and Hopper's eyes narrowed in surprise.

'Yes. How did you know?'

'The lady on the front row said she told Barb to put him in a home.'

'That's Mrs Korbel. And I imagine she did. So did I. But Mrs Pugh – that's Barb – wouldn't do it. Couldn't do it, I guess. They'd been married forever.'

'Who found the body?'

Again Hopper looked surprised. 'She did.' He pointed to the other side of the crime scene where a woman stood alone, watching. She stood with her arms crossed over her chest, her expression unreadable. But there was a fragility to her, a palpable tension, as if she was barely holding on.

She was tall, five nine or ten. The long hair she'd pulled back in a simple ponytail was a reddish gold that flickered under the bright CSU lights, like little licks of fire. She was very pretty, her features so classically fine that her face could have graced a statue. Or perhaps it was because she stood so motionlessly that he thought so.

She wore a windbreaker, running shorts and a pair of hi-tech running shoes. That she'd been allowed proximity to the scene suggested she was more than a simple bystander, but he'd never seen her before. That face he'd remember.

Those legs he'd certainly remember.

'Who is—?' he started to ask, then she turned and met his eyes.

And in a flash of painful memory, JD knew exactly who she was. 'Dr Trask,' he said quietly. Lucy Trask, the ME. *Lucy will know what to do.* 'She found him?'

'Just before dawn,' Hopper said. 'The doc . . . well, she's a nice lady, that's all.'

JD found he had to clear his throat. 'I know. Where is Mrs Pugh?'

'My partner Rico went to find her. He got no answer when he knocked on their apartment door. The super was waiting with the key. By then the whole building was out here. Everybody but Mrs Pugh. Rico searched the apartment, but no sign of the missus. Her car's not in the parking lot.'

'No sign of foul play in the apartment?'

'No. Rico says it looks like she left. There were a couple extra bowls of cat food on the kitchen floor, and all the kitchen appliances were unplugged. The super's getting emergency contact info off the rental agreement now.'

JD had been listening to Hopper, but hadn't taken his gaze off Dr Lucy Trask. She'd looked away, but not before he'd seen the devastated grief in her eyes.

He looked back at Hopper. 'Get Rico on the radio. Tell him not to call the emergency contact. Give the info to me. I don't want anyone else informing the wife.'

Hopper frowned. 'Barb Pugh isn't involved. She's almost seventy.'

'I hear you.' It was unlikely that an old woman could produce that kind of damage. 'But I have to proceed like she is involved until I know differently.'

Hopper's frown lessened slightly. 'All right. I'll get Rico on the radio.'

'Thank you.' JD crouched next to the victim, studying him up close. Someone had done a real job on Mr Jerry Pugh. The weapon

11

used had been blunt and hard. The attack had been relentless. Every feature of the man's face had been crushed.

Rage, he thought. Or maybe a drug-induced frenzy. He'd certainly seen enough of that in Narcotics. This was no garden-variety mugging. Someone had totally lost it.

CSU's Drew Peterson crouched beside him. 'Hey, JD. You got here fast. You finally sell your place way out in the burbs?'

JD and Drew had been assigned to the same precinct right out of the Academy, but they hadn't seen much of each other since Maya died. JD hadn't seen much of anyone since then. His assignment in the Narcotics division had mercifully swallowed him up. But this move to Homicide was a clean break. A fresh start. And as much as he pitied the poor old man slumped over the chess table, JD was looking forward to the change.

'Not even a nibble.' After a frustrating year on the market, JD was about to give up trying to sell the house he'd once shared with his wife. 'You find anything?'

'Not a lot so far. We just finished taking pictures. The ME has to do their thing, then we'll get started. Where's Stevie?'

'On her way.' As soon as she lined up someone to watch her little girl. JD's partner Stevie Mazzetti normally had all her bases covered when they were on call, but her childcare backups had backfired today. He didn't mind covering for Stevie. Her need for being covered was rare. She was a good cop. And JD owed her a lot.

JD pointed to the grass around the chess table. 'He wasn't killed here. No blood on the grass or on the beige overcoat. Any idea how he got here?'

'My best guess, by wheelchair. I found tracks in the grass. We'll take impressions if we can. Chair's gone, though. Whoever dumped him here took it with them.'

'No tire tracks from the path to this table,' JD said. 'He was dragged or carried, which would have left somebody pushing an empty wheelchair from the scene. If he was dragged, he might have grass on his shoes.'

'If he does, it's stuck to the soles. Did you see his shoes?' Drew asked.

JD leaned to see beneath the chess table. The victim's wingtips were new and had been shined recently. 'No scuffing. Doesn't look like he was dragged.'

'Do you know how much those shoes cost?'

'A lot.' The shoes appeared to be very expensive. Maybe even custom-made. JD looked over his shoulder at the apartment building. It wasn't low-rent, but it certainly wasn't the Ritz. 'I guess what he saved on rent, he spent on shoes. I wonder what Mr Pugh did for a living, before the dementia.'

'The doc will know,' Drew said. 'She lives in the building too.'

'She knew him personally?' he asked, and Drew nodded again. That explained both her grief and why she was running here, in this particular park. She still stood motionless, staring at the body, and sympathy tugged at his heart. 'That had to have been a huge shock. She's not going to do the exam, is she?'

'No. She called for techs and a rig. She appears to be holding it together.'

'But not by much,' JD murmured. 'I'm going to interview Dr Trask, then see if we can find the vic's wife and any witnesses. Call me over if you find something.'

'Will do.'

Lucy Trask straightened when she saw him coming. Her eyes were dry, but her face was very pale. She fixed her gaze on the dead man in the chair, not glancing up.

'Dr Trask? I'm Detective Fitzpatrick.'

'I know,' she said tonelessly. 'You're Mazzetti's new partner. Where is Stevie?'

'On her way. Can I ask you a few questions?'

'Of course.' She spoke, but her lips barely moved.

'Why don't we go sit in my car? You'll be more comfortable there.'

Her jaw tightened. 'No. I'll stay here. Please, just ask your questions, Detective.'

There was a thread of desperate fury in her voice. She had the smallest trace of an accent. It wasn't quite Southern, but she wasn't from the city. At least not originally. 'Okay. You knew the victim?'

13

She jerked a nod, but said nothing.

'I'm sorry, Dr Trask. I know this is beyond difficult. You found him?' he asked and she nodded again. 'When?'

'At about five-thirty. I was running. I saw Mr Pugh in his chair.' She recited the words, as if giving a report. 'I thought he'd wandered away from his apartment again.'

'Because he had dementia,' JD said and her glance swung up to his. Her eyes were a clear, piercing blue, not easily forgotten. At the moment they churned turbulently with grief and anger and shock, but he knew they were capable of great warmth and compassion. He'd remembered her eyes for a long time after the day he'd first seen her. The only time he'd seen her.

And he'd only seen her eyes. The rest of her had been masked and gowned. He hadn't seen her face, but he'd never forgotten her eyes.

'Mr Pugh had Alzheimer's disease,' she confirmed.

'How often did he wander away from home?'

Her shoulders sagged wearily. 'Recently, three or four times a week. Barb has to sleep sometime. When he wandered off at night, I was usually the one to find him.'

'And you would take him home?'

'Yes.' She said it so quietly he barely heard the word.

'He would go willingly with you?'

'Yes. He wasn't violent.'

'Some Alzheimer's patients are,' JD noted.

Her chin lifted a fraction. 'Some are. He wasn't. We were able to calm him.'

She had more than known the victim, JD realized. They'd been close. 'You were out early this morning.'

'Yes. I always run before dawn.'

'Did you see the victim sitting there when you started your run?'

She looked angry. 'No. If I had, I would have taken him home right then.'

'So he wasn't there when you started your run?'

Her eyes flickered, as if now understanding his question. 'Oh. No. He might have been, but I wouldn't have seen him. I start from the other side of the building and run the perimeter of the neighborhood before cutting back through the park on my way back.'

'Did you see anyone else?'

'Only the other runners. I don't know any of their names. Officer Hopper might.' She looked toward her building. 'Where is Officer Rico? He went to check on Barb.'

'It looks like she's gone.'

Trask's gaze shot up to him, wild panic in her eyes this time. One slender hand grabbed his arm in a vise-like grip. 'Gone where? Gone dead?' she demanded and he immediately regretted the words he'd chosen.

'No, no,' he soothed, covering her hand with his. Her skin was like ice. He pulled her fingers from his sleeve and sandwiched her hand between his palms, rubbing them to warm her. 'It appears she left. The apartment is empty and her car isn't in the lot.'

Panic became disbelief and she stood there, her hand motionless between his. 'No. Barb would never leave him alone like that.'

'But she is gone.'

Jerking her hand free, she took a step back, the remaining color draining from her face. 'No. Absolutely not. She would not leave him of her own free will. Somebody must have taken her. Oh, my God.'

'She unplugged all the kitchen appliances,' JD said and watched as his words penetrated her disbelief. 'Did she do that when she traveled?'

Trask nodded, numbly. 'Yes. But I won't believe she left him alone. She was devoted to him.'

'Sometimes people under stress do things they wouldn't normally do,' JD said carefully. 'Caring for a spouse with Alz—'

'*No*,' she interrupted, fury giving her voice authority. 'No. For God's sake, Detective, Mr Pugh couldn't even dress himself. He couldn't even tie his . . .' She faltered suddenly, her brows furrowing.

JD leaned in closer when she didn't finish the sentence. 'Tie his what?'

But she was already moving toward the body. 'His shoes,' she said over her shoulder. 'He's wearing shoes with laces.'

JD hurried after her, ready to pull her back if she got too close, but she stopped, crouching where he had minutes before. Something had clicked and she was no longer numb. Now there was an energy around her. The air all but hummed.

Fascinated, he crouched beside her, staring at her profile as she stared at the victim's feet. Color had returned to her face, her cheeks pinking up before his eyes.

No, he could never have forgotten her face.

'Mr Pugh hasn't worn regular shoes in five years,' she murmured, dragging his attention back to the dead man in the chair. 'He wears an orthopedic shoe with Velcro. Barb's fingers were too stiff to tie his laces.'

'Maybe he had two pairs,' JD said, but she shook her head.

'These are Ferragamos. Mr Pugh never had that kind of money, and if he had, he wouldn't have spent it on shoes.'

'What did he do for a living? I mean . . . before the Alzheimer's?'

She glanced up at him, her eyes sharp. Alert. And relieved. 'He was a high-school music teacher who bought his shoes from J.C. Penney's. This is not Jerry Pugh.'

She sounded utterly certain. 'What makes you so sure?' he asked.

'These shoes are the wrong size,' she said. 'These are size ten. Mr Pugh wore size twelve.' She closed her eyes, pursing lips that trembled. 'Oh, God. Oh, God. Wears. *Wears* a size twelve. He's still alive. This isn't him. *This isn't him.*'

'Are you all right, Dr Trask?'

She nodded, trembling, her hands clenched into fists. 'I'm fine.'

He wasn't sure about that, but hoped she'd know if she were about to faint. 'How do you know Mr Pugh's shoe size?' he asked, unconvinced.

'I see a lot of feet in my business, Detective. I know my sizes.'

He pictured the bodies in the cold room at the morgue, with just their feet sticking from beneath the sheet, tags on the toes. 'I guess you do. But how do you know *his*?'

She moved her shoulders a little uncomfortably as she stared at the victim's battered face. 'In February I found Mr Pugh sitting right here, in his chair. He'd left the house without his shoes and his feet

16

were almost frozen. I called 911, massaged his feet and covered them with my coat. I know what size his feet are. This man's are too small. This man is not Mr Pugh.'

'That was very kind of you, massaging the feet of an old man,' he murmured.

'It was what anyone would have done.'

He doubted that. 'You call him "Mr Pugh", but you call her "Barb". Why?'

That took her aback, he could see. She hesitated. 'Old habits die hard, I guess,' she finally said. 'I didn't realize I did that.'

'How long have you known Mr Pugh?'

'Twenty years. He was my teacher. In high school.' She said the phrases haltingly, as if reluctant to divulge the information. Briskly she rose, and he followed. 'This man is not seventy years old. If I hadn't been distracted, I would have seen that.'

'You had a right to be distracted,' JD began, but she waved his words away.

'He might be fifty, if that. He's taller than Mr Pugh too, by a good two inches.' She leaned over the dead man's head carefully. Dried blood was thickly crusted over the scalp. 'He's bald, like Mr Pugh. Or his head's been shaved. I'll let you know which when I get him on a table.'

'Okay, let's assume you're right and this man is not Jerry Pugh. What made you originally think he was?'

'First, he was sitting in Mr Pugh's chair.'

'You said that before. What do you mean, "his" chair?'

'When he wanders, he always comes here, to this chair. Before the Alzheimer's he was quite a chess player. He'd come here every day after school and there were always people waiting to take him on.' She shook herself lightly. 'Plus there was that.' She pointed to a tweed hat on the ground. 'Mr Pugh wears one just like it. It was pulled over his face, like he was asleep. It fell off when I touched his shoulder and he fell forward.' She paused, biting her lower lip. 'Mr Pugh has a similar trench coat, too.'

JD frowned, not liking that. 'Who knows that Mr Pugh wanders out here?'

Slowly she turned, looked up to meet his eyes. Hers were troubled. 'Everyone in our building. Everyone in any of the buildings nearby. He wanders out at different times during the night and day. Why?' She asked the question even though he thought she already knew the answer.

'Who knows you run every morning before dawn?'

'Other runners. Anyone who's up at dawn. Why?' she repeated.

'Because he wasn't killed here. Drew thinks he was transported by wheelchair from the front of your building. Somebody went to a lot of trouble to have him found.'

She looked back at the hat. 'You think someone wanted me to find him.'

He thought exactly that, but didn't want to jump to any conclusions. 'For now, let's leave it at someone going to a lot of trouble to have him found.'

'Hands are in his pockets,' she observed quietly. 'His face is destroyed. Someone wanted him found, but not identified. I think you'll find his fingertips are . . . altered.'

'Or gone,' JD said grimly.

'Or gone,' she repeated evenly. 'Rigor's passed. He's been dead at least two days. I'll get you a better time of death after the exam.' She leaned forward a few inches, studying the facial injuries. 'Blunt object was used. I'll have a better idea—'

'After the exam,' he finished. 'So let's get him transported. I want to check his pockets for ID, but I don't want to chance any evidence falling on the grass here. Can we check his pockets as soon as you unload him at the morgue?'

She studied him, clearly sizing him up. 'Either Stevie's been training you or you just have common sense. A lot of cops would want me to lay him out here.'

Her approval made him feel . . . good. Just as it had the other time they'd met. He didn't think she remembered it and he wasn't in any hurry to bring it up.

A door slammed behind them and as one they looked over their shoulders to see an ME tech pushing a gurney with a folded body bag lying on top. 'I'm just coming back from two weeks out of the office,' Trask said. 'I may have a heavy load, so I may not be able to do the cut today. But if you want to meet me at the morgue, we can do a cursory exam and go through his pockets right away.'

'I appreciate it. I'll work on locating the Pughs. I want to be sure they're all right.'

'Thank you. I'll suit up and get started.' She looked back at the body slumped over the chess table. 'I want to believe I came along by coincidence, that the placement of this man's body had nothing to do with me.'

'But you don't.'

'Do you?'

He wanted to put her mind at ease, but wouldn't lie to her. 'No.'

She sighed. 'Neither do I.'

TWO

Monday, May 3, 6.20 A.M.

Well. That had gone much better than he'd dared to hope for. He'd held his breath for a while, hoping Trask would come along, hoping she'd follow her usual path.

He needn't have worried. Lucy Trask was as predictable as the sun she hated so much. She'd found the cocksucker, just like he'd planned.

He'd enjoyed the precious minutes when she'd thought the cocksucker was the old man. Unfortunately she'd figured it out too soon. *I should have changed his shoes*. Stupid mistake. *Could have drawn her torment out a lot longer*. She truly loved that old man, Mr Pugh. *Good to know*.

He took stock of the two detectives talking. The man had been first on the scene. The woman had just arrived. Now that he knew who was investigating, he could put Plan B in place – setting up a distraction in the unlikely event that things went sour and he needed to get away fast. Cops had families and he had no qualms about using theirs. *Just like they used mine*.

He'd get his justice, one body at a time. His mouth curved in a satisfied smile. The next name on his list was already taken and stowed. He couldn't wait.

Monday, May 3, 6.35 A.M.

Lucy drew a steadying breath as she leaned against the morgue rig, stepping into a pair of coveralls. Her heart was still pounding. *It isn't him. Not Mr Pugh.*

20

Then who is it? And why had he been left there, in Mr Pugh's chair?

For me to find? A shiver raced across her skin as she zipped the coveralls up over her running clothes. It was already seventy degrees, but she was freezing cold. Shock, she thought. She'd come close to hyperventilating, especially there at the end.

Rubbing her hands together, she remembered Detective Fitzpatrick doing the same thing. That had been kind. And effective. The man had hands like a furnace.

She wondered if he made a habit of warming the hands of those who discovered the bodies. She imagined he hadn't had many opportunities to do so, not yet anyway. Stevie Mazzetti's former partner had retired only three weeks before and this new partner hadn't been in Homicide before. He'd come from Narcotics, and— *Oh.*

'Narcotics,' she said aloud. *The little girl. Two years ago.* He alone had come to witness the autopsy of a child, the victim of a stray bullet in a drug-related shooting.

That's where I saw him. She'd been trying to remember while he'd intently studied her face as she'd studied the victim's shoes. He'd been trying to remember too.

'You got that right,' murmured the woman standing to her right. 'That man can addict me any time.'

Lucy looked up and immediately rolled her eyes. ME Tech Ruby Gomez was openly ogling Detective Fitzpatrick as he stood several vehicles away, engaged in a serious conversation with Stevie Mazzetti, who'd just arrived on the scene.

'Ruby,' Lucy hissed. 'Put your eyes back in your head.'

Ruby didn't move. 'Why? You're the one who said he was a narcotic.'

'I said "Narcotics". He came from Narcotics.'

'I know. In fact, I know everything there is to know about that man.'

'Like what?' Lucy demanded, sounding petulant even to her own ears.

'Like he's hot.' Ruby shot her an amused look. 'What more do I need to know?'

21

'That it's time to work. We've got a dead man slumped over a chess table. Focus.'

'I am. On the live hot cop who has a very nice butt,' Ruby replied tartly, then swung around with a resigned sigh. 'Fine. Let's go get the dead guy.' She closed the back doors of the rig, taking a last look at Fitzpatrick. 'That is one fine-lookin' man.'

Lucy shook her head, although she privately agreed. JD Fitzpatrick had tall, dark and handsome all sewn up in a very tidy package, and there was something about the way he moved. He was lean where a lot of cops were bulky. Still, he filled the space around him, his air confident. Almost dangerous. That he was kind made him more so.

The handsome, arrogant ones were easy to spot. Easy to avoid. The kind ones snuck under your radar, then . . . *bam.* She hefted her field exam kit and started walking. 'Men that look like that are invariably a lot more trouble than they're worth.'

'In the long term, absolutely,' Ruby said, her very red lips twitching. 'I sure as hell wouldn't marry one. But short term, their brand of trouble is well worth it.'

Red was Ruby's trademark because she was anything but subtle. She wore it on her lips and on the long fingernails that she pressed on at the end of each shift. Men buzzed around her like bees to a queen and Ruby proudly held court.

Lucy liked her. They had a business-hours friendship that left most people shaking their heads. *Oil and water*, the others would say. It didn't take a rocket scientist to get which was the water. Ruby was flashy and vivid where Lucy was contained. Bland.

Or so they all thought. Not even Ruby knew what Lucy did when she left the office. None of them did. And if Lucy had her way, they never would.

'Well, make trouble on your own time,' Lucy said briskly. 'I promised Detective Fitzpatrick we'd process this guy as soon as we got him back to the morgue. How many cases do I have today, anyway?'

'Maybe four,' Ruby replied absently, stealing looks over her shoulder. 'He's coming. Detective Hot Cop. Stevie Mazzetti's with him.'

'Ruby,' Lucy snapped and Ruby sighed again.

'See, that's the difference between us,' she said.

'What, that I'm a professional?' Lucy asked sarcastically.

Ruby just grinned, unoffended. 'That too. You've got to get out, kid. See some men that don't have tags on their toes.'

'Right now, the victim in the chair is my main concern.'

Ruby puckered her lips. 'Ooh. And now we get prim.'

Lucy stopped short. 'Someone meant for me to find him,' she said quietly. 'Dressed him so that I'd think he was someone important to me. Finding out who he is and how he died so that the cops can find out who did this . . . that's my priority.'

Ruby sobered. 'I'm sorry. Why don't you go in to the lab? Alan and I can bag him.'

'If it had been my friend I'd let you, but he's not and the cops need answers.'

Ruby nodded once. 'Then let's get busy.'

'Thank you.' Ruby walked to where ME Tech Alan Dunbar waited, casting glances over her shoulder at Detective Fitzpatrick along the way. Lucy was tempted to sneak one last peek herself, but there was work to do.

A man to identify. And a question to answer. *Why set the victim up for me to find?*

'Lucy! What is this? Are you all right?'

The voice behind her was as familiar as her own and when Lucy turned, she automatically looked down. At five-feet-nothing, Gwyn Weaver was ten inches shorter than Lucy in her sock feet. When she wore her work boots, Lucy towered even higher.

Lucy was surprised it had taken her best friend this long to get out here. Usually Gwyn was on the front row of any crowd. This morning her smooth voice was shrill and panicked and Lucy opened her mouth to reassure.

'I'm—' Startled, Lucy cut herself off, her chin lifting and eyes widening at the sight of Gwyn's companion. 'Royce.' Who stared at her coveralls with the big 'ME' stenciled on the back. Royce, who only knew her from the club. 'You . . . you both came.'

Shit. Lucy had known when Gwyn moved into her apartment

23

complex that this would happen eventually, that at some point one of Gwyn's boyfriends would see her in her day job attire. She had just expected it would be her nice prim suit, not her coveralls. And she certainly hadn't expected it this morning.

Although she should have. They'd gotten in so late from picking her up at the airport last night. It made sense Royce would sleep over at Gwyn's place. On any other morning it wouldn't have mattered. Except this morning it did.

'He knows, Lucy,' Gwyn said under her breath. She was searching Lucy's face, her own panic receding. 'I had to tell him. But he's not going to tell.'

'I promise,' Royce said, seemingly taking her day job in stride. 'I take it that you didn't really go to California for a sales conference.'

'No,' Lucy admitted. 'It was a forensic pathology symposium.'

'Why lie?' he asked, more curious than annoyed.

'Some people can't deal with what I do. It's easier this way.'

'I guess I can understand that,' he said with a comforting smile. 'What happened here?'

Gwyn looked around Lucy, straining to see the scene. 'The neighbors said it was Mr Pugh. But you're here, suited up, and not upset. So it can't be.'

'I thought it was, but it's not. We don't know who it is.'

Gwyn looked up at her, dark eyes troubled. 'But you're sure it's not Mr P?' she asked, so honestly concerned that Lucy couldn't stay annoyed.

'I'm very sure. Look, guys, I have to get to work. I'll catch you later?'

'Tonight,' Gwyn said, giving her a pointed nod. 'Everyone's missed you.'

And she'd missed them. Lucy had never been away so long before, and every night she'd wondered what the gang was up to. 'I'll try. I may be backed up at work.'

'Which we need to let her get back to,' Royce said to Gwyn. 'Come on. You came, you saw, so you can go back to sleep now.' He gave Lucy a warm smile and her shoulder a squeeze. 'If you need anything, let us know. I'm glad it wasn't your friend.'

'Thanks.' She watched them go, Gwyn small and doll-like at Royce's side. He'd put his arm around Gwyn, shielding her from the unpleasant crime scene and Lucy felt a tiny pang of loneliness. Gwyn always thought the next guy might be the one, but up until now it had never worked out and they were still single girls together. But this time, Lucy thought Gwyn could be right. Things would change. *And I'll be alone again.*

Which I will worry about later. Get to work.

When she reached the body, Lucy put her field kit on the ground next to the gurney that Alan had already prepared with a body bag. She looked up at Alan who stood grim-faced, staring at the body. 'You okay?' she asked.

Alan was a little green. 'Somebody did a real number on him, didn't they?'

'Indeed,' Lucy said, feeling a tug of guilt. Alan had been with them for only a few months, and he'd never seen a corpse this mutilated. 'I should have prepared you.'

'It's okay. The cops said that you thought it was your friend. I'm glad it's not.'

'Me too,' she murmured. Pulling on gloves, she motioned Alan and Ruby to follow. 'He's past rigor, so he'll be limp. Try to keep his hands in his pockets.'

'Why?' Alan asked.

'His face is messed up, honey,' Ruby said. 'Chances are his hands are too.'

'Oh.' Alan swallowed. 'Okay.'

Lucy lightly touched the victim's head, studying the dried blood with a frown.

'What?' Fitzpatrick asked.

Lucy looked up. He and Mazzetti stood a few feet away. 'The texture of the dried blood is wrong somehow. But I can tell you that his head has been shaved.'

Stevie leaned close to see. She was a petite brunette, and at thirty-four she was a year younger than Lucy, but had always seemed much older. 'Are you okay?' Stevie murmured over the dead man. 'I heard you had a shock. We could call another pathologist.'

25

'No. I'm fine.' Lucy managed a smile. She respected Stevie a lot, even though the woman's side-gig creeped her out. Grief counseling. The thought made her want to shudder. All that focus on death. When someone was dead, they were dead. *I should know.* Talking about it week after week was futile and just plain strange. 'But thanks.'

Stevie smiled back, then straightened, back to business. 'Does he have any ID?'

Lucy patted the victim's coat pockets lightly then grimaced when her fingers met with no resistance where there should have been bone. 'No wallet. No fingers either.'

'At all?' Fitzpatrick asked.

'Left hand, they're gone at the second knuckle. Right hand, the same. Except . . .' She touched a single finger through the coat. 'He still has his ring finger.' She looked up at Fitzpatrick who watched her intently, and she realized she was holding her breath. Detective Hot Cop, Ruby had called him. *Indeed.* Quietly she exhaled. 'It's got a ring on it.'

Drew Peterson crouched beside her and she could focus again. 'Can we get it off once he's on the bag?'

'We can try.' She probed the victim's legs through his trousers, then grimaced again. 'Multiple breaks. His knees feel like mush. This guy was tortured.'

'I hate tortures,' Stevie muttered.

'I imagine he hated it worse,' Fitzpatrick said dryly.

Lucy stepped back from the body. 'Alan, Ruby, he's all yours.'

Ruby was a pro, but Alan looked queasy enough to have Lucy worried. She was watching to see if anything fell from the body to the ground as they moved him, when a new shiver ran down her back. Where she'd been freezing, she was now warm. Fitzpatrick stood behind her, his body blasting heat.

'I found the Pughs,' he said softly. He'd bent down so that he spoke in her ear, and she could feel the tickle of his breath against her neck. 'They're both fine.'

A combination of relief and awareness had her knees wobbling but she held herself straight, keeping her eyes on Ruby and Alan. 'Thank you. Where are they?'

'The emergency number the super had was Mrs Pugh's sister. They've been there for two days. I'm sending a squad car by to check, just in case.'

'Thank you. I've been out of town a few weeks and when I got back last night it was too late to check on them. I didn't know they were gone, but it makes sense they're there. Barb visits her sister often.'

He was quiet a moment, still standing way too close. 'Who knew you were gone?'

She thought about the two weeks of silence the other tenants had enjoyed in her absence. 'Everybody in the building and at work. I went to a training symposium, then lectured at a university in LA.'

'You didn't post anything on your Facebook page about being away?'

She looked over her shoulder, annoyed. 'Of course not.'

His nose was about two inches from hers. This close she could see that his eyes were dark, dark blue, not black as she'd thought before. 'Some people do,' he said.

'Some people are stupid. I am not.'

'*Ugh!*' Alan's grunt had everyone looking back at the body. The victim's hands had fallen from his pockets as they'd placed him on the gurney. Luckily the hands had flopped straight down, falling on the unzipped body bag, so no evidence had fallen to the grass.

'Like you said,' Fitzpatrick said grimly when they'd surrounded the gurney. 'Just his ring finger, complete with a ring. Missing the tip.'

'His teeth appear broken too,' Lucy added. 'I don't think you're going to find ID.'

'The ring on his finger's the ID,' Stevie said. 'Whoever did this left it behind for a reason. Can you get it off?'

Lucy tugged at the ring and held it up to the morning light. 'University of Maryland Medical School,' she read.

Fitzpatrick frowned. 'Wonder what the doc did to get his knees capped?'

Lucy dropped the ring into the evidence bag Drew held open, then gingerly pulled the victim's sleeve back, revealing a gold

27

wristwatch. 'It's a Rolex.' She removed it and placed it in Fitzpatrick's outstretched gloved hand.

'Not a robbery,' he said and studied the back of the watch. 'Inscription says "Thanks for the memories." They spelled "memories" with an extra "m". Wait.' He squinted at the inscription, then rolled his eyes. 'Make that "Thanks for the mammaries."'

'I'd say you're looking for a plastic surgeon,' Ruby said dryly, and Lucy felt an appalling urge to laugh out loud. Gratefully, she stifled it. This was not funny.

'A plastic surgeon who really got on someone's wrong side,' Fitzpatrick said.

'Dr Trask?' Alan said quietly. 'He's got something in his mouth.'

The object was dirty white and looked like it might have been a handkerchief. Stevie and Fitzpatrick bent closer but Lucy put a hand between them and the victim. 'I need to remove it in a protected environment.'

Fitzpatrick straightened with a scowl. 'We know, we know, back at the morgue. Look, he probably doesn't, but at least see if he's got a wallet in his breast pocket.'

'That I can do.' Lucy probed the man's chest with her fingertips, then flinched, her hands stilling abruptly when what she felt wasn't anywhere close to being right.

'What else?' Stevie asked in a tone that said she really didn't want to know.

Lucy pressed a little harder against the beige trench coat to be sure. Once again there was no resistance where there should have been a rib cage. *This is very bad*.

'They're not supposed to do that, are they?' Fitzpatrick asked blandly. 'I mean, your fingers sinking into his chest like that.'

'No, they're not.' She looked up grimly. 'I don't know if this is your cause of death or not, but there's a big hole here where his heart used to be.'

Stevie let out a breath. 'I think this guy just moved to the top of your priority list.'

Lucy nodded. 'Indeed.'

Monday, May 3, 8.15 A.M.

Clay Maynard hung up his phone with a frown. He'd had one hell of a night last night and this morning wasn't looking much better.

'Well?' his assistant asked from the doorway of his office.

'Evan missed checking in both last week and this morning, he's not answering his cell, and he's not where he's supposed to be. The foreman at the construction site just said he never showed up for work last week so he fired him. What did you find?'

'The landlord of the place Nicki rented in his new name said he hasn't shown up yet.' Alyssa Moore bit her lip. 'This doesn't sound good. Could Margo have found him?'

'Not if he did what Nicki told him to do.' A headache was brewing. 'He said Margo would kill him if she found him.'

'She's already tried twice. Maybe three times was her charm.'

'Dammit,' Clay hissed. 'We gave him a new life. All he had to do was claim it.'

Alyssa sat in the chair next to his desk, crossing long legs that made his headache even worse. He'd been engaged to her older sister Lou four years ago when he first met Alyssa. Back then Alyssa had been a scrawny tomboy always getting into scrapes. Now she was a leggy eighteen year old getting into a whole different kind of trouble, which was why Lou asked him to hire her as his assistant. Though Lou and he called off their wedding, they'd stayed close – close enough that she didn't mind hitting him up for favors, like keeping an eye on her baby sister.

Luckily Alyssa was a decent assistant, because keeping his promise to keep her out of trouble was turning out to be a *lot* more trouble than Clay had bargained for.

'Do you *mind*?' he snapped at Alyssa, gesturing to her skirt. 'I pay you enough to buy clothes with more material than that.'

Alyssa rolled her eyes and tugged at the skirt. 'Oh, my God. You sound just like Lou. Or my dad. I'm not sure which is worse.'

'I don't know,' Clay muttered. 'They both carry a gun.'

Alyssa's older sister and father were cops. Lou was a Maryland sheriff and Mr Moore had retired from a Boston beat. That Clay was a former cop was the reason Mr Moore had allowed his younger daughter to come to work at Clay's PI agency.

That and he'd wanted his daughter as far away as possible from the teenaged Romeo who Alyssa had been convinced she couldn't live without. One month in Baltimore and Alyssa had forgotten all about the boy back home. Unfortunately, she'd discovered a whole new crop right here. But that was the least of Clay's concerns.

'You didn't mind my skirt last night,' she said. 'That creep never even suspected you were planting a tracker under his car. He was too busy staring at my legs.'

Clay closed his eyes and blindly searched a drawer for his bottle of painkillers. He'd nearly had a heart attack when he'd seen Alyssa leaning against her car, where his much more experienced partner, Nicki, should have been.

Except Nicki was on vacation at the beach an hour away and had not answered her phone all day yesterday.

'Yes, I did mind,' he said. 'I was going to go it alone, but you were already there, waiting for him. What were you thinking, showing up like that?'

'That you needed help,' Alyssa said quietly. 'That the little boy needed help. You had one chance to plant that device. If you hadn't, where would that little boy be now?'

'Probably halfway to Mexico,' Clay admitted.

He'd been hired by a woman desperate to find her son. Her estranged husband, a dangerous foreign national, had grabbed the boy and the cops hadn't been able to find either of them. Clay had been able to draw the husband out with a message from the wife, knowing the man wouldn't risk bringing the child.

He'd wanted Nicki to pretend to have car trouble, distracting the husband with her cleavage while Clay planted the tracking device, hoping the husband would lead them to the boy. Alyssa had done the distracting instead while Clay had done his job, and now the boy was safe with his mother. The husband was in jail, awaiting arraignment on a whole laundry list of charges.

It had been risky. But that's why desperate people hired Clay and Nicki.

Nicki was also a former cop – and Clay's first patrol partner. She'd left DCPD years after Clay had started his agency, right about the time Clay's old PI partner had married and moved to Chicago. Clay and Nicki now shared the agency and a mission. They helped desperate people when the cops couldn't. Or wouldn't.

Sometimes that meant breaking a few rules. They were good with that.

Nicki had been dependable, but Clay had been fixing a lot of her mistakes lately. She'd been preoccupied. Moody. He hoped she was using this vacation to work through whatever shit that was messing with her mind.

'We saved the day,' Alyssa said. 'I did a good job.'

'You did. But you could have been killed. Promise me you won't do that again.'

'Promise to train me.' She lifted a brow. 'And I won't do it again until I am.'

Clay ground his teeth. 'I'll think about it.' He resumed his search for the painkillers.

'Left bottom drawer,' Alyssa said. 'I reorganized your desk.'

He blinked into the drawer. So she had. 'Wow. Thank you.'

She inclined her head regally. 'You are welcome. So, back to Evan?'

'Yeah. Evan.' Nicki had asked him to keep an eye on her clients while she was away, but he'd gotten wind that the child's father was about to bolt hours after Evan had first missed a check-in. The search for the boy took priority. Now, Evan was two days more missing than before. 'Something's wrong.'

'Should we assume the crazy-assed stalker bitch from hell found him?'

'Shit.' Clay shook out his last three tablets. Seemed like he'd just bought that bottle. Probably because he had. 'I don't want to, but we have to now.'

'You're gonna eat a hole in your stomach,' Alyssa chided mildly.

He ignored her, chasing the pills down with cold coffee. 'Margo couldn't have found him if he'd followed Nicki's instructions. He must have gone back.'

Alyssa sighed. 'I thought Evan was smarter than that.'

'He has kids, and that always makes people stupid. He probably wanted to see them one more time before he became Ted Gamble.'

'So what are you gonna do?'

'Go look for him. If he's dead, we need to report Margo. If he's changed his mind, we need to recover all of his new ID.' He checked his watch. It was a five-hour drive to southern Virginia with traffic. 'I can be in Newport News by mid-afternoon.'

'I'll get the name of the hotel Nicki used when she went down there.'

Alyssa went back to her desk while Clay reread the contents of the file written in Nicki's precise hand. Evan Reardon had made some stupid choices. The most stupid was cheating on his wife with Margo Winchester, a pole-dancing floozy, but a close runner-up was thinking he'd be able to walk away when he was done with her.

Margo made good on her threat to expose their affair. Evan's wife left him, taking their three kids. She was staying with her folks and all she'd told Nicki was that Evan was not the man she'd married. Then she'd shut the door in Nicki's face.

Evan still hadn't married Margo and the woman had become violent. He'd approached the police, but that hadn't gone so well. Margo's dad, like Alyssa's, was a cop. Unlike Alyssa's dad, Margo's was not a good cop. Evan had been harassed, followed by the police who seemed to be looking for something to use against him.

So Evan hadn't reported the stalking and it had become worse. He'd finally come to Nicki when Margo began threatening his kids. He wanted to draw her away from his children. He wanted Margo to think he was dead. Drastic, but he'd been desperate.

Helping people start over was what Clay and Nicki did best. New identities were harder in the post-9/11 world, but still possible if one had the right skills. Clay and Nicki had the skills. They always made sure the client was telling the truth, checking out all aspects of the story. This one was stickier as bad cops were involved.

Bad cops existed, Clay knew. It was the main reason he himself was a former cop. He'd been unable to look the other way and made the wrong bad cop mad.

He sighed, wishing again that Nic hadn't picked this week to get away from it all. They'd had some close calls, but had never lost a client. Maybe until now. He closed and locked his briefcase. He needed to find out what happened to Evan Reardon.

Three

JD waited behind his car while Stevie parked hers in the garage adjacent to the morgue. The ME's rig had left the scene an hour before, so hopefully Dr Trask had some new information for them. He and Stevie had spent the time interviewing the neighbors, but no one had seen anything.

Stevie locked her car. 'I meant to thank you for covering for me this morning.'

'Not a problem. I may need you to do the same for me some day.'

They were nearing the morgue door and JD steeled himself. He really hated the morgue. He didn't know how the MEs stood working here every day.

'I'd say this case is a trial by fire for you,' Stevie said.

'Don't worry. I've seen worse.'

'The man's been pounded into pulp, his fingers removed, and his heart cut out. And that's before we've looked under his clothes. And you've seen worse.'

'I've seen worse,' he repeated mildly. And he had. Which was sad.

'You ever work a torture case in Narcotics?' she asked.

'No,' he said and she rolled her eyes.

'Dammit, JD, are you gonna make me dig this out of you with a grapefruit spoon?'

His lips twitched, just a little. 'Sorry. I'm not used to all the questions.' He was not used to having a partner try to get into his head, but he'd known Stevie would. Getting into minds was her thing.

'You say you've seen worse. In Kandahar?'

JD frowned. She knew where he'd been. And what he'd done. Not many people knew, but her husband – JD's best friend – had. 'Yes.'

'Paul said you gave him permission to tell me.'

He had. Paul never would have said a word if he hadn't given the okay. 'Back then I never thought we'd be partners.'

Stevie smiled sadly. 'I can forget. Pretend I never knew.'

'No, it's okay.'

'You do know you have nothing to be ashamed of, right? You served your country, JD. You did right.'

JD thought of all those lonely days and nights, sitting alone, his sight trained on the spot through which his target would eventually pass. And of the self-loathing that inevitably followed once he'd pulled the trigger. He'd been alone when he came back home, even though he'd had Maya. He'd gone through the motions, working his job, even participating in sports. He'd been a hell of a shortstop. But he'd still been alone.

Until the night Paul beaned him with a softball and insisted on driving him to the ER. To this day JD wasn't certain it had been entirely an accident. Paul became his first real friend. Earned JD's trust. Welcomed him into his family.

The night Paul was murdered, JD had found himself alone again. Then Maya had died, taking away even the illusion of having someone. But those days were past. Like Kandahar, they were memories he rarely allowed himself to access.

He opened the morgue door for them. 'We're here.'

Stevie looked like she wanted to delve deeper, but thankfully she let it go. 'I didn't know you'd met Lucy Trask already.'

Her new topic made him uncomfortable again, but in a different way this time. 'I hadn't really. Dr Trask did an autopsy I witnessed when I was in Narcotics. I was with her for maybe thirty minutes. We never actually spoke until today.'

'Really? I never would have guessed that,' she said shrewdly.

'Lucy's a good pathologist. Thorough. I don't think I've ever seen her as shaken as she was today. Thinking that vic was her friend was hard. Lucy doesn't get close to many people.'

She pushed the door open to the autopsy suite where Lucy Trask stood behind an exam table. She was covered head to toe – a gown over her scrubs, a mask over her face, and her hair with a surgical cap. She looked just like she had the first time he'd seen her. Except this time the body she stood over was full-sized.

Her head was bowed, her attention focused on the victim on the table.

'Whatcha got?' Stevie asked and Trask abruptly looked up, startled. Her eyes met JD's for an unguarded moment before dropping back to the victim. But in that moment he'd seen surprise – and something else.

Interest. It had been a long time since he'd spent time with a woman, but not so long that he could no longer recognize interest when he saw it flare. She'd been aware of him before, at the scene. Now she was wondering. He found himself standing a little straighter even as his chest tightened. Because he was wondering, too.

'Quite a lot,' Trask said, her voice brisk. 'I was preparing to do the cut.' She pulled the mask away from her face, leaving it to dangle around her neck. 'But now that you're here, you can look at him before I get started. What's left of him anyway.'

She wasn't exaggerating. There was almost too much damage to take in. The two focal points were the victim's damaged face and the huge hole in his chest. His missing fingers just added to the macabre sight.

Stevie grimaced. 'What did they use on him, anyway?'

'All kinds of things. I told you at the scene that his legs were broken. X-rays showed three breaks in his right femur, two in his left. I'm thinking a bat was used. This hole in his chest is post-mortem. The removal of his eyes, tongue, and the finger amputations were not.'

'The tongue was in the handkerchief?' Fitzpatrick asked and she nodded.

Stevie sighed. 'So, what was the cause of death?'

'I don't know yet. I can tell you this guy had some work done on his face.'

'I kinda figured that one on my own,' Stevie said dryly. 'And me, not even a doc.'

Trask shook her head. 'I mean, he had plastic surgery.'

'How can you tell?' JD asked. 'Looks like every bone in his face is smashed.'

'Every bone is smashed, but he's got cheek implants. Showed up on the X-ray.'

'We can get serial numbers,' Stevie said excitedly. 'And then ID this guy.'

'We can,' Trask said. 'I'll get the implants out when I do the cut. The killer must not have known about them.'

'Could be why he took the heart,' Stevie mused. 'Maybe it was traceable too.'

'I wondered that,' Trask said. 'We'll know when we get the victim's name.'

'How did he cut out the heart?' Stevie asked. 'That's not an easy thing to do.'

'No, it's not. Determining that will take more time than I've had so far, but whatever he used was powerful enough to cut through all the muscle and the bone. The lines of the cut are pretty smooth. He didn't hack his way through.'

'There's a surprising lack of blood,' Stevie noted.

'That's because the body was washed before being re-dressed.'

'And the hole in his chest?' Stevie asked.

'Stuffed with a hand towel, your basic white cotton blend.'

'Anything else?' JD asked.

She lifted her brows. 'Oh, I'm just getting started, Detective. I took his core temp. Fourteen degrees Celsius. That's about fifty-eight Fahrenheit.'

JD and Stevie shared a confused glance. 'He was frozen?' JD asked.

Trask nodded. 'Yes, he was.'

'Well that shoots time of death to hell,' Stevie grumbled. 'How did he get the guy in the chair if he was frozen?'

'He thawed his extremities out. Maybe in water. Kind of like when you thaw a frozen turkey in the sink and the wings and legs thaw first. That made him poseable. It would explain how the blood below his neck was washed away, because the blood on his face and scalp is still here, just dried.'

'How long was he frozen?' JD asked and watched Trask's eyes grow troubled.

'To freeze and partially thaw? A week. Maybe longer.'

'Maybe two weeks?' he asked quietly.

She looked down at the body, then back up again. 'Maybe.'

Stevie sighed. 'The length of time you were gone. You get back last night, and this morning this dead guy just happens to end up in the park along your jogging route.'

'Dressed like your friend,' JD added, 'who you often found sitting in the same spot and often returned to his home.'

'Not good,' Stevie murmured. 'Not good at all. Lucy, you said you were just getting started. What else?'

Carefully Trask lifted the body, just enough for them to glimpse the victim's back, and JD squinted. 'What is it?' he asked.

'Cigarette burns,' she said, 'in a very definite pattern. Done pre-mortem. Tap the top of that computer monitor on the counter. I took a digital before you got here.'

JD did as she asked and the screen saver disappeared, revealing the photo. A single thought hit him hard as he absorbed what he saw. *Maybe I haven't seen worse.*

Stevie bent to study the screen. 'It's a letter I.' She looked over her shoulder at JD, her mouth tight. 'Or a Roman numeral I. We could be looking at more.'

He looked at Trask, saw that she'd already come to the same conclusion. 'Get those implants out of his cheeks, Doc. We need to know who this guy is.'

you belong to me

'Not what I wanted to hear, people.' Lieutenant Peter Hyatt stood at the window in his office, glaring down at the street. He was a burly man who rarely smiled and seemed to get a charge from making the clerks in the office jump at his commands.

Stevie had told him that Hyatt's bark was worse than his bite. Still, JD didn't think he liked his new CO. Of course, liking the man had nothing to do with anything. What mattered was whether the big guy would support them when they needed it.

JD thought about the victim. *I.* They would need all the support they could get.

Hyatt turned from the window, worry etching lines around his mouth. 'But then again, I don't want to hear about ninety-eight per cent of what's said to me. So you think the ME was supposed to find this guy? Why?'

'We don't know,' Stevie said. 'Yet.'

'This Trask . . .' Hyatt perched on the corner of his desk, folding his arms across his massive chest. 'Tell me about her.'

'She's good,' Stevie said. 'She's got an eye for detail and a logical mind. And she doesn't have a protocol broom stuck up her ass like some of the other MEs.'

Hyatt shook his head. 'You paint such pretty pictures, Stevie. What about her private life? Boyfriends, irate fiancés? Any reason to think this could be personal?'

Stevie frowned. 'I don't think she's involved with anyone. But I don't know her outside work. She's kind of a private person.'

JD didn't realize he'd been holding his breath. Not involved. That was good. 'I got that as well,' he said. 'She figured out that the victim wasn't the man she knew because his feet were too small. Which she knew because she'd cared for the old man's feet this winter when he wandered out of his house without shoes. But she didn't want to tell me that. I had to pry it out of her and I'm not sure why.'

Hyatt frowned. 'That doesn't make sense. Find out why. If she was squirrely about revealing that, she could have other secrets,

39

ones that might be reason enough to set her up to find a body. So does she know the vic? What's his name?'

'Christopher Jones,' Stevie answered. 'Trask removed the cheek implants and called it in while we were waiting. She says she's never heard of him.'

Hyatt's gray brows lifted. 'Did you believe her?'

'Yes,' JD said, probably a little too quickly, earning him a sharp glance from Hyatt. Feeling his face heat, he shrugged. 'I saw her expression when she thought she knew the guy. I don't think she's lying.'

Stevie nodded her agreement. 'She's cooperating, Peter. We don't have any reason to think she had anything to do with this.'

'Other than being set up to find the body,' Hyatt said sarcastically. 'Which is just a tiny little detail. What do we know about the vic?'

'Lives in Columbia,' Stevie said. 'We're going out there after we brief you.'

'So Mr Jones was a doctor?'

'No,' JD said. 'A divorce attorney, which bothers us.'

'Divorce attorneys bother me too, every month when I write two alimony checks. But I suspect you're more bothered that your dead attorney wore a med school ring.'

'And a Rolex that said "Thanks for the mammaries",' JD said.

Hyatt snorted a surprised laugh, then cleared his throat. 'Sorry. Hadn't heard that detail yet.' He pulled a sober look back to his face. 'Go check out Lawyer Jones. Find out why he was wearing a doctor's ring and why he's dead. And find out how he connects to Dr Trask. Even if it's an answer you don't like.' He gave Stevie a pointed look. 'You two friends? Is this going to be a problem for you?'

She shrugged. 'Lucy and I are not *un*friendly, but no, we're not best friends or anything. So no, it's not going to be a problem for me.'

Hyatt turned his gaze to JD. 'And you? You were quick to defend her.'

JD shook his head, feeling more like he was defending himself. He didn't like that. 'I spoke to her for the first time today. So no, not a problem for me either.'

Which he hoped was true. But when he remembered the way she'd looked at him when he'd entered the morgue and the way it had sent his pulse scrambling, he knew it would be a very big problem for him.

'Then go. Find out why there's a "I" burned into his back. If I have to tell the brass that we have a serial on the loose, I want as much detail as I can get.'

Monday, May 3, 10.20 A.M.

'You rang?'

Lucy looked up from the microscope. Dr Craig Mulhauser had stuck his head in the door to the lab. Her boss now, he'd been one of her professors in med school and one of the myriad of reasons she'd chosen pathology.

It had either been pathology or busking on a downtown street corner.

And wouldn't that have made her mother so proud? Lucy could almost hear her mother's wailing lament. *All those years of music lessons, gone to waste! Playing show tunes for nickels like a beggar on the street.* Lucy had almost chosen busking for the drama alone. She thought of the club that was her second home. In a way, she had.

She motioned Craig into the lab. 'I'm not seeing what I should be seeing.'

He pointed to the microscope. 'The John Doe you found this morning?'

'Christopher Jones. He had a core temp of fifty-eight degrees.'

Craig's shaggy brows shot up. 'That's something you don't see every day.'

'Exactly. His arms and legs, hip joints – all thawed. I should have realized something was different when he went down on the chess table. Now I remember the way his body went . . . *thunk*. Not . . . *squish*.'

Craig's lips twitched. 'Thunk and squish?'

She narrowed her eyes. 'You know what I mean.'

'I usually do, which kind of scares me. Seriously, though, you

41

thought it was a friend. That you didn't pick up on thunk versus squish is understandable. So what are you not seeing that you should?'

She gestured him to look through the microscope. 'No desiccation,' she said as he peered through the lens. 'I thought I'd see cellular damage to a much greater extent.'

'But you don't,' he murmured. 'Where did you take the sample from?'

'His thigh, but samples from his abdomen and arm showed the same absence of damage. There should be damage.' Any time the water in human cells was frozen and thawed, there was evidence of crystallization and dehydration. But here there was none.

Craig glanced up. 'And?'

'He was frozen,' Lucy said, 'but not conventionally. I know this sounds crazy, but it looks like this guy was flash frozen. Like frozen corn.'

'Doesn't sound crazy at all. Flash freezing takes the temp down so fast that there would be minimal dehydration. Which is kind of the point of it. No cellular damage, flavor is retained. In corn, anyway,' he added. He leaned against the counter. 'But you're talking one hell of a large piece of equipment.'

'I know. The victim was five eleven.' She shrugged. 'At least it's a lead. How many gargantuan flash freezers can be lying around?'

'I'm more interested in why the victim was frozen to begin with.'

'Detective Fitzpatrick believes the killer targeted me to find the victim. That's why Mr Jones was sitting at the chess table, dressed like my friend. I've been out of town for a few weeks and I guess the body wouldn't keep. So he froze him.'

Craig's face went dark as if all the pieces had just fallen together. 'Why would a killer do that? Target you? Why you?'

She fought the urge to childishly fidget. 'Probably because he figured an ME finding the body would give him more attention. I wouldn't worry about it. It's not like I actually knew the victim.'

'True, but why you? And how did the killer even know about you? You're not a celebrity, Lucy. You've never even been on the news. I'm always the one to go to press conferences. How would this guy even know you exist? That you run in the park? That you were out of town. How?'

She thought about the people who knew what she did for a living, the ones who'd known she'd gone away from home. Her apartment building. Here at the morgue. The university at which she'd spoken the week before. The hotel where she'd attended a training session the week before that.

And the club. She couldn't forget the club.

'Lots of people knew I was out of town. Lots of people know I'm a pathologist.'

'But who knew you ran every morning? Who knew the old man was your friend?'

'I don't know.' And she honestly did not. Lots of people knew a few details of her life, but there were only a handful who'd know every detail. Unless that person had made it his business to know.

'I want you to be careful,' Craig said, his voice low and urgent.

'I will be. I am. You're giving me the creeps.'

'Good.' With a weary sigh he stood. 'Call me when you get home tonight.'

She hesitated. 'It'll be late. I don't want to wake Rhoda.'

'You won't. She sleeps like the dead.' He shook his head. 'Sorry. Bad pun.'

Lucy smiled. 'You've been making bad puns for as long as I've known you and you're only apologizing now?'

Craig didn't smile back. 'I'm serious. You call me when you get home. Even if it's late. Call from the landline in your apartment, not your cell. And don't text. I'm old-fashioned enough to want to hear your voice, to be sure that you're home safely.'

She sighed. She'd planned to text from her cell from the club. *Guess that's out.* 'Okay. I'll call. From home,' she added when he glared.

'All right.'

Monday, May 3, 10.35 A.M.

'This is the place,' Stevie said, looking out the passenger window. JD had driven to Christopher Jones's house while Stevie had navigated the telephone maze of departments at the university. After four transfers and fifteen minutes of elevator music – which JD was more than a little disturbed to find she actually enjoyed – Stevie had been connected with the right person with access to the right university records.

Christopher Jones had not attended the university's med school.

JD pulled to the curb. 'There's a wheelchair ramp in front.'

'And a handicapped tag on the van in the driveway,' Stevie noted. She pulled a coin from her pocket to flip for the chore of notifying next of kin. 'Heads or tails?'

'Heads.'

She flipped and made a sympathetic face. 'Tails. You want me to take this one?'

JD shook his head with a frown. 'I'm no welcher, Mazzetti. Let's do this.'

They went up to the house and JD pressed the bell. The door opened, revealing a middle-aged man in a wheelchair. His hair was streaked with gray, his nose a little off-center. 'Yes? Can I help you?'

'I'm Detective Fitzpatrick and this is my partner, Detective Mazzetti. We'd like to speak to Mrs Christopher Jones.'

'I'm Mr Christopher Jones. What's this about?'

JD blinked in surprise and from the corner of his eye saw Stevie do the same. 'You're Christopher Jones?' he asked.

The man rolled his eyes. 'I don't have time for this.'

'Wait.' JD put his hand on the door when the man started to close it. 'Sir, your name has come up in a homicide investigation. May we come in?'

The man's face drained of color. 'Oh, my God. He did it. He really did it. I thought he was just blowing smoke, trying to get her to back off on her custody claim. I didn't think he'd really . . .' His shoulders sagged. 'When? When did he kill her?'

Again JD blinked. 'Sir, I think you've misunderstood. Your name came up in our investigation as the deceased.'

The man narrowed his eyes. 'But I'm not dead.'

'We can see that,' JD said. 'May we come in, Mr Jones?'

Christopher Jones backed his chair into a large foyer, still frowning. 'Please.'

'Mr Jones, have you ever had plastic surgery on your face?' JD asked.

Jones touched his face, the gesture a self-conscious one. 'Yes. I was in a car accident five years ago. Crushed my face and severed my spinal cord. Why?'

'Did you have cheek implants?' JD persisted.

'Yes. I did. *Why?*' Jones repeated testily.

'Because implants registered to you were found in a body discovered this morning.' JD studied the man's face, watching surprise flicker in his eyes.

'It's a mistake,' Jones said. 'I still have my implants, thank you very much.'

'Who did your surgery?' Stevie asked.

'Dr Russell Bennett,' Jones said. 'He has a practice downtown.'

'We'll talk to him,' JD promised. 'Thank you.' He opened the door to let them out, but Stevie didn't move. She was looking at Christopher Jones.

'Sir,' she said, 'this isn't our business – yet. But just now you seemed like you really thought your client's husband had killed her. Even if you think he's blowing smoke, your client should report the threat. I'd hate for it to become our business.'

Jones nodded reluctantly. 'I'll suggest she does that.'

'Thank you,' Stevie said. 'You have a good day.'

As soon as they got to the car, Stevie was back on the phone, dialing the university. After a few transfers she got their answer and flipped her phone closed. 'Russell Bennett graduated from University of Maryland's medical school.'

'A plastic surgeon who went to Maryland. He could be our vic.' JD started the car. 'But if we get there and *he's* still alive, what's Plan B? If he goofed and switched implants, he could get into

45

trouble. He's going to be cagey about answering questions.'

'Yeah, I know.' Stevie pulled down her visor mirror and studied her reflection. 'You think I have enough wrinkles to make Bennett believe I'm there for a consult?'

JD choked on a laugh. 'I think I'm taking the Fifth on that one.'

'Probably a wise move on your part.' She peeked down her blouse, then looked over at him with a grin. 'Let's throw in a boob job. That he'll believe.'

He had to grin back. Stevie's smile was infectious. 'What's my role?'

'You're my spouse. Rich, indulgent, and dissatisfied with my lack of curves.'

JD sobered abruptly. 'Paul wasn't dissatisfied with a single thing about you.'

Her smile faltered. 'I know. I was lucky.'

'Anyone who knew him was.' There weren't many who'd met Paul Mazzetti who hadn't counted him a friend.

Except for the punk who'd killed him. Paul had been shot down in cold blood for being in the wrong place, wrong time and having the nerve to disobey a convenience store robber's commands in order to protect his child. A pregnant Stevie had buried her husband and son, and it was only the knowledge that the child she carried needed her that helped her go on. Five year old Cordelia never met her father.

Stevie had persevered, using the tragedy to help others. The grief support groups she sponsored for cops changed lives. *Including mine.* JD owed Stevie one hell of a lot. Maybe his very life.

Stevie's lips tipped up sadly. 'Let's go meet Dr Bennett, unless we already have.'

He was about to pull away from the curb when his cell buzzed. 'Fitzpatrick.'

'Detective, this is Lucy Trask.'

Reflex had him sitting straighter in his seat. 'Yes, Dr Trask. What do you have?'

'I think the victim was flash frozen. Are you familiar with that?'

'Like they do to vegetables?' he asked. 'Flash frozen,' he said to Stevie.

'Exactly,' Trask said. 'The freezer would have to be huge – industrial-sized. If I were you, I'd start with food packaging plants.'

JD relayed the information to Stevie who was already on her laptop, searching for local food packaging facilities. 'That has to be helpful,' he said to Trask. 'Oh, and we've just left Christopher Jones.'

'You mean his house?'

'That, too. He was there, in the cheek-implanted flesh. He was very annoyed to find we thought him dead.'

'But . . . that doesn't make sense, Detective.'

'It does if the surgeon goofed,' he said. 'The surgeon's name is Russell Bennett.' JD heard the sharp intake of her breath, then silence. 'Dr Trask?'

'Bennett? Russell Bennett? Are you sure?'

He frowned. 'Yes, we're sure. Why?'

'Him, I know,' she murmured.

Four

Lucy fumbled as she hung up the phone, unable to look away from the mutilated body on her exam table. JD Fitzpatrick's voice still echoed in her ears. Russell Bennett.

Russell Bennett. No, it's not possible.

But it was. He was about the right age, height and weight. He'd gone to Maryland's med school. She remembered seeing the diploma on the wall of his living room. It was entirely possible. 'Oh, my God,' she whispered.

It was impossible to see Russ's face in the obscene mass of blunt trauma that lay before her. Still she stared, trying to connect some detail of the man she'd known with the body that had been so abused. Other than basic size, there was none.

'Hey, kid.' Ruby poked her head in the door. 'You free for lunch?' She came into the room, her brows furrowed. 'You don't look so good. What happened?'

Lucy swallowed hard, then dropped her eyes back to the dead man. He didn't look back. He had no eyes. Whoever killed him had taken his eyes. *Why?* 'I knew him.'

'You knew Christopher Jones? How?'

'I was wrong,' Lucy said numbly. 'Christopher Jones is alive.'

Ruby came around the table and grasped Lucy's chin, tilting her head so that their eyes met. 'You're whiter than he is, girl. Sit down.'

'I'm fine,' Lucy said, but found herself pushed down to the stool.

'I said, sit down.' Ruby sat on the other stool. 'Now tell me what this is about.'

48

Lucy told her what Fitzpatrick had said about the cheek implants and Ruby blinked.

'Wow. Who could have predicted that? But you don't know this body is the surgeon, this Russell Bennett character. You just know he did Jones's implant.'

Lucy shook her head. 'I knew him. There's a connection now.'

Ruby's eyes widened. 'Knew, or *knew*?'

'Just knew. I didn't *know* him.' *But I might have. Eventually.* 'I know his parents. The Bennetts are good people.' *This will break their hearts.*

'So what are you gonna do?'

'Nothing. I'm going to sit here until Stevie and Fitzpatrick get here. If you wouldn't mind, take . . .' *Russ.* No, it wasn't Russ Bennett anymore. She drew a shaky breath. 'Take the deceased back to the cold room. I shouldn't have any more contact with this case. I found him, I knew him.' *And we had words.* She wanted to wince. She'd had a lot more than words with him. 'I might be a suspect.'

Ruby scoffed. 'You were set up to find him. The cops will see that.'

When everything was known, Lucy imagined they would. *But everything would have to be known.* She struggled to keep her voice calm because every muscle in her body had clenched. 'I'm sure you're right. But for now, remove the deceased. Please.'

Ruby stood up and yanked on a pair of gloves. 'Fine.' She wagged a finger at Lucy's face. 'But don't you say one word to those detectives, I don't care how hot that Fitzpatrick is. You say nothing without Dr Mulhauser here. Or your lawyer.'

Lucy's gut churned painfully. Lawyer. *I might need a lawyer.* Luckily she knew one. 'You might be right.'

'I'm usually right,' Ruby stated. She covered the body with a sheet, then looked back at Lucy. 'I'm sorry, kid. This has to be rough. He was your friend.'

He was never my friend. He lied to me to try to get me to sleep with him. But that she wouldn't tell Ruby. 'Thanks.'

'Well, when this is over, we'll go out and have martinis for lunch, okay?'

Lucy forced her lips to curve. 'It's a date. Except you can have my martini.'

Ruby's sigh could have launched a ship. 'Let me guess. You just autopsied a pickled liver.'

'Not "just". I get a steady stream of diseased livers. Booze'll kill you.'

'Honey, something's gonna kill us all. I'd rather it was something fun.' Not waiting for a reply, Ruby rolled the body back to the cold room, leaving Lucy alone.

For a moment Lucy simply sat, wondering what to do next.

I should call a lawyer. I should tell Craig. Someone should tell the Bennetts that Russ is gone. But the last one would be the detectives' job.

They'd be here soon, to do their job. It wouldn't be personal and they'd ask her a lot of questions she wouldn't want to answer. *Terrific.* Well, at least it would get Fitzpatrick to stop looking at her the way he had earlier. The man was too intense.

And she'd learned long ago that intense men were way too much trouble. But then again, calm, seemingly sedate men were a hell of a lot of trouble, too. Exhibit one, Russ Bennett. *He sure fooled me. Fooled us both.*

Gwyn needs to know. Before Lucy knew it, she was dialing.

'Mel's Morgue. You stab 'em, we slab 'em,' Gwyn deadpanned.

On any other day Lucy would have laughed. Today she had to swallow back a sob. 'It's Lucy.'

'Well, duh. I can see the caller ID. You think I answer that way for everybody?'

'No. Of course not.' Lucy had to stop. Suddenly her heart was beating way too fast again as her mind raced. *What am I doing?*

You can't tell her. If the cops find out you told her Russ is dead, you could both be in trouble. Because Gwyn had also known Russ. *Known,* as Ruby would have said, and that hadn't been pretty. At all. Gwyn needed to know Russ was dead, but not until the Bennetts had been informed. And not until the cops knew it all.

Gwyn had not done this. Lucy had never been more sure of anything in her life. But Gwyn would still be a suspect. *Just like me.*

You can't let them blindside her. She'll be so hurt. She'll hate you forever.

No, Lucy knew that wasn't true. Gwyn wasn't capable of hating anyone forever.

Not like I have. But that was an issue for another day.

'Lucy? What's wrong? Are you okay, honey?'

She couldn't tell Gwyn, not yet. 'Um, I need to talk to Thorne.'

'What happened?' Gwyn demanded.

'Don't be mad, but I can't tell you yet. Please, put me through to Thorne.' Thomas Thorne was Gwyn's boss, their friend, and one of the best bass players in the city. Today Lucy cared more that he was also one of the best defense attorneys in the city.

'He's in court,' Gwyn said worriedly. 'But I'll have him call you as soon as he gets out. This is about that body this morning, isn't it? The one you were supposed to find.'

Normally Lucy admired Gwyn's quick mind. Today, not so much. 'Yes.'

'Lucy, just tell me you're okay. Are you in any danger?'

'No. I'm here in the morgue. I'm okay, I promise. And I'll tell you as soon as I can.'

'Okay,' Gwyn said doubtfully. 'Come to the club tonight. It'll make you feel better.'

After the day she'd had, the club sounded like nirvana. 'If I can, I will.'

'Mowry says people have been calling to ask if you're coming in.'

'If I can, I will.' *If I'm not in jail. Again.* The thought terrified. *Again.*

'Look, I'm meeting Royce for lunch. Why don't you join us? I'll ask him to invite one of the guys from his office for you.'

Lucy wanted to scream. *No, I cannot meet you for lunch. I am in trouble here.* But of course she did not. 'No thanks. I've got a ton of work. You two have a good time.'

'Mel's Morgue is always bursting at the seams,' Gwyn said fretfully and Lucy knew her friend had not been convinced. 'You've got to eat.'

No, I don't. I really don't. Nausea was clawing at the back of her throat and she swallowed it back down, injecting a calm smile into her voice so that Gwyn would stop worrying. 'I ate a really late breakfast so I'm not hungry. You have fun with Royce, and thank him again for me. It was sweet of you two to wait around for my late flight last night. I appreciated the ride.'

She looked up when the door opened. It was Craig Mulhauser, and he looked upset. Not angry, but very, very concerned and both the smile and the calm she'd conjured disintegrated. 'I have to go, hon. Have Thorne call as soon as he can.'

She put her phone on the counter, squared her shoulders. 'I was calling my attorney,' she told him.

'Probably wise, just to be on the safe side. Ruby told me that it's Bennett. I'll stay here with you until the detectives come. Then we'll play it by ear.' He smiled, but his was as forced as hers had been. 'I wouldn't worry, Lucy. You're an innocent bystander here. You haven't done a thing wrong.'

This time, was his unspoken implication. Grimly she remembered her last exchange with a living and livid Russell Bennett. She thought of the blood gushing from Russ's nose and the very public place in which she'd said some very unwise things.

Things that were now about to come back and bite her in the ass. Or worse.

Craig cleared his throat. 'If they ask me about it, what should I say?'

Lucy sighed quietly. 'The truth.'

Monday, May 3, 11.00 A.M.

'I liked it a helluva lot better when she didn't know the vic,' JD muttered as he drove away from Christopher Jones's neighborhood.

'I know.' Stevie Mazzetti studied her partner's face. He'd been taken aback by Lucy's admission that she knew Russell Bennett. He'd been taken aback by Lucy in general, and while under any other circumstances that might be a good thing, under these circumstances it was not. 'Why didn't you ask her how she knew him?'

He'd just told Lucy to stay where she was, that they'd come to her.

'I almost did,' he said. 'But I figured Hyatt would have our asses for not doing it in person and he'd be right. The woman's not quick to share, but her eyes say a lot. We need to be in the room with her when we talk to her about Bennett. Plus, we need to make sure it actually is Bennett.'

It wasn't a bad answer, Stevie thought, even if it wasn't the whole truth. Even though they'd been partners only a few weeks, she'd known JD a long time and knew when he wasn't spilling all. He'd been relieved in Hyatt's office when she'd said Lucy didn't have a significant other. And he'd been stunned and annoyed just now when he found out she'd known Bennett.

He glanced over at her. 'What?' he asked petulantly. 'You're thinking again. I don't like it when you do that.'

She smiled wryly. He knew her, too. 'She's cute. Lucy, I mean.'

This time his glance was a glare. 'Stevie,' he warned.

'JD,' she mimicked. 'So, apart from the obvious, you're right. We need to talk to her in person. But she didn't do this. She's being used for some reason. Let's go by Bennett's place, see if he's home.'

'He'd be at work by now.' He frowned. 'But if he's alive, he's got some explaining to do about those implants. He'd be able to tell us who got Jones's cheeks, but he probably won't. If he's dead, we're going to want to see his files. We're going to need a warrant for his office either way. Gray's not going to like us today.'

'Gray doesn't like us most days,' Stevie said, although that really wasn't true. DA Grayson Smith was one of the nicest guys a body could meet – outside the office. But at work he tolerated no bull. It would be terrifying to be on the wrong side of the courtroom when he was prosecutor. He was more dedicated than any DA she'd ever met.

Even more than the one she'd been married to, for which she'd been grateful. At least she'd seen Paul during the years they'd had together. Paul had understood the balance between his family and his job. Gray either didn't or didn't feel he needed to, as he had no family waiting at home. It was hard to say. Because even she, probably one of Gray's oldest friends, had a hard time cutting through the steel exterior he'd forged.

'I'll call for Bennett's address,' she said, 'then I'll start the warrant. You call Hyatt.'

JD's lip curled in a soft snarl that made him look like James Dean. She'd often wondered if that was what the JD stood for, but the one time she'd asked, he'd deftly sidestepped the topic. So she'd left it alone.

Stevie understood the value and necessity of boundaries.

'Fine,' he grumbled. 'I'll call Hyatt. I suppose it's marginally better than requesting a warrant from Smith. Check and see if Bennett's been reported missing. Hyatt'll ask.'

'He's not been reported missing,' she told JD when she'd hung up with Records, and gave him Bennett's home address, a luxury condo overlooking Inner Harbor.

'Pricey neighborhood,' he noted. 'Fits with the Rolex and the shoes.'

'That's a lotta mammaries,' she said and he swallowed a snort, turning it into a cough. 'Now, you call Hyatt and I'll beard Gray in his den.'

Her call to Gray's office line was picked up by Daphne Montgomery, a woman in her early forties who hailed from tiny Riverdale, West Virginia, a fact she told everyone the first time she met them, by way of apology for the 'dang twang'. Stevie liked her a lot but knew that the woman was driving Grayson crazy with her big hair and the homemade casseroles and cobblers she brought in every day to tempt him to eat.

You go, girl. The man needed a keeper.

'Hey, Daphne, it's Stevie Mazzetti.'

'Stevie. How's that precious girl of yours?'

Stevie smiled. 'Cordelia is just fine, thanks. Is *he* about?'

'Yes, but he's in one terrible mood today.'

'He always is. Put me through, please. Tell him I said it was important.'

'It's your funeral, baby girl.'

54

A moment later Grayson's annoyed voice came over the line. 'God help me, Stevie, I'm going to scream.'

'What is it today?'

'Peach. I'm allergic to peach. Gives me hives.'

'Did you tell her you were allergic the last three times she made it?'

'No,' he said, sounding like her five-year-old daughter. 'I will.'

'She's a nice lady, Gray. Put it aside and I'll take it home. Peach is Cordy's favorite of all Daphne's cobblers. Look, I have a situation that needs a warrant.'

'You always have a situation that needs a warrant,' he said sourly.

'This one needs a special one. It's for a doctor's office.'

Gray sighed. 'And on a Monday, too. Let's have it.'

She gave him the details. 'So we need a warrant either way.'

'We're nowhere close to having enough for a warrant. It's possible that your vic ended up with somebody else's cheeks through an honest paperwork error.'

She'd known he'd say that. 'Then if Bennett's not dead, he knows who our vic is. He'll cite doctor–patient privilege crap.'

'But you think he's dead.'

She thought about the ring and the watch. And the Roman numeral 'I' burned into the victim's back. *We don't have time for this.* 'Yeah, I think the stiff is Bennett. If he's missing, can we get a warrant for his residence?'

'We should be able to. I'm due in court in fifteen minutes, so call Miss Montgomery once you find out if he's alive and kicking or not. She can get the paperwork started.'

She hung up at the same time JD did. He was rolling his eyes.

'Hyatt has already decided Lucy Trask is involved,' he said.

'And you've decided that she's not,' Stevie said mildly.

JD flashed her an irritable look. 'So did you.'

'I don't think she killed him, for God's sake. But she is involved, JD, on some level. She was set up to find that man's body, whoever the hell he is. The sooner we find out how she knows him, the better. I hope to hell she's got an alibi.'

'That would be ideal,' he said dryly, slowing to turn onto Bennett's street. 'We're almost there. Did we get a warrant for Bennett's place?'

'Nah. Grayson wants to know if Bennett's dead first.'

'That would be ideal,' he repeated. 'Maybe this guy can tell us.' JD pointed to a uniformed doorman standing in front of Bennett's condo building.

'Sorry,' the doorman called when JD parked on the curb. 'You can't park there.'

Stevie showed him her badge and the doorman frowned. 'I'm Detective Mazzetti and this is Detective Fitzpatrick. We're looking for a Dr Russell Bennett.'

The doorman's eyes narrowed suspiciously. 'He's not here.'

'Not here, as in he doesn't live here or he isn't here at the moment?' JD asked with an easy smile. Stevie liked that about him. He could be good or bad cop with ease, and that Irish smile of his had disarmed many an unwilling witness in the three weeks they'd worked together. Lucy Trask didn't stand a chance against that smile.

'He lives here,' the doorman conceded grudgingly.

Stevie took a notebook from her pocket. 'Your name, sir?'

'Herrigan. Dennis Herrigan. What d'ya want with Dr Bennett?'

'We just need to talk to him,' JD said smoothly. 'It's with regard to an ongoing investigation. We can't say more than that. You know how that is.'

'Yeah, I know,' Herrigan said with a big sigh. 'But he's not here. He's on vacation.'

'Oh.' JD looked disappointed. 'Do you know when he'll be back?'

'Should be soon. He's been gone for two weeks.'

'That's some vacation,' JD said with a shake of his head. 'Wish I had two weeks to go off and party.'

'Don't we all,' Herrigan said. 'But he needed it. The doc works hard.'

JD frowned. 'We're going to catch . . . you know, from our boss if we come back empty-handed. Is there a Mrs Bennett? Could we maybe talk to her?'

56

Herrigan's expression went dark. 'Haven't seen her in weeks.'

'You don't like her,' JD said, his voice gone quietly conspiratorial.

Herrigan darted an apprehensive look Stevie's way. 'It's not my place to say.'

Which, of course, said it all. JD was in the zone with this witness and Stevie knew the man would speak more freely if she weren't there. She held up her phone. 'I'm getting a call. Wait till I get back.'

She stepped away and put her phone to her ear, pretending to take a call when she was really listening to JD, who blew out a breath. 'Sorry, man,' he whispered. 'She's . . . you know how it is. But she's senior and I gotta keep my nose clean.'

'I know,' Herrigan muttered. 'Got one at home.'

'So what about Mrs Bennett?' JD clicked his tongue lasciviously. 'I heard she was a looker.'

Stevie bit back a smile. JD had been a top narcotics detective, going undercover from time to time. He was almost too good at this.

'Bennett don't date the ugly ones,' Herrigan whispered loudly.

'I heard he . . . you know, *supplemented* her figure, *if* you know what I mean.'

Herrigan's laugh was raunchy. 'That he did. Not that she appreciated it. Bitch. She's trying to take him for every cent he's got. Luckily the doc had a pre-nup. I stopped her from going up last month when he wasn't home. The doc had to get a court order keeping her out because she was stealing all the artwork he'd collected.'

'She hasn't tried to come up while he was on vacation?'

'Not that I've seen.'

'When did he leave?'

'Let me think. Two weeks ago Sunday. I don't normally work Sundays but I'd traded with one of the guys who had Orioles tickets. Third base line.'

'Sweet. Wish I could take the time off for a game, but boss-lady over there won't let me. So you saw the doctor in the afternoon?'

'Yeah. I called him a cab.'

'To the airport?'

Herrigan hesitated and Stevie turned enough so that she could see him from the corner of her eye, the phone still at her ear. He was frowning. 'No. I can't remember where, but it wasn't to the airport.'

'Did he tell you where he was going on vacation?' JD asked.

'No. Well, yes, but not me directly. He called the desk the next morning. I wasn't on duty yet. Said he'd gone down to the Virgins and to make sure we stopped the paper and the mail. So we did.'

'When you put him in the cab, did he have a suitcase?'

'A briefcase. He must've come back for the suitcase when I was off duty.' Herrigan straightened, his eyes narrowing suspiciously once again. 'Why?'

JD smiled again, but Herrigan had caught on. 'We're just looking to talk to him.'

Stevie walked back to where the men stood. 'Sorry that took so long.'

'Not a problem,' JD said, then took a card from his pocket and wrote his cell on the back. 'Mr Herrigan, please call me if you see him or if you remember anything at all.'

Herrigan's eyes widened at the 'Homicide' on JD's card. 'Is she dead? Mrs Bennett? 'Cause if she is, the doc did not do it. That woman had all kinds of men, bad ones. Any one of them coulda done it.'

JD's brows lifted. 'We could use some names, a place to start.'

'Don't know their names,' Herrigan said, now surly. 'She'd meet them down the street when she lived here and they'd go off to do God knows what. But I saw them.'

'What about the wife's name?' JD asked.

'Brandi, with an i,' he said scornfully. 'Signed for things with a little heart over the i. Was about as mature as a seventh-grader. Bitch.'

JD wrote it down. 'If you see them again, call me. Thank you.'

Once they were in the car, Stevie nodded approvingly. 'Good guess that the wife had supplements.'

JD shrugged. 'Thanks for the mammaries. It just made sense. Bennett must give that guy one hell of a Christmas bonus to inspire such loyalty.' He pulled away from the curb, his hands tense on the wheel. 'So do we talk to the wife or Dr Trask first?'

'We know Lucy didn't do this. Let's head back to the morgue and see what she can add. I'd like any background we can get before we talk to the wife.'

Monday, May 3, 11.45 A.M.

A few hours' sleep and a good cup of coffee were all he'd needed. Feeling downright chipper, he parked his Lexus near his dock, pulled out his cell phone and opened up Trakamatik's website. The little blue dot blinked at the morgue, just where it was supposed to be, because that's where Lucy Trask was.

He didn't expect her to bolt today, but she would once the bodies began to stack up and she knew her jig was up. He imagined she'd turn tail and run when she realized she'd be found out for the liar she was and the crimes she'd committed, and he wanted to be able to find her when she did. Thanks to modern technology, that was as simple as the tracking device he'd slipped in the lining of her purse. It had been so easy. Women were completely careless with their handbags.

Which was good for him. He could log into the website from anywhere, on any computer. Or even his phone. For now, little Lucy was where she was supposed to be.

Locking his car, he paused at the end of his dock, taking a minute to admire his handiwork. He'd repaired the broken planks and cleared away the junk. The property was shaping up, if he did say so himself.

James Cannon had owned this place, but he hadn't deserved it. He certainly hadn't taken care of it.

Cannon's name had been the first on the list provided by Malcolm Edwards, two months ago. Getting the list had been an amazing rush. Killing Malcolm and his wife . . . simply unforgettable. He'd psyched himself up for the Malcolm kill, and the high had lasted for *days*.

But when he'd taken James Cannon out on Malcolm's boat to slit his throat, it was just . . . *bleh*. No finesse. No panache. And nobody to know what he'd done. He realized that some of the rush had been Malcolm's horror in watching his wife die.

They deserved that horror. Every name on his list deserved it. So when he'd killed Cannon alone, it had been a shallow victory. Nothing to savor.

Except Cannon's two properties. This place here on the water and Cannon's upscale condo in downtown Baltimore. He'd use them until he was finished. Having a center of operations plus a cushy place to crash after a day of killing was a boon.

Cannon had certainly had an eye for real estate. Luckily he was a virtual recluse. He was cut off from his family. He had no friends. Nobody missed him. *None of his neighbors even blinked when I told them I'd sublet his condo*. He'd simply taken the key off Cannon's body and moved himself in. No one asked where James was. No one cared.

Nobody around this place on the water asked either. He'd found the deed in Cannon's drawer, and when he'd driven his Lexus out here to check it out, he'd been thrilled. It was a fish processing plant, or it might have been if Cannon had managed to finish what he'd started. Inside the plant were equipment and tools. Power saws and freezers. And the best part – a dock with a harbor deep enough for his boat.

He continued down the dock and jumped to the glossy deck. Gone were all traces of Malcolm Edwards and his wife. No one would ever know *Carrie On* had once been painted over the bow.

World, meet the *Satisfaction*. If anyone thought to look it up, the *Satisfaction*'s altered registration would come up obviously fake, but it wouldn't come up as Malcolm Edwards's boat, either.

Because it's my boat. I have my own boat again. Finally. He thought of the boat they'd once had. The *'Vette*, named for his mother. His father had loved that bucket of rust. *So did I*. They'd spent many a long day pulling crabs from the bay onto the deck of that old fishing tub. For some, crabbing was a diversion, a way to spend a sunny Sunday afternoon. For his family, it had been their livelihood.

But it was all long gone. The *'Vette*. The crabbing business. The family. All long gone. Because of Malcolm Edwards and James Cannon and Russell Bennett and all the others. They'd taken the heart of his family. They'd taken their fortune. They'd taken everything. He wanted them to pay.

And he'd found he wanted people to know what he'd done to each and every one of them. Slitting Cannon's throat and dumping his body in the Bay had given him no satisfaction. Nobody had seen. Nobody would have cared if they had.

So he'd plotted and considered and reordered the names on his list. Russ Bennett had moved to the top and become his lab rat of sorts. He'd played out every twisted fantasy he'd ever had and it had been so good. *So very good.*

And the cherry on top – like Malcolm Edwards, Bennett had been loaded. Torturing their bank account IDs and passwords out of them had been mere child's play. Transferring all their money to his own accounts, easier still.

Now their money belongs to me. He was racking up property and wealth faster than a kid playing Monopoly. *And I'll take care of it. I know what it's like to go without. Because of them.*

They weren't using their money any longer. *I might as well enjoy it. Besides, they owed me this, the life I should have had.* The life he would have had.

The life Lucy Trask now does have, actually. For that alone, she'll pay. Soon.

Now he had a different fish to fry. So to speak.

He went down the steps to the *Satisfaction*'s cabin and opened the head door. There she was, naked, tied, gagged, and perched on the toilet seat, just where he'd left her. Her eyes were wide and terrified. The barbiturate cocktail he'd used to knock her out had worn off. She was hyperventilating around the gag. Most excellent.

'Hello there, Mrs Gordon,' he said quietly. Her sixty-five-year-old face was tighter than a drum thanks to cosmetic surgery. 'Do you remember me? No? That's okay. I don't think we've ever been formally introduced. But who I am isn't nearly as important as who my sister was. And who your son is. And what he did twenty-one years ago.'

Her eyes flickered wildly and he knew Russ Bennett had told

him the truth. Janet Gordon knew what had happened then. She'd kept it quiet all these years. Mostly.

Hatred boiled up from his gut. This woman didn't deserve the air she breathed. He balled his hand into a fist, so wanting to smash the face she'd placed above everything else. Above everything *right*. But he controlled himself. *In due time*. She'd be sorry.

'Russ Bennett told me all about you,' he whispered harshly. 'That you *knew*. That you blackmailed him into doing your little nips and tucks. I didn't believe him at first. You know, the quality of information extracted through torture is typically pretty low.'

She shrank back against the head's wall, her eyes filling with tears. She should have been pitiful, but the sight of her tears made his rage boil even higher.

'I kept thinking, how could a woman – a *mother* – benefit from the suffering of an innocent girl? And how stupid were you to trust Bennett not to let the knife slip or give you a little too much anesthetic? But you did trust him and here you are, with your perky tits and your tucked tummy and your face stretched tighter than a trampoline.' He grimaced. 'Can you even blink?'

She blinked, but barely, sending tears streaking down her cheeks.

'Oh, you poor, poor thing,' he crooned. 'How are you feeling? Terrible? Well, don't worry. It's about to get a whole lot worse. And when you're dead? Your son will come running all the way from Colorado to ID your body. And then I'll get my turn with him.'

'No!' she cried, the word muffled, but understandable.

'*Yes*,' he hissed. 'After all these years of living free, Ryan's finally about to get what's coming to him.'

'*No*.' She thrashed to get free and he simply watched, waiting until she tired. Within a few seconds her shoulders sagged, her chin dropping to her chest. He waited until she wearily lifted her eyes to him. He wanted to be sure she understood what was going to happen to her. He wanted to see the terror in her eyes.

He'd waited twenty-one years to see the terror in all their eyes. All the nights he'd lain in his bed, hearing his mother's sobs, his parents' angry words, his father's drunken shouts. Because of what Janet Gordon's son and his friends had done. And not done.

'I killed Malcolm pretty mercifully, all in all, because he cooperated. Once I'd convinced him it was in his best interest, anyway. He gave me the list of names, all the people who watched and did nothing. Like your son. Ryan just stood and watched and never lifted a finger to stop it. But at least he's had a lousy life too. Hasn't he? *Hasn't he?*' he repeated viciously and she nodded, her body trembling.

'Your son's been in and out of jail, drugs, depression, can't hold down a job. Russ Bennett, on the other hand, was rich and successful. That just didn't seem fair to me. Does it seem fair to you?' He grabbed her shoulders and shook her, hard. '*Does it?*'

Squeezing her eyes tightly closed, she shook her head.

He took the filleting knife from his pocket and unsheathed it. Pressed the tip under her chin, then tugged the gag from her mouth. 'Does any of this seem fair to you?'

'What . . .' She trembled so violently he pulled the knife back a fraction of an inch. *Don't want her to cut her own throat, for God's sake.*

'What what, Janet?'

She cringed, pressing back against the head's wall. 'What do you want from me?'

He leaned in so close he could smell her fear. 'I want satisfaction.'

'But I wasn't even there!' she cried. 'I didn't *do* anything!'

'That's exactly right. You. Didn't. Do. Anything.' He put the gag back in place and lifted her chin, studying her face. 'I tried everything on Russ, everything I've always wanted to do to all of you but couldn't, because I never knew who you were. Thanks to Malcolm, I now have the list. But thanks to Russ, I have you.'

And Lucy Trask, he thought. He'd altered his plan yet again when he'd heard everything Russ Bennett had to say. Bennett had been right about Janet Gordon. There had never been any doubt in his mind that what Bennett had said about Lucy was also true. She'd been a bully and a bitch, which went without saying as she was a Trask. She'd been a thief and even though she hadn't raised her own hand, by her silence she was as guilty. *And she'd profited.* Just like Janet. As far as he was concerned, Janet was simply practice for Lucy.

And practice did make perfect.

He tilted Janet's face, assessing. 'Let's see. Russ watched, so I gouged his eyes out. He said nothing, so I cut his tongue out. He never lifted a finger to help, so I cut off all of his fingers. And for fun I broke every bone in his face, and all his teeth, as was done to her.' He smiled. 'And the heart he claimed not to know about? I cut it out, too.'

His smile sharpened when she began to mewl in terror, tears now flowing steadily down her taut cheeks. 'I don't feel sorry for you, Janet, because my sister cried too. She begged. For mercy. For help. For somebody to do something. But your son did *nothing*. You did worse than nothing. At any time in twenty-one years you could have spoken, gotten justice. But instead, you *profited*.'

He squeezed her chin hard and she whimpered. 'For this *face*. I will enjoy every moment of killing you.'

He shoved her away in contempt, sheathed his blade. 'Quite frankly, I'm torn. I'd like to break every bone in your face, just like I did to Russ. On the other hand, I've got to leave a little something for your son to identify in the morgue.'

He backed out of the head, pausing outside the door. 'I'll be back later and we'll take a little sail. I'll take you up on deck, where I have more room to work. Cleanup's easier up there too. I'll take the gag off. And then you can scream all you want.'

Five

Monday, May 3, 12.05 P.M.

Dr Craig Mulhauser closed the conference-room door. 'Let's get this done so we can get on with business,' he said briskly. He was an older man who'd stood next to Lucy Trask like a bodyguard, making JD wonder what the two had been expecting.

She'd known Russ Bennett. *How?* And how well?

JD took the seat across from Trask. Mulhauser took the chair to her right with a protective air, while Stevie sat to her left. For a moment Trask ignored them all, studying her hands primly folded on the table. Then she looked up, resolutely. It was a face-the-executioner look, and JD got a bad feeling about what was to come.

'Do we know if Russell Bennett is alive?' she asked.

'No,' Stevie said. 'It doesn't look good. His receptionist said he wouldn't be in the office today when I called, posing as a patient confirming an appointment. She said that all his appointments had been cancelled. We drove by his condo on our way here. Pretty fancy place. His doorman told us Bennett had been on vacation for the last two weeks.'

'Herrigan,' Trask said with distaste. 'He keeps a good eye on the place for Russ.'

So she'd been to Bennett's place. And she called the victim by his first name. JD sat back, watching her. 'How did you know Dr Bennett?'

She drew a fortifying breath, her cheeks growing pink. 'I dated him for a while.'

JD tamped down his irritation at the disclosure while Stevie's eyes opened wide.

'You dated him?' Stevie asked. 'While he was married?'

Trask's face became redder. 'Until I found out he was married. I hadn't known. I never would have done that. I don't date much, period, and never married men.'

JD exhaled silently, relieved. 'Okay,' he said. 'So what happened?'

Trask looked away, rubbing her temple. 'You'll hear it when you start investigating, so I might as well tell you myself. I was supposed to meet him for dinner one night. He . . . ah . . . wanted to take our relationship to the next level. He'd been asking, but low key. Actually he'd been kind of patient. A really nice guy.' She said the last sarcastically.

'I take it that he wasn't,' JD said and she flicked an embarrassed glance his way.

'No,' she said. 'I was leaving my apartment when this woman ran up to me and slapped me right across the face. Hard. Called me a whore and a home-wrecker and husband-stealer and several names that my neighbors whispered about for months.'

'That would have been Mrs Russell Bennett,' Stevie said. 'Brandi.'

'No, this was the first Mrs Bennett,' Trask corrected. 'This was five years ago. He's been divorced and married again since then. But her slapping me was how I found out he was married. She'd been following him, had seen him kiss me good night in front of his condo after dinner the night before, and followed me home.'

JD pushed 'kiss me good night' and its resulting mental picture to one side of his mind. *Focus.* 'But she didn't slap you until the next night,' he said. 'Why did she wait?'

'I think she was too hurt and maybe too stunned the night she found out he was cheating on her. The night she slapped me, she was very drunk.'

'So I take it she didn't live at the apartment,' Stevie said.

'No. They had two places, which I also didn't know before. One in the city and one way out in the burbs, which I found out after I'd calmed her down. I told her that I didn't know he was married, swore to her. Maybe I looked so shocked that she believed me,

I don't know. She was too drunk to drive, so I called her a cab.'

'That was kind,' JD murmured. 'Considering she'd hit you. Hard.'

Trask shrugged uncomfortably. 'She was hurting.'

'As were you,' Stevie said kindly and Trask shrugged again.

'I was more mad than hurt.' She sighed. 'Which was the problem. I went to the condo. I'd met Russ there after work a few times. We'd grab dinner in the neighborhood. Herrigan saw me coming and got this panicked look. The next thing I know Russ is coming out of his building with yet another woman on his arm.'

JD winced. 'He was not a wise man.'

'You have no idea. The *other* other woman was my best friend, Gwyn. She didn't know about me, either. Or, as it turned out, the existing Mrs Bennett.'

JD shook his head, confused. 'Wait. You're best friends, but you didn't tell each other about who you were dating?'

'We weren't best friends then. We had been, when we were kids. We went to the same elementary school. We grew apart, because . . . life just happened. We actually became friends again because of that night. Gwyn's no dummy. She saw me standing there totally pissed off, saw Herrigan panicking and put it together. Russ tried to schmooze his way out of it, but we wouldn't let him. When I said I'd met Mrs Bennett, Gwyn lost it.' She hesitated. 'Because she had taken it to the next level with him.'

JD winced again. 'Ouch.'

'Which was what Russ said next, because Gwyn slapped him.' Trask stopped, a frown furrowing her brow. 'But then he hit her back, really hard. With his fist. Knocked her down on the pavement. Bloodied her lip, called her a whore. I hadn't expected that.'

'Hell of a guy,' Stevie murmured. 'Made friends all over the damn place.'

Trask's eyes had dropped back to her folded hands.

'What did you do?' JD asked.

'Nothing for a second. I was too shocked.' She met his eyes and he could see her apprehension. 'But then he reached down to hit her again. I think he'd forgotten that he was standing on a busy street. I put myself between him and Gwyn. He got in my face and I was really mad, so I got right back in his. I don't get mad often,' she said. 'But I was that night. He pulled a fist like he would hit me and I let him have it, right in the nose.'

JD felt the urge to high-five her, but restrained himself. 'And?'

'I broke his nose,' she said unapologetically. 'Blood was gushing. Gwyn was crying. Russ was cursing, I was yelling at Herrigan to call 911. People were gathering, some with their camera phones out. It was a zoo.' She glanced at Mulhauser.

The older man shrugged. 'You've told them this much, Lucy. You might as well.'

'True. I told Russ that if he ever lifted a hand to me or any other woman again that I'd make him sorry he was born. Then I said that he was lucky somebody hadn't killed him before now. It was stupid, and I really didn't say I'd kill him, but then . . .'

'He shows up in your back yard, dead, sorry he was ever born,' Stevie finished.

'Exactly,' Trask said. 'When you told me his name, I had Ruby Gomez put his body away. I was done with the cut, but was still looking at slides. Dr Mulhauser will go over my findings and corroborate everything.'

'Lucy did not do this,' Mulhauser said firmly.

JD's gut knew that was true, that she'd had nothing to do with this, but he had to ask. 'Where were you two weeks ago? Exactly?'

'In LA,' she answered. 'I flew out Sunday morning and stayed in the conference hotel all week. The following week I guest-lectured at UCLA. When did Herrigan say that he'd last seen Russ Bennett?'

JD and Stevie shared a quick look and Stevie gave a little nod.

'Sunday afternoon,' JD said and watched Lucy Trask's shoulders sag in relief.

'I was in the air by then and I never left LA. I imagine the airline and the hotel can confirm that, as can attendees at the conference and the class I taught. Lots of people saw me, every day. I can get you fifty names, easily.'

'That's good,' Stevie said. 'That should be an easy alibi to verify.'

'Your altercation with Dr Bennett happened five years ago,' JD said. 'Have you seen him since?'

'Once, at a party, two years ago. That's how I knew he'd been divorced since that night. The second Mrs Bennett was about twelve, I think,' she said grumpily.

'Lucy,' Mulhauser cautioned softly.

'Well, she was young. Maybe twenty. Large . . . attributes. The Mrs Bennett who slapped me was older than Russ. She'd had so much plastic surgery, trying to keep herself looking young,' she said bitterly, 'for a husband who cheated on her anyway. I hear Russ and the new wife were separated. I hadn't seen him in two years. Until today.'

'Why do you think he was left for you to find, Dr Trask?' JD asked softly and she looked up, the same troubled look in her eyes that she'd worn that morning.

'I don't know,' she said softly. 'I just don't know. He was not a nice man, but I can't see anyone angry enough to do that to him. This was brutal and inhuman. I can't see anyone dressing him like Mr Pugh. That was brutal, too. To me.'

'Who knew that you knew Bennett?' Stevie asked.

'Gwyn, of course. I told her boss, who's a defense attorney, and I told Dr Mulhauser. Mr Herrigan knew. And anyone who was standing outside Russ's condo that evening. I don't know who Russ told. Or who the first Mrs Bennett told.'

JD frowned. 'Why did you tell a defense attorney?'

'Same reason she told me,' Mulhauser answered. 'Because Bennett filed an assault complaint. The asshole knew it wouldn't stick, but he just wanted to fuck with her career. Sorry,' he added belatedly, while Trask patted his hand.

'Did anyone else here at the morgue know about the two of you?' Stevie asked. 'Anyone who would also have known that you were out of the office?'

'Nobody besides Dr Mulhauser knew. I think everyone here would be surprised to find I'd worked up enough gumption to date anyone, much less hit them.' Again she met JD's eyes, this time with a spark of defiance. 'Because I'm typically very boring.'

'Boring' was not the word JD would have chosen. Lucy Trask fascinated him. That she'd feel the need to warn him away fascinated him more. 'What's your friend Gwyn's last name?' he asked and watched the defiant spark in her eyes flash hot.

'She's not involved,' she said, her jaw gone taut. 'She was with her mother that weekend. They went shopping. I'm sure they'll have receipts. But I know you have to talk to her. Her name is Gwyn Weaver. She works for Thomas Thorne.'

'He's the defense attorney?' JD wrote it down, wincing on the inside. The one time he'd testified against a defendant repped by Thorne had not been fun. He didn't relish tangling with the man again on any level. 'Did you tell your friend about Bennett today?'

Some of her ire dissipated. 'I wanted to, but I didn't. I called her, but changed my mind before I said anything. I don't want her to look suspicious.' And it had cost her, he could see. She returned her gaze to lock with his. 'Because she is not involved.'

'I heard you the first time,' JD said mildly. 'Do you know what the killer used to cut out the vic's heart?'

She blinked, startled by the topic change. 'A Sawzall. Probably.'

It made sense. The power saw boasted the ability to cut through almost anything and was readily available at most hardware stores. 'Why do you think so?' he asked.

'From a visual inspection of the abrasions on the remaining bone. The blade size and serration is right and it has the power to do the job. Even the cordless models can cut through bone. With more time I could have given you a better description of make and model. I'm sure one of the other MEs still can.'

'How do you know it has the power to do the job?' Stevie asked.

'Trauma doctors use it in the field. For amputations. When necessary.'

JD had known that. He'd seen it done, in the field. But there was something in the way she'd said it – a restless discomfort – that piqued his curiosity. 'Have *you* used it in the field?' he asked and watched her eyes flicker.

She looked away. 'Yes.'

Mulhauser stared at her, surprised. 'When was this, Lucy?'

'After I finished my first residency. I was in Mexico and there was a car accident ahead of us. A little girl's leg had been crushed and she was bleeding out. The Sawzall was the only device that would have allowed me to free her in time.' She swallowed hard, the memory clearly a painful one. 'So your killer could easily have used one to cut through bone and sinew. Any other questions?'

'Did the little girl live?' JD asked softly and her lips twisted bitterly, surprising him.

'Yes. Any *other* questions?'

Tons. But he'd save them for another time. 'How did you meet Russ Bennett?'

'He wrecked my Big Wheel,' she said flatly.

JD wasn't sure he'd heard correctly. 'Your big wheel? What wheel?'

'You know, that big tricycle thing that kids ride. You must have had one.'

'No,' JD said, 'I actually didn't.' That wasn't the kind of childhood he'd had. 'How did Bennett wreck your Big Wheel?'

'I was four and his family had just moved in next door. A few days after they moved in, I was riding my Big Wheel down the hill in front of our house and the wheel came loose. I crashed into a parked car and broke my arm. One of the other kids heard him laughing and bragging about loosening the bolt.'

'How old was he?' JD asked, wondering why at four years old she'd been allowed to ride unsupervised in the street to begin with.

'Only seven. My dad marched over to his parents and told them what happened. Mr and Mrs Bennett grounded Russ even though he always insisted he hadn't done it, that the other kid had lied. Then later I found my favorite Barbie hanging by a rope from the swing set in our back yard. Again he was punished. After that he left me alone.'

Hell of a guy, JD thought. That Russell Bennett would use his fists on a woman made sense. He'd been violent from childhood. It looked like the man had pushed the wrong person too far this time.

'So you were neighbors?' Stevie asked.

71

'Yes. If possible, I'd like to go with you when you notify his parents. If this is indeed Russ.'

'We'd have to get that approved through our captain,' Stevie said. 'Lucy, I'm a little confused. If this guy was a jerk, why did you go out with him five years ago?'

'Time passed,' she said lightly. 'People can change. I wanted to believe he had.'

'Who contacted who?' Stevie asked.

'He looked me up when I moved to Baltimore for this job. I didn't want to see him, but he kept asking me out. One day I came home and found a box wrapped in gold paper on my doorstep. It was a Barbie – Doctor Barbie, actually.'

'Nice touch,' Stevie said dryly, and Trask's lips curved self-deprecatingly.

'Wasn't it? I agreed to go out once and thought he was nicer than I remembered, so I kept seeing him. I thought he was nice until his wife came up and slapped me.' She pulled her vibrating cell phone from her pocket. 'It's my attorney. Will I need him?'

'If your alibi checks out, no,' Stevie said, and Trask put the phone on the table without answering it.

'When will you check it?' Mulhauser asked. 'Because until you do, I'm down one medical examiner.' He shot Trask an awkward look. 'I can't have you touching anything new until you're cleared. I'm sorry.'

'I know,' she murmured. 'It's okay, Craig. I expected this.'

'I'll start making calls as soon as we leave here,' Stevie promised, then lifted a shoulder. 'Besides, we still have to positively ID this victim, Lucy. If it's not Russ Bennett, none of this is relevant.'

Mulhauser frowned. 'Unless there's a scar or some other identifying feature on the remains, we'll need to use DNA. The dental records will be unusable.'

'Are there any scars on the body that pre-dated this attack?' JD asked.

'Yes,' Trask said. 'There is scarring from an old burn on the left hand, and the right forearm shows some remodeling. It was broken within the last five to seven years. He also has a mole on his right shoulder blade. Perhaps you can ask one of his wives about this before asking his parents. If Russ really is on vacation, I'd hate to upset them for nothing. Mrs Bennett had a heart attack a few months ago.'

The affection in her voice was unmistakable. She'd obviously kept up with the Bennetts, despite her issues with Russell. 'Where do the Bennetts live?' he asked.

'Same place they've lived for thirty years. Anderson Ferry, on the Choptank River. It's a ninety-minute drive if there's no Bay Bridge traffic.'

Which meant that Anderson Ferry, Maryland, was where Lucy Trask had been raised. Which explained the hint of Southern in her speech. He'd met residents of Maryland's Eastern Shore who spoke with an unexpected twang. JD wondered if her family still lived there, but before he could ask, she opened a folder of autopsy photos.

'Here's one of the shoulder-blade mole,' she said, sorting the photos. 'And one of the scar from the burn. Neither of these pictures shows any of the assault injuries.' She looked up, her expression grim. 'And believe me, that wasn't easy to do.'

Stevie took the two photos. 'Thanks, Lucy. We'll start with the old and new Mrs Bennetts to find out if Russell had any of these marks before we go to the parents.'

'I have the first wife's address,' Trask offered.

JD's brows went up. 'You two keep in touch?'

'More like a one-way thing. She sent flowers after I broke his nose and I get a Christmas card every year.' Trask found the address in her phone and wrote it down. 'She kept the house and the kids. She's kept in touch with Russ's folks so the kids can have a relationship with their grandparents. The Bennetts like her.' She handed the paper to JD, careful not to touch him. 'They're good people and this is going to tear them up. Please don't forget to ask your captain if I can be there when you notify them.'

JD held her gaze and for a moment saw the flicker of awareness he'd seen before. It was quickly extinguished, her eyes going cool. But he'd seen it.

'I won't forget,' he said quietly. 'I promise. But you have to promise something too.'

He reached across the table, brushing her fingers briefly as he took the autopsy folder she still held, not missing the subtle twitch of her hand or the quick intake of her breath at the contact. Within the folder he found the photo of the 'I' burned into the victim's back and turned it so she could see it.

'This is a threat, Lucy,' he said softly. 'You were set up to find this man's body, whoever he is. Someone went to a lot of trouble to make that happen. You didn't do the murder, but you're connected. Until we find out how, you stick with people you know.'

Her cool control snapped, emotion churning in her eyes. He saw the awareness return, but also saw fear and anger. That was good. She needed to be afraid. *Just not of me.* Still, he got the feeling she *was* afraid of him and he didn't know why.

'I get it,' she said roughly. 'No dark alleys.'

'Or running before dawn,' he added. 'Promise me, Dr Trask.'

She nodded once, her eyes not leaving his. 'I promise.'

He handed her one of his cards. 'Both Stevie's and my cell numbers are on the back. Call us if you need us.'

She took the card gingerly, again avoiding his fingers. 'I will. Thank you.'

'Then we'll get to work,' Stevie said. 'We'll be in touch.'

Lucy watched them leave, her heart pounding wildly. Stevie had patted her shoulder comfortingly as she'd pushed away from the table, but Fitzpatrick hadn't touched her again. He hadn't needed to. Her hand still tingled from that brief brush of their fingers. Her cheeks still burned from that last long look he'd leveled before he'd closed the conference room door on his way out.

Fitzpatrick was very interested. Her 'boring' warning had had the opposite effect, only intensifying his not-so-subtle study of her face as he'd sat across the table. *I don't want him to be interested.*

But of course she did. *Goddamn me.* She gritted her teeth. *Won't you ever learn?*

'That went better than I thought it would,' Craig said.

She realized he'd been watching her. 'Yes, it did,' she murmured. 'I have an alibi.'

'I could see they didn't think you had anything to do with it from the moment they walked in,' Craig said. 'Especially Fitzpatrick. I think he likes you,' he added slyly.

She wanted to wince. 'It doesn't matter if he likes me or not.'

You, Lucy Trask, are a big liar. Having a man like JD Fitzpatrick interested mattered a great deal. He was sexy, kind, and had a magnetism that drew her gaze despite her best intentions. Ruby had called him a narcotic, which was probably the most accurate description.

He'd be amazing in bed. The thought sent a new shiver across her skin. *Oh, God.*

Which was precisely why she needed to keep her distance. Even if every nerve in her body was telling her to run closer. *Maybe just once.* What could it hurt?

Everything. Unbidden, the squeal of tires and the sickening crunch of metal filled her memory. Her mind went quiet, until all she could hear was the baby's wail that still invaded her worst nightmares. What could it hurt, indeed? *Everything.*

Craig frowned, still watching her. 'Whatever you say,' he said skeptically.

'So, what about me? Am I on leave?'

'Yes. Until you're officially cleared. Luckily you were just back and hadn't had time to start any other cases.'

'But we're so behind.'

'That's mine to worry about. I'll figure something.' He rose, tugging his suit coat into place. 'Go home for now. And remember what they said about being alone in dark places. I don't want anyone finding you slumped over a chess table.'

Lucy followed him from the conference room, the memory of this morning's chess table pushing the baby's cry from her mind. She thought about the body back in the cold room. The man had no face, no fingers, no tongue. *And no heart.*

It was Russ. Every instinct she possessed told her it was.

Fitzpatrick was right. *I am involved, somehow.* But how? And why? *Why me?*

Monday, May 3, 1.00 P.M.

Lucy headed to the parking garage, looking over her shoulder every few feet. She was suddenly conscious of how empty the garage was, even in the daytime. And she was suddenly conscious of how isolated she was. Her back went rigid and she picked up her pace, her key clutched in one hand.

She passed a parked car with a man in the driver's seat. *Watching me.* He got out and, ignoring her, pulled an armful of books from his trunk. *Okay, not watching me.*

'Lucy.'

She heard the voice a split second before hitting a hard body full on. Stifling what would have been a shriek, she looked up. And up some more.

'Thorne,' she breathed in relief. 'You scared me.'

He'd gripped her shoulders to steady them. Thomas Thorne was a huge man, at least six six. Even Fitzpatrick would have to look up at him. Right now Thorne's handsome face was scowling. 'You didn't pick up your phone.'

She thought of the call she'd left unanswered. 'I was talking to the detectives.'

His scowl deepened. 'Without me?' he growled. He had a deep, gravelly voice that carried through a packed courtroom without a microphone.

If she hadn't known him so well, she might have been unnerved. 'I had an alibi.'

His eyes narrowed. 'Famous last words. Are you that stupid?'

Annoyed, she took a step closer, lifting her chin. 'No. Any other questions?'

Did the little girl live? She heard Fitzpatrick's quiet voice in her mind. That's what he'd asked after she'd told them she'd cut off a human leg with a Sawzall and once again she thought of the first time she'd seen him, standing across her autopsy suite. His feet had been spread solidly, arms crossed over his chest, his face stoically stern. She especially remembered the tears in his eyes. They'd startled her that day.

The victim had been a three-year-old girl. He'd cared, just like he'd cared today.

JD Fitzpatrick was a very dangerous man indeed.

'What?' Thorne asked, giving her a little shake. 'You just went somewhere.'

Lucy refocused on his face. 'I'm fine. I've had an eventful day.' She told him what had happened, leaving out the missing body parts that the police wanted kept under wraps.

'Shit,' he murmured, but even a murmur from Thorne vibrated like a shout.

'Indeed,' Lucy said. 'Mazzetti and Fitzpatrick are verifying my alibi. I had a class full of students every day last week and had room service delivered almost every day. There was no way that I could have made it from Baltimore to LA and back again to kill Russ Bennett, or whoever that victim really is.'

'They'll come to talk to Gwyn,' he said and she sighed.

'I didn't tell her. I thought it would be worse for her in the long term if I did. But I did tell them she was with her mom the day Bennett disappeared.'

Thorne winced. 'She's gonna be pissed that you kept this from her.'

Lucy lifted on her toes so that she could pat his cheek. 'You'll sweeten her back up,' she said, hoping it was true. 'Just give her a new whip. She's worn the old one out.'

'I'll put it on your tab,' he said dryly, but he'd stopped scowling. 'I've got to run. Let me see you to your car. Let's go.' He started walking and she had to nearly skip to keep up with his long stride. 'If the cops want to talk to you again, you call me,' he ordered. 'And next time, do not say a word until I am physically at your side.'

She nodded dutifully. 'Yes, sir.'

'I've met JD Fitzpatrick,' he added crossly. 'I didn't like him.'

Her brows lifted, surprised. 'Why not?'

Thorne's mouth curved ruefully. 'He's a straight cop. I grilled him for a long time on the stand, but he never slipped once. Told the goddamn truth.'

Lucy frowned, unsurprised to hear that Fitzpatrick had integrity, but disliking the thought of him being grilled. She and Thorne argued about his career many an evening. Lucy's feelings were mixed. As were Thorne's. 'Did you get your client off?'

'No. He was guilty.' Thorne shrugged. 'But he got a fair trial so I slept that night.' He stopped when they got to her old Chevy. 'Call me when you get home.'

'Okay.'

He waited until she'd unlocked her car door. 'See you tonight at the club?'

'I'll try,' she said. 'I'm sorry I worried you, Thorne. Thanks for coming out.'

'It's all right, I was out anyway.' He backed away, doing the phone sign. 'Call me.'

Lucy knew that a lot of women would love to be getting the phone sign from Thomas Thorne, and at one time she might have been one of them. Not any more. Now she went for nice, sensible men who weren't trouble.

Fitzpatrick's face popped into her mind and she sighed. *Not like him*. He was trou—

Her thoughts scattered, her hand freezing on the car door. There was a box. On her floorboard. Wrapped in foil, it glittered. And around it was tied a big red bow.

The car had been locked and no one else had a key.

She snatched her hand from the door. 'Thorne?' she called, her voice trembling.

He was back in seconds, looking over her shoulder. 'What's that?'

'I don't know. I didn't leave it there.' She looked back at him. 'Did you?'

His expression was grim. 'No. Don't touch it.'

'I'm not stupid, Thorne.' She pulled her cell phone from her purse, commanding her hand to be steady as she searched for the card Fitzpatrick had given her.

'What the hell are you doing?' he asked, his own phone in his hand.

'Calling Fitzpatrick.' Heart pounding, she crouched down to better see the box. It was about the size of a softball. 'What are you doing?'

'I was going to call 911. Back up, Luce. You don't know what's in that box. It could be a bomb, for God's sake.'

Lucy aimed her keychain penlight at the box, illuminating the foil design and her pounding heart dropped to her gut. *No, not a bomb*. Not a conventional one anyway.

'I don't think so,' she whispered.

Thorne crouched behind her. 'Looks like somebody had wrapping paper left over from Valentine's Day.' He paused, studying her. 'You know what's inside, don't you?'

She dialed Fitzpatrick's number. 'I have a good idea.'

'So . . .' Thorne made an exasperated noise. 'What's inside?'

'Same thing that's on the outside,' she said, then held up her hand for quiet when Fitzpatrick answered, his voice low and urgent. 'Detective, it's Lucy Trask.'

'What's happened?' Fitzpatrick demanded. 'Are you all right?'

Slowly she rose, careful to touch nothing. 'I'm fine, but you need to come back. He's left a gift in my car. The box is wrapped in paper with purple, pink and red hearts.'

She heard him draw a breath. 'Shit. Where are you?'

'In the parking garage across from the morgue, second floor, east entrance.'

'Alone?'

She should have found the slightly accusatory note in his voice offensive. Instead she felt warmed. 'No. Thomas Thorne is here with me. We haven't touched anything.'

'Good. I'll send Drew and the CSU team right away. Stevie and I will be there as soon as we can. Will Thorne stay with you until the uniforms get there?'

She found herself wishing Fitzpatrick would turn around and come straight back, but knew Drew would have to do his thing before the detectives could do theirs. She looked up at Thorne. 'Can you stay a few minutes? Just until the cops get here?'

Thorne glared. 'Try to make me leave,' he growled.

'He'll stay,' she said to Fitzpatrick. 'What should I do when they get here?'

'Stay put. We'll be there soon.'

Monday, May 3, 1.10 P.M.

JD snapped his phone shut and returned his eyes to the road. His hands gripped the wheel, itching to turn them around and immediately return to the garage. And to Lucy Trask. But they were almost at Brandi Bennett's apartment. Squad cars could get to Lucy a lot faster.

'Dammit,' he muttered, reaching for the radio.

'What happened?' Stevie asked.

'The prick left a gift-wrapped box in her car.' He called Dispatch, requesting that squad cars, CSU, and a bomb detail be sent to the parking garage.

'How do we know it's from the prick?' Stevie asked when he'd finished.

'The wrapping paper is covered with hearts.'

'Oh.' Stevie grimaced. 'That's really nasty.'

'Really nasty? He cut the vic's heart out. I think he was already really nasty.'

'But he kept the heart. This is personal against the doc. How did Lucy sound?'

'Like she's keeping it together.' *Barely*, he added to himself as he thought about the little tremble in her voice as she'd asked him to come back. *She'll be fine. She's trained to keep a level head.* 'At least she's not alone. She was with Thorne.'

Which made his eyes narrow. He well remembered Thomas Thorne. The man had turned every female head in the courtroom, including the judge's.

'Well, politics aside, he is a big guy. Nobody's gonna bother her with him around.'

'You know him?' JD tried to make the question nonchalant, but he could see Stevie was not fooled. Stevie was rarely fooled.

'Only to be in court with him,' she said. 'He's a real piece of work, although I've never known him to out and out lie. If Lucy's with Thorne, she's okay for now.'

JD still wished he could turn the car around and be sure she was all right. But he had work to do. They were here. He pulled into a space in front of Brandi Bennett's apartment building. She'd been easy enough to find. She'd filed for a business license, citing this as her primary address. The nature of her business had been a little less easy to determine. The state's business directory said 'Modeling'. They'd have to see exactly what Mrs Bennett was showing off.

'You want to take the lead with the wife?' he asked.

Stevie shrugged. 'The doorman said she liked men. If you can soften her up with that dimple of yours, be my guest.'

Six

Newport News, Virginia
Monday, May 3, 1.25 P.M.

Clay could see the gray water of the Bay and boats bobbing in the distance. On any other day he might have been thinking of a quiet day fishing. But not today.

He pulled into the run-down subdivision where Evan had last lived. According to Nicki, it was all the man could afford after his wife had kicked him out.

Which, Clay thought, she'd been more than entitled to do. By his own admission, Evan had cheated on her multiple times with multiple women. The last of his women was the game-changer. Margo Winchester was certifiably insane, but would she—

Oh, God. Yes, she would. Clay slowed his car as he passed the little frame house which Evan had rented. It was gone. Burned to the ground. A Condemned sign was planted in the front yard, yellow crime-scene tape across what had been the door.

Margo had made good on her threat. Part of it anyway. She'd told Evan she'd kill him, then lay waste to everything he owned, including his children. She'd sent him letters, included photographs of his house, of his children at play in the schoolyard.

She'd meant business.

Clay dragged one hand down his face. He was tired. Which didn't matter at the moment. He needed to check the local death notices. Find out if Evan's body had been found. He needed to have a chat with Ms Margo Winchester. Because if Evan was still alive, Clay needed to get him to safety.

It was what Evan Reardon had paid for. Safe passage to a new life.

Of course, if Evan was dead, Margo needed to pay, and Clay would have to bring the matter to the attention of the police.

Without bringing attention to me. He pulled his cell from his pocket and dialed Alyssa, who answered on the third ring. 'Evan's house is a pile of charred rubble.'

'Oh, no.' She sighed. 'The crazy-assed bitch really did it. She killed him.'

'Perhaps. I need you to get me the address of the local newspaper. I need to find out if Evan's body's been found.'

'I'll text it to your phone. You can click on the address and it'll go to your GPS.'

He blinked. 'Really? Since when?'

'Since I loaded the app onto your phone.'

'Thank you. I need some more information. Check the back issues of all the local papers. I want the details on the fire at Evan's place before I hit the newspaper.'

'Are you gonna be you or somebody else?' she asked.

Clay hesitated. 'Not me, not yet. If Evan's still alive and just hiding somewhere, I don't want to give him away. And if Margo Winchester's cop daddy is involved, I don't want to show my hand too soon. For now I'm a fire insurance investigator. But I need the details on the fire first, plus who holds the mortgage on that house, if anyone does. Evan only rented it. Find out who their insurance is actually with, if you can. Do you know how to do those searches?'

'Nicki showed me once.'

'Good. While you work on that, I'm going to find Margo.'

Baltimore
Monday, May 3, 1.35 P.M.

Lucy stood outside the parking garage next to a squad car, her cell phone to her ear, wincing as Gwyn ranted. Drew was inside the garage with the bomb squad, who were checking out the box in Lucy's car. The growing crowd behind them was getting angrier by the minute because the garage had been temporarily shut down.

It had been the sight of the bomb squad that had snapped Lucy out of her shock, making her think of Gwyn's car. What if it wasn't a heart? What if it was a bomb? What if Gwyn had been left one too? They'd both been involved with Russ at one time.

Gwyn had been understandably upset when Lucy had called to tell her to check her car. And angry. And hurt. Gwyn had hung up to check her car, but was now back and rarin' to go.

'Why didn't you tell me it was Bennett?' Gwyn's voice shook. 'I would have come, sat by you when the cops grilled you. My God. Mr Pugh is like your father. No,' she amended, 'not like *your* father. Like *a* father. You wouldn't harm a hair on his head. You shouldn't have been alone when the cops were questioning you like a criminal.'

I wasn't alone, Lucy thought. *Fitzpatrick was there.* The thought startled her for a second, but then she admitted it was true. He'd made her feel safe. And not alone.

'Craig Mulhauser was there,' Lucy said wearily. 'And Thorne already yelled at me. Please don't yell at me anymore. I'm having a really bad day.'

Gwyn sighed. 'I'm sorry. But I should have been there. I would have come.'

'I know. But I'm an old hand at being questioned for murder. I was fine.'

Gwyn grew sullenly silent. 'That's not funny, Lucy.'

It was Lucy's turn to sigh. 'You're right. I promise that next time I'm under the bright lights, I'll call you. Are you okay?'

Gwyn laughed shakily. 'Yeah, now I am. I was so scared when I got your call that I left half a cannoli on my plate at Mama Rosina's.'

'Cannoli?' Lucy said wistfully. Her stomach had started to growl and she realized she'd eaten nothing all day. Suddenly she was starving. 'And Mama Rosina makes such a good one.'

'And ravioli,' Gwyn said, and Lucy frowned.

'Now you're just being cruel.'

'I would be if I hadn't brought you any.'

Lucy jumped when someone tapped her shoulder and she wheeled around to find Gwyn and Royce grinning behind her.

Hanging up her cell phone, Gwyn held out a large paper sack. For a moment Lucy could only stare, then the wonderful aroma from the bag smacked her in the face.

'You brought me lunch?'

'Of course.' Gwyn reached up to hug her hard. 'You can't be finding bodies and hearts on an empty stomach. And cannoli's always good for what ails you.'

Lucy peeled the foil from the tin and inhaled. 'Mmm. Thank you. Is there a fork?'

Royce handed her one. 'Sorry. It's one of those spork things. I guess they're worried you'll stab yourself.'

'No problem.' She dug in. 'You're sure there's nothing in your car?'

'No boxes,' Gwyn said. 'Royce and I checked twice.'

'She didn't tell me anything,' he said. 'But she got so pale that I wouldn't let her do it alone. Do we need to have the bomb squad check her car?'

'I don't think so. I'll let them know you looked already. This probably isn't a bomb either.'

'Are you all right, Luce?' Gwyn asked.

'I'm okay. Just . . . overwhelmed. Thorne stayed with me until the cops came.'

'I know. He called to check on me before he went back into court. He said you were in good hands with the cops.' Gwyn's chuckle was dry. 'And *that* statement alone shows what a fucked-up day this really is.'

Lucy laughed, then realized how much she'd needed to. 'The day Thomas Thorne felt safe with the cops . . . mark it on the calendar.' Abruptly she sobered. 'The bomb squad's coming out. I think we're clear. I gotta go.'

'I have to be getting back,' Royce said. 'Come on, babe. I'll take you to work.'

'Walk her in, will you, Royce?' Lucy asked. 'Make sure she's safe.'

'Hey,' Gwyn said, waving her hand in Lucy's face. 'I'm down here.'

But Royce nodded soberly. 'After all this? You bet. What about you? Who's making sure you're safe?'

Fitzpatrick. But even though she felt it was true, she wasn't about to say that out loud, so she gestured to all the police cruisers. 'They are, so don't worry.'

Gwyn reached up to hug her hard. 'Come tonight,' she whispered fiercely. 'I think I need to see that you're safe more than you need to be there. So please, indulge me.'

Lucy hugged her back. 'After all this? You bet.'

Monday, May 3, 1.35 P.M.

Stevie pounded on Brandi Bennett's apartment door again. 'Mrs Bennett,' she called loudly. 'Please come to the door.'

'Maybe she's not home,' JD said.

'Her car's outside,' Stevie said.

A door opened behind them and a middle-aged woman stuck her head out. Her expression was dour. 'She's home.'

Stevie gave her an encouraging smile. 'Thank you. And you are?'

'Dorothy Camellini.' Her eyes narrowed. 'You two cops?'

'Yes, ma'am,' Stevie said. 'I'm Detective Mazzetti and this is my partner, Detective Fitzpatrick. How do you know Mrs Bennett is home?'

Dorothy's brows shot up. '*Mrs* Bennett? I had no idea she was married. Her husband must either be very dead or very forgiving.'

'What do you mean?' JD asked. 'And how do you know she's home?'

'Because the walls are paper thin. I could hear them in the back room, just before you knocked, then they went quiet. Trying to wait you out.' Dorothy's mouth tightened. 'They *do* things in there, all day long. Her and those men. Sometimes all night. *Things*.'

Stevie leaned closer. 'You mean sexual things?' she murmured.

'Yes. It's disgusting. They're making porn in there.'

JD was unsurprised. When he'd seen 'modeling' on Brandi Bennett's business license, it had been the first thing he'd thought of. 'They might think we're Vice.'

'They may wish we were,' Stevie murmured. She pounded on the door again. 'We are not Vice,' she called loudly. 'Now all your neighbors know that too.'

Abruptly the door opened and a young woman appeared, clutching a short silk robe around her very augmented body. Her face was caked thick with makeup, her blond hair teased within an inch of its life. There was a fresh hickey on the side of her neck. 'Thank you,' she snapped. 'Now all my neighbors know the cops are after me.'

Stevie looked over her shoulder to where Dorothy watched, wide-eyed. 'We're good, ma'am. Thank you for your help.'

Dorothy gave Brandi a snide look before closing her door firmly.

Brandi looked at them defiantly. 'If you'd opened your door when we first knocked,' JD said mildly, 'we wouldn't have kept banging. May we come in?'

'No you may not,' she said nastily. 'Please hurry, I'm very busy.'

I'm sure you were. But JD kept his voice mild. 'You're Mrs Brandi Bennett?'

Her lip curled in contempt. 'Only until that prick of a husband of mine signs the divorce papers. Did he send you? Asshole. Tell him he's not getting these back.' She lifted her breasts high, and when she dropped them they didn't bounce at all.

Whoa. Okay. JD wondered if Brandi had given Russell Bennett his Rolex. 'He wants them back?' he asked carefully and she sneered.

'He wants everything back. I don't get back the gifts I gave him. No, sir. Asshole.'

'The Rolex,' JD said and she nodded.

'I even had it engraved.' She huffed, pouting. 'So if you're here because he said I stole something, he's lying. These' – she grabbed her breasts again – 'are the only things I walked away with, and you can tell him that he's not getting 'em back. Asshole.'

'We get the picture,' Stevie said. 'But we're not robbery detectives. I'm Detective Mazzetti and this is my partner, Detective Fitzpatrick. We're Homicide.'

Brandi's pout abruptly disappeared, her jaw going slack. 'H-h-homicide? Why?'

'We have reason to believe Dr Bennett is dead,' JD said.

Brandi's lipsticked mouth worked like a beached trout. 'Russ? Dead? When?'

'When was the last time you saw your husband, Mrs Bennett?' Stevie asked.

'Three weeks ago,' Brandi murmured. 'At his divorce attorney's office.' The shock slid from her eyes, replaced by panic. 'I didn't do it. I swear.'

'We didn't say you did,' JD said. 'We're just gathering information right now. Can you tell me if Dr Bennett had any distinctive moles or scars?'

She nodded numbly. 'Yeah. He had a mole on his back, near his shoulder blade. I kept telling him to have his partner remove it. It was disgusting.'

It was enough of an ID to get a warrant for Bennett's apartment, JD thought. 'Who is your husband's partner?' he asked, taking out his notebook.

'Leon Renquist. He does mostly faces. Did my nose. Russ was the breast man. He only did faces when Leon went on vacation.' She tried to look over JD's arm to see what was being written in the notebook, but he lifted the notebook higher and she scowled.

'Did Dr Renquist ever do any procedures on Dr Bennett?' JD asked.

She nodded. 'Once. Some bitch broke Russ's nose and Leon fixed it for him. Gave him some more cheekbone and shaved his chin while he was at it. I used to be mad at the bitch that broke his nose, but if I met her today, I'd give her a medal.'

Go, Lucy, he thought. 'Because Dr Bennett was—'

'An asshole,' Brandi supplied helpfully. 'I swear I didn't kill him. Lots of times I wanted to, but a whole hell of a lot of other people wanted it too. Looks like somebody finally wanted it enough. Did it hurt? When they killed him, I mean. I hope it really hurt.'

JD had to clear his throat. The lady wasn't the brightest bulb. 'Mrs Bennett, when did you and Dr Bennett separate?'

Brandi looked away, an angry flush heating her cheeks. 'About two months ago.'

'Why?' he asked. Stevie had stepped back, giving him the lead.

'He came home early one day. That damn doorman. Ratted me out.'

'Mr Herrigan told Dr Bennett that you had a lover in the condo?' JD clarified and she nodded angrily.

'Like the asshole didn't have his share of women. I mean Russ, not Herrigan. Herrigan couldn't get any from a blow-up doll, he was such a troll. I knew about Russ's women, I just didn't care. But what was good for the goose wasn't good for the gander.' She faltered. 'Or the other way. I guess he's the gander. Anyway, it must have hurt, because you're not sure it's his body. Whoever did it must've worked him over good.'

'But that wouldn't have been you,' JD said, and her cheeks darkened further.

'No. I have an alibi. I've been here, shooting movies because the prick cut off my credit cards and cleaned out my bank account.'

'Who might have wanted to hurt Dr Bennett?' JD asked. 'Besides you?'

Again she sneered. 'Any one of the six women he was doing on the side. Russ had a real addiction to sex. Couldn't get enough. But any woman who bedded him wanted his money. The guy sucked in bed. And not in the good way.'

JD had to fight the urge to clear his throat once again. 'Do you have names?'

'No, but Herrigan will. They all have to sign in with the little weasel. I think he used that sign-in sheet to get favors from Russ. Russ tipped him very well. I don't think Herrigan ever had to make a threat. Russ took care of his buds. Just not his wives.'

'So you get no settlement from the divorce?' Stevie asked.

'I signed a pre-nup.'

'Sometimes the pre-nup allows for a settlement of cash or assets,' JD said.

She glared. 'I know that. Do I look stupid? But Russ wouldn't agree to that.'

'You married him anyway,' JD said. 'Why?'

'Because he was *rich*,' Brandi said, as if JD was the stupid one. 'I figured I could sock away a nest egg to tide me over till I got a new sugar daddy, but the asshole found my stash and cleaned me out of that too. That's why I'm doin' porn. I got *nothin'*.'

Interesting. When she got agitated, Brandi had the same little twang that Lucy Trask did. Lucy's was just more refined. 'Where did you meet Dr Bennett?' he asked.

'At my high-school graduation party,' she said, daring him to comment. 'I was eighteen. He was visiting his parents and dropped by to see my uncle who was letting us use his place. I flirted, one thing led to another and we did it in my uncle's wine cellar. After that, Russ moved me to the city, set me up with a real nice place. Took me on trips to his ski chalet and his beach house on Hilton Head and bought me presents.'

'Where did you go to high school?' JD asked and her eyes flashed contempt.

'Little town in the middle of nowhere.' She lifted her chin. 'And I'll never go back.'

'Anderson Ferry,' JD said quietly.

Brandi nodded grimly. 'Like fucking Mayberry. Nothin' to do but sit on the front porch in a rocker and scratch your ass. I was eighty before I was eighteen.' She grabbed the doorknob. 'I didn't kill the sonofabitch, but when you find out who did, give 'em a big ole wet kiss from me.'

She started to step back, but JD put his hand on the door. 'One more question. Did you know of any injuries Dr Bennett had? Any broken bones?'

'Yes. He skied into a tree in Montana. Broke his arm.'

'Scary for a surgeon,' JD commented. 'He needed his hands to function.'

She shrugged. 'He got a good doctor. Sports guy. All the ball players use him.'

'You remember his name?' Stevie asked.

Brandi's lips curved mirthlessly. 'They must've done a real number on his face. You're asking about scars, broken bones. His doctor was Hampton. Hodgins. Started with an H. Can I go now? I've got work to do.'

'Yes,' JD said, 'but we'll want to talk to you again.'

'I got nothin' to hide. Literally.' She slammed the door in their faces.

Stevie knocked on Dorothy's door and it immediately opened, the neighbor's eyes wide. 'Here's my card,' Stevie said, handing her one. 'It's got both my and my partner's phone numbers on the back. If you see anything, hear anything, please let us know.'

Dorothy nodded. 'Are they allowed to do that?' she whispered. 'You know, make movies like that, in an apartment? Next to decent people?'

'They have to be licensed,' Stevie told her. 'We'll make sure the right people check into them. Thank you for your help.'

They waited until they were back in the car before Stevie whistled quietly. 'The doctor seems to have had quite a fascination with women from his home town.'

'Lucy, Gwyn and Brandi,' JD agreed. 'Maybe there are more.'

'I never would have guessed that Brandi and Lucy were from the same hometown.'

'I thought they might be. Brandi's voice has a similar cadence to Lucy Trask's.'

Stevie frowned. 'No way. Lucy sounds nothing like that woman.'

'Not normally. But when she was upset this morning, she sounded a little like that.'

Stevie was regarding him with a mixture of respect and curiosity. 'So I learn something new about you both. You've got a good ear.'

'Thanks.' He waited, but she said no more. 'What did you learn about Dr Trask?'

Stevie's expression became thoughtful. 'That she can lose her composure.'

He thought of the tremble in Lucy's voice when she'd called about the box. She'd been rattled, as anyone would be. But she'd kept her cool. *And she called me.*

'She can and did. Why is that surprising?' He sounded annoyed and didn't care.

Stevie's smile was knowing. 'I've worked with Lucy on maybe fifty cases and I've never seen her so much as break a sweat. I've certainly never seen her upset until today. But she's entitled. Most people would have cracked, but she didn't. That she let you see her vulnerable, well, that's just . . . unique. So, where to now?'

Mollified, JD started the car. 'For now, let's go check out the box in Lucy's car, then get a warrant for Bennett's condo. We'll need something for the lab to do a DNA. Then we need to talk to his partner. He might know who wanted to see Bennett dead.'

'My money's on one of the six women he was cheating with,' Stevie said. 'Or the first ex-wife. A woman scorned and all that. Plus there's the whole heartless thing. Ripping out his heart is a hell of a metaphor for betrayal. I bet Herrigan will sing like a bird when he finds out Bennett is dead. We'll have those six names in ten minutes.'

'I give Herrigan less than five to spill all.' JD merged into traffic, thinking about Bennett and his heart, or lack thereof. 'The missing fingers and the broken bones feel like torture, like maybe he had something someone wanted. But taking his heart . . . It was done post-mortem. That's not torture.'

'Like I said, it's a metaphor. A statement. It's personal.'

'And it's personally targeted at Lucy Trask,' JD said grimly. 'Why?'

'She knew the victim, grew up in the same town.'

'As did at least two of Bennett's other women.'

'But why would he hate Lucy Trask?' Stevie frowned. 'It doesn't make sense.'

JD sighed. 'Unless she's hiding something, like Hyatt said.' He didn't want to believe that. 'She's seemed upfront, though.'

'Maybe she doesn't know what she knows. Maybe Bennett didn't either. Seems that a man who was that concerned about himself wouldn't last too long under torture.'

'He would have caved. Maybe he did. Maybe this killer just likes to maim. Bennett has no heart because he was a betrayer. But the tongue . . . That was done while he was alive. Without a tongue he couldn't tell them what they wanted to know.'

'Also a statement?'

'I think so. He either said or didn't say something that he should have.'

'We need to know what that was. Especially if that mark was a number "I".'

'Especially if he's picked Lucy Trask to be number two.'

Stevie sighed. 'We've told her to be careful, and she's not stupid. Nor has she ever struck me as a woman who would take unnecessary risks.'

'No,' he murmured. *Which would be good for her safety and potentially bad for me.* Because mixed in with the interest he'd seen in her eyes had also been an apprehension that he didn't understand. It had almost bordered on fear. But that he'd deal with later. Number one priority was ensuring Lucy Trask did not become number two on a sadistic killer's list. 'But she's his target.'

'I know. We could put her in a safe house, but I'd rather have her close by to help us with the forensics.'

'What about police protection?'

Stevie shook her head. 'Not likely. If she were a witness against the mob for the state, then maybe, but not for this.' She shrugged when his frown deepened. 'Look, I don't like it any more than you do. Let me call Hyatt, give him an update. Maybe he can give us a few more bodies to do some of this legwork so we can find this guy faster and Lucy won't need protecting anymore anyway.'

Not likely. 'Ask him if Lucy can go with us to notify Bennett's parents.'

Stevie considered it. 'By now we should have the faxed affidavits from her hotel and the university saying she was in California the past two weeks. He might go for it.' Her brows lifted. 'And then she'd be with us. *Voilà*, police protection.'

JD inclined his head, saying nothing.

She smiled at him. 'Way to work the system.'

'I learned a thing or two in Narcotics,' JD said mildly. 'If Hyatt balks, tell him that three of Bennett's relationships were with women from his hometown. There's something there. Maybe Lucy can help us find it. Tell him she could be a consultant. At no charge to the department, of course.'

Stevie's smile widened to a grin. 'Now you're getting cocky. She can be our native guide into the wilds of Anderson Ferry and point out all the lions and tigers and bears, oh my.' She grimaced. 'Sorry, Cordelia's been on a *Wizard of Oz* kick. We've watched it four times in the last two weeks. I hear Munchkins in my sleep. Gives me a twitch.'

JD chuckled. 'I doubt we'll find lions, tigers or bears across the Bay Bridge, but at least Lucy can point out a place for decent crabcakes.'

Monday, May 3, 2.15 P.M.

Arms crossed tightly over her body, Lucy watched as Drew Peterson and the CSU team loaded her car onto a flatbed truck. They'd closed off the parking garage until the bomb squad had arrived, angering many car owners. But better angry than dead.

Luckily there was no bomb. The X-ray had shown the box to hold only a fist-sized mass of muscle, just as she'd suspected. Russ Bennett's heart was now on its way to the CSU lab. The very thought made her sick.

That Russ's killer had free access to her car made her far sicker. *How?* And why?

That her car was also on its way to the CSU lab was the icing on top. 'How long do you have to keep it?' she asked wearily.

'A few days, maybe longer,' Drew said. 'I'm sorry, Dr Trask.'

'Sorry for what?' asked a low voice behind them and Lucy tensed, her heart starting to pound all over again. Fitzpatrick was back, standing mere inches behind her and a hard shiver prickled her skin. The man was so warm and she had been so cold, all day. She had to hold her shoulders stiff to keep from leaning into him and all that delicious heat. Wouldn't be safe. Wouldn't be right. *Don't do it, Lucy*.

'We have to take her car,' Drew told him. 'I'd be surprised if this guy left any fingerprints, but we're going over it with a fine-toothed comb.'

'I guess I'll just rent a car until you're done with it.'

Fitzpatrick cleared his throat. 'I have an extra car that's just sitting in my garage. You're welcome to borrow it, Dr Trask, for as long as you need it.'

Startled, Lucy turned to look up at him over her shoulder. 'You're joking.'

He held her gaze, his eyes totally serious. 'Nobody drives it. It just sits.'

'I cannot borrow your car, Detective,' she said, but even to her own ears she sounded unsure.

His smile was quick and easy, his dimple flashing. 'Sure you can. No reason to waste your money on renting a car. Unless you've got money to burn. Do you?'

She hesitated, that dimple drawing her gaze like a magnet. A little panic bubbled up into her throat. She squelched it firmly. Just because she was attracted to Fitzpatrick did not mean she had to do anything about it. *It's still my choice. And I choose no.*

'You don't even know me. Why on God's earth would you trust me with your car?'

'You have any traffic tickets?' he asked.

'Of course not,' she said stiffly. 'I don't speed. You know how many autopsies I do on idiots who drove too fast?'

He blinked, nonplussed. 'I imagine more than I'd like to count.'

'Exactly. So no, I don't have any tickets.' She frowned when he pulled his key ring from his pocket. 'What are you doing?'

'Giving you the key.' He pulled it off the ring, took her hand and pressed the key into her palm. 'Your hands are freezing again.'

She watched as his hand closed her fingers into a fist around the key, the metal warm from being in his pocket, next to skin. His hand was temptingly dark against hers. He probably worshipped the sun. Skin cancer, just waiting to happen. 'You're crazy,' she murmured, 'you know that?'

His hand lingered a moment longer. 'It's just a car, Lucy,' he said softly.

She looked up, found his gaze intense and her body clenched in a way it hadn't in a very long time. It was just a car. He was just a cop. This was just . . . expedient. *And I am such a liar.* She let out a quiet breath. 'What can I say? Thank you.'

'I'll take you to it later.' He looked over at Drew. 'The box?'

The box. Warmth fled, cold fear returning, the distraction provided by his car over.

'Not a bomb,' Drew said. 'We'll unwrap it in the lab.'

'It's Russ's heart,' Lucy said hollowly. 'The killer got into my car in a public parking garage. How? And why? Why leave *me* the box?'

'For the same reason he left you the body,' Fitzpatrick said. 'This is personal.'

She closed her eyes, wishing she could start the day over again. 'But *why*?'

His warm hand squeezed her shoulder. 'We'll find out. It'll be all right. So will you.'

This was craziness, hearts in boxes and bodies on chess tables. But crazier still was that she believed Fitzpatrick when he said it would be all right. 'Okay.'

'We got the tape from the security office,' Drew said. 'I was about to look at it.'

'Let's do that now,' Fitzpatrick said.

'Where is Stevie?' Lucy asked as they walked toward the CSU van, where one of the techs had the tape cued.

'In the car, talking to Hyatt. She'll be along shortly. Where is Thomas Thorne? I thought he was going to stay with you.'

'He had to go to court. He stayed until Drew got here, but had to go.'

'Okay. Do you park in the same place every day?'

'Of course,' Lucy said, weary again. 'Just like I run at the same time every morning. I guess I won't be doing either of those anymore.'

'You're not to blame,' Fitzpatrick said firmly. 'You have the right to park anywhere you choose and run any time you choose. However, your routine made it easier for this guy to anticipate how to get close to you. How to terrorize you,' he added quietly.

She thought about the body slumped over the chess table, how terrified she'd been when she'd thought it was Mr Pugh. 'He's certainly done that. Drew, I got here at eight fifteen.'

'That's what I figured.' Drew started the tape and ratcheted up the speed. 'Here you are, arriving. You locked your car.'

Lucy watched herself on the monitor. 'Of course I did. I always lock up.'

Drew sped through minutes of inactivity, slowing when a figure came into view.

'Stop,' Fitzpatrick said. The tape rewound and restarted in slow motion.

Lucy watched, stunned when a boy on a bicycle appeared. 'It's just a kid.'

'A teenager,' Fitzpatrick said, bending close to the screen. 'He's not afraid, not looking over his shoulder. There's the box.'

The boy took the box from his backpack and a piece of paper from his pocket. He unfolded the paper and a small object slid into his hand.

Shocked, Lucy's knees went weak. 'Is that . . . ? That can't be . . .'

'Yeah, it is,' Fitzpatrick said grimly. 'Kid's got a key to your car.'

The kid checked the license plate, then used the key to open Lucy's driver-side door. He placed the box on the floor, fluffed the bow, and relocked the car. He then pulled a phone from his pocket, punched in a text message, and bicycled away.

'Can we get a better look at his face?' Fitzpatrick asked, his voice low and urgent.

'There's a camera at the entrance,' Drew said. 'Maybe we can get a better angle.'

Lucy lowered herself to the CSU van's back bumper. Her chest was so tight she could barely draw a breath. 'He had a key to my car,' she murmured. 'How?'

Fitzpatrick crouched so that he was looking up at her, his expression as urgent as his voice had been. 'Does anyone else have a key to your car?'

'No,' she whispered.

'Have you ever lent your car to anyone?'

'No.' To her mortification, tears stung her eyes. 'Never.'

He took her hands, held them tight in his. 'I need you to stay calm, because this will be okay. You're safe. Listen to me. Cars come with two sets of keys. Where's your other set?'

She closed her eyes, focusing on his deep voice. *You're safe.* The tears seeped from beneath her eyelids, sliding down her cheeks. 'Locked in the fire safe, in my apartment.'

'That's good.' He squeezed her hands gently, then wiped the tears from her cheeks with his thumbs. 'What about the safe? Does it have a combination or a key?'

She fixed her gaze on his, clutching at his hands when they reclaimed hers. Anchoring herself. 'A key. One is on my key ring in my purse. The other is in my safe deposit box.'

'Very sensible.' His mouth curved in a wry smile. 'I would have expected no less.'

She managed to smile back, understanding what he'd done and surprised that it had worked. The stranglehold of terror had loosened, at least enough so that she could breathe. 'I'm nothing if not sensible and predictable,' she said, forcing a lightness she might never feel again. A killer had her key. *He was close enough to me to get my key.*

What other keys does he have? What if he had the key to her apartment? *What if he came in? While I was sleeping?* The picture of Russ Bennett's mutilated chest flooded her mind and she went cold, shuddering out a breath as terror renewed its hold.

Fitzpatrick squeezed her hands again, sobering. 'If he has the key to your car, he may have other keys.'

'My apartment,' she said hoarsely.

'Maybe. Maybe not. Regardless, you need to find another place to stay for a while. Can you stay with a friend? Maybe Gwyn?'

She nodded shakily. 'She has a sofa I can use. She's hardly ever there anyway.'

He smiled and she knew it was to help her stay calm. 'She has a boyfriend?'

'She always has a boyfriend. I'm sure she'll let me stay.'

'Stay where?' Stevie crouched to look up into Lucy's face. 'What happened?'

Fitzpatrick told her and Stevie's cheeks darkened with anger. 'Sonofabitch,' she muttered. 'Don't worry, Lucy. We've got your back.'

Lucy swallowed hard. 'Thanks.'

Stevie patted her knee. 'I do have some good news. You're no longer a suspect.'

Lucy choked back what would have been a hysterical laugh. 'Thank you.'

'I've got the kid's face,' Drew said and stepped back from the monitor. 'Look.'

Fitzpatrick rose, still holding Lucy's hands. With a gentle tug, he pulled her to her feet and turned her around so that she could see. His hands covering her shoulders, he tugged again, still gently, pulling her back against him. This time she gave in to the urge. *Because I'm shaken up. Because he's so warm and I'm freezing.*

Because he feels safe. Even though deep inside she knew he'd be anything but. His hands clenched on her shoulders, but briefly. Then his hips shifted so that their only contact was above the waist, but not quite quickly enough. Lucy sucked in a breath. It hadn't been so long that she'd forgotten what an aroused man felt like.

'Do you know him, Lucy?' Fitzpatrick murmured urgently.

Concentrate. The kid was Asian, maybe eighteen. Five nine or so, with short, spiked hair. And a face she'd never seen before.

She shook her head, watching as the kid got off his bike and walked it around the exit arm, waving to the guy in the ticket booth. 'I don't know the boy on the bike. But that's not the man who's usually on duty,' she said, pointing to the man in the booth.

'He's not the one we talked to,' Drew agreed. 'That's a different guy.'

Fitzpatrick turned to a waiting uniform. 'Can you ask the man working the booth to come talk to us? Thanks.'

'He's a courier,' Stevie said. 'Back up the tape, Drew, and watch him again.'

The young man walked his bicycle out of the garage then remounted, one foot on the ground. He took an envelope from his backpack, glancing at it before returning it.

'The camera didn't get what was written on the envelope,' Lucy said, disappointed.

Fitzpatrick gave her shoulders another squeeze. 'Can we get a still of his face?'

Drew printed one and handed it to him. 'Maybe a lobby receptionist can ID him.'

'Detectives.' The uniformed officer was back, a middle-aged man at his side. 'This is Mr Joe Isaiah. He mans the booth.'

Joe had a very worried look on his face and Lucy could see he was deliberately avoiding her eyes. She knew this man. Said hello to him every day. He was kind. But today he was also scared. *Join the club*, she thought.

'I already talked to the officers,' Joe said defensively.

'We have a few more questions.' Stevie pointed to the monitor where Drew had already rewound the tape. 'That's not you in the booth, Mr Isaiah. Why isn't it?'

Joe's nerves grew. 'My cousin was minding the booth. I was only gone an hour.'

'Why didn't you tell the other officers that?' Stevie asked.

'I didn't want the building manager to know. I was at the doctor with my wife. She's sick. I've missed a lot of work and I was scared to ask for more time off. I can't lose my job, my health insurance. Please. My cousin knows how to run the register.'

'He let a courier in,' Stevie said, 'who unlawfully entered a vehicle in this garage.'

Joe licked his lip nervously. 'But the bomb squad left. There was no problem. It was just a present. I didn't think . . .' He stopped, regrouped. 'I messed up, didn't I?'

'This is a homicide investigation, sir,' Fitzpatrick said. 'We want to talk to your cousin to see if he recognizes this young man.' He held up the picture and Joe blinked.

'That's Jimmy Yee. He does deliveries here two, three times a week. He can't be involved in any murder. Jimmy's a nice kid.'

Fitzpatrick wrote it down. 'Do you know who he works for?'

'It's a family business. Yee's Express. They do deliveries around town.'

'Thanks, Mr Isaiah,' Stevie said. 'We appreciate your help.'

Joe nodded miserably. 'Do you have to tell my boss?'

Stevie glanced at Fitzpatrick. 'I think we have what we need for now.'

Fitzpatrick nodded. 'Will you be available in case we have more questions?'

Joe's shoulders slumped. 'Anything you need. Thank you.' He looked at Lucy for the first time, guilt in his eyes. 'Dr Trask, I'm so sorry. Are you okay? You're not hurt?'

'I'm fine, Joe. I hope Dinah gets better.' She could feel Fitzpatrick watching her. He was surprised that she knew Joe, more so that she knew the man's wife.

'Let's get to Yee's Express,' Stevie said, 'and see what they have on this delivery.'

'What about me?' Lucy asked. 'Can I go back to work now that I'm cleared? I can't go home until you check out my apartment,' she added when they hesitated, sharing a glance. 'You said I have to stay with my friend.'

'Someone will take you home while we check out this delivery boy,' Fitzpatrick said. 'You can pick up what you need for a few days.'

'And then after that,' Stevie said, 'we want you to come with us to Anderson Ferry. We need to notify the Bennetts about their son before they hear it from Brandi Bennett.'

Lucy nodded, relieved and suddenly more tense all at once. *I'm going home.* Except it hadn't been home in a very long time. 'Good. Thank your captain for me.'

'I will,' Stevie said. 'While we're chasing down the courier, can you check out the heart in the box to see if it's Bennett's?'

'I can tell you if it's human and if the blood is Russ's type.' The thought of handling the heart of someone she'd known made her cringe. 'I'll need DNA for an exact match.'

'You should have that within an hour,' Stevie said. 'We've got a warrant for Bennett's condo and our captain is sending someone over to gather up hairbrushes, toothbrushes, all the usual suspects.'

Fitzpatrick met her eyes. 'Stick with one of the officers until I come for you.'

She probably should have been offended at his possessive tone, but found she was not. And she was no longer cold, at least for the moment. 'Okay.'

Seven

Newport News, Virginia
Monday, May 3, 2.45 P.M.

Somebody was home. Clay stood outside the condo door, listening. Nicki's report said she'd met with Margo Winchester here, at this address. Margo lived here with a roommate, another young woman who'd looked scared. Nicki had told Clay that she thought the girl had a right to be scared. Margo had gone off on a crazed rant that had unnerved Nicki, who'd seen nearly everything as a DC cop.

Bracing himself for a confrontation, Clay knocked with the little brass knocker that said KLEIN. The door was opened promptly by a woman who appeared to be about eighty. She had soft white curls and a sweet face. She'd also had a recent open-heart surgery, based on the scar peeking over the neckline of her shirt. She looked up at him warily, fear flickering in her eyes, magnified by the Coke-bottle lenses she wore.

'Yes? Can I help you? If you're selling something, don't even bother.'

He smiled to put her at ease. 'I'm not a salesman, ma'am. I'm an investigator and I'm looking for a woman named Margo Winchester.'

'She doesn't live here.' The woman started to close the door.

'Mrs Klein, wait. Please. Margo was living here, two months ago.'

'No, young man, she was not. I've lived in this condo for fifteen years and no one named Margo has ever been here. Now please leave.' She closed the door in his face.

For a moment he stared at the knocker, a bad feeling forming in his gut. He took the photo of Margo Winchester from his briefcase and knocked again.

Mrs Klein opened the door, irate. 'Do I have to call 911 on you, sir?'

'No, ma'am. I'm so sorry to bother you, but this is very important. I'm searching for someone who's missing and this woman may have been the last person to see him alive. Can you at least look at a picture?'

She frowned at him, but stuck out her hand. 'Fine.' She brought the photo close to her nose, squinting as she studied it thoroughly. Then she handed it back. 'Never seen her before. I can't help you. Maybe you have the wrong building. They do look alike.'

'I don't have the wrong building.' Nicki was meticulous about such things. 'There was another woman here too. Do you live alone?'

Her face paled and he wished he could take the question back. The door slammed in his face again. 'I have the phone in my hand,' Mrs Klein said through the door. 'I'll call 911 if you are not gone in five seconds.'

He'd frightened her and he hadn't meant to.

'I'm sorry,' he called back. 'I'm going now.' He headed down the stairs and to his car, taking comfort in the fact that her glasses had been so thick she hadn't a prayer of reading his license plates.

He drove away, parking at a convenience store parking lot where he opened the file and looked at the photos Nicki had taken of the condo building when she'd been here before. It was the same place. Margo Winchester had been there along with her roommate, but there had been no old lady.

It was reasonable to assume Mrs Klein could have been in the hospital then. Her scar looked recent enough. So why was Margo using the condo? Was she a squatter? Who had the other young woman been?

He called his office. 'Have you found anything about the fire?' he asked Alyssa.

'Not everything you asked for, but you're not going to like what I did find.'

103

'I kind of expected as much. Well, let's have it.'

'The fire occurred a week ago and is a suspected arson. A victim was found inside, an adult male. As yet unidentified. This was all the newspaper had.'

His heart sank. An adult male. 'Evan. Shit. What about the house? Who owns it?'

'The bank. It went into foreclosure six months ago, Clay.'

He sat up straight. 'What?'

'The bank owns it. If Evan was living there, he was squatting.'

Not good. 'And the condo where Margo was living has been the residence of an eighty-year-old woman for the last fifteen years. She's never heard of Margo.'

'What are you gonna do?'

'I'm going to pay a visit to Evan's ex-wife, then check into a hotel and grab a nap before Margo Winchester's club opens. If she's not dancing tonight, maybe one of the other dancers can tell me where she really lives.'

'What should I do?'

He thought hard. Fatigue was catching up to him. 'Check out a Mrs Klein.' He gave Alyssa the condo's address. 'Find out about her relatives. Especially any female relatives about thirty years old. Nicki's got a note here that Margo called the woman Linda, and that Linda had a tattoo of a cobra striking on her upper right arm.'

'Lovely,' Alyssa said with disgust. 'Not.'

'It might help ID her. And find out when Mrs Klein had open-heart surgery. If my hunch is right, it'd be about the time Nicki came down here two months ago to check Evan out, right before she took his case.'

'You think Margo was squatting too.'

'Yeah. I just don't know why.'

Monday, May 3, 2.45 P.M.

'The coast is clear, Dr Trask,' the female CSU analyst said. Her name was Cherise Taylor and she seemed very capable. She was also nearly six feet tall and built like a brick. Lucy felt safe and intimidated at the same time.

Relieved, Lucy let out the breath she'd been holding as she'd stood outside her apartment door. 'No more boxes with heart wrapping paper?'

'None that I see. A CSU team will be by later to do a complete sweep, but I see no evidence of an intruder. You can come in and gather your things. I'll stay with you.'

Lucy entered her apartment, chills pebbling her arms. She'd left this morning feeling secure. Now, she felt violated. And scared. She walked through each room, looking to see if anything had been disturbed. 'Nothing looks out of place.'

'That's good,' Cherise said. 'Can you open your fire safe? We need to know if your spare set of keys is there.'

Her hands trembling, Lucy managed to get the key in the lock. 'They're here.'

'I'll take the safe and its contents. We'll see if it's been handled.'

Because a killer could still have been in my place, made a copy of the key and put it back. It was enough to make a sane person paranoid. 'I'll just pack my things.'

'I need to come with you,' Cherise said apologetically.

Lucy sighed. 'I know.' In her bedroom she took a suitcase from her closet, then looked over her shoulder. 'How long should I plan to be gone?'

'Hard to say. A few days, maybe.'

'Okay.' Lucy pulled several suits from the closet, then hesitated before she grabbed one of her little black dresses. It was black and it was little. It was also leather. Kind of a must-have for the club. She slipped the dress between the suits, grabbed a few pairs of shoes, and put the lot in her suitcase.

She packed her toiletries, then stood at her dresser, staring at her treasures. She ran her fingers over the worn violin case that had graced her dresser top for the five years she'd lived here. The violin had belonged to Mr Pugh, but Barb had given it to her for safekeeping when Mr Pugh had no longer been able to play.

If there ever was a fire, it would be one of the three things she'd grab on the way out. The second was a silver picture frame, hinged to hold two photos – a dark-haired teenage boy with a serious face and a football helmet under his arm, and a smiling blond man astride a motorcycle, his helmet also under one arm.

The boy had been her brother, Buck. The man her first fiancé, Heath. Both were dead. Both had left her alone, just in different ways. *I'm tired of being alone.*

Lucy got a duffle bag and put the violin case and the picture frame inside. From her jewelry box she took an old cardboard box. Opening it, she let out another relieved breath. The bracelet was still there. It was the third thing she'd take with her, a gift from a brother to the sister who'd loved him. Needed him. The engraving on the cheap charm still made her smile sadly. *#1 Sister.*

Then the '#1' made her frown as the image of Russ's back intruded. She put the box in the duffle, hefted it on her shoulder, then turned to Cherise. 'That's all I need.'

She waited in the hall while Cherise locked her front door and padlocked it with a crime-scene lock.

'Lucy? What's all this?' Mrs Korbel stood on the landing above, her wrinkled face concerned.

'It's okay,' Lucy soothed. 'The police are just investigating what happened this morning. I'm fine. Really.'

Mrs Korbel's eyes narrowed skeptically. 'Very well, as long as you're all right.'

'I am. Thank you for asking. I checked on Barb and Mr Pugh. They're fine, too.'

'I know. I called Barb this morning. She's staying with her sister, you know.'

'Yes, ma'am. Well, I need to be going now.' She'd gotten to the next landing when Mrs Korbel called her name again. She looked over her shoulder to find the old lady looking sad. 'Yes, ma'am?'

'I hope you come back soon, Lucy. We've missed your concerts the last few weeks you were gone.'

Startled, Lucy cast a quick glance at Cherise who looked interested, but who said nothing. She looked back up at Mrs Korbel. 'I didn't know you were listening.'

Mrs Korbel looked surprised that Lucy was surprised. 'We all do, child. For Barb's sake nobody wants Jerry upset, but hearing you play to calm him down is . . . well, it's good for the soul. Come home soon.'

For a moment Lucy didn't know what to say. 'Thank you. I will.'

Monday, May 3, 2.55 P.M.

Mr Yee of Yee's Express was an elderly man with a pencil-thin mustache. His eyes darted nervously from his files to JD and Stevie as he searched for a record of the morning's delivery. 'My nephew is a good boy.'

'We didn't say he wasn't,' JD said calmly. 'But somebody hired him and we need to know who that was.'

'He's on his way in. He's over at the harbor, so it'll take him a few minutes. Here's the record you want.' Yee pulled a piece of paper from the folder. 'It was arranged by Dr Russell Bennett. Charged to his Visa.'

'Chutzpah,' JD murmured and Stevie nodded.

'Sir,' she said, 'how did the box arrive? Did anyone drop it off?'

'No. I remember that one now that I saw Bennett's name. I got a call from Dr Bennett saying he'd been delayed on a business trip out of town and didn't want to miss his anniversary with his ladyfriend. He sent the box through the mail with instructions to deliver it today. He didn't want his ladyfriend to be angry.'

'When did you receive the box?'

'Saturday afternoon, last mail delivery.'

'What about the key to her car?' Stevie asked.

'Came with the box. There was the wrapped box with a bow and a little envelope with a key and a note saying where we could find the car.'

'Where's the note and the key?' JD asked.

'Jimmy's got them. He'll bring them back when he comes in.'

'Okay,' JD said. 'And the shipping box? Where is that?'

Yee looked bewildered. 'Cut down and put out with last night's trash.'

'Did the garbage truck come yet?' JD asked, hoping.

'No, not yet.'

Yes. 'We'll want to search for that box.'

Yee's bewilderment grew. 'Why?'

Stevie ignored his question. 'Didn't you think it odd that he wanted the box delivered to a lady's car and not her house or office? And that he'd have her key?'

'And that he'd send it to you through the US mail?' JD added.

Yee shrugged. 'Dr Bennett sometimes does strange things.'

'So you've done business with him before,' JD said.

'Sure. He's a good customer.' Yee looked rueful. 'Lots of lady-friends.'

'Did you know he was married?' Stevie asked.

'Yes, but . . .' He shrugged again. 'Not my business.'

'What kind of things does he ask to be delivered?' JD asked.

'Usually roses, candy, theater tickets. Once there was a bucket of sand with some oyster shells. Turned out one of the shells had a pearl and diamond ring in it. Worth about four thousand bucks. So I didn't think anything about this.'

The bell on the door rang and the three of them turned toward it. 'Jimmy,' Yee said, relieved.

The young man took in the scene, warily. 'What's wrong?'

'I'm Detective Fitzpatrick and this is my partner, Detective Mazzetti. We'd like to ask you a few questions about the package you delivered to that car this morning.'

Jimmy looked to his uncle, panicked. 'You're not in trouble,' his uncle said. 'Is he?'

'Not right now,' JD said. 'First, can we see the note and the key?'

The boy produced them from his backpack. 'I didn't do anything wrong.'

'It's okay,' Stevie said. 'We're not after you. We're after the guy who sent this box.'

'Dr Bennett?' Jimmy asked, stunned. 'Why? I mean, the guy's a total douche, but he never did anything illegal.'

'Jimmy,' his uncle scolded. 'I will not tolerate that language.'

'Why did you say he was a douche?' JD asked and the boy shrugged.

'All those women, none of them knowing about the others. I felt bad doing those deliveries. Made me feel . . . responsible. Like I should have told them. But I didn't. My uncle said it was none of our business. To just do the deliveries.'

JD looked at Stevie. 'We don't have to get those names from Herrigan,' he said.

One side of Stevie's mouth lifted. 'Silver lining. Mr Yee, we're going to need a list of all the women you've delivered to for Dr Bennett.'

Yee blew out a breath. 'How far back?'

'Five years,' JD said. 'Maybe six.'

'That's a lot of women, Detective,' Yee said, alarmed.

'And we appreciate the work it will take,' JD replied. 'We need the most recent six names now. We'll wait. Here's my card with my email and fax number. We need the less recent names as soon as possible.'

Yee took the card, clearly upset. 'Anything else?'

'Yes,' Stevie said. 'You talked to Dr Bennett yourself? Did he sound like himself?'

Yee frowned. 'I don't remem— Wait. He had a cold. I remember saying it was a shame he had a cold in the summer. He said, "You have no idea." And he laughed.'

JD thought about Bennett's body, flash frozen. 'What number did he call from?'

'It must have been his cell, which I have on record. Otherwise I would have written it on the order. That's procedure. Just in case their card doesn't go through.'

'Detective?' Jimmy asked quietly. 'Is Dr Bennett okay?'

'We're not sure yet,' JD averred. 'But son, next time somebody asks you to deliver something to a car, don't.'

'What was in that box?'

'That's part of our investigation, Jimmy,' Stevie said. 'We're not at liberty to say. But the garage was closed down for an hour while law enforcement searched the car.'

Unsteadily the boy moved behind the register. 'We have deliveries for the last five years in our system. Anything older and we'll have to go to storage to get the records.' He looked up, his eyes shadowed. 'There's no courier–client confidentiality, is there?'

The question was asked so gravely, JD had to keep his lips from twitching. 'No, son,' he said, equally gravely. 'We appreciate this.'

In two minutes Jimmy handed JD a list. 'There are a few men on it,' Jimmy said. 'I remember those were regular envelopes, maybe for business.'

There were about forty women on the list. JD flipped to the last page, angered to see Lucy's name. Written in the 'Item Delivered' column was 'Barbie Doll' and he remembered her saying that was how Bennett had broken through her defenses. Bastard.

'Thanks, Jimmy,' he said. 'Call me or my partner if Bennett makes any further contact with you.' JD drew Stevie aside. 'I'll search for the shipping box if you want to start checking on those names. See where they come from.'

'Be it ever so humble,' Stevie murmured to let him know she'd be checking for any connection to Bennett's hometown. 'Hurry. We still have the first ex to notify before we drive out to see the parents.'

'We'll pick up Lucy on the way.'

Stevie checked her watch. 'I'll take my own car and follow behind you, in case we run late. Cordelia's got that thing at school tonight.'

'Not just a "thing",' JD said. 'It's not every day a girl graduates from kindergarten. And your whole clan will be on hand, hankies in one hand, camcorders in the other.'

Stevie flashed an amused grin. 'Exactly. So get busy dumpster diving.'

Monday, May 3, 3.20 P.M.

'It's a beautiful day.' And it was. The sun was shining and the wind was just strong enough to cool his face without rocking the boat too much.

He looked down at the deck where Janet Gordon lay bound and quivering. 'Where should we start?' he asked and she shrank back

110

against the deck, tears on her face. Her tears did not move him. They were selfish tears, cried only for herself. Leaning over her, he sliced the gag from her mouth with his very sharp filleting knife.

'Well?' he asked quietly.

'Please, don't kill me,' she sobbed. 'Please. I didn't do anything.'

He stared down at her, shaking his head. 'Unbelievable. You still don't get it, do you? That you didn't do anything is exactly why you're here.'

He turned the knife one way, then the other, making sure she could see his blade in all its sharpened glory. She sucked in a breath and screamed at the top of her lungs, which made him smile. He lifted her up in his arms so that she could see where they were.

'Look around you. Nothing but open water. So scream all you want. I like it.'

He dropped her and she blinked, temporarily disoriented. 'Please. I'm begging you.' Then she drew a deep breath, her struggle for control a fascinating sight. She still thought he might let her go. 'You won't get away with this,' she said ominously, although her desperation was clear. 'I wrote a letter.'

He cocked his head, interested. 'Really? To whom?'

'To the DA. It had everything in it. Everything I knew. Everything that happened that day. Everyone that was there.'

'And where is this letter?'

'With my attorney. If anything happens to me, he's to mail it to the DA.'

'Hm. So Bennett was telling the truth about that, too.'

She stared, stunned. 'You knew?'

'Yes. When Bennett told me about you, I said I didn't believe anyone would be so stupid as to let someone who was blackmailing them around them with sharp knives. He said you'd shown him the letter, that he had to keep you alive. And happy.' He lifted his brows. 'How *happy* did he keep you, Janet?'

'It wasn't like that,' she spat. 'That's disgusting.'

He threw back his head and laughed. '*That*'s disgusting? You use the murder and rape of an innocent girl to get a nose job, and having sex with Bennett is disgusting?'

111

'She wasn't innocent,' Janet blurted from behind clenched teeth.

He abruptly went still, inside and out. 'What did you say?'

She also went still. Maybe she was finally getting it. 'Nothing.'

He crouched down, his temper ice cold. 'You think she wanted to be assaulted? Beaten until she was unrecognizable? You think my sister wanted it? That she asked for it? Maybe her skirt was too short. Maybe she slept around?'

Janet pursed her lips and said nothing.

'Tell me,' he said, 'is your son's name in that letter?'

She closed her eyes. 'No,' she whispered.

'How will he feel when he finds out what you traded for your silence?'

'It won't matter. He won't care. He hates me.'

'Really? Why?'

'Because I wouldn't tell the police what he'd done.'

This surprised him. 'Really? Ryan wanted you to tell the cops?'

'That's why he told me. He wanted to be punished, but he couldn't turn himself in. Wanted me to do it for him.' There was contempt in her voice that made him feel the tiniest bit sorry for her son. But not that sorry. Ryan was, bottom line, a coward.

'And you said no.'

'It would have ruined our family, and it was too late to help anyway. The killer was dead and those boys . . . they had families. Futures. We couldn't tell.'

He sat back on his heels, studying her as his anger grew even colder. *I had a future once*, he thought. *Nobody thought about me or my family.* 'We? Who's "we"?'

She opened her eyes to stare up at him. 'If I tell you, will you let me live?'

What a piece of work. 'No.'

Her eyes flashed hate. 'Then go to hell,' she spat and he smiled.

'That's what Bennett said. After a few fingers, he changed his tune. So will you.'

'That letter will come out,' she said desperately. 'Everyone will know what happened. She was your sister. You'll be the most likely suspect.'

'I don't think so. Because I don't exist anymore.' He leaned in close, pressed the tip of the knife to the hollow of her throat. 'Because I'm dead.'

Monday, May 3, 3.20 P.M.

Stevie wrinkled her nose. 'Drew should send a van for this. You reek enough.'

JD brushed the remnants of trash off his clothes. 'I got a lot smellier on one of my Narc undercover assignments. I had to play a guy who hadn't bathed in way too long. This is not that bad.' He'd found Bennett's box sandwiched between two larger boxes that had been knocked down flat. 'I want Drew to get this ASAP. We can put it in the trunk.'

'You're right. Sooner the better. I'm just glad it's your car and not mine.'

At the car, JD popped his trunk. And sighed. 'I forgot about this.'

Stevie peered inside at the pile of clothes and sports equipment. 'What is all this?' She gave him a measured look. 'Are you giving Maya's stuff away?'

Stevie had been urging JD to deal with his dead wife's things for a long time. And he had. Mostly. 'This is all my stuff. Sports equipment, video games. I found it when I was cleaning out my storage unit last weekend. It's all stuff I packed away before I went into the army. I'm going to donate it, I just haven't had the chance.'

'You're donating video games you had before the army?' She reached in the bag, pulled out a few and laughed. 'Nobody will want these. They're ancient.'

'They're classics,' he corrected. 'Vintage. Collectors will pay through the nose.'

Stevie was looking through the games curiously. 'They're all shooting games. No jumping plumbers even.' She eyed him shrewdly. 'Did the games prepare you?'

No, he thought. It was a hell of a lot different to take a bead on a live man than a cartoon. No game had prepared him for what it had been like when his first target's head exploded. Or his last target, or

113

any of the ones in between. It was real. And horrifying. And it stayed with you. *Forever*. He put the games back in the bag and answered her original question to change the subject.

'I gave all Maya's stuff away last year when I put the house up for sale.'

She nodded, accepting his avoidance. 'You've come a long way, JD.'

Not really. It had taken a year to stand the thought of anyone else touching his wife's things, and a year more to give them away. Three years after her death, despite the urging of his friends, there had been no one who made him feel . . . alive.

Until today, when Lucy had met his eyes and everything changed. 'I'm moving on.'

'I could see that back in the parking garage,' she said wryly. 'Just don't move on too fast. And roll the car windows down. Please.'

Monday, May 3, 3.40 P.M.

'Well?'

Lucy looked up from the CSU lab's microscope to find Stevie Mazzetti standing in the doorway holding a man's suit in a dry-cleaning bag. 'It's a human heart,' Lucy said, 'still mostly frozen. It's the same blood type as Russ's. We'll run the DNA to confirm, but it's his. Drew's got the container and is checking for prints, but he's not hopeful.'

'How was the heart stored?' Stevie asked.

'Bagged in a generic ziplock bag and shipped in a cheap plastic bowl – like the ones you get takeout soup in.'

'Dime a dozen,' Stevie said.

'Which is why Drew wasn't hopeful.' Lucy tried to keep her eyes on Stevie's face, but she kept glancing over the woman's shoulder to the hall beyond.

Stevie smiled slightly. 'He's coming, Doc. Don't worry.'

'I wasn't—'

Stevie interrupted her with a wave. 'Don't even try.' She hung the suit on a hook next to the door and pulled up a stool. She looked straight ahead for a moment, then turned to meet Lucy's eyes. 'We've been friends for years, JD and I.'

'Then he's a lucky man,' Lucy said quietly and Stevie gave that slight smile again.

'He might disagree. JD's a good guy. He's had a rough time the last few years.'

Stevie's tone held a warning and made part of Lucy want to run away. But she also wanted to know more about JD Fitzpatrick. Curiosity won out. 'How so?'

'He's a widower. His wife died in an accident three years ago.'

That took her by surprise. Somehow he hadn't seemed like the married type. Not that she was the best judge on that. *Russ Bennett, Exhibit A.*

Then Lucy remembered the child's autopsy, JD's stoic silence and the tears in his eyes. That had been two years ago. Dread settled on her shoulders. Had he also lost a child in the accident that claimed his wife? Was that why he'd been moved to tears?

'Did they have any children?'

Stevie looked surprised by the question. 'No. Maya wasn't a kid kind of person.'

'Oh.' So why had he been there that day? *Get a spine, Lucy, and ask him yourself.*

Stevie was staring at her intently. 'He took Maya's death hard and hasn't had anyone since. I've been telling him to get out there. Meet someone.'

'That's hard to do after losing someone you love,' she murmured, thinking of the pictures in her duffle bag. Losing her brother had simply devastated her, changing her life. After losing her first fiancé, she'd had a lot of trouble letting her guard down again, but she had, eventually. Strangely enough, the departure of fiancé number two had been more an inconvenience than a devastation. Still, it had been years until she'd opened her heart again. And that time to Russ Bennett. *And that turned out so well.*

Part of her was still terrified. Part of her yearned, though. *I'm tired of being alone.*

'We all heal at our own pace,' Stevie said. 'I might not have said anything at all, but I saw the way he looked at you. And you at him. I wanted you to know he's a good man, but you could hurt him. So don't hurt him. Please.'

'Please what?' Fitzpatrick filled the doorway, carrying a stack of flattened boxes in a clear trash bag. He'd taken off his suit coat and tie, and his white shirt clung to his arms and back, damp with sweat. His dark hair was slicked back and there was a smudge on his cheek. Muscles rippled under the almost transparent shirt as he flexed, trying to maneuver the boxes into the room.

Lucy tried not to stare, but it was a futile effort. *Oh, my.* Then the odor hit and she started coughing. 'What is that?'

Fitzpatrick gave her an annoyed look. 'You do autopsies all day, yet gag at this?'

'I'm used to *eau de* corpse,' she shot back from behind her hand. 'What *is* that?'

'A cross-section of the garbage dumpster behind Yee's Express delivery service,' Stevie said, her dark eyes twinkling.

'Stevie,' Drew chided, coming in behind him. 'You sent him into the dumpster?'

'Hey, he volunteered. Besides, he's got a change of clothes.' Stevie pointed to the dry-cleaner bag. 'I've got to go to Cordelia's graduation tonight with his stink on me.'

'It'll have dissipated by then,' Fitzpatrick said. 'Don't be a whiner. Where do you want this shit, Drew?' Drew pointed to an empty corner and they all followed Fitzpatrick as he carefully placed it on the floor.

'I hope it really isn't shit, Stevie,' Drew said mildly. 'Not again.'

'That was bad,' Stevie agreed. 'No, this is regulation garbage. The heart box arrived at the courier's on Saturday in a shipping box that they cut down and threw in the dumpster. After which an entire frat house had pizza and beer and threw the leftovers on top,' she finished cheerfully, and Lucy had to purse her lips to keep from smiling.

Fitzpatrick noted her effort and grinned, his dimple appearing beneath the smudge on his cheek. 'It's okay. Go ahead and laugh. I imagine you can use it after today.'

'Did you have to bring the whole dumpster?' she asked, giving in to the smile.

Fitzpatrick's eyes flashed dark, sending a now-familiar shiver down her spine. Then he shrugged, breaking the moment. 'Who knows what might have been in the outer box when it was tossed? I took a few inches above and below, just to be safe.'

Lucy grimaced. 'You put that in your car?'

'Hell, I've had an addict puke all over my backseat more than once. This trash is clean in comparison.' He started sorting. 'Here's the shipping box, Drew. It was mailed locally, even though the guy claiming to be Bennett also claimed to be out of town. Yee didn't notice the local postmark. He just saw the return label with Bennett's name on it.'

Stevie took two plastic evidence bags from her pocket containing a folded note and a key. 'I don't think you'll get prints except Jimmy and his uncle, but we can try.'

'They're coming in to get printed for elimination,' Fitzpatrick said. 'We told them to ask for you, Drew. Have you gotten anything from Bennett's condo? Hyatt put Skinner and Morton on the search.'

'So far, a hairbrush and a toothbrush for DNA matching,' Drew said. 'I've got a team over there too, but from what I hear there were no signs of struggle.'

Stevie nodded. 'That's what Hyatt said. We're pulling Bennett's phone records to see who he might have talked to the last day he was seen. The doorman said he got into a cab with only his briefcase, so it's sounding like he was lured away. We have a status meeting with Hyatt in fifteen. Can you be there, Drew? It shouldn't take long.'

'I'll be there.'

Fitzpatrick rose, brushing dirt from his trousers. 'Lucy, he wants to talk to you about Bennett. You can go with Stevie. I'm going to shower and change and meet you up there. Do we know anything more about that heart?'

'Only that the blood is the same type as Russ's, which we expected.'

Stevie waved Fitzpatrick away. 'We need to hurry and you still stink. Go clean up.' She handed him his suit. 'You're just lucky the cleaners had this one ready for pickup.'

'See you in fifteen,' he said and was gone, leaving Lucy to watch his very fine rear end as he rushed away. Ruby had been right that morning. The man did have an amazing butt. A narcotic, she'd called him. JD Fitzpatrick was certainly that.

Nope, Lucy wasn't cold anymore.

Eight

Monday, May 3, 4.00 P.M.

By the time JD got to Hyatt's office, it was standing room only. But that was mainly because Hyatt kept only one guest chair in his office and JD had learned pretty quickly that one sat in the chair only when one was invited. Usually only the brass was invited.

JD wasn't sure if Hyatt kept them standing to keep them in their place or if he held to the belief that standing meetings were short meetings. The bald man achieved both.

'Close the door, Detective,' Hyatt said formally. 'We've been waiting for you.'

JD wanted to roll his eyes. He was exactly on time, to the second. He'd hurried not to impress Hyatt, but because he'd wanted to get back to Lucy.

She'd smiled at him back in Drew's office, a quick, unfettered smile that had lit up her face and stopped his heart. Something about her had changed in the hour between the garage and the CSU lab. He didn't know what had happened and wasn't sure he cared. At that moment it had been all he could do not to reach for her, but they'd been at work and he'd been covered in dumpster filth.

He closed Hyatt's door and instantly felt the chill. Something was up. Stevie and Drew were there, along with Elizabeth Morton and Phil Skinner, the other detectives assigned to the case.

To his surprise, Lucy sat in Hyatt's extra chair, turned around to face the group. At her side was ADA Daphne Montgomery, who JD hadn't yet met in person, but had spoken to on the phone. Daphne was forty-ish, with big blond hair and a hot pink suit with a short skirt that showed off a magnificent pair of legs. Rumor had it that she'd been a Vegas showgirl back in the day, and Daphne hadn't done anything to quell the mill. JD liked her a lot. Daphne was an optimist in a land of career pessimists.

But at the moment Daphne wore a frown, her hand on Lucy's shoulder almost protectively, sending the hackles on the back of JD's neck straight up. Hyatt sat behind his desk like a drill sergeant, revealing nothing. Her expression shuttered, Lucy met JD's eyes, seeking answers he didn't have.

'What's going on?' JD asked Hyatt quietly. 'I thought you wanted to ask Dr Trask a few questions about Dr Bennett.'

'I do,' Hyatt said. 'Just not the ones you think.'

JD opened his mouth to protest, but Stevie cut off him with a sharp warning glance and a shake of her head. JD folded his arms across his chest, not liking this a bit.

Hyatt noted the silent exchange, then stood. Now only Lucy sat and she was looking increasingly pissed. JD could relate. Hyatt was known for grandstanding, and there was little doubt that that was where this was headed.

'Lieutenant Hyatt,' Lucy said, her voice level but tight. 'I was under the impression that I'd been cleared of suspicion in Russell Bennett's murder.'

'Your alibi checked out. But given that my detectives have requested your presence at the notification of a victim's family, I thought I should know more about you.' He lifted an arrogant brow. 'It seems you've been keeping secrets, Dr Trask.'

JD thought he saw her eyes flicker, but it was over so quickly he couldn't be sure.

'I have not, Lieutenant,' she said coolly. 'I was candid with your detectives. I told them that I'd dated the victim for a short time and that I'd broken his nose.'

Hyatt nodded. 'Five years ago, true. I'm talking about further back than that. Try August, fourteen years ago.'

Her eyes didn't flicker this time. They flashed in shocked fury before she quickly reined herself in. 'I have nothing to hide, Lieutenant.'

'I should think not,' Hyatt said dryly. 'It took Detectives Morton and Skinner less than an hour to dig it up. Ms Montgomery found the court records faster than that.'

Daphne Montgomery's jaw tightened while Morton briefly closed her eyes and Skinner shook his head, a slight movement that made JD realize that whatever this was about, they hadn't meant for it to go down this way.

Lucy lifted her empty hands before folding them in her lap, the gesture one of contempt. 'Then you know it all. Anything I'd provide would be . . . simply extraneous.'

Hyatt sat on the edge of his desk close to Lucy, deliberately crowding her space. 'Humor me,' he said. 'What happened, in your own words?'

She met Hyatt's gaze head-on. Her voice was calm, but her hands clenched tightly in her lap. 'I was arrested, charged, tried before a jury of my peers, and acquitted. The charges were then dropped, my record expunged.'

JD looked to Stevie and saw she was as stunned as he was, but Hyatt appeared unsurprised, his mouth curving in a half-smile of appreciation. 'Succinctly delivered, Doctor,' he said. 'But I'd like a little more meat with my bones.'

'I owe you no explanations,' Lucy said coldly. 'May I leave?'

'You could, but I don't think you'll want to,' Hyatt said. 'It was an accident, right?'

She nodded, tight-lipped. 'Lieutenant, I—'

'Your fiancé was killed,' Hyatt interrupted, 'was he not?'

She'd been engaged. Of course she'd had relationships, so had he. He'd been married, for God's sake. Still, it left JD unsettled to think of her so attached. Her fiancé's death still caused her pain. It was plain on her face before she closed her eyes, recovering her composure.

'He was.' Then she opened her eyes and they were empty. 'This has no bearing on anything related to this case or to any of you. I've had a very long day. I'm leaving now.' She rose, but Daphne pressed her back into the chair.

'Lucy, the lieutenant's approach is vile.' Daphne looked straight at Hyatt as she said the words, making JD want to cheer. 'But you need to stay, sugar. And Peter, you need to get to the goddamn point.'

Hyatt's glare was annoyed. 'Thank you, Miss Montgomery.' He blew out a frustrated breath. 'Tell me what happened, Dr Trask. If you truly have nothing to hide.'

Once again Lucy's eyes flashed as she battled for control. 'Fine. But I will not sit here like I'm in the defendant's chair. Been there, done that.' She stood, straightened her skirt, and walked to the window before turning to face them. 'I was with my fiancé. I'd had a glass of wine, he'd had way more. I tried to get his keys, he pushed me out of the car. A minute later I heard a crash, ran to the scene. He'd been thrown from his convertible and was already dead, but he'd hit another car.'

'In which two people were hurt,' Daphne supplied softly.

Lucy's nod was stiff. 'Yes. A mother and her child. The mother was critically injured, the child bruised, but strapped in a car seat and therefore alive. I went for help, but through a misunderstanding was accused of being the driver. I was charged with vehicular homicide of my fiancé. The evidence supported my assertion that I was not in the car at the time. I was cleared.' She drew a breath. 'That is all.'

Hyatt's smile was wry. 'I don't think so, but we'll leave it at that for now. For the record, I had no intention of making you feel like you'd been seated in the defendant's chair. As you noted, you've had a long day. I was trying to be nice.'

Lucy's expression showed her skepticism as to Hyatt's intent. JD agreed with her.

'So to get to the point, Peter,' Daphne said, articulating each word. 'The file.'

Lucy looked around the room. 'What file?'

'What file?' JD and Stevie said at the same time.

'The file we found in Bennett's condo when we did our search,' Elizabeth Morton replied. 'It was on his desk. It's a file about you, Dr Trask.'

Hyatt reached backward to pull a thick folder from his desk. 'Copies,' he said and handed the file to JD.

JD put the file on Hyatt's desk and began sorting. Lucy stood at his side, looking over each page as he did. 'Oh, my God,' she murmured. 'What is this?'

'Looks like everything you ever did,' JD said, turning the pages. 'College transcripts, articles on your arrest and trial, your move here to Baltimore. Everything.'

She leaned over his arm, riffling through the pages. 'No, not everything. The articles about the trial are here, but the one on the verdict isn't.' She turned to look at Elizabeth Morton. 'Did you remove it?'

'No,' Elizabeth said. 'We saw the article on the trial and called Daphne over to see it.'

'I was there in case they found any patient records,' Daphne said when Lucy frowned at her, puzzled. 'We have to protect doctor–patient confidentiality. We all made a few calls and dug up the story in a short time. We pretty quickly determined you'd been fully cleared of any wrongdoing in the accident.'

'Then why this?' she asked, anger making her voice tremble. 'Why sandbag me?'

Hyatt sat behind his desk. 'I wanted to be sure you truly had nothing to hide. If you'd minimized your role or denied it happened, then I wouldn't have approved your participation in this case. But if anything, you made yourself look worse.'

'Worse than what?' Stevie asked.

'Worse than she needed to,' Daphne answered cryptically.

'So I'm to participate?' Lucy asked sardonically. 'To what do I owe this honor?'

'I asked him if you could be our native guide,' Stevie said. 'Bennett had ongoing ties to his hometown – your hometown. We wanted your help.'

'But if he'd had cause to blackmail you, I couldn't approve it,' Hyatt said. 'You were upfront about it. No danger of blackmail.'

Lucy's pale cheeks darkened in anger. 'Good to know. And if I refuse?'

Hyatt shrugged. 'Somebody left a human heart in your car today. I'd think you'd want that man caught.'

'Like it or not,' JD murmured, 'you're a key to this. This killer picked you. And for what it's worth, Stevie and I didn't know about this.'

She jerked a nod. 'I believe you. Thank you.'

Relieved, he turned to Morton and Skinner. 'Was this the only file? Or did he have others on his other women?'

Lucy winced. 'How many other women?'

'At least forty in five years,' Stevie said and Lucy winced again.

'What's the hometown tie?' she asked.

'At least three of you are from Anderson Ferry,' JD said. 'We're checking the rest of the names on the list.'

'Three of us? Gwyn, me, and who else?'

'Brandi Bennett,' he said and her eyes widened.

'Brandi Bennett is from Anderson Ferry? No way.'

'You didn't know her there?' Hyatt asked.

'No, but she was much younger than Gwyn and me. What was her last name?'

Stevie checked her notes. 'Stackhouse.'

'I knew of the family. They had a lot of kids. I didn't really know any of them.'

'Did he have files on the other women?' JD asked again.

'Not that we found,' Elizabeth said. 'Only Dr Trask. Why would he have a file on her?'

'Hate's the easy answer,' JD said. 'Because she broke his nose. But I'd ask why now? The articles were stamped by the Anderson Ferry newspaper just three weeks ago. Was anything else found in the condo?'

'Nothing to indicate a struggle,' Elizabeth said. 'We got his credit card and bank records. Guy paid a hell of a lot of alimony to the first wife.'

'What about the crime scene, Drew?' Hyatt asked.

'We took casts of the tire tracks we found in the grass,' Drew said. 'The tracks were made by a wheelchair, like I thought. But we never found the chair.'

'He didn't ditch it after setting up the body,' Stevie said, 'but pushing an empty wheelchair around the park seems like a risk. If anyone saw him, they'd remember that.'

'He could have ridden away in it,' Drew said. 'But then there are no tracks leading from the scene. He had to stay on that path all the way back to the parking lot or he stashed the chair in one of those apartments.'

'No surveillance cameras in the parking lot?' Hyatt asked.

'None that work,' Drew replied. 'Your apartment security sucks, Dr Trask.'

She nodded, but said nothing.

'What about the body, Dr Trask?' Hyatt asked.

'So far, only the injuries I've already reported.' Her tone was cool, clearly unmoved by Hyatt's explanation of his actions. She was still very pissed. 'We're waiting for DNA confirmation that this is indeed Russ Bennett.'

'His current wife, Brandi, corroborated the scar and the broken bone,' Stevie said.

'It's him,' Hyatt said. 'Mulhauser called me. He spoke with Bennett's orthopedist who confirmed that Bennett had broken his arm in exactly the same way and same place. We'll do the DNA to dot the i, but we can be confident that Bennett is dead.'

'His body was flash frozen,' JD said. 'We need to get a list of area food processing plants with freezers. His killer had to have had access to a big one.'

'Skinner and I will follow up on that,' Elizabeth Morton said.

'And my clerk will run checks on the women on Bennett's delivery list,' Hyatt said. 'Any one of them may have had motive. What about the first ex-wife?'

'She had motive five years ago when he was cheating on her,' JD said. 'But why would she kill him now? He was paying her a lot of alimony.'

'She's too small a woman to have moved the body,' Lucy added.

'But we're going to see her before we go out to the parents,' Stevie told Hyatt. 'To do the notification and check her out.' She looked over at Daphne. 'What about Bennett's medical office?

Do we have a warrant to search there too?'

'Grayson's working on it,' Daphne said. 'That's more complicated than the condo. We'll call you when we get a judge to sign. Peter, if you're through grilling Lucy for shits and giggles, I'll be on my way,' she said to Hyatt, who once again looked annoyed.

JD's respect for Daphne increased tenfold.

'You all know what you have to do,' Hyatt said irritably when Daphne had departed in a cloud of gardenia perfume. 'Everybody go. Except Mazzetti and Fitzpatrick. You stay. And close the door.'

'Wait for me outside the office,' JD said to Lucy in a low voice. He watched her go, then closed the door and turned to a placidly staring Hyatt. 'That was a test, wasn't it? Not just of Dr Trask, but of us.'

'And you passed,' Hyatt said. 'Barely. You,' he pointed to Stevie, 'did okay. You, Fitzpatrick, are a hothead and you lead with your emotions. Get your head in the game, and I don't mean the one you've already engaged. Now get to work. Be back at oh-eight.'

Fuck him. Lucy marched toward the ladies' room, hands clenched into fists, too angry for much more articulate thought than *fuck Hyatt*. It was all she could do back there to keep her voice civil, and she'd only done so for Fitzpatrick, who'd seemed as furious with his boss as she'd been. Hyatt had manipulated her past for his own benefit.

Use me. *Test* me. *Bring up my dirty little secrets like that. Fuck you, Hyatt.*

'Lucy, honey, wait up.'

It was Daphne. Lucy had to force herself to stop, draw a breath so that she wouldn't be sharp with the assistant DA, who she'd come to appreciate the first time she'd testified on one of Daphne's cases. The woman was smart, sassy, and used her twang to put people at ease and sometimes to make them underestimate her. Then, if they were guilty, she decimated them.

They were three for three, Lucy and Daphne. Three cases so far, and three convictions. Daphne Montgomery was new, but she was good.

Daphne put an arm around Lucy's shoulders. 'You okay, baby girl?'

It made Lucy wistful. *Nobody's called me that in a long time.* 'Yeah, I'm okay.'

'I just wanted to be sure you knew that nobody appreciated that dickhead Hyatt.' Daphne grinned when Lucy laughed in spite of herself. 'See, I knew I could make you smile. Seriously, Mazzetti and Fitzpatrick did not know. You got that, right?'

'I got it. I just don't understand why he did it.'

'Well, if it makes you feel better, he's that way with everybody. Don't take it personally.'

'You're joking. Why is he allowed to get away with that?'

'Because he's a good cop. Look, we all hated what he did in there. JD looked like he wanted to smack Hyatt upside his bald head. But it's good he didn't. That was as much a test of JD as it was of you. You got that too, right?'

Lucy stared at her. 'Why would he test Detective Fitzpatrick? Why do any of it?'

'Well, I didn't know either, until JD walked in the room and looked at you.'

Stevie's words came to mind. 'How did he look at me?'

'Like you were all that mattered. If he'd sprung to your defense, he would've been off the case. For your sake, I'm glad he didn't. You need him. If a tenth of what I hear about him is true, you won't find a braver cop.' Daphne pushed at Lucy's mouth with her thumb, making Lucy realize she was frowning. 'Plus, he's hot. And he's coming up the hall.'

'Thanks, Daphne. I appreciate it.'

'I know,' Daphne said quietly. 'And you need to find a different way to tell that story of yours, sugar. You make yourself sound only slightly less guilty than Ma Barker.'

'It wasn't any of their business,' Lucy hissed, feeling her ire rise all over again.

'No, it wasn't. But now it is, because some killer's made it our business. So help JD and Stevie find him so I can put his ass away forever.'

127

Lucy drew a breath. 'Okay.' She was calm now. 'Thank you.'

'Good girl. Here's my cell and home numbers.' Daphne slipped her card into Lucy's jacket pocket. 'You call me if you need me. I mean that.' She turned them both around so that they could watch Fitzpatrick and Stevie approach and gave a low hum of approval. 'I wish I were you, baby girl. That man is somethin'.'

He was indeed. Showered and clean-shaven, he could easily have graced the cover of a magazine. There was something about him, and every last bit of it was masculine. Then again, her first fiancé had been the same. *And look how that ended up.*

'You might want to try breathing,' Daphne whispered. 'I'm told it's good for you. Now I've got to go. Call me.' She patted Fitzpatrick's arm as she passed.

When Fitzpatrick was two steps from Lucy, he shoved his hands in his pockets. His gaze was intense and he leaned forward slightly, as if he'd have his hands on her if he could. 'I'm sorry,' he said simply. 'That shouldn't have happened.'

'It's not your fault,' Lucy said. 'Did you pass *your* test?'

'Barely. Stevie's the star pupil, but I'm learning the ropes. Are you ready to go? We need to get to the first wife so we can get over the Bay Bridge to the Bennetts.'

You're going home. Lucy wished she hadn't asked to go along. But she owed the Bennetts a lot. Their son was dead. They'd need support, someone they could lean on.

'I need to get the bag I packed when I went back to my apartment.'

'I'll meet you at the first Mrs Bennett's house,' Stevie said. 'I need to get the list of Bennett's girlfriends to Hyatt's clerk so she can run them. I'll make you a copy, Lucy.'

'Because I'm your native guide,' Lucy said dryly. 'You know, you could have just asked. I would have been happy to help, especially, as Hyatt so noted, because the killer left a heart in my car.'

'It wasn't a done deal,' Stevie said with a sigh. 'Hyatt said he wanted to talk to you first. I didn't know he had an ulterior motive. We *are* sorry.'

Lucy studied their faces. 'You haven't asked me what really happened.'

'Because it's your business,' JD said. 'You've had enough for one day.'

'And it ain't over yet,' Stevie added. 'I'll meet you there, JD.' With a wave she was gone, leaving Lucy alone with JD Fitzpatrick for the very first time.

No, that wasn't true. They'd been alone that day in the autopsy suite. When he'd cried. 'Who was the child to you?' Lucy asked softly, before she could lose her nerve.

His eyes widened. 'Excuse me?'

'Two years ago you witnessed the autopsy of a child. Who was she to you?'

He looked uncomfortable. 'A victim,' he said so quietly she had to lean closer to hear. 'I didn't know her. I found her dead in the street.'

'No one else came. Her parents didn't come to ID the body. There was no one.'

'Which is why I was there.' He took her elbow gently. 'Let's get your bag.'

She let him walk her to CSU where she fetched her bags. Fitzpatrick reached for them both, but she held on to the bag that held her violin case. 'I've got this one.'

Fitzpatrick lifted her heavy suitcase as if it weighed nothing. 'Then let's go.'

They said nothing until they got to his car and he opened the trunk. Lucy leaned forward and sniffed. 'It still stinks.'

'Then we can put your bags in the backseat.'

She wrinkled her nose. 'Where addicts puke?'

He laughed, his dimple appearing. 'That was in the car I drove in Narcotics. So far nobody's puked in the back of this car.' He put her bags on the seat next to a pile of old clothes. Then he winked at her. 'That I know of, anyway. Anything could have happened before I got the car.'

'Ha, ha,' she grumbled, surprised when he opened the passenger door for her. But she supposed she shouldn't have been. JD Fitzpatrick had been the epitome of good manners all day. Which would make his bad-boy mode even more enticing, she knew. That he had a bad-boy mode was not even in question. Of course he did.

And the thought of it turned her on. A lot. *Dammit*.

He said nothing more, taking them northwest, out of the city. They had at least a half-hour drive ahead of them and she suddenly found herself edgy. It had been a roller-coaster day, and as Stevie had said, it wasn't over yet.

'Why did Stevie drive separately?' she asked.

'Her daughter graduates kindergarten tonight. If we run late, she's going to take off so that she doesn't miss it.'

'Kindergarten graduation? They do that?'

He nodded, smiling wistfully. 'Yeah, it's really cute.'

'I thought you didn't have kids,' she said, then wished the words back.

He glanced over at her. 'Been asking about me?'

Her cheeks heated. 'Yes.'

'Good.' He glanced at her again, a little longer this time before returning his gaze to the road. 'I was there when Stevie's son graduated from kindergarten.' He cleared his throat harshly. 'I've known Cordelia since she was born. I wish I could be there for her tonight, but she'll have tons of family there for her.' He handed her his wallet. 'Her picture's in there.'

Lucy opened his wallet hesitantly, feeling awkward handling his things. But the awkwardness fled when she saw the little girl's sweet smile. 'She's adorable.'

'And happy,' he said, a little too fiercely. 'Stevie's a good mom.'

She remembered him saying he'd had no Big Wheel as a child and wondered if he'd not had happiness either. Or a good mom. She wanted to ask, but he'd respected her privacy about her trial. She'd respect his. If he wanted to talk about it, he would.

Besides, if she asked about his mom, he'd ask about hers. She gave him back his wallet and he slipped it in his pocket.

'So what are my responsibilities as your native guide?' she asked.

'To keep your eyes and ears open, tell us if the people we talk to in Anderson Ferry have relationships that aren't obvious.'

'I haven't lived there in a long time. There will be a lot I don't know.'

'You've kept up, though. You knew Bennett's mother had a recent heart attack.'

Lucy barely remembered telling him that, but he was a detective. Of course he'd pick up on details. She'd have to keep that in mind. 'Because I talk to her on the phone and visit with her when she has her doctors' appointments, here in the city. I haven't been back to Anderson Ferry in years.'

Again he glanced at her. 'Why not?'

She hesitated, then shrugged. 'There isn't anything there for me anymore.'

'No family?'

This time she didn't hesitate. 'No. None.'

'I'm sorry.'

'It's okay.' Although it really wasn't. 'And you? What about your family?'

'None to speak of.'

So it was as she'd thought. 'I can respect that, Detective.'

'JD,' he said. 'My name is JD.'

'What does it stand for?'

'Just Deserts,' he said lightly, a diversion tactic, she knew.

'No wonder you don't wish to speak of them,' she said dryly. 'I wouldn't either, if they'd saddled me with a name like that.'

This drew a chuckle. 'JD is just initials,' he said. 'Doesn't stand for anything.'

She didn't believe him, but let it go. 'Okay. But you still haven't honestly answered my first question. Why am I here? I don't think I can help you with anything in Anderson Ferry. You never even asked me who I still knew. So why am I here?'

'You asked to come. To be there when we notified the family.'

She studied his profile, noting that he was careful not to look at her now. A muscle twitched in his taut jaw. 'You're afraid,' she murmured. 'For me. Aren't you?'

'Aren't you?' he countered. 'Because if you're not, you damn well should be.'

That gave her pause. And then she understood. 'You're my bodyguard?'

131

'No. We are not bodyguards.' He said it as if reciting from a handbook. 'That's why you're our consultant. Unpaid, of course. Donating your time out of the goodness of your heart, a desire to support your community and to catch the psycho who had a human heart delivered to your car.'

'Of course,' she murmured. 'Your native guide.'

Now he looked at her. 'Yes. Do you want to quit?'

She thought of Russ's brutalized body. Of the number 'I' burned into his back. Fitzpatrick and Stevie had manipulated the system to keep her safe. 'No. I think I like this arrangement just fine. I certainly won't fight you on it. And I'll be the best native guide you could ever want.'

'Okay. Now, can I ask you a question?'

She steeled herself for a question about her trial. 'You can ask.'

'Are you involved with Thomas Thorne? Specifically, I mean romantically.'

She blinked. 'No,' she said firmly. 'Friends only. We're not at all compatible. Thorne keeps a veritable harem and I . . . haven't.'

'Good. Are you involved with anyone?'

'No.'

'Would you?'

'Become involved with someone?' She still studied his profile. *He's as nervous as I am.* She'd expected confidence. Swagger. She hadn't expected nerves. Maybe he wasn't as dangerous as she'd imagined.

No, Lucy. He is. To you, he is. Say no. Just say no. But her mouth would not cooperate. Just saying no had left her alone for too long. 'Maybe. It would depend.'

'On what?'

Think, girl. About the killer leaving you a human heart. You don't need JD Fitzpatrick distracting you. It would be nice if he stayed focused, too.

'Lucy?' he asked when she said nothing. 'What would it depend on?'

She sighed quietly. 'Well, for starters, on whether I'm some killer's number two.'

Monday, May 3, 5.00 P.M.

He lifted his face into the wind, letting it cool him. Then he looked down at his feet. Janet Gordon was done. He hoped she found hell to her liking, because that's exactly where he'd sent her. She'd died beautifully, with much screaming and weeping and begging.

Just as he'd hoped. He turned the *Satisfaction* back to shore. He'd take care of her worthless heart back at his plant. The wind was kicking up and he needed a steady hand. Plus, the cement floor would be easier to clean than the deck of his boat. He'd learned the hard way with Bennett – cutting out a human heart, even after death, produced a lot more blood than even he'd anticipated.

But he hadn't been thinking, and cleaning up the deck of the *Satisfaction* after Bennett's kill had taken hours and tons of bleach – which couldn't be good for the hardwood finish or the marine life in the Bay. So this time he'd planned ahead.

He had a Shop-Vac set up in one of the rooms designed to clean fish. It had a drain, so he could easily empty all the blood he vacuumed out as he cut. He'd have just enough time to prepare the body before delivering Janet.

She didn't need to be frozen, which was a shame. It'd been fun sending Russ through that big freezer. Kind of an experiment, just to see how he'd come out. Boys and their toys. But Janet would keep until he got her where she needed to be.

Which was wherever Lucy Trask planned to be tonight. The woman was a total creature of habit, thank the good Lord. So if good old Lucy's habits held firm, he knew exactly where he'd find her. And then she'd find Janet.

Then the cops would come and there would be much brouhaha. A second one, they'd say. A serial killer, they'd moan. The press would go wild.

It would be easy to identify Mrs Gordon. He'd left her breasts. Kind of. They'd find the serial numbers easily enough, which would lead them right back to Bennett. Her son Ryan would come straightaway – if for no other reason than to be certain his inheritance was well tended.

Of course the bank accounts had been cleaned out. *By me.*

Ryan had no money of his own, poor guy. Mama Janet kept him on a tight financial leash, with a teeny little allowance that barely fed his methadone habit. He'd come back east, and quickly. He'd want the money. And maybe because Ryan would want to prove to himself that Mama really was dead. *And I'll be waiting.*

'Too bad she fucked you over, Ry,' he murmured. 'Because even if I let you live, which I will not, you'd be answering to the cops for what you did.'

Because murder had no statute of limitations.

He crouched next to dead Janet and yanked her up by her throat. 'Right, Mrs Gordon? No fucking statute of limitations. *But I didn't do anything,*' he mimicked cruelly and flung her away. He rose, dusting off his jeans. 'No, you didn't. So I did.'

He grabbed the pack of cigarettes from the table next to his tools. One left. He'd bought this pack specifically for Janet. Virginia Slims. They made a smaller burn mark, a benefit since her back was a lot narrower than Bennett's. He'd used all but one burning the 'L' into her skin.

She'd screamed all kinds of useful information, like her bank account passwords, her son's cell number, and the name of her attorney – the one who held her confession letter. All of which would come in very handy.

He lit up the last cigarette and took a nice long drag. He had time for one smoke before heading back.

Monday, May 3, 5.00 P.M.

Fitzpatrick's fists had tightened on the steering wheel, his mouth flattening at Lucy's cool assessment of her possible fate. 'You're not going to be any goddamn killer's second victim, Lucy. It's not gonna happen. I won't let it.'

There was the confidence she'd expected. He was nervous about the personal stuff, like whether or not she'd want to be involved with him, but he was completely secure in his duty as a cop. And as her protector. 'Good to know,' she murmured.

'So tell me, what would your becoming involved with me depend on? Please.'

The *please* undid her. 'I don't think you'd understand if I told you.'

The muscle in his jaw was twitching again. 'Try me.'

Lucy looked away, staring out the window at the I-95 traffic as she searched for an answer. Finally she decided on the truth. 'It would depend on how exciting you are.'

He was silent for a long moment. 'I don't understand.'

Lucy's smile was rueful. 'See? I told you.' She gathered her courage and turned to look at him. 'I'm a lot of trouble, JD. I'd advise you to keep moving on.'

He frowned, but said nothing and she found herself disappointed. A piece of her wished he'd argue, but another piece of her was glad he didn't. He might be sweet and he might be kind, but every instinct she had said he'd be a thrill-seeker.

And then she'd become one too. Again. Which couldn't be allowed to happen. Again. Hyatt had actually done her a favor by dredging up Heath's death and her trial earlier. It was just the bucket of cold water she'd needed to focus on reality.

Lucy settled back for the rest of the drive to the first Mrs Bennett's house. Then sat up when Fitzpatrick exited the highway a few exits too early. 'Where are you going?'

His expression was grim as he pointed. 'There.'

There was a gas station at the end of the exit ramp, but instead of pulling in, he drove behind the building and parked the car. Pocketing his keys, he came around to her side, opened the door, and popped her seat belt free.

'What is—' was all she had time to say before he took her by the shoulders and pulled her to her feet. She stared up at him, her skin buzzing and her pulse pounding. He was angry. But he was also aroused and that fast, so was she.

'Is this exciting enough for you?' he growled before digging his fingers into her hair, a second before his mouth came down on hers.

Coherent thought fled. *Yes. Please. More.* He was hot and

135

demanding and hard. Her hands were on his chest, then around his neck as he pressed her against the car. Oh, God, he was hard, in all the right places. He ate at her mouth, nips and bites that made her moan. His hands slid down her back, detouring to grab her hips just before they would have closed over her butt. She lifted on her toes, cursing the straight skirt that kept her from wrapping her legs around his waist.

Narcotic. The man was a narcotic. She ripped her mouth away, struggling for control where there was none. *This is why you don't get involved. Not even a little bit. It's like an alcoholic having 'just one drink'. You can't. No maybes. Just no.*

His breathing was strident against her cheek, sending new shivers down her spine. 'Is this exciting enough for you?' he repeated, much more quietly.

'Too much,' she whispered, her arms still around his neck. She needed to move, to push him away but she could not. He felt too good. Smelled too good. Made her feel too good. *Alive.* Wearily she leaned her forehead against his chest. 'Way too much.'

'I should apologize,' he said roughly. 'But I'm not sorry. I've wanted to do that since this morning.'

'Do you always do everything you want?' she asked, a little bitterly.

'No. Not nearly. And I get the impression that neither do you.'

He was right. She swallowed hard, wishing. 'What do you do in your spare time?'

'What?'

She lifted her head, met his dark eyes. 'Your spare time. How do you spend it?'

His jaw tensed. 'Are you asking me if I'm involved with anyone? Because if you think I could do this when . . . I'd be no better than Bennett.'

'No. Stevie told me that you'd had no one since you lost your wife.'

His eyes narrowed. 'What else did Stevie say?'

'That you were a good man. A good friend.'

His anger disappeared like mist. 'Oh.'

136

'I need to know, JD,' she urged, her voice low. 'Please. Your spare time?'

'I don't have a lot of spare time. I sleep. Sometimes I do weekend coaching.'

'What do you coach?' *Please say something normal. Something safe.*

'Now a little baseball. In the fall, it'll be football. Why?'

She let herself breathe. That was normal. Americana. *I can do that. I can sit in the stands and cheer him on without losing it.* She hoped. 'I just needed to know.'

He was studying her intently. 'I don't understand.'

'I know,' she murmured. Eventually, if this worked out, she'd tell him. She'd have to. But for now, for this moment, he held her in his arms and she was warm, her body needy. It had been a very, very long time. She lifted on her toes, fitting her mouth to his, her kiss light, tentative.

For about five seconds. Then he took the kiss deeper, made it richer. So much hotter. He kept his hands on her hips, but he tightened his grip, as if the effort cost him. He ended the kiss gradually, giving her mouth a little nudge as he pulled away.

'We have to go,' he whispered. 'I have to work.'

'I know,' she whispered back. He helped her into the car and buckled her in with a tenderness that made her want to sigh.

He'd pulled the car back onto the highway before clearing his throat. 'For the record, in the future, that's how I'd like to spend my spare time.'

He was nervous again. It was sweet. 'I won't fight you on it.'

He glanced over with a wry smile. 'Good to know. We're almost at the first Mrs Bennett's house. Tell me everything you can remember about her.'

Nine

Stevie checked her watch again. There was no way she was going with JD to notify Bennett's parents. She'd never make it back in time for Cordelia's graduation.

Which Stevie would not miss, no way, no how. *Ah, finally.* JD parked behind her car. 'What took you so long?' she asked when he and Lucy got out.

'Traffic,' he said, but Stevie was no fool. There was something different about him. About Lucy Trask, too. Her lips were a little puffier than they'd been before. Which would have been fine, except that Hyatt had let them know he was watching JD.

That JD and Lucy had stopped for some quick nookie was *not* a good thing.

Stevie sighed. 'Let's get this interview done. I'm not going to be able to go with you to the Bennetts' in Anderson Ferry. You want to put it off until tomorrow?'

JD shook his head as she'd expected. 'The parents need to hear it from us before they see it on the news. I'm surprised the story hasn't already broken.'

'It did, but the network said they wouldn't disclose the name until the family had been notified. So far they've only reported the body in the park this morning.'

'That's good, at least. Do you want to lead with the missus?'

'Sure. What about Lucy?'

'I can stay outside,' Lucy said. 'I'm fine with that.'

JD frowned. 'Okay, but lock up,' he said, as if the woman were Cordy's age.

To Stevie's surprise, Lucy just smiled dryly. 'I'll be fine.'

Stevie got a piece of paper from her car. 'It's the list of Bennett's girlfriends from the courier. I got backgrounds on a few of them. Three more on that list are from Anderson Ferry. See if you know them. We'll want to check them out.'

Lucy read the list, wincing. 'I'm here too, with Doctor Barbie. I'll see what I remember.' She shot JD a meaningful look. 'Because I'm the best damn native guide there is.'

He chuckled and gave her his keys. 'Don't play with the radio.'

'Lucy seems . . . comfortable,' Stevie said as they walked up to the front door.

'She's not as rigid as you might think,' he murmured.

'Just be careful, JD,' Stevie warned. 'Hyatt's watching you.'

'I know,' was all he said, then knocked on Mrs Bennett's door.

'First name is Helen,' Stevie murmured just before the door swung open, revealing a chicly dressed woman who'd undergone way too much plastic surgery.

'Can I help you?' Helen asked.

'Yes, ma'am. I'm Detective Mazzetti and this is Detective Fitzpatrick. We're here to talk to you about your ex-husband, Dr Russell Bennett.'

Helen looked confused. 'They sent detectives? I never expected that. Come in.'

Stevie swallowed her frown. 'What were you expecting, ma'am?' she asked.

Helen led them into a very nicely furnished living room. 'Well, I expected a phone call at the most. You'll want the details for your report. Let me get the papers for you.'

'Wait.' Stevie gently held the woman's arm. 'Why do you think we're here?'

'Because of the fraud report I started with the bank this morning,' she said, then frowned. 'But you're not.' Her expression changed to panic. 'Is it one of my boys?'

'Sshh,' Stevie soothed. 'Not your kids. This isn't about your kids.'

Weakly, Helen sank onto a sofa. 'Thank God. Then what is it? What kind of detectives did you say you were?'

'We're from Homicide,' Stevie said. 'We're here about your ex-husband.'

Helen Bennett's face lost all its remaining color. 'Russell? He's dead?'

'We believe so, ma'am.' Stevie sat next to her. JD took a chair across the room.

'You believe so?' Helen repeated, her voice hollow and shocked. 'What does that even mean, you believe so? Is he or isn't he?'

'We're still working on a final identification,' Stevie said gently. 'But scars and bone breaks match. Your ex-husband was beaten too badly for a visual identification.'

Helen covered her mouth with a hand that shook. 'Oh, my God.'

'I need to ask you some questions, Mrs Bennett, and they might not be comfortable ones. For that I apologize. Can you tell me about the fraud report?'

'Our bank funds were stolen. Russell kept a bank account for the boys, separate from my alimony and child support. It was for big, special things.'

'And you tried to use that account?' Stevie prompted.

'Yes. My oldest son is twelve today. I used the debit card for his gift this morning, but the card was denied. The bank said the account was empty. I called Russ, but only got his voicemail. I was furious. I thought he'd cleaned out the account again.'

'Again? He'd done this before?'

'A few times, if one of his floozies wanted something expensive.'

'When did you last speak with your ex-husband, ma'am?'

'Two weeks ago. Our youngest had a special recital and wanted Russ there.'

'Did Dr Bennett go to the recital?'

'No. He had some excuse, as usual. This time he was meeting a new client.'

'Which day did you talk to him?'

'Sunday, two weeks ago. Russ said he'd come, but then he called a few hours before the recital and said he'd gotten tied up. My son cried himself to sleep that night.'

'What time did he call you?'

'It was just after one. I should have known something was wrong.'

'Why?'

'Normally he just wouldn't show. But this time he called, said he was tied up and told me to tell the boys he loved them.' Tears rolled down her face. 'I told him to go to hell.'

Stevie patted her hand. 'Did he call your house phone or your cell?' Proof of the call would cement Lucy's alibi. Lucy would have been halfway to LA by then.

'My cell. Do his parents know?'

'No. We're going to tell them when we leave here.'

She nodded uncertainly. 'I should call them first.'

'We'd appreciate it if you wouldn't,' Stevie said softly. 'This is a police matter now. We need to talk to them. Do you know of anyone who wanted to hurt your husband?'

'Only every woman he two-timed, every patient he cheated. The only people who'll cry about his death are his parents and my boys – and me for their pain.'

'Tell me about his patients. You say he cheated them?'

'He'd been sued more than once for shoddy work. If you want to make a list of people who hated him, you're going to need a lot bigger pencil.'

'Do you know any names of disgruntled patients?' Stevie asked.

'None from after our divorce, only patients from five years ago who actually sued.'

'I can get those names,' Stevie said. 'Ma'am, where were you on Sunday night?'

Her smile was thin-lipped. 'Same place I am every night. Right here, with my sons. And no, I can't prove it. Am I a suspect?'

'Right now everyone is,' Stevie said, 'until we can cross them off the list.'

'I wouldn't kill him. I hated him for what he did to me, but he was still the father of my sons, and even if he was a lousy father, they needed him.' Her thin smile grew bitter. 'Besides, now that he's gone, my alimony dries up, as does any child support.'

'There will be life insurance,' Stevie said and watched Helen's eyes flash.

'No, there won't be. Russell stopped payments on his policy last year. He *said* he could barely afford his malpractice premiums. I'll have to find a job and daycare and . . . Oh, God.' Her panic returned. 'I can't believe this. How am I going to tell my boys?'

Stevie took out her card and wrote a name on it. 'This is a child psychologist who specializes in kids who've lost a parent violently. He's good. My cell is on there too, if you remember anything that might help.' She looked at JD, who had been surreptitiously checking the display on his own cell phone. 'Do you have anything for Mrs Bennett?'

'Just a few things,' JD said. 'When you told him to go to hell, what did he say?'

Helen looked away. 'He said "That's where I'm headed." I didn't understand then.'

'Why would you?' JD asked, understanding in his voice. 'Do you remember anything special about that call? Any sounds? Anything you were thinking?'

Helen drew a breath. 'There were birds. Seabirds. I could hear them. I accused Russ of ditching our son's recital to have brunch at the harbor with one of his floozies.'

'And what did he say to that?'

'Nothing. He hung up on me.'

'Did he mention the name of the client he planned to see?' he asked.

'No. I assumed it was a woman for that reason, too. I should have known something was wrong, should have called 911.' New tears began to roll down her face.

JD took the chair next to her. 'I'm sorry, Mrs Bennett, but just a few more questions. Tell me, how did you first meet Dr Bennett?' he asked, in a way that told Stevie that he knew something.

Helen hesitated. 'I was his and his sister's babysitter,' she said and Stevie had to fight the urge to blink in surprise. 'I was home

142

from college for the summer and earning every cent I could for school. But we didn't really meet until years later, at a party. We were introduced by a mutual friend and were so surprised to find we knew each other from before.'

'So you grew up in Anderson Ferry too,' JD said.

'No, I grew up here. My parents divorced and my mother moved there to share a house with a friend, when I was in high school. She moved out a few years later. Why?'

'Just gathering the facts, ma'am,' JD said. 'If you think of anything else, please don't hesitate to tell us.'

Helen haltingly walked them to the door. 'His parents will be devastated. Even though he was a disappointment to them, they loved him.'

JD paused at the door. 'One more thing. What would you say if I told you that Lucy Trask found your husband's body in the park behind her apartment this morning?'

Helen staggered back a step. 'What? Lucy found him? Oh, my God. Poor Lucy.'

'Dr Trask was also threatened,' JD said. 'Who might hate them both?'

'Oh, my God,' Helen repeated, horrified, then forced herself to calm. 'If Lucy was threatened, I can't see any of Russell's floozies doing it. We all love Lucy.'

'Because she broke his nose,' Stevie said.

'Partly. And partly because she stood up to him when he hit her friend.' Helen sighed wearily. 'Russell was a terrible husband. He'd hit me when he got angry. I stayed for the boys, but when I found out about the cheating . . . well, I couldn't stay, for me. If Lucy was threatened, it wasn't by one of the women.'

'Thank you, Mrs Bennett,' JD said. 'We are very sorry for your loss.'

Stevie waited until they were back at their cars. 'Now how did you know she had lived in Anderson Ferry?' she demanded. 'That woman had no accent.'

'Lucy texted me with it while you were asking Helen questions. I'd asked her to tell me everything she remembered about Helen

Bennett, but she didn't know much. I don't know how she found out about this.' He tapped on the car window and Lucy rolled it down.

'Well?' she asked.

'She lived in Anderson Ferry for a short time,' JD said. 'How did you know?'

Lucy handed him her phone. 'Facebook. You can find people who went to your high school. I was looking for people on this courier list when I got a what-if hunch. I checked a few years further back and saw her listed as Helen Anderson Bennett.'

'Wow,' Stevie said. 'Really good work, Lucy. How many others did you find?'

'Of the forty names on this list, so far there are twelve. That includes Gwyn, Brandi and Helen. Plus me.'

'That's a whole helluva lot,' Stevie said. 'Why?'

Lucy shrugged. 'Don't know. Ages range from Helen, at fifty-two, to a girl younger than Brandi. She's barely eighteen. I wrote down the names for you.'

Stevie nodded. 'Fine by me. You two go to the parents and I'll start running backgrounds on these Anderson Ferry names. Even if Mrs B thinks they're all members of the I-love-Lucy club, one of these women could have knocked him off.'

Lucy coughed. 'The I-love-Lucy club?'

'She says her husband's floozies think you're the bomb,' JD said dryly. 'We need to get moving. Oh, I almost forgot.' He pulled a small silver gift box from his pocket. 'This is for Cordelia. I wanted to give it to her myself, but . . . Tell her it's from me.'

Stevie smiled up at him, noting from the corner of her eye the look on Lucy's face – curiosity and a touch of awe. 'You got her a graduation present? Thank you, JD.'

He frowned for a minute. 'You know, on second thought, you may want to check it before you give it to her. It seemed like a good idea at the time.'

Stevie waited until they'd driven away before opening the box. She sucked in a stunned breath. *Oh.* Tears sprang to her eyes as she lifted a silver locket from the box. The locket was open, revealing Cordelia's school picture on one side and Paul's face on the other.

Nestled against the cotton was a small framed photo of a dirty but grinning Paul and JD – a copy of the photo from which JD had cut Paul's face.

Stevie remembered the day the picture was taken. The men were playing baseball, the women watching. JD's wife had still been alive. *So was my son.* The pain that never died stabbed deep, taking her breath away. She missed her son, her husband. Every day of her life. But as she preached to her grief groups, life went on. *And so do we.*

She swiped her thumb over the photo, a caress of Paul's smiling face. Cordy would love the locket. It was so thoughtful of JD. Lucy Trask was a lucky woman.

Newport News, Virginia
Monday, May 3, 5.15 P.M.

Clay Maynard knocked at the door of the small house, hoping his luck would be better with Evan Reardon's wife who'd left him than it had been trying to track down Margo Winchester. The house belonged to Frank Parker, Evan's father-in-law.

The father-in-law opened the door, suspicion on his face. 'Yes?'

'My name is Clay Maynard. I'm an investigator. I need to talk to Sandy Reardon about her husband.'

Parker's expression darkened. 'She's got nothing to say about him.' He started to close the door and Clay knew he had to get the man's attention.

'Wait. I'm concerned about the safety of her children.'

Parker's face flashed pure fury. 'You take these kids over my dead body.'

'Whoa.' Clay held up one hand. 'Who said anything about taking her kids?'

Parker's eyes narrowed. 'You're not from Children's Services?'

'No, I'm a private investigator. I need to ask her some questions about Evan.'

'Like what?'

Clay hesitated. 'Like if she's seen him lately.'

Parker's expression became shrewd. 'You don't believe he's dead either.'

Clay played dumb even though he knew that Nicki had fabricated Evan's demise, an accident in a rented catamaran off the coast of Mexico. The boat was found floating aimlessly, no Evan to be found – presumably lost at sea. 'He's dead?'

'That's what we were told. I don't buy it. Evan was too good a sailor. Man don't work his way through college on a fishing charter and get swept off a catamaran. But as long as the SOB stays away from Sandy and the kids, I don't care.'

Parker stepped outside and closed the door. 'She's been through hell. It's taken five years, but we can finally hug her without her flinching. The kids are settled. They've made new friends and don't cry themselves to sleep. Please, just leave her alone.'

Five years? Evan had told Nicki his wife had left him months ago, not years. And because he'd cheated. But Parker was talking like Sandy had been battered. Clay felt sick. This wasn't the picture he'd gotten from Nicki's report. They didn't help just anyone wipe out their past. There had to be a very strong case. After talking to a crazed and threat-spewing Margo Winchester, Nicki had been satisfied that Evan's was.

Nicki's interview with Sandy Reardon had been short and to the point. Sandy's anger had been cold, her demeanor reserved. She'd answered only the questions Nicki had asked and had volunteered no more information. *Yes, I left Evan. No, I do not intend to take him back. The children are safe with me. They will stay here. With me.*

There had been no indication of abuse, of a flinching wife, of crying children. The bad feeling plaguing Clay intensified. 'I really need to know why she left Evan.'

Parker narrowed his eyes. 'Last time an investigator came, she told my daughter she was checking out Evan's references for some job, but we knew better. That woman didn't take my grandchildren and neither will you, by God.'

'I am a private investigator. I work with the woman who came here before. Why would Sandy think we wanted to take her kids? That doesn't make sense.'

'Because the state office called Sandy, dammit. Told her that Evan had reported her for neglect. That they'd be sending someone to interview her. Then that investigator shows up, asking her if her kids are okay. What should she have thought?'

'Hell,' Clay muttered, wondering who'd made that call. He'd asked about the kids' safety because he'd been worried that Margo would hurt them as she'd threatened. Now he wondered about the veracity of that threat, too. 'Why did your daughter leave Evan?'

Rage burned in Parker's eyes. 'He beat her years ago, back when he lived here in town. If I'd known, I'd have torn his fucking head off. But she stayed then, because she was too proud to tell us. She didn't leave until he got mean with the kids. Still hasn't divorced the prick. But he kept up support payments until he "died", so I didn't push.'

Clay briefly closed his eyes, the scenario becoming all too clear. 'Did your daughter report the assault to the police?'

Parker's jaw clenched hard. 'No. I wanted her to, but she said no. Evan's got a friend in the police department and Sandy was afraid he'd make trouble for her.'

'*Evan's* got a friend in the department?'

'That's what I said,' Parker spat. 'Are you deaf?'

'No, sir. I was just led to believe that Evan was afraid of the police.'

'Like hell. He only left town because I threatened to blow his balls off.'

'Where did he go?'

'Eastern Maryland. Cambridge, I think. He got a job in a hospital there, but the support checks he wrote were off a bank in DC. Which stopped coming after he "died".'

Hell. This was majorly fucked up. Nicki had talked to a cop when she'd been here before. A real cop, with real credentials. The cop had given her the same story as Evan had about Margo Winchester being a cop's daughter – and that Margo's daddy wasn't to be crossed. But now Evan's friend was a cop? *Please don't be the same guy.*

'What's Evan's friend's name? The cop, I mean.'

'Ken Pullman.'

Hell. Same guy. Either Evan had lied or Parker was now. *My money's on Evan for the lie.* Still, somebody had died in that house fire. Clay stood for a moment, trying to decide what to tell this man. Something was very, very wrong here.

'I can't say much, but Evan is missing and that's no lie. It appears there's been foul play. If you have a gun, keep it handy and loaded. Watch your daughter and the kids.'

Parker paled. 'What the hell is this?'

'I really wish I knew,' Clay said. 'And that's no lie either. One more question. When was the last time any of you saw Evan?'

'Three months ago, at his mother's funeral. He came back for it. Sandy thought it was important for the kids to go. I went to make sure Evan stayed away from them. Evan was in a mood, mad at everyone. Worse than we remembered. After that, he went through his mama's things, then left. Next we heard, he was "dead" in Mexico.'

'Thank you,' Clay said. 'Take care.' He got into his car and called Alyssa. 'What have you found on the old lady, Mrs Klein?'

'She did have surgery two months ago.'

'When Nic was here. How do you know?'

'I called the local florist, pretending to be the granddaughter of one of Mrs Klein's friends. I told them my grandma had made a mess of her checkbook and I was trying to figure out what one of the checks was for, that it looked like it had been written to them. They confirmed that Mrs Klein had been in the hospital then and had received other flowers, but none sent by sweet granny. I chatted them up some more and found out Mrs Klein has a granddaughter. Wild child, always in trouble, causing her sweet granny a lot of heartache. Maybe that's the girl Nicki saw with Margo.'

'Nice work, Alyssa,' he said. 'I just found out the real reason Sandy left Evan.'

'From the tone of your voice, you're not happy about it.'

'No. He beat her and hit the kids.'

'Oh, God. Evan was lying?'

'So it would seem. Add in the fire at the house he was not really renting and the fact that Margo was only squatting at Mrs Klein's while she was in the hospital . . .' And the cop who'd corroborated Evan's story. *This is very bad.*

'What have we done, Clay?' she whispered.

'You've done nothing. Nicki should have checked harder, but everyone she talked to backed up Evan's story. Now that I look at it this way, I can see how she was manipulated.'

'Somebody died in that fire. What if it *was* Evan?'

A dull, vicious throb had started at the base of his skull. 'What if it wasn't?'

For a minute neither of them spoke. Then Alyssa sighed. 'What should I do?'

'I want you to start calling hotels in Ocean City. It's where Nic goes when she goes to the beach. Find out where the hell she is.' He hesitated. 'If you reach her through her hotel and she sounds drunk, call me right away. She's been sober for a few years now, but this has happened before.'

Alyssa was quiet a moment. 'Okay. I will. What will you do next?'

'I'm going to pay a visit to the morgue. I need to know if that body is Evan Reardon. Then I'm going to Margo's dance club. I want answers and I want them now.'

Monday, May 3, 6.30 P.M.

Dropping the tracking device in Lucy Trask's handbag had been the smartest thing he'd done. He now knew where she was at any given moment, day or night.

At the moment she was on her way to Anderson Ferry and he wondered why. After disposing of Janet's body, he'd returned home, cleaned up, then checked his tracking website. The little blue dot was east of the Bay Bridge. If she was bolting, he was going to be majorly pissed, considering she was supposed to find Janet later tonight.

Maybe it was because of Russ Bennett. His murder was all over the news, but they weren't releasing his name until the family had been notified. Maybe that's where she was going. Bennett had told him that Lucy kissed up to his parents.

149

He doubted she was bolting yet, but if she did, he'd be able to find her. *She can't hide from me.* For now he'd keep one eye on the little blue ball on his tracking screen while he kept the other on the home of Detective Mazzetti. Luckily there weren't many Mazzettis in Maryland. It had taken him all of five seconds to find her home address.

He was looking for insurance, in case the unexpected happened and the detectives got too close. He needed a distraction to throw in their paths if he needed to bolt. There were few better distractions than family.

Five seconds after parking on Mazzetti's street, he knew he'd picked the right detective to distract, should the need arise. Not only was she the more experienced of the two homicide detectives, but there was a swingset in her back yard and a small kid-sized bike on the front porch. A mom would get mighty distracted if something were to happen to her child. The kid was a girl, if the Disney Princess stickers on two upstairs windows were any indication.

The front door opened and a little girl raced out. Cute kid. She stood by the van, dancing in place on the curb, a backpack slung over one small shoulder.

'Mommy!' she shouted. 'We're gonna be late. Hurry!'

Mazzetti appeared at the door, wearing a pretty dress, an indulgent frown, and curlers in her hair. 'Come inside, Cordelia. I need a few more minutes to get ready.'

Mazzetti disappeared from view and he knew he might have no more perfect time. He slipped from his car and up the sidewalk where Cordelia was dancing her way back to her house. A well-placed foot had her stumbling forward.

'Oh, dear,' he said, catching her before she hit the sidewalk, nudging the backpack off her shoulder. Deftly he slipped the zipper open an inch and dropped the tracker from the tissue in which he'd wrapped it so he'd leave no prints. He crumpled the tissue in his hand. 'I'm sorry. I'm so clumsy. Are you okay?'

The child looked down at her pretty dress to make sure she hadn't dirtied it. 'Yes.'

He smiled. 'Here's your backpack. You dropped it.' He put it on the sidewalk and walked away, whistling a tune softly, his pulse pleasantly racing.

'Cordelia,' Mazzetti called from the door. 'Come inside. I need to braid your hair.'

He didn't plan to hurt the kid, didn't even want to snatch her. But if the detectives got too close, he would take her in a heartbeat and stow her somewhere. By the time the cops found her, he'd be long gone. It paid to have insurance.

Monday, May 3, 6.30 P.M.

Lucy had fallen asleep a half-hour outside of Baltimore, her dead cell phone in one hand, the courier's list in the other. JD was afraid to take them from her hands for fear of waking her up. She'd looked up each Anderson Ferry woman using her phone's Internet connection until it beeped menacingly, out of juice. JD imagined that Stevie had done the same thing, and more efficiently, but it kept Lucy's mind busy and the fear from her eyes.

And it kept his lust backburnered, a bit. Stevie had been right. Hyatt was watching. *I shouldn't have kissed her.* Not then, anyway. But her saying that getting involved with him depended on how exciting he was had tripped a trigger he'd thought himself well over. *I guess not.* He should have waited, but he couldn't be too sorry he hadn't. She'd responded in his arms like fire. There was nothing cold about Lucy. Nor boring.

At the moment she slept deeply, leaving him to study her, undeterred. Her hair was picking up the rays of the setting sun, going all gold within the red as it tumbled over her shoulders. The severe twist she'd worn all day had fallen down as she'd slept, making him want to reach out and touch. She was a beautiful woman.

With kind eyes. Actually that had been his very first impression. Now he knew there were layers to Lucy Trask that he could spend a very long time uncovering.

Except her layers weren't the only thing he wanted to uncover. *Do you always do what you want?* she'd asked. Hardly. Since she'd smiled at him over a pile of smelly garbage, he'd had to struggle to keep a lid on what he really wanted, which was to see her out of that prim blue suit.

She wanted the same thing. Her body had revved like a finely tuned engine, and that was just with a kiss. What would she be like in his bed?

He reached out to touch her smooth cheek when the buzzing of his phone in his pocket had him jumping. 'Fitzpatrick,' he answered quietly.

'JD? It's Stevie. Are you okay?'

'I'm fine. Lucy's just asleep.'

'That's good. Doc's had a busy day. I checked the women on the courier's list who were from Anderson Ferry. None have records and none appear to be big enough to move Bennett's body unassisted.'

'The second part I knew,' he said softly. 'Lucy checked them out on Facebook. If their photos are real, most of them aren't taller than five five. She's by far the tallest of all of them.'

'Who needs fancy police databases when we have Facebook and a phone?' Stevie asked dryly. 'Don't hang up yet. Somebody here wants to talk to you.'

A minute later a little girl piped up. 'Hi, JD.'

'Hi, Cordelia.' He smiled. 'How's my girl?'

'I'm fine. Thank you! I love my locket!'

His smile became a grin. 'I'm glad. I wish I could have given it to you myself.'

There was a beat of silence. 'You mean you're not gonna be here with me?'

He winced at the disappointment in her voice. 'No. I have to work.'

'You always have to work, JD,' she scolded. 'You need to get some priorities.'

'I know. But I'm working tonight so that your mom can be with you. That's a good priority, isn't it?'

'I guess so.'

'Have your Aunt Izzy take lots of pictures.'

'She already has. She's making Mommy crazy. Oh, I gotta go now. I love you, JD.'

His heart squeezed as it always did when Cordelia said the words. She'd been the first female in his life who'd said them and meant them. 'Love you too, squirt. Have fun.'

Cordelia hung up and all he heard was the sound of the road. Then Lucy stirred, shifting in her seat so that she stared at him in a way that made him want to squirm.

'I think you must be a nice man,' she said, her voice throaty from sleep.

The huskiness in her voice wreaked havoc on his self-control. 'Not really,' he said. 'I can be a sarcastic SOB.'

'But a little girl loves you. Kids can spot the posers, you know?'

'Yeah. And Cordelia's a pretty smart kid.'

'Not that you're biased or anything,' she said, smiling at him and his heart nearly knocked out of his chest. 'What did you give Cordelia?'

'A locket. I put a picture of her dad in it. He died before she was born. I thought she might like it, but I didn't want to upset her.'

'Which was why you asked Stevie to check it first.'

He shrugged self-consciously. 'I never get those gifts right.'

For a couple of hard beats of his heart she said nothing at all. Then she cleared her throat. 'I imagine Cordelia will cherish it forever. I would have.'

'Hope so. Stevie's a great mom, but the dad Cordy lost was one of the good ones.'

'I'd heard that Stevie's husband died.'

'Gunned down in a store robbery.' He exhaled. 'Her son, too. He was five.'

'Oh, my God.' Lucy sat up, horrified. 'How does someone come back from that?'

'Like Stevie did,' JD said. 'She was pregnant with Cordelia at the time. She made herself go on, for Cordy. Being a cop, it's hard to work through shit like that. You gotta be strong. Invincible. But losing someone, especially like that . . . It cuts you down.'

'That's why Stevie does the grief groups.'

'Yeah. She needed help to move on and knew other cops would too. So she started the groups. Now it's kind of her thing. She's the grief guru.'

'I always thought that was creepy. Now that I know the story, well, it's lovely. How did you meet Stevie?'

'Through Paul, her husband. We played on the same baseball team. I remember feeling so damn helpless when he died.' He hesitated. 'And then my wife died.'

'I'm sorry,' Lucy murmured.

'Yeah.' He needed a moment. Their deaths didn't hurt like they once had. Time did heal. But the guilt never really went away. 'I was on a bad road after Maya died.'

'So you went to Stevie's grief group.'

He nodded. 'She set me straight again.'

'Then the grief group is even more lovely.'

He smiled. 'I don't think I've ever heard it called lovely. More like a ribbon of gristle in a steak. You just chew your way through it and spit out what you can. Speaking of steak, let's get dinner when we're done here.'

She winced. 'I don't know. I was hungry. Now, not so much.'

'You cut up dead people all day and a little gristle bothers you?'

She looked annoyed. 'You know, if you didn't say the "You cut up dead people all day" thing again, I could live with that.'

He grinned at her. 'It gets you all riled. You're cute that way.'

'I am *not* cute.' She drew a sudden breath when he turned off the highway toward Anderson Ferry, looking like she was startled to be there. 'We're here.'

'We made good time while you were sleeping. Which way?' he asked when he came to the town's main street. She gave him directions, saying no more until they'd stopped in front of a very normal-looking suburban house. He turned to study her. She had grown paler with each mile, sick-looking even. 'You're sure you want to do this, Lucy? You don't have to.'

'Yeah. I owe the Bennetts a lot. Kind of like you owe Stevie.' And with that cryptic remark she got out, straightened her skirt, and looked straight ahead. 'Let's do this.'

Monday, May 3, 6.45 P.M.

'Your steak, sir. Rare.'

He eyed the plate put before him curiously. Blood oozed from the beef, exactly as he'd ordered it. After spending the afternoon wading through Janet Gordon's blood, the sight of a really rare steak should probably make him a little queasy.

But it didn't. He cut into the meat with gusto, giving the waiter a nod. 'I'll have another glass of that.' He pointed to his almost empty wine glass. 'What was it again?'

'Pinot Noir. An excellent red.' The waiter departed, leaving him to sit back and enjoy the fruits of his labors. It was a very nice restaurant, with white tablecloths and extra forks. If the receipts in Janet's purse were any indication, she'd come here often.

He liked having money. The alternative totally sucked ass.

It was good he'd started with the rich ones. It was nice to live well while he checked the next few kills off his list, as they wouldn't be contributing as much to his unofficial retirement account as Malcolm, Russ and Janet had.

He pulled the list from his pocket and scanned the names he'd convinced Malcolm Edwards to share. He could recite this list from memory, but seeing it, holding it, made him feel good. Seeing the names with the check marks made him feel better. They all deserved to die. His eyes dropped to the bottom of the list.

Lucy Trask. Of all of them, she deserved it most.

She'd known. All this time. She'd known and done nothing. Worse than nothing. Like her father, Lucy was a liar and a cheat. A bully. Like Janet Gordon, Lucy had profited. *She purchased her dreams with my sister's blood.* For that she would pay.

'Your wine, sir,' the waiter said.

He folded the paper and slipped it into his pocket smoothly. 'Thank you.'

'Thank her.' He pointed to a woman sitting at the bar. 'Compliments of the lady.'

'Oh?' The woman was a looker, her long dark hair curling around her shoulders. Her short skirt and low-cut sweater left little to the imagination. He wanted to believe she wanted him, but thought it more likely she'd been attracted by the roll of cash he'd flashed at the bar when he'd first arrived. Either way, she was hot. Suddenly, so was he.

A minute later she slid onto the chair beside him. 'Hi,' she all but purred.

'Thank you,' he said, lifting his glass to her.

She smiled, leaning forward to give him a good view of the girls. If she twisted the right way, a lucky guy could catch a glimpse of nipple, a fact of which he was certain she was well aware. 'I haven't seen you here in a while,' she said.

He assessed her coolly. She was bullshitting him, but with such style he could hardly mind. 'That might be because I've never been here before.'

She laughed, unperturbed. 'Me neither, but I thought it was worth a try. I'm Susie.'

'Ted,' he said, and it was probably closer to the truth than the name she'd given. Ted was the name on his driver's license and credit cards. Ted Gamble was the name he'd paid Nicki Fields a hell of a lot of money to create.

'I'm here for a convention,' she said and he laughed.

Any man knew that was code for *I wanna get laid*. 'I'm not,' he said.

She looked at him, her mouth curving in a feline smile. 'You play hard to get.'

'That's because I'm not interested in sex-for-hire.'

She blinked, having the good sense to play insulted. 'Me neither.' She rose abruptly, her eyes filling with tears. He had to give her props. The girl could kind of act. 'You know, you're a real jerk. This wasn't easy for me, coming onto you.'

He leaned back in his chair, aware that several people were watching and that made him nervous. 'Sit down,' he said calmly and she did. From the corner of his eye he could see the other diners going back to their meals and he began to relax again. *Don't worry*, he thought. *It's not like any of them were looking at me anyway, not with those tits practically falling out of her sweater*. 'Now tell me what this is really about.'

Her lower lip trembled. 'My boyfriend cheated on me. In our bed.'

'Then he's scum,' he said mildly. 'So this is payback?'

She nodded defiantly. 'Yes. I saw you and you looked good. I'm going to do this, but it doesn't have to be you. I don't want it to be you anymore.' She blinked, sending two big tears down her cheeks. God, she was really good.

If she was half as good at sex as she was at lying, it might be worthwhile. 'I'm sorry,' he said. 'I didn't mean to insult you. But are you sure you want to do this?'

She nodded again, a little less resolutely. 'Yes. He did it with my best friend. I want him to know he can't get away with it.'

'So you'll have sex with a stranger to pay him back?'

'Absolutely.'

'Wouldn't it be better to have sex with *his* best friend?'

She bit her lip. 'His best friend is a disgusting troll. You're not.'

His lips twitched. 'High praise. I think I might blush.'

She laughed, again at ease. 'So what'll it be? You scratch my back, I'll scratch your . . .' She let her eyes drift down to his crotch, which had very understandably come to attention as soon as she'd jiggled her tits in his face.

He considered it. It would be a just reward for a hard day's labor, and he did have a few hours to kill. 'Just don't draw blood,' he said. He pushed his empty plate away and threw enough bills on the table to pay for his dinner. 'I can't stand the sight of blood.'

He walked her to his car, his eyes on her very visible breasts. 'It's not too late to change your—' Then he groaned when she slid her body against his, kissing him open-mouthed and hot. She had his fly unzipped and his cock in her hand before he could think and then he couldn't think at all when she dropped to her knees, taking him into her mouth. All the way down like Sandy had never done.

Oh, my God. His eyes rolled back in his head.

Then sanity returned. He yanked her up by her hair, plundering her mouth with his. 'Are you crazy? You can't do that here.'

'Then find a place where I can. Where to?' she murmured against his lips.

Alarms went off in his mind but he ignored them. Today he'd killed without mercy. Tonight he'd take what he wanted. And if she crossed him, he'd just kill her too.

'The closest hotel,' he said, trying to get control, but her hand was inside his pants again, stroking him.

'Okay,' she said breathlessly. 'Will you drive?'

'Get in,' he growled, pushing her to the seat. 'Let's do this.'

Ten

The Bennetts were in the middle of dinner when JD knocked on the front door. It smelled like pot roast and reminded him that he hadn't eaten in a very long time.

Mr Bennett answered the door, surprise on his face. 'Lucy? Come in.'

Obviously they hadn't been warned by either of the ex-wives, JD thought.

'It's been so long since we've seen you,' Bennett went on, taking Lucy's arm. 'Who is this you've brought to meet us? I assume you've come to give us good news?'

'Mr B, wait.' She looked inside the house uncertainly. 'Is Mrs B here?'

Bennett nodded, his smile disappearing. 'Lucy, what's wrong? Who is this man?'

'This is Detective Fitzpatrick. He's from Baltimore.' She took the old man's hand in hers, drew a deep breath. 'He's a homicide detective. I'm so sorry. Russ is dead.'

The old man's face drained of color and he stumbled back. 'No.'

'I'm so sorry,' Lucy said again. 'Can we come in?'

Bennett stared at her for a moment, numb. 'Of course,' he mumbled.

Lucy helped him to a sofa and looked up at JD. 'Stay here. I'll be right back.'

'Jason?' a woman called from the kitchen. 'Who's there?'

Lucy squared her shoulders. 'It's me, Mrs B. Lucy Trask.' She

159

disappeared into the kitchen, where for a few moments there were happy sounds.

Then silence. Lucy reappeared, supporting a tiny woman who leaned heavily against her, her face a disturbing gray. 'Get her a glass of water,' Lucy said. 'Quick.'

JD complied and when he got back to the living room, Lucy was kneeling next to the sofa, shaking a pill from an amber prescription bottle. She placed the pill under the elder Mrs Bennett's tongue and began taking her pulse. She glanced up at Mr Bennett. 'Is she still seeing Dr Jameson?'

'Yes,' Bennett whispered.

Holding Mrs Bennett's hand, Lucy made a call on her cell phone. 'Dr Jameson's on his way,' she said. 'I should have had him meet us here. Her pulse is leveling out, thank God. Mrs B, talk to me.'

Mrs Bennett turned dull eyes on Lucy's face. 'My Russell . . . dead? How?'

Lucy took Mr Bennett's hand, so that she held onto both. 'He was murdered.'

Mr Bennett collapsed back against the sofa, his face as gray as his wife's. 'How?'

Lucy hesitated. 'He was beaten. I'm so sorry.'

Mrs Bennett gasped. 'Beaten? My Russell? Was he robbed?'

Lucy looked up over her shoulder at JD, wordlessly asking for help. *A little late for that*, JD thought. He hadn't expected her to do the notification herself, just to observe while he did it. *I should have been a lot clearer*. Lesson learned.

'No, ma'am,' JD said calmly. 'It appears to be a crime of rage. Perhaps revenge.'

The Bennetts looked lost. 'Revenge?' Mrs Bennett whispered. 'But why?'

'That's what we need to understand,' Lucy said with quiet urgency. 'You talked with him often. Did he mention anyone who might have threatened him?'

Mr Bennett closed his eyes. 'No.'

'I'm sorry,' Lucy said softly. 'I'll call Renee for you.'

'Who's Renee?' JD asked.

'Their daughter. She lives in Oxford, not too far from here.'

'Good gracious.' A large woman pushed through the front door without knocking. 'What's going on?' she gasped dramatically. 'Lucy Trask, what are *you* doing here?'

Lucy rose slowly and immediately the mood changed. Lucy's hands clenched into fists and red spread across her cheeks. The woman eyed Lucy shrewdly and JD realized that the gasp had been for theatrics only. She'd known Lucy was here.

For a moment Lucy and the woman stood staring at one another and the tension in the room grew. 'Mrs Westcott,' Lucy said formally. 'This really isn't a good time.'

'That I can see for myself. What is going on, Hildy? What has she done to you?' Mrs Westcott roughly pushed Lucy aside and sat next to Mrs Bennett. 'You're as gray as old flannel. Did you take your pill?'

'Yes, she did,' Lucy said between her teeth. 'You need to leave.'

Westcott glared. 'You have no rights here. I don't care how many initials you have after your name.' She turned to Mrs Bennett, her mouth drooping. 'What's happened?'

Mrs Bennett began to cry. 'It's Russell. He's dead. Murdered.'

Westcott blinked. '*Well.*' She gathered the frail Mrs Bennett to her very ample bosom and patted her back. 'You poor dear. It was his hard living, Hildy. It was bound to catch up to him.' This made Mrs Bennett sob harder and Mr Bennett look like he wanted to bodily throw the woman out.

JD considered doing it for him, but then the woman began to talk.

'A shame it is, just a shame. I wonder who'll be next.'

'Next?' JD asked and Mrs Westcott looked up coolly.

'And you are?'

'Detective Fitzpatrick, Baltimore Homicide. And you are?'

'Myrna Westcott. *I* live next door. *I* chair the Neighborhood Watch. *I* make sure *undesirables* don't hurt my neighbors.' She gave Lucy the evil eye as she said this.

Lucy seemed to grow taller, her spine even more rigid, and for a moment JD thought she might strike the woman. But Lucy turned on her heel to walk away. 'Bitch,' she muttered under her breath, shocking JD into an open-mouthed stare.

'I heard that,' Westcott declared loudly. 'Your mother would be so ashamed.'

'Which would be nothing new,' Lucy said through clenched teeth. It had been as if a cork had popped as she stood, practically vibrating. Then she drew a breath and turned back to Mr Bennett. 'I'm sorry. I'm going into the kitchen to call Renee. I'll be back.'

Feeling like a spectator on a soap opera set, JD pulled his wits together. 'What do you mean, who's next?' he asked politely. He crouched, pressing his fingers to Mrs Bennett's wrist. Her pulse was weak but steady, so she hadn't yet been smothered by Westcott's bosom. He looked up to find Westcott studying him with venom.

'Are you with Lucy Trask?' She said Lucy's name like she'd say *Hitler*.

Yes, he wanted to snap, but did not. 'I'm a detective, ma'am,' he said blandly. 'I'm here because someone's dead that should not be. What did you mean, who's next?'

'Just that these things come in threes. Everyone knows that.'

'Dr Bennett was the second one to meet with harm?' JD asked.

'Oh, yes,' Westcott said with glee at being able to share juicy news. 'Two months ago Malcolm Edwards and his wife went out for a sail and,' she leaned closer to JD, bringing the still sobbing Mrs Bennett with her, '*never came back.*'

From the corner of his eye JD noticed that Mr Bennett had gone still as stone.

'Who was Malcolm Edwards?' JD asked and Westcott shrugged.

'A boy who grew up in the neighborhood. Bought himself a fancy yacht and took up a fast life that was the death of him, just like Russell.'

Mr Bennett swallowed. 'He had cancer, Myrna. It's not the same.'

'He was *lost* at *sea*,' Westcott sniffed. 'Then Russell is taken from us.' She patted Mrs Bennett's back. 'Don't you worry, Hildy. I'm here.'

Lucy came back into the room, her composure regained. 'Renee's on her way.'

'Thank you, Lucy,' Mr Bennett said faintly. He stood, and for a moment JD thought he'd fall down. But he didn't, surprising JD by taking Lucy's arm and escorting her to the door. 'I appreciate you coming all this way, Lucy,' he said quietly. 'But Mrs Bennett isn't well. Perhaps you and the detective should go now and let her rest.'

Over her shoulder Westcott gave Lucy a triumphant glare, while Lucy stared at Bennett, her eyes filled with stunned hurt. 'I can stay. For as long as you need me.'

A car pulled up outside. 'That's Dr Jameson. He can make sure Hildy gets the proper care. Thank you for coming, Lucy dear. Thank you, Detective.'

For a moment JD debated saying he was going to stay, but decided against it. He gave Bennett his card. 'Thank you, sir. This news will take a while to sink in. You'll have questions and may remember something later that might be of value to our investigation. Please feel free to call. Come, Dr Trask. I'll take you home.'

Westcott sniffed loudly. 'Good riddance to bad rubbish, I say.'

JD wanted to tell the old biddy to shut her damn mouth, but he was watching Lucy who was searching Bennett's face with near desperation. She closed her eyes briefly and squared her shoulders, reaching up to give the old man a hug he did not return. 'This has been a shock. You know my cell. Call me and I'll come. You know that.'

'I know. I'll call you soon.' And with that he shut the door in their faces.

Lucy walked to the street, her hurt palpable. JD opened the car door for her, then frowned, the hackles on the back of his neck rising. He turned, scanning the street to find the source of his unease. In the house next door to the Bennetts', a pair of eyes stared through the blinds in the living room window.

'Lucy, someone's watching you.'

'Someone's always watching you here,' she said bitterly. 'Let's go.'

Monday, May 3, 7.15 P.M.

'I'd like a room,' he said, Susie in tow.

The guy behind the hotel desk looked up. 'How long will you be staying with us?'

'Maybe a night. I'll pay cash.'

'You have to use your credit card, sir. The system won't let me dispense a key card without a credit card on file.'

'I'll pay for the room in advance.' He peeled two hundred dollars from his money roll and threw it on the counter.

'I'm sorry, sir, I have to have a credit card for damages, the minibar. I'm sorry.'

'You and me both.' He had credit cards in his wallet, but they belonged to his victims and wouldn't match his ID. He did have a card issued to Ted Gamble, the identity Nicki had developed for him, but he didn't want to use it. He didn't want anyone to know he'd been here as Gamble. When the killings were done, he would pop up in a different part of the world altogether.

Susie sidled up beside him. 'What's wrong, baby?' She leaned up on her toes so that she could whisper in his ear. 'I'm hungry for more of what I tasted outside. Hurry.'

All the blood in his head rushed to his groin. He leaned on the counter. 'Look,' he lied, 'I got a wife. She can't know I was here, and she checks the statements.'

'I see your dilemma. I can run your card but hold charges until you check out. If you pay cash, I'll tear up the charge record. Nobody has to know you were even here.'

He gave the clerk his Ted Gamble Visa. 'Give me a room. I don't care where.'

Susie purred. 'As long as it has a bed.'

The clerk handed him a key. 'Room 323, on the third floor. Elevators are—'

He heard no more, taking his card, the key, and Susie's hand, dragging her to the elevator. Beside him, she chuckled throatily. 'Hurry, Ted. I need to fuck.'

Monday, May 3, 7.45 P.M.

JD drove away from the Bennetts' neighborhood, watching Lucy as closely as he could while still keeping his eyes on the road. Her expression was one of numbed misery, her face pale, hands clenched into impotent fists in her lap. *Good riddance to bad rubbish,* Westcott had said. And Mr Bennett hadn't said a word in Lucy's defense. Bennett had just hustled her out the door. *And that pisses me off.*

The man had just found out his son was dead, so JD could cut him some slack. Except . . . JD thought of how still Bennett had gone at the mention of the other dead man. Malcolm Edwards. That had bothered Bennett nearly as much as hearing his own son had died. There was something there. JD was certain of it.

It was also clear that Lucy had left some major baggage behind in the old neighborhood. For a moment there he'd seen the flash of temper that had ended in Russ Bennett's broken nose. He'd thought she'd strike the bad-mannered Mrs Westcott and he wouldn't have really blamed her had she done so.

But Lucy had pulled herself back under control, and still held herself together, but barely. Her emotions churned so close to the surface that he could feel them. She was trembling, whether from hurt or rage he wasn't sure. Probably both.

Waiting until they were well away from the neighborhood, JD pulled into the lot of an abandoned strip mall, stopped the car and got out. Lucy's gaze followed him as he walked around the car, but when he opened her door she closed her eyes, her pale cheeks heating from embarrassment.

'I'm sorry,' she whispered. 'I was unprofessional and rude. I messed things up.'

As he'd done before, he popped the lock on her seat belt and pulled her to her feet and into his arms. But this time he just held her. She stood stiffly, not leaning into him, but not pulling away either. Her trembling had become shivering despite the heat of the evening, so he shrugged out of his coat and draped it over her shoulders.

165

All at once she shuddered, her hands coming up to clutch the fabric of his shirt. 'I'm sorry,' she repeated miserably. 'I don't know what came over me.'

He rested his cheek on the top of her head, realizing how very well she fit in his arms, tucked under his chin. The last time he'd held her like this he'd been too busy kissing her to notice. He hoped he'd be too busy kissing her again later to notice, but now he wanted to make her hurt go away if he could. If she'd let him.

'Old Lady Westcott called you an "undesirable" and you got mad. I would have been mad too. Who is she to you?'

'Just a neighbor. An old harpy. Has been for as long as I can remember.'

'Why was she so rude to you?'

Against his chest she sighed. 'We go back a way. I . . . I don't like her very much.'

'Yeah, I kind of got that. You muttering "bitch" was my first clue.'

She covered her face with her hands. 'I can't believe I said that. Mr Bennett was in shock and I said *that*. I made things worse when I wanted to make them better.'

Personally, he thought Westcott had made things worse for Bennett by bringing up Malcolm Edwards, but he'd get to that in a minute. 'Why did she call you an "undesirable"? What happened between the two of you?' he asked.

For a moment she said nothing. Then she lifted one shoulder wearily. 'She's a difficult woman. I don't know why she does anything.'

He had a hunch and played it. 'She was involved in your trial.'

Lucy jerked back to stare up at him, wide-eyed. 'How did you know that?'

'I didn't, not until just now. Honestly, I guessed.'

Her blue eyes flickered, narrowing. 'You tricked me.'

He smoothed her hair away from her face and rubbed his thumb over her lips which had turned down in a frown. He was regretting having brought it up. At least right now, when she was so upset. 'I'm sorry. I didn't mean to trick you.'

'Sure you did,' she said flatly. 'You're a detective. It's what you do. Let's get back. You have work to do and I still have to find a place to stay tonight.' She pulled away from him, getting into the car. 'We native guides need our sleep to stay sharp.'

JD obeyed, heading them back to Baltimore and away from Anderson Ferry and its rude gossips and creepy eyes that watched from windows. Lucy stared straight ahead, arms crossed over her chest, fingers clutching the lapels of his jacket as she held it closed around her like a shield. *Note to self: don't use interrogation techniques on prospective girlfriends.* It really didn't help.

'I'm sorry, Lucy,' he said quietly. 'It's really been too long since I've been in a relationship. I'm completely out of practice. I should have just asked you.'

'It's all right,' she said, no longer sounding angry. Just . . . deflated. 'I probably wouldn't have told you had you asked. I don't really like to talk about it.'

'Okay, then. A different question. Who was Malcolm Edwards?'

She turned to look at him, confused. 'I don't know. Why?'

'Because he's dead too. While you were calling Bennett's daughter, Mrs Westcott said he ran with Russ Bennett back in the day and that he recently died in a boating accident. She claimed that bad things come in threes, that Bennett was number two.'

Lucy frowned. 'Odd, considering the killer marked him as number one.'

'So you didn't know Malcolm?'

'I don't remember the name. If he ran with Russ's crowd, he'd have been older than me. Plus all those guys had nicknames. You want me to check him out?' She was already retrieving her phone from her purse.

'If your phone has juice,' he said, sensing she needed to keep her mind off what had transpired at the Bennetts' house. 'Otherwise I'll call Stevie and have her check.'

She plugged his car's charger into her phone. 'This works.' She punched keys and waited. 'I got a couple of hits on Malcolm Edwards.'

He glanced over, saw her fully absorbed in the screen she was reading. Her energy was back, her focus. He could feel it hum, just as he'd felt her hurt only minutes before. That she was able to completely concentrate so effortlessly was impressive.

It was something he'd had to learn to do in the army, back when he'd sat behind cover for hours, waiting for his target to pass through his sight. In those days he'd had to call upon his focus in the blink of an eye and it hadn't been easy. Then again, no part of his job back then had been easy. Which was why he didn't like to think about it.

'Malcolm Edwards has a Facebook page too?' he asked.

'No, but there are some articles about his accident. This one says he was last seen boarding his yacht, the *Carrie On*. Carrie, as in a woman's name.'

'His wife?'

'Yes. She disappeared at the same time. There was speculation that he'd committed suicide, but consensus is that he never would have risked her life.'

'So what happened?'

'A storm blew in. A source close to the investigation said that in Malcolm's condition, he wouldn't have been able to handle the rigging. He had terminal cancer.'

'That's what Mr Bennett said, back there. What about the wife, Carrie?'

'Nobody's sure where she went. This article speculates that she was with him at the time. She hasn't turned up to claim any assets.'

'And the boat?'

'The Coast Guard did an extensive search, but found nothing.'

'Huh,' JD said. 'You'd think they'd find something.'

'You'd think. But this says the Coast Guard had warned boaters of strong currents. They think the boat got dragged out to sea and went down.'

'You'd think that something would wash ashore. Wood or something.'

She shrugged. 'You'd think. It says here that he left his estate to his wife, but that because she died with him, it went to the Church of Divine Forgiveness.'

That two men who'd known each other as boys had died within months of one another could be a simple coincidence. Except that Russell was murdered and his father had gone so very still at the mention of the other man's name. Being 'lost at sea' could be a convenient way to kill someone. Then again, simple coincidence was highly possible.

'If it was a big enough payoff,' he said, 'the church might have had motive.'

'Maybe. Here's his obit. His and Carrie's memorial service was just last week. "Malcolm Edwards was born in Anderson Ferry, Maryland, where he attended Anderson Ferry High School, lettering in football and . . ."' She faltered, trailing off.

'And?' JD prompted.

'He was on the All-Star team,' she said, her tone oddly strained. 'They won the championship his senior year.' She cleared her throat briskly. 'He is survived by no one. He and Carrie had no children and his parents died years ago.' She fell silent, staring at the phone screen, biting her bottom lip.

'What's so important about that championship football team, Lucy?'

She folded her hands in her lap primly. 'My brother played on it. He was MVP.'

'Really? Where is your brother now?'

'He died when I was fourteen. The year the team won the championship.'

'I'm sorry,' he said, but thoughts were already rolling around his mind. Edwards and Lucy's brother had played ball on the same team. A killer was taunting Lucy after murdering Russ Bennett, who'd known Edwards.

'It was a long time ago,' she said. 'The obit has a picture of Malcolm in his high school jersey. I knew him as Butch. He played defense. He was my brother's friend.'

'Did Russ Bennett play on the team?'

'No, although I imagine he wanted to. It was the big thing in Anderson Ferry. It was a way to get out, if you were a boy.'

'And the girls? How did they "get out"?'

'Some married. I went to college. Gwyn joined the—' She stopped abruptly, then continued. 'A sorority.'

He glanced over at her. That wasn't what she'd been about to say. 'I see. So, how did your brother die? If you don't mind my asking.'

She clutched his jacket around her more tightly. 'In an accident,' she said stiffly.

'I guess you do mind my asking,' he said ruefully and she sighed.

'I'm sorry. It was twenty-one years ago and I'm long over it, but . . .'

'Sometimes old hurts don't die.' Of this he was well aware.

She nodded. 'Yes.'

'And I imagine going back to your old neighborhood didn't help.'

She grimaced. 'No, it didn't.'

'Were your brother and Russ Bennett the same age?'

She turned to study his profile. 'Yes, they were in the same grade. So was Malcolm Edwards. Why did you ask me about Malcolm to begin with?'

'I told you. Westcott brought him up.'

'She also called me an "undesirable". I would have thought you'd be more worried about that instead of some seemingly coincidental death, especially after . . . well, after what happened earlier today.'

'You mean when I kissed you? And you kissed me back?'

Her cheeks heated. 'Yes. Maybe you shouldn't have. Maybe I am an undesirable.' She said it in a defiant way, as if challenging him to agree.

'I know you're not.'

Her brows lifted. 'And how could you possibly *know* that?'

He shrugged. 'Because *I* desire you.'

She started to smile, then shook her head hard. 'No, I'm serious. How do you know Westcott wasn't right? I could be . . . just plain bad. You can't know.'

'I don't think so. If you were bad, you wouldn't have cared for an old man's feet.' He hesitated, then shrugged again. 'Or cried over the body of a girl you didn't know.'

'So did you,' she murmured.

He kept his eyes straight ahead. 'I know. And I've wondered how many others you cried over when no one was watching.'

'A lot,' she said, so quietly that he almost didn't hear. 'Why did you ask about Malcolm?'

The topic change was intentional. He'd ventured too close, again. He decided to venture even closer. 'Because when Westcott said his name, Mr Bennett reacted.'

She frowned. 'Reacted exactly how?'

'He froze. Looked guilty.' He met her gaze. 'And then he ushered you out.'

'You think there's a connection between Russ's murder and Malcolm's death? And that Mr B knows what it is?' She shook her head. 'No. Just . . . no.'

'Okay,' he said quietly, refocusing on the road.

'Okay,' she repeated forcefully. 'So what are you going to do next?'

Check into Malcolm Edwards and Russ Bennett's father, he thought. 'Check out the old girlfriends,' he said, 'find any food processing plants with huge freezers, and hope Drew finds a usable print on that shipping box and/or your car.'

'You really think this guy left his prints?' she asked dourly.

'No. Hopefully by the time I get back I'll have Bennett's LUDs.' Hopefully the phone company's Local Utilization Detail would offer up a clue. 'I need to find out who he was meeting the Sunday he disappeared. Hopefully you'll find something more on Bennett's body tomorrow.'

'Drop me off at the morgue. I've got some time yet tonight I can work on him.'

'No. I don't want you there alone.'

'I won't be. Alan and Ruby are on duty and we have a security guard. You have to leave me alone sometimes.' She lifted a brow. 'Unless you want to stand next to me while I cut up dead bodies. Mulhauser says he has four in the freezer with my name on them.

171

You can hold the bowl when I remove their brains. They kind of go . . . *plop.*'

He tossed her a wry glare, swallowing hard. 'That was for tricking you earlier.'

'Pretty much,' she agreed magnanimously.

'Are we even now?'

She smiled at him and he took heart. 'Pretty much.'

'Fine. I'll leave you to your bone saws. I've got LUDs to check.'

She nodded, amused. 'I thought so.'

Monday, May 3, 8.00 P.M.

He rolled onto his back, breathing hard. He'd been wrong. Susie was much better at sex than she was at lying.

'Incredible,' Susie purred and he almost believed she meant it. 'Both times.'

'So did you get back at him?' he asked.

'At who?'

'Your boyfriend. The one who cheated on you.'

She huffed a chuckle. 'Yeah, I did.'

'How will he know?'

She sat up, looking down at him with a confused frown. 'What?'

'How will he know you've gotten your revenge?'

'Why do you care?'

He shrugged. 'Call it a hobby.'

'You're cute, but strange,' she said. She pulled her hair back and touched the rapidly darkening bruise on her neck lightly. 'Feels like a decent hickey.'

'Decent enough,' he drawled. 'That's your proof?'

'It'll do,' she said, then rolled over, hanging halfway off the bed and giving him a very nice view of primo ass. He heard the jingle of keys and pushed himself up on one elbow to peer over the bed to see what she was up to.

And none too soon. She was riffling through his pants pockets. His temper exploded and he grabbed the bitch by the arm, dragging her onto her back. 'What the hell do you think you're doing?' he snarled and her eyes widened in fear.

She brought her arm up, revealing the pack of Marlboros clutched in her hand. 'Looking for a smoke.' She jerked her arm away. 'What are you, some kind of psycho?'

If you only knew, baby. He drew a breath and pried the squashed pack of cigarettes from her hand. 'No, but you shouldn't go searching a man's pockets.'

She nodded, inching away from him. 'I'm sorry,' she whined. 'I smelled smoke on your jacket earlier. I figured you'd have some smokes.'

'You can't smoke these.' The Marlboros he'd bought especially for Ryan, for when the man came to claim his mother's body. He hoped Ryan would appreciate the symbolism. Marlboros for a man who worked a ranch.

They'd burn the next letter into Ryan's back. *And I'll make sure it hurts. A lot.* Susie was looking at him suspiciously and he realized he'd spoken too urgently.

'It's a non-smoking room,' he added, more quietly. He rolled to his feet, gathering his clothing from where it lay strewn across the room. 'I'm going to take a shower.'

She looked away. 'Can I use the bathroom first?' she asked stiffly.

He blew out an annoyed breath. 'Hurry. I've got places to go.' *Bodies to deliver.*

She picked up her miniskirt and the thong that had ended up under the bed. Grabbing her purse and blouse, she rushed into the bathroom. 'I'll hurry.'

He shoved the squashed Marlboros back in his pants pocket. He'd have to buy a new pack now. She'd bent them. He needed nice, straight cigarettes to make nice, uniform burns in Ryan's back. He started to pull his hand out of his pocket, then froze.

Something was missing. His credit card. He'd been in such a hurry to fuck Susie that he hadn't put it back in his wallet. Had he? It wasn't in his pocket. And neither was his wallet. *The bitch stole my wallet.*

He stared at the bathroom door, his fury cold. She must have lifted it when she was pushing his pants down in supposed sexual abandon, then hidden it with her skirt.

All the credit cards and ID he'd taken from his victims were in that wallet. It was only a matter of time before one of their names turned up on the news. And she'd seen his Ted Gamble ID. She couldn't be allowed to tell.

Get her out of here. Quietly. He pulled on his pants, then took two items from his jacket pocket and casually opened the bathroom door.

She was still naked, kneeling on the floor, using the lid of the toilet as a desk. She twisted, her squeal of outrage faltering when she saw what he held in his hands. Her eyes grew wide again, first with fear, then with a kind of furious acceptance.

'Goddamn it. I can usually smell a cop a mile away.' She lifted her brows. 'You got a lot of other people's cards here, Officer Pullman. I wonder why.'

He used the gun in his right hand to point to the bed. 'Sit on the bed with your hands where I can see them.' Sullenly she obeyed. He dropped the Newport News PD badge in his jacket pocket and retrieved his cards and the paper she'd been writing on.

She'd been scribbling, more than writing. His Ted Gamble card had been under the paper and she'd used a pencil to make an old-fashioned tracing of the number. He tossed her clothes to the bed. 'Get dressed,' he said, still holding the gun.

She pulled on her thong, her jaw taut. 'Are you going to arrest me or what?'

'That depends on you. I'm going to check out downstairs, pay for the room in cash and get that clerk to cancel the charge on my card. If you cooperate, I'll let you go.'

Her eyes narrowed suspiciously. 'No record?'

He smiled. 'No record anywhere.'

She considered it. 'I can live with that.'

Newport News, Virginia
Monday, May 3, 8.00 P.M.

Clay sat in his car outside Mrs Klein's condo for the second time that day, frustrated and tired. He was no closer to finding Margo Winchester than he'd been when he'd arrived hours ago. In fact, he'd taken several steps back in that department.

The last few hours had not gone well. The clerk at the morgue had, unfortunately, done her job. In other words, she'd revealed nothing of use to him. He'd gone in looking for word on his 'brother-in-law' who'd 'disappeared while on vacation'. Clay told the clerk he was checking all the hospitals and morgues. He'd given Evan Reardon's description, but the clerk had no record of any such John Doe.

The body found in the house fire had to have been brought to this morgue. That there was not even a spark of interest in the clerk's eyes told him that either the description of Evan was so far off that they could immediately eliminate the possibility or they had an idea of who the fire victim really was.

Which meant that Evan probably wasn't dead. Which bothered Clay more than Evan falling victim to an insane female stalker. If Evan was alive, he had much to explain. Any way Clay cut it, he was nowhere and Evan was still missing.

His cell phone began to ring. Clay grabbed it, hoping it was Nicki, but it was Alyssa. His sense of dread began to climb. Where was Nicki? *And what had she done?* She couldn't have missed all these clues. Something was so very wrong.

'Have you found her yet?' Clay asked without greeting.

'No, and I've been calling hotels for three hours. If Nicki's in Ocean City, she's not staying at any of her usual places or any of the major hotels.'

'She could be staying with someone, or not checked in under her own name.'

'What if something happened to her, Clay? She could be hurt somewhere.'

Or worse. The picture had already formed in his mind. She could be lying in a morgue, murdered by one of her one-night stands. Or by her own hand. He closed his eyes. She'd been behaving so strangely before she left. *I should have known. I should have asked. I should have pried.*

'Try Nicki Triton. It was her married name, years ago. Sometimes she still uses it.' But the last time had been when she'd been forced to leave DCPD and gone on a bender that had lasted for days. Clay had been the one to find her after her parents contacted him, frantic because they couldn't find her. Clay had dried her out, offered her a job with his agency. A second chance. Things had gone well. Until recently.

Now everything had gone to hell. 'We have other problems. I found Margo.'

'How?' Alyssa demanded.

'I tracked her cop father. He's on the force in the next town.'

'So that's good, right? You found her.'

'No, it's not good. Margo's been locked up for four months, in rehab. She's in a private facility her parents are apparently mortgaging their home to afford. One of the parents' neighbors filled me in. The real Margo does have a record for assault and does look like the woman Nicki met here two months ago. But she is not the woman we're looking for. And Evan's not the man killed in the fire here last week.'

Alyssa let out a slow breath. 'Evan played us.'

'He played Nicki,' he said. 'And me. You've done nothing wrong here.'

'So what next?'

'I find the woman who Nicki actually met. She danced at a club on the beach, but they don't open until nine. I'm going to try to find Klein's granddaughter right now.' He looked up at Mrs Klein's front door and hoped this visit would go better than his first.

'What should I do?'

'Keep calling hotels around Ocean City. Focus on the area near the boardwalk.'

'How do you even know she's there, Clay?'

'Her car is there.'

There was a moment of silence. 'You can track her car?'

'Yes. And she can track mine. It's for protection, in case we run into a situation we can't handle. We're not tracking your car, if you're worried.'

'I was, a little. Clay.' She hesitated. 'Should I call the hospitals or police?'

A worry nagged at him, the knowledge that Nicki should have seen any one of the inconsistencies in Evan's story. *What did you do, Nic?* 'Not the police. Not yet. But try the hospitals.' He made himself say the words. 'I'll call the morgues.'

'I'm sorry,' Alyssa whispered.

'It's nothing you've done,' he said roughly. 'I have to go. Call me if you find anything.' Forcing the thought of the morgue from his mind, he climbed the stairs to Mrs Klein's apartment and rapped the knocker. Inside he heard nothing. He'd seen her car parked outside, so she was probably home.

'Mrs Klein?' he called. 'I don't mean to bother you, but I'm still looking for the same woman. I really need to talk to your granddaughter. I think she knows her and I know they were both here. Your granddaughter has a cobra tattoo.'

There was no response. 'Mrs Klein? Are you all right?' He froze at the sound of a footstep behind him. He turned slowly to see two uniformed cops cautiously climbing the stairs. *How the hell did they get here so fast?* Unless the old lady had better eyes than he'd thought and saw his car in the lot below.

'Sir?' one of them said. 'Is there a problem here?'

'No. But I'm assuming I've frightened the resident,' Clay said. 'That was not my intent. I'm looking for information on her granddaughter.'

'So we heard,' the first cop said. 'Would you step away from the door, please?'

Clay complied, holding his hands where they could see them. Behind him the door opened and he looked over his shoulder to see Mrs Klein peering out.

'I told you I'd call the cops,' she said, satisfied.

Clay sighed. 'Fine. I'll leave. I don't want any trouble.'

'It's a little late for that, sir,' the second uniform said. 'You need to come with us.'

Clay took a step back. 'Where? Why?'

'To the precinct,' the second cop said.

'Am I under arrest?' Clay asked.

'No,' the first cop said. He was older and, Clay hoped, wiser. 'Mr Maynard, you match the description of a man who visited the morgue a short time ago.'

Clay's brows lifted. His questions had gotten someone's attention. 'I've committed no crime.' Technically. He'd bent the truth a bit, that was all.

The older cop nodded, soberly. 'Then you shouldn't have any issues coming in and answering a few questions.'

Clay dropped his hands to his sides. The man had handled it just like Clay might have when he'd worn a badge. 'Okay. I'll follow you in, driving my own car.'

The younger cop started to protest, but the older one cut him off with a sharp glance. 'That would be fine, Mr Maynard,' the older man said. 'This way, please.'

Clay sighed again. *This day is really starting to suck.*

Eleven

J D shook his head as he took the highway exit for the morgue. 'You are not going to change my mind, so don't even try.'

Lucy's stunned discovery of a local band's CD in his car had spurred a lively discussion on the merits of all the local bands, and for an hour she'd simply enjoyed talking with a man for the first time in a very long time.

The last hour had been . . . fun. They'd stopped at a drive-thru for dinner. Nothing fancy or pretentious. They'd listened to music and talked, about everything and nothing at all. But especially not the case or Mrs Westcott or her brother or his friends. Which she had deeply appreciated.

She also appreciated that he knew music, all types. It made her wonder what he'd think about hers. If things went well, then . . . *someday I might trust him with it.* Someday.

But now she shook her head at him, disagreeing with his assessment of local talent. 'You can't really prefer Bromo Bay to Silver Fish. Please.'

He shrugged. 'Bromo's lead guitar's got superior finger control.'

She sighed. 'You're missing the point, JD.'

He pulled into the parking garage next to the morgue. 'Which is what?'

'That finger control is just technique. Any decent musician can master technique. Bromo's missing heart, and there is a world of difference between technique and heart.'

'I guess I'll have to concede that point to the musician in the car.' He found a parking place, then reached over to take her hand, running a thumb over her calloused fingertips. 'I felt the calluses earlier. You said Mr Pugh was your music teacher.'

Suddenly the easy conversation was over and he was looking at her with an intensity that assured she'd never be cold again. 'In high school,' she said.

'What do you play?'

'Violin, mostly,' she hedged, unnerved by the overwhelming urge to tell him about the club. About her music. To see his response. Maybe to gain his approval.

'You took only a few belongings from your apartment today. One was a violin.'

She frowned. 'The CSU cop told you what I took from my apartment?'

'Procedure,' he said. 'Don't be upset. She also said that one of the neighbors commented on your "concerts". What did she mean?'

'I play for Mr Pugh when he becomes agitated. It calms him. I made a recording for Barb to play for him when I can't be there.'

He studied her a moment more, then got out of the car. 'I'll walk you to your office.'

He opened her door and once again pulled her to her feet. But this time he simply stood, studying her face. Her cheeks heated under his scrutiny and she dropped her gaze to the knot of his tie, her heart starting to pound in her ears.

'Thank you,' she whispered. 'I needed to be there for the Bennetts, even if it didn't end as I planned. Thank you for taking my mind off unpleasant things for a little while.'

'Lucy.' He hooked his finger under her chin and lifted it until she met his eyes. He didn't smile and she could see he was as nervous as she was. 'All the way back I kept thinking about earlier. When I kissed you. And you kissed me back.'

Blood rushed low and her deepest muscles clenched. 'I did do that, didn't I?'

'Yes, you did.' He leaned closer until all she could see was dark, dark blue. 'I'm hoping you'll do it again.'

'I . . .' She was unsure of what she might have said, but it didn't matter. His mouth was on hers, warm and demanding and so very sexy. His hands in her hair, he moved her head one way then another, layering on sensation after delightful sensation.

But there was something missing. She needed more. She heard herself whimper and he exploded, his mouth going from skillfully seducing to ravaging. His hands ran down her sides, pausing to cup her breasts, his thumbs flicking her nipples through too many layers of fabric before skimming her body to close over her butt, kneading almost desperately.

He hauled her up on her toes, trapping her between a hard car and a very hard man. His hips surged and she sucked in a harsh breath as she felt him. All of him. He'd said he found her desirable. He had not been lying. Not one little bit.

She tried to wriggle closer, cursing her straight skirt for the second time that day. A growl of frustration vibrated in his throat and he ripped his mouth away, his breath hard against her temple. For a moment they hung there, panting.

His hands flexed, his fingers drawing her skirt higher. 'I hate this skirt,' he said.

'So do I.'

He pulled back far enough to pin her gaze with his. His dark eyes were intense. Hot. Lucy stared, mesmerized. *Narcotic.*

'I want to see you out of it,' he whispered.

She swallowed hard. Her heart was pounding, her body needing. She wanted him. A lot. Way more than was wise. 'So do I.'

His eyes flashed. Dangerously. 'It's been a long time for me. There's been no one, nothing but work. And then this morning I saw you and . . .'

'And?'

'It was like a freight train. All of a sudden . . . It's like . . . Hell, I don't know.'

'All of a sudden it's like you're alive again?' she asked quietly.

Relief flickered amid the heat in his eyes. 'I'm afraid I'll rush you. That I'll blow it.'

'I know. I don't date much. I'm not sure how to handle this.'

He rested his brow on hers. 'But you want me?' he murmured smoothly.

Everything inside her clenched, then went liquid. 'Yes. God help me. But it's late. We've both had a very long day. Why don't you go home, get some sleep?'

'I was going to say the same thing to you.'

'I can't go home. I've got to get a key from Gwyn for her apartment.'

He hesitated. 'I've got a big place. Lots of room.'

Lucy closed her eyes, fighting the urge to do as she pleased. It had been a very, very long time for her, too. 'Do you know how tempting that is?'

'Hell, yeah,' he said wryly and she opened her eyes to his crooked smile. 'Too much, too soon?' he asked and she nodded. 'Then let me at least take you to my house so you can pick up the loaner car and I'll follow you to your friend's apartment.'

She winced a little. 'You mean the car that belonged to your wife?'

He blinked. 'How did you know that?'

'I didn't, not until just now,' she said dryly. 'Honestly, I guessed.'

He frowned. 'I thought we were even. You know, brains plopping into bowls.'

She laughed. 'I said "pretty much" before. Now we're even.'

'Okay,' he grumbled, but his eyes smiled. 'But you need a car. CSU could have yours for days, especially if they find something.'

'Which we know they won't,' she said. 'But I still couldn't borrow yours. Driving your dead wife's car is too creepy. Thorne has an extra one.' She reached in her jacket pocket for her phone. 'He sent me a text while we were driving back. His car is parked in slot 62 and he left the key with Alan in the morgue.'

'Will you call me when you're ready to leave, so that I can at least make sure you get to Gwyn's safely? I won't stay. I won't even ask. I promise.'

She thought of the number 'I' burned into Russ's back and nodded. 'Yes.'

'Then I'll go back to my office and run LUDs till you're ready to call it a night.'

She waited until he'd moved the larger bag from his backseat to the concrete before she reached in for the smaller bag, the one that held her violin case. 'I'll get that one,' she said. She moved aside some of his clothing that had toppled from its pile in the backseat to cover her bag. 'It's not—'

Lucy stopped abruptly. The pile of clothing wasn't all clothing. Beneath brightly colored pants and jackets was a helmet. She stared at it as if it was a snake, coiled to strike. Her body had gone ice cold, her heart pounding in her ears.

She knew exactly what it was. She'd seen hundreds of helmets just like it. She'd worn helmets just like it. He raced. Motorcycles. He raced motorcycles.

She grabbed her duffle and took a step back, trying to remember what she'd been saying. 'Um, heavy,' she said. 'My bag's not heavy. Whose helmet is that?'

He looked over her shoulder, puzzled. 'Mine. Why?'

I knew it. She'd sensed the thrill-seeker in him from the moment they'd met. *Why didn't I listen to my gut?* Because she'd been listening to other parts of her anatomy.

'Just curious,' she managed. *Walk away fast.* She started toward the morgue, clutching her duffle bag to her chest which was so tight she could barely breathe.

'Lucy? Lucy, wait.' Behind her he slammed the car door and ran to catch up, his steps echoing in the quiet. 'Lucy.' He appeared beside her, his stride easily matching hers, a frown on his face. 'You left your purse.'

She faltered a step, then shouldered the duffle, took her purse from his hands and kept walking. 'Thank you. I really need to go.'

'And I really need to walk you up,' he said, his tone gone harsh. 'What is wrong with you? What just happened?'

'Nothing,' she lied. 'I just remembered some tests I started this morning that are past due for being read. If I don't read them soon, I'll have to do them again.'

Just get away. And for God's sake do not kiss him again.

JD grabbed her arm, tugged gently. 'Lucy, stop.'

They were almost at the morgue. 'Can't. Gotta save those tests or you'll be an unhappy detective come morning.' With a forced smile she pulled away. For a moment he stood his ground, then he jogged to catch up with her at the door. She swiped her badge through the reader and yanked open the door.

'Lucy. Goddammit.' JD held the door open when she would have pulled it closed. 'Stop. What the hell is wrong? And don't tell me nothing. You took one look at that helmet and started running. What just happened?'

She drew a breath. And counted to ten. 'Do you race moto-cross?'

His brows crunched. 'Yes, in the past. Why?'

She straightened her spine. 'Will you race again?'

His eyes narrowed. 'Maybe. I don't know. *Why?*'

She gathered her calm and searched for an answer he'd accept. 'Do you know how many autopsies I do on idiots who race motorcycles?'

He frowned, offended. 'I wore a helmet. *That* helmet.'

'So?' she said, forcing her tone to be ruefully brisk. 'That just means you'll courteously contain your scrambled brain in the helmet for someone like me to examine, versus creating a colorful smear on the highway for my morgue tech to scrape into a baggie. Either way, you're just as dead. I need to go.' She took her suitcase from his hand and rolled it into the building. 'Thanks for the evening. I won't keep you.'

'Whoa, wait.' He grasped her shoulder and held firm. 'Call me when you're ready to go, okay? I'll come and walk you to your car and see you to Gwyn's.'

She nodded brightly, having no intention of calling him back. She'd find someone else to walk her out. 'Thanks.' She quickly went to the elevator, dragging her suitcase behind her. In a minute she was going up, her last sight that of JD Fitzpatrick staring bewilderedly as the elevator doors closed.

Lucy sagged against the cold steel wall. A narrow escape. Except she hadn't escaped intact. He'd kissed her and she'd kissed him back. He was a good man who had a good heart. But he was dangerous. A lot more so to her than to himself.

Newport News, Virginia
Monday, May 3, 9.15 P.M.

Clay drummed his fingers impatiently on the metal interrogation table. He'd been waiting for an hour now. The older, wiser cop had taken his gun, given him a receipt, searched his briefcase then returned it to him with barely a word. Clay was grateful he'd had the presence of mind to lock Nicki's case file in his hotel room safe. The only thing he carried in the briefcase was a notepad and a photo of 'Margo Winchester'.

I don't have time for this. The club where 'Margo' danced would be open by now. If she was there, he needed to talk to her. He needed to find Evan Reardon so that he could get to Ocean City and start looking for Nicki.

The door finally opened and in walked a tall, dark man in a navy suit. He was in his late thirties. His tie was loosened and his top button undone. He held a Styrofoam cup in one hand and a manila envelope in the other. He put the cup in front of Clay.

'It sucks, but I assume you're used to bad coffee since you used to be a cop,' the man said and sat down across from him. He slid a card across the table. 'I'm Sherman.'

Detective Richard Sherman, Homicide, the card read.

Interesting. 'Whose body is that in the morgue?' Clay asked.

Sherman's mouth curved, but not nicely. 'Not your brother-in-law's. Unless you've got a different ex-wife than I just talked to. She's got no brothers and you got no sisters.'

Clay stared. 'You called my ex-wife?' They hadn't spoken in years. 'Hell.'

Sherman shrugged. 'You lied to my morgue clerk. I know you used to be a DC cop. I know that now you're a PI and licensed to carry that weapon. What I want to know is who you're looking for.'

'I'm working on behalf of a client.' Clay hoped like hell Sherman didn't know he'd visited Sandy Reardon. There was little chance of that, unless Mr Parker reported him. Clay thought Parker trusted the police less than he did, so he was probably okay.

'Uh-huh.' Sherman opened the manila envelope and shook a photo onto the table, then pushed it to Clay. 'Who is she?'

Clay took one look at the close-up of a face, then abruptly pushed it away, bile rising to burn his throat. *Margo*. Or what was left of her. 'God.'

'A few days in the Bay'll do that to a body.' Sherman turned it over. 'You have a photo in your briefcase that resembles this woman.'

Clay said nothing for a moment, thinking. It wouldn't make sense to deny it. It might even help him. 'The cop that brought me here has a good eye.'

'That he does. Helped that we'd posted an artist's sketch of what the girl might have looked like, based on what's left of her. He also has a good ear, and heard you tell Mrs Klein that you were looking for a woman. Who is she?'

'I don't know.'

'Mr Maynard, please don't try my patience.'

Clay smiled thinly. 'I wouldn't dream of it. I know who she claimed to be, but I found out tonight that she'd lied.'

'She's connected to your "brother-in-law"?' Sherman asked, punctuating the air.

'Maybe. I don't know anymore.'

'Ironic. You go to the morgue looking for one body and find another.'

'Oh, yeah,' Clay said bitterly. 'But I really don't know who she was.'

'Then who did she claim to be?'

Clay hesitated, then shrugged. 'A woman named Margo Winchester.'

'How did you know she wasn't Margo?'

'Her father's neighbor told me Margo was in rehab and had been for some time.'

'I see. I need to know who your "brother-in-law" is. You must

186

believe he could be dead, since you went searching at the morgue.'

'I can't tell you. PI–client confidentiality and all that. I'm sure you understand.'

'I don't give a shit about your PI–client confidentiality,' Sherman said coldly. 'I've got a dead woman in my morgue and she's somehow connected to a guy you're looking for. If I don't get an answer, I could hold you.'

'But you won't,' Clay said, keeping his voice calm. 'I had nothing to do with this girl's death.' At least he hoped so. 'I've been in Maryland until today. You can't hold me. You'll let me go, then follow me.' He shrugged. 'It's what I would do.'

Sherman didn't look impressed. 'You're an ex-cop. I'd think you'd want the person who did this' – he tapped the dead girl's photo – 'brought to justice.'

'I do. I just can't help you.'

'Your client could have done this.'

'How do you know she didn't just drown?' Clay countered.

Sherman pushed a different morgue photo across the table, a close-up of the victim's neck in profile. 'The gaping wound across her throat was my first clue.'

Clay made himself look at it. There wasn't much left, but he could see that the knife had sliced side to side, coming up to curve around the woman's right ear.

'I see.' Clay studied Sherman while the detective studied him right back. There was something more here, something the detective wasn't saying. Sherman was edgy, too intense. 'Who died in the fire?' Clay asked quietly.

'A cop named Ken Pullman,' he said and tilted his head. 'That surprises you.'

Clay knew his shock had been visible. Ken Pullman had been the cop Nicki had talked to months ago. The one who'd backed up Evan's claim that 'Margo' was a dangerous stalker. The one Sandy Reardon's father had said was Evan's friend.

'That wasn't in the paper. Had I known, I wouldn't have gone to the morgue.'

'Ken Pullman's body was burned so badly we had to use dental records. We just made the ID today. But his throat was also slit.'

'Same detail around the ear as the woman?'

Sherman nodded grimly. 'Now you can see why I have to have your client's name.'

Clay closed his eyes. A dead cop, a dead woman. And Evan was connected. 'Vaughn Stanley,' he said, giving Sherman a name that would buy Clay time. It was a shell-ID he'd developed with the partner he'd had before Nic, a name he could provide in just such an emergency. This was the first time Clay had used it.

Sherman rose. 'Thank you. I'll be in touch. You can go now.'

Baltimore
Monday, May 3, 9.45 P.M.

'Can you hear me now?' Gwyn asked, talking on her cell. The background noise abruptly quieted. She'd gone into the club's office.

'Yeah,' Lucy said, having called Gwyn as soon as she'd entered the morgue. 'You have a crowd tonight.'

'Everybody knows you're back in town. They're hoping you'll come in.'

Lucy frowned. 'How do they know I'm back in town?'

'They saw me leaving with Royce last night to pick you up from the airport. I didn't think it was a big secret.'

'It wasn't, until bodies and hearts starting showing up around me.'

'You found more?'

'No. Just the one.' Lucy massaged her aching head. 'God, I've had a bad day.'

'I think we established that. Now come on in and play. You know you want to.'

'I do. Gwyn, I went to Anderson Ferry today.'

There were a few beats of silence. 'Why?'

'To inform the Bennetts about Russ. I owed them that much.'

'So what happened when you got there?'

'I got ambushed by Mrs Westcott.'

'God, that old bitch? Isn't she dead yet?'

'Unfortunately for me, no. She called me an "undesirable" in front of JD.'

'Who's JD?'

'Detective Fitzpatrick.'

'We'll come back to him later. For now, we focus on you. Did you see *them*?'

'No, but they saw me.' She sighed. 'They were watching at the window. They didn't come out. Didn't say a word.'

Gwyn echoed the sigh. 'That sucks, babe.'

'Doesn't it, though? And then, to top it all off, JD Fitzpatrick kissed me. Twice.'

'Whoa, back to him. Did you kiss him back?' Gwyn asked eagerly.

'Yes. I did. And then I saw the motorcycle helmet on his backseat.'

'Ooh.' There was a wince in Gwyn's voice. 'Maybe it's somebody else's?'

'He said it was his. And not just any helmet. Motocross.'

'Mmm,' Gwyn hummed. 'Can I have him if you don't want him?'

'Gwyn,' she snapped, 'this is serious.'

'It certainly is. So put on your dress and get out of the morgue. Thorne will follow you over. He'll meet you next to your car. His car, I mean. The one he's loaning you.'

'Thanks,' Lucy said. 'You guys are the best.'

'All for one, babe.'

Baltimore
Monday, May 3, 9.45 P.M.

JD drained the last of the stale coffee from his cup and grimaced. The caffeine jab better be worth the bad taste that now filled his mouth. It had been the last cup in the pot and God only knew how long it had been there. The homicide bullpen was deserted and he didn't plan to stay long enough to warrant making a fresh pot.

He scrubbed his palms over his face, starting when his cell buzzed in his pocket. Lucy must have read those tests, he thought, then saw the call was from Stevie.

189

'So is our girl all graduated from kindergarten?' he asked and Stevie laughed.

'Graduated and high on sugar from the ice cream we had afterward. My mom's trying to get her to sleep now. Cordelia loved your locket. JD, that was the sweetest gift. Thank you.'

JD shifted, uncomfortable with her praise. 'I'm glad. Did you get my message?'

'I did. Sounds like you had some excitement at the Bennetts'. What happened?'

He gave her the details and she whistled softly.

'And Lucy didn't see the connection between Edwards and Bennett? Her brother's been dead a long time, but she is the one who was set up to find Bennett's body.'

'I don't think she wanted to see it,' JD said. 'That Westcott woman did a real number on her. And Mr Bennett didn't help.'

'She'll come around. She might just need to sleep on it. How did her brother die?'

He wasn't so sure Lucy would come around so quickly. He could still see the overly bright smile she'd pasted on her face as she'd waved good-bye. His helmet had sent her running away as fast as that damn skinny skirt would allow. But at least he knew why.

The first thing he'd done on returning to his desk was a search on her brother's death. The terms 'Trask', 'accident', 'death', 'Anderson Ferry', and 'survived by Lucy' had brought up her brother's obituary, and he'd seen his hunch had been right.

'Motorcycle accident. I sent you an email with a link to his obituary,' JD said.

'I'm not at my computer. What does it say?'

JD clicked the window on his screen and winced once again at the headline. 'He was known as Buck, but his real name was Linus.'

Stevie coughed. 'Her parents named them Lucy and Linus? Really?'

'Yeah.' *And I thought my real name was bad*, he thought. Well, it still was, but for different reasons. 'Linus died in a motorcycle accident twenty-one years ago. He was survived by his parents, Ron and Kathy, and his sister, Lucy. Lucy was fourteen.'

Which explained a bit. She'd been catapulted rather rudely into her past tonight. Seeing his helmet in the backseat was probably the icing on the cake.

'So he wasn't murdered,' Stevie mused. 'Seems like a long shot now that the three are connected, but it's something to go on. What do we know about Edwards?'

'Just what I've found online. The Edwardses were a society couple, active in the community. I found pictures of them at trendy events.' JD riffled through the pages he'd printed out. 'Edwards was a golfer, did all the charity tournaments. He was also a yachter. Competed on a team. His name's listed a lot on the local yacht club's website for placing in one race or another. But all the events seemed to stop a year ago.'

'Maybe that's when he was diagnosed with cancer.'

'Probably. A year ago his name started popping up linked to donations. Big donations.' He pulled those printouts to the top of the pile. 'Here's one for a half-mil to the cancer society. Another half-mil to fight domestic abuse. And that's just what I found with a few clicks. I have a dozen more news stories to look through.'

'More donations?'

'Mostly.' JD started clicking on the links in his results screen, then frowned. 'Here's another news story.' He skimmed the first paragraph and his pulse kicked up. 'Stevie, Malcolm Edwards' bank account was cleaned out.'

She was quiet a moment. 'Just like Bennett's. That's why Helen Bennett thought we were there this afternoon, because she'd filed a fraud report.'

'Exactly. This says that the money was wired out electronically. The police traced it to an offshore company and the trail stopped.'

'Does it list a contact?' she asked, excitement in her voice.

'No. Just Delaware State Police.'

'Let's call first thing in the morning then. Now we have a real connection.'

'And a number two,' JD murmured.

191

'What?'

'If this Edwards is connected, he'd have been number one and Bennett would have been number two.'

'You're right. So why burn a "1" into Bennett's back?'

'And why drag Lucy into all of this?'

'Right again. I'm surprised you aren't with her now.'

'I dropped her off at the morgue to check some tests. She's supposed to call me when she's done, but I think I'll head over there now, just to be sure.'

'Call if you need me. I'll see you tomorrow before Hyatt's oh-eight.'

'I'll be there.' JD began shutting down windows on his computer screen. Why target Lucy? Her only connection was a brother who'd died more than twenty years ago. He started to close the final open article on his screen, then froze when a detail jumped out at him. He bent closer, squinting. *What the hell?*

The article was Linus Trask's death announcement. He re-read the address listed for Linus at the time of his death. The street was the same as the Bennetts', which wasn't too big a surprise. Lucy had said they were neighbors. But the house number was only two off the Bennetts'. They'd been next-door neighbors.

JD thought about the eyes he'd seen watching them as they'd gotten into his car. Who lived in that house? He brought up the county tax website and typed in Linus's last address, then sat back, frowning at the result.

The house was still owned by Ron and Kathy Trask. Lucy had said her parents were dead. Hadn't she? *No. She'd said she had no family.* Yet that was her parents' house and likely had been her parents watching them.

JD gathered the printouts and tossed them in his briefcase. He'd finish reading the articles after he saw Lucy safely to Gwyn's. For now he wanted to know why she'd walked past her parents' house and never indicated she'd known them.

And why, when they saw their own daughter, they hadn't come out to speak to her.

Mrs Westcott had called her an 'undesirable'. Said her mother would be ashamed. And in her anger, Lucy had replied that that would be nothing new.

Hyatt was right. Lucy was keeping secrets. JD wanted answers. Now.

Monday, May 3, 9.45 P.M.

'You've been driving around for a half-hour,' Susie complained. 'You could have just dropped me off back at the restaurant.'

'So you can rip off another mark?' he asked, amused. He'd been looking for the best place to dump her body. Oh, and a public telephone booth. Not necessarily in that order. 'What kind of cop would I be if I dropped you back off at your hunting ground?'

'Hopefully the kind that'll give me cab fare back,' she grumbled.

'Yeah, right.' He spotted a deserted alley with a large dumpster. *It'll do.* He pulled up next to the dumpster. 'Get out.'

'Here?' she cried. 'This is a bad neighborhood. You can't leave me here.'

He went around to her side of the car and yanked her out by her hair. 'I said, get out.'

She paled, flinching. 'Okay, okay. But you can't just leave me here.' Her eyes darted side to side. 'They'll slit my throat before I walk two blocks.'

'No they won't,' he said, dragging her around to the trunk. 'But I will.'

'Stop it! Let go of me!' She struggled to get free and he slapped her, hard. Dazed, she staggered, her knees buckling. Then he popped the trunk open and she gasped at the sight of Janet Gordon's body, completely ignoring the extra-sharp filleting knife he grabbed from the wheel well. 'Oh, my God,' she whispered, her horrified gaze fixed on Janet. 'You . . . she . . . she's dead. Oh, my God.'

Susie drew a chest full of air to scream but the sound never made it out of her throat. But a lot of blood did. He laughed as it spurted, spraying the brick alley wall as he'd had the presence of mind to spin her around before he'd sliced her from ear to ear. He was getting a lot better at slitting throats. Now he knew to aim the body away.

It was a lot less messy that way. Still, he had her blood on his hands and his face. He looked down with a scowl. And his new clothes.

Luckily he'd brought a change of clothes for later. He hadn't planned to wear these nice new clothes while moving Janet's body to where she'd be found by Lucy Trask. He tossed Susie's body in the dumpster, then shrugged out of his shirt and used it to clean his blade. The blade he carefully stored back in the wheel well with his other tools. There were a few fishing reels in there too, in case he was ever stopped.

Nobody would think twice about him carrying a filleting knife next to reels. Of course they might if they were in the same trunk as a dead body, which was why he had to get rid of said body soon. No use in tempting fate. It'd be just his luck to get stopped for a routine traffic violation while carrying dead Janet Gordon in his trunk.

He balled up the shirt and shoved it next to Janet's body. He'd find a place to dump the shirt, far away from here. No use in giving the police clues.

Well, unless it suited him. Which was why he needed to find a pay phone. He checked his watch. Lucy would be on soon. He had to get Janet set up.

Monday, May 3, 10.10 P.M.

It was a short drive to the morgue. JD pulled into the same slot in which he'd parked earlier. Since he hadn't yet heard from Lucy, he'd go inside and wait for her.

He'd walked past two cars when the door leading to the elevator bays opened and two people came out. JD had to blink, not believing his eyes at first.

There was a security guard pulling a suitcase. Next to him walked Lucy. But not as JD had left her. Gone was the long, skinny, prim blue skirt. Now she wore a white lab coat that hit her legs mid-thigh. Her very bare legs. He scowled. *What the hell is she wearing under that lab coat?* From where he stood, it didn't look like much of anything.

She led the guard to slot 62 and a sleek Mercedes. That must be Thorne's 'extra' car, he thought, annoyed. She'd had a security guard walk her out. She hadn't called.

She's avoiding me. And then something she'd said earlier made sense. When he'd asked her what her involvement with him would depend on, she'd told him it would depend on how exciting he was. He'd thought she craved excitement, but he'd been wrong. The thought of his racing must have brought back a lot of old memories of her brother's death. She'd wanted him to be *un*exciting.

Boring, like she'd claimed to be. He narrowed his eyes at her long bare legs. But obviously was not. At least he'd been right about that from the beginning. Lucy Trask was not boring.

He'd stepped forward to let her know he was there when the door to the black SUV parked in slot 63 opened. His hand was on his gun when Thomas Thorne emerged. Lucy didn't look surprised to see him. In fact she looked relieved.

She'd called Thorne. *And not me.*

Thorne took her suitcase and put it in the car's trunk while the security guard gave the lawyer a visual inspection with a suspicious eye. The guard turned to Lucy for confirmation and she nodded, sending the guard on his way.

Thorne had opened the Mercedes' doors and was shining a flashlight throughout the interior while Lucy stood by the trunk, rummaging in her suitcase. They appeared to be arguing now. JD could hear their tone, but not the words. They were too far away and the garage echoed every noise. But they didn't appear to be . . . together.

She'd denied being romantically involved with Thorne. Over the day she'd omitted some truths but had not told an outright lie. He'd believe her on this, until he had better reason not to. *She also said she'd call you.*

Then Lucy toed off the sensible pumps she wore and took off the lab coat and JD nearly choked on his tongue. She was wearing a . . . dress. No, not a dress. He wasn't sure what it qualified as, but it was black and leather and bared all of her shoulders and most of her midriff. And it had studs. Lots of silver studs.

She bent to slip on a pair of five-inch stiletto heels and JD stifled a groan. The dress left very, very little to the imagination. And he had a damn good imagination.

He let out a breath that he was sure they could hear, but they were too busy arguing to pay attention to him. Thorne checked the car's interior once more before helping Lucy in and closing her door, his expression forbidding. He got in his SUV and waited until she had pulled out of her parking place, then followed her out.

Without giving it another thought, JD got in his own car and followed them both.

Monday, May 3, 10.20 P.M.

'Goddamn it, Thorne,' Lucy muttered, looking in her rearview. The man was crawling up her ass in his SUV. The bully.

Commanding me not to go to the club tonight. She'd feel a lot safer in a room full of people she knew than sitting alone in Gwyn's apartment waiting for the boogeyman to come snatch her. Thorne had been annoyed that she hadn't listened to him. Sometimes he treated her like she was stupid. *And that pisses me off.*

But he'd come when she'd asked him. Thorne always came when she asked him. They'd forged a friendship. Having a life-altering event in common tended to do that.

You've got a life-altering event in common with JD Fitzpatrick, too. They'd both lost loves. Then she thought of the helmet in his backseat. She had a lot more in common with Fitzpatrick than was comfortable or wise.

You said you'd call him. He'd be angry that she'd gone without him. *Get it over with.* At the next red light she reached for her cell and dialed his number from memory.

'Fitzpatrick,' he answered on the first ring.

She pursed her lips. Just hearing his voice made her body throb in all the most unwise places. 'It's Lucy.'

'You ready for me to pick you up?'

He sounded tense. Aloof. *Well, you did run away from him like a lunatic. What did you expect?* The light changed and she started driving. 'No. You don't need to do that. Thorne was in the neighborhood and he's going to see me to Gwyn's place.'

There was a half-beat of silence. 'Thorne?' Another half-beat. 'Okay.'

He was hurt. Goddammit, she'd hurt him and that was the last thing she'd wanted. But, she had to admit, it was what she had intended. *Push him away. Far away.*

'It's not what you think,' she said quietly.

'What do I think, Lucy?' he asked and her chest got tight.

'That I'm a tease. That I lied about Thorne and me just being friends.'

'Did you lie?'

There was a sober note to the question that had her frowning. 'No.'

Once again, that beat of silence. 'Call me when you get home. From a landline. I'd like to be sure you're safe. On a cell you could be calling me from anywhere.'

'You sound like Mulhauser,' she grumbled. 'Calling from a damn landline.'

'Bennett's killer let him call his ex-wife from his cell phone to tell her he wasn't going to make their kid's recital,' JD said sharply, 'because Bennett's killer didn't want anyone missing him for a while. You could call me from anywhere and I wouldn't know you were in trouble until you showed up missing. Or slumped over a chess table.'

Lucy drew a breath. 'I get your point. I'll call you from Gwyn's home phone.' She hesitated. 'I'm not going straight there. I've got something I need to take care of first.'

'Is Thorne still with you?'

She looked in her rearview and rolled her eyes. 'Thorne's practically crawling up my bumper, so I'm safe. I'll be careful. I promise.'

'And tomorrow morning? How will you get to work? You shouldn't drive alone.'

Her mind spun. She hated to ask Thorne to accompany her again. She'd put him to a lot of trouble today. 'Maybe . . . maybe you and Stevie could come by. Together.'

This time the silence stretched on.

'Are you still there?' she asked.

'Yeah. Call when you get to Gwyn's, it doesn't matter how late.' He hung up.

And what did you expect? You kissed him back. Twice. Told him you wanted him.

I do. But it didn't matter. She didn't always get what she wanted.

She hoped the music would be really loud tonight. She needed it to drown out the voice in her head that was telling her she'd just made a huge mistake.

Twelve

J D once again had to fight to keep from choking on his own tongue. Lucy was getting out of her car, aided by Thorne. She put her purse in her duffle bag, zipped it up, and handed it to Thorne. But JD wasn't looking at Thorne. He could only stare at Lucy.

She'd changed her appearance still further, and if he hadn't seen her take off that lab coat back in the garage, he never would have recognized the woman who walked confidently into the club on five-inch stilettos, Thorne at her side.

Her eyes were lined in black, her lips a rich wine. Her golden-red hair fell to her shoulders and around her throat she wore a choker. With spikes. *I should be disturbed.* Instead he found himself intrigued. Painfully aroused. And totally confused. She'd freaked over his helmet, yet walked into a club looking like some . . . dominatrix.

'Lucy,' he murmured, 'you have some splainin' to do.'

'Excuse me, sir?' It was the valet, a college-aged kid.

JD pulled his badge from his pocket. 'I need to self-park, kid.'

The valet rolled his eyes, seeing his tip go up in smoke. 'Over there.'

JD parked, then dropped a ten on the podium. 'I parked cars for a long time.'

'How long?' the valet asked in a polite way that said he couldn't care less.

'About an hour.' JD grinned when the kid looked surprised. 'I revved some guy's Ferrari and got myself fired.'

199

The kid grinned back. 'But it was worth it, wasn't it?'

'Oh, yeah. Tell me, what goes on in there?'

The kid's brows went up. 'Dark scene. Heavy metal. No drugs,' he added a little too forcefully. 'I really meant that, even if it sounds like I'm sucking up.'

'It did sound that way, actually. Who is the woman that just walked by?'

The kid got a lecherous look and it was all JD could do to keep from knocking it off his face. 'That's Lu*cin*da,' the kid said. 'Emphasis on the "sin". She plays E-V.'

'E-V? Who's that?' he asked, knowing what the kid meant but playing dumb.

The kid gave him the pitying look that the young reserved for old people who were terminally uncool. 'Electric violin, man. She doesn't play every night, but when she does, the place goes wild. You have to see her. She's really good.'

'I fully intend to. Thanks, kid.'

Newport News, Virginia
Monday, May 3, 10.45 P.M.

Clay walked by the unmarked car that had followed him from Sherman's precinct to the convenience store. Inside the store Clay bought a prepaid phone. The police had handled his cell phone while he'd been waiting. He could no longer trust its security.

'You got a pay phone?' he asked the clerk, who pointed to the back wall, bored.

Clay found the phone and dialed his office, relieved when Alyssa answered. 'I'm glad you're still there,' he said. 'I need you to go online and activate this prepaid for me.' He read the instructions on the box.

'It's done,' she said. 'I've called the hospitals around Ocean City. Nobody's been admitted matching Nicki's description. Did . . . did you call the morgues?'

'Not yet.' He'd been a little busy. Now, he was terrified to hear the answer he might receive. There were two bodies in Sherman's morgue. Evan was connected. He might even have killed them. And Nicki was missing.

Please, let her be drunk somewhere. Please. 'I need you to run Nicki's credit cards, business and personal. Find out where she's been.'

He had to find Evan. When he did, he needed to find a way to turn him over to the cops without sacrificing all the good he and Nic had accomplished. They'd helped a lot of people in the past. They would again. But first he had to take care of Evan. *I might have to . . .*

Clay blew out a breath, not liking where his thoughts were taking him. He had never killed except when his own life or the lives of others were at stake. *Think about all the lives you'll never protect if the cops find out Nicki made Evan a fake ID.*

Yeah, Clay thought bitterly. Right. He'd just be protecting himself from jail. But the thought of Evan's new identity spurred an idea. 'When did you run the Gamble card?'

'This morning,' Alyssa said. 'It hadn't been used.'

'Run it again. Evan's going to need money sometime. Call me if you find anything. I'm going to the Pussycat Lounge, where "Margo" worked. I want her real name.'

Baltimore
Monday, May 3, 11.05 P.M.

Whoa. JD had to get used to the darkness in the club, which was called Sheidalin. His eyes were drawn to the stage where a band played loud but strangely melodious music. It shouldn't have been. It should have been crashing, dissonant, cacophonous.

But it wasn't. And at center stage was Lucy, with an electric violin tucked under her chin. It was only a frame of an instrument, an ornate S with a neck and finger-board.

The music swelled around them, fast and nearly frantic. She stood with her eyes closed, playing like a woman possessed. And maybe she was. But he didn't care. She was beautiful and he couldn't rip his eyes away.

'She's something, isn't she?'

JD glanced up at Thorne, irritated at being made to look away from Lucy for even a few seconds. He looked back at the stage where the band was growing frenzied. Yet somehow she managed to stay apart from it all, almost as if she were in a bubble. Untouched. 'Yes, she is. Why did she lie to me about this place? About her music?'

'Did she? Did she specifically say she was not coming to a club tonight and playing with a band?' Thorne asked and JD's eyes rolled.

'I forgot for a minute who you are.' A defense attorney, for God's sake.

'The burden of proof, Detective,' Thorne said, amused. 'It's on you.'

'Why didn't she tell me?' he asked.

'I assume because she didn't want you to know. That you're here will upset her.'

The threatening tone in Thorne's voice made JD frown. 'I'm not leaving.'

'If she says you will, then you will. This is my place. I can remove you if I choose.'

JD looked up, his frown deepening. 'Your place?'

'Well, I'm a co-owner. Me and Gwyn. And Lucy.'

JD's mouth fell open. 'Lucy owns this place?'

'About a third. We started it together, the three of us.'

'When?'

'We've been open for three years, but we started planning right after I met her.'

'Five years ago, when she broke Bennett's nose.'

'Yes. Gwyn had just started working as my receptionist, and when Bennett filed charges, Lucy called me in. We hit it off, Lucy and I.' Thorne just smiled when JD glared. 'Not like that. We have an event common in our past.'

'Which was?' JD asked acidly.

'We were both unjustly accused of murder.'

'Lucy was acquitted, her record expunged.'

'As was mine,' Thorne said. 'But there are always those who wonder and whisper. Was it really true? How did that person get off? A dark cloud follows you. Oh, dear.' His tone moved from harsh to softly sardonic. 'She's seen you. And she is not pleased.'

No, she was not. She still played, but her posture had changed, as had the music she created. No longer fluid, it was now angry. Compelling in a different way. Her eyes narrowed, latching onto JD. Her cheeks were red and she smoldered where she stood.

'My God,' JD breathed. 'She's like . . . fire.'

Thorne chuckled darkly. 'See you don't get your fingers burned. Or broken.'

Startled, JD looked up. 'Are you threatening me?'

'Absolutely not. But they will.' He pointed to a few of the dancers crowded up against the stage, gyrating to the music. 'They'll know Lucy is angry and hurt. And they won't like that.' Thorne met his eyes and JD was surprised to see the tiniest bit of fear. 'Fitzpatrick, nobody here knows who she is in the daytime. Don't blow it for her.'

The fear was for Lucy, JD realized. 'What do you mean?'

'I mean, nobody knows who she is in the daytime.' Thorne enunciated each word. 'It's. A. Secret. This is her escape. Don't ruin it. If you haven't already by being here.'

'But why? Why the secret?'

'Ask her.'

With that Thorne walked away and JD turned back to Lucy, who had drawn the last note from the violin. She calmly placed it and the bow on a stand, came down the stairs at the edge of the stage and started towards him, fury in every long-legged step.

JD's mouth watered. This was the hum of energy that he'd felt at the crime scene, then later every time she focused. Now he knew that hum was a pale shadow of what she really was. And he wondered why she hid such a light under a bushel.

He didn't have much time to wonder. She'd crossed the small room and now stood before him, eyes flashing. The five-inch heels put her mouth only an inch below his own, her angry eyes nearly level with his. She literally took his breath away.

'You followed me,' she said quietly, but he heard.

'Yes, I did,' he said, unapologetic. His heart was pounding, his blood rushing. Every cell in his body was screaming for him to reach out and grab her. To take her. *To have her.* 'I need to talk to you.'

She lifted her chin. 'I don't want to talk to you.'

'Fine, then we won't talk.' He took her elbow and started for the door, a little surprised when she went willingly. If she'd said no, he would have respected that. But at this moment . . . It was all he could do to keep from throwing her over his shoulder.

He walked her out the door, past the bouncer, grimly guiding her around the building, his arm around her waist. As grim as he, she kept up with him step for step. He turned the corner into the alley and finally alone, dug his fingers into her hair and ground his mouth into hers, desperately, taking what he wanted. What he needed.

With a growl that sent his pulse spiking, she grabbed the lapels of his coat and yanked herself higher, meeting his mouth with a desperation of her own. 'Damn you,' she muttered between kisses. 'Why did you follow me here?'

For a full minute he didn't answer, devouring her mouth. His palms slicked down the back of the amazing excuse for a dress, hesitating only for a moment when he encountered bare thighs before sliding up under the skirt. He groaned. Her butt was also bare, only a tiny strip of material disappearing into the cleft between her cheeks. His fingers flexed once in anticipation and then he filled his palms with smooth, soft skin. Her body jerked against him, her arms coming around his neck, one leg bending so that her thigh rubbed against his as she struggled to get closer.

His fingertips slid higher, encountering slick, wet, hot flesh and she moaned, deep in her throat. She was open to him. He could have her. Here. *Now*.

Now. Now. Now. The word banged in his mind as he pulled her closer, grinding his body against her, wishing they were anywhere but here. *Here is good. Now is better.* He nipped at her throat, grimacing when the spikes on her choker poked him.

'Take it off. Take it off now.'

She let go of him to reach behind her neck then dropped the choker on the ground. Her hands slithered back up his chest, yanking at buttons until she could put her hands on him, flattening, rubbing all over his skin while her mouth ate at his. All while her wet heat teased and beckoned. He could smell her, wanted to taste her. Needed to have her. *Mine. Mine. Mine.*

He sank his teeth into the curve of her shoulder as he plunged two fingers up into her and she went rigid, arching back with a strangled cry of pleasure that fired his blood.

'I want you,' he growled into her ear. 'Now.'

'Yes.' She gritted it, her head thrown back as he savaged her throat. 'Now. Do it now.' She opened her eyes and he was lost. 'Do it.'

He backed her against the wall, yanking her higher against him, groaning when she lifted both legs, cinching them around his waist. Her thighs were bare, beautifully bare, all the way to her hips across which the strings of her thong stretched taut.

She held his gaze, hers molten. Her eyes narrowed, challenging. Mesmerizing. 'Just do it,' she mouthed.

His control snapped and so did the string of her thong when he ripped it. He freed himself and plunged hard and deep, groaning as she tightened around him. *Good. So good.* 'Oh, my God.' He plunged again, harder, faster, unable to stop. 'Lucy.'

Her nails dug into his shoulders and she thrust against him, unrestrained. Then she arched back with a strangled cry, her body going rigid as she came, hard. She was beautiful. Intensely, wildly beautiful.

Mine. It filled his mind as he plunged a final time, letting himself follow.

He rested his forehead against the wall, turning to press a kiss to her jaw. She was panting, her legs gone lax around him. Slowly he lowered her until her feet were on the ground. His body shuddered as he withdrew. She trembled, her knees locking as she leaned against the wall, keeping herself upright.

She closed her eyes, swallowed hard. 'Oh, my God,' she said on a quiet exhale.

It didn't sound positive.

JD braced his hands on either side of her head, pushing back so that he could stare down at her. 'Don't ask me to say I'm sorry,' he whispered. 'Please.'

'I won't. I need to go.' She pushed at his chest and he stepped away. She tugged her dress back down over her hips and started walking.

'Lucy, wait.'

She stopped, her back to him. 'Why did you follow me?'

'Why did you lie to me?'

'I didn't,' she said hoarsely. 'I *never* lied to you.'

'You kept secrets.'

'They're mine to keep. Until I choose to share them, they are mine to keep.' She was shivering again.

Quickly he shrugged out of his jacket and draped it over her shoulders, then moved to stand in front of her, needing to see her face. 'Tell me, Lucy, and I want the truth. When you said you wanted me, were you lying?'

She cocked her jaw, annoyance flaring in her eyes. 'I did not lie to you.'

'So you do want me. You wanted this.'

She was quiet a moment. 'Yes. But you are not good for me, Detective.'

He was frustrated and confused. 'I can't accept that I'm not good for you. I won't.'

'You don't understand.'

'So explain it to me,' he said urgently.

'I can't,' she said, panic inching into her voice.

He cupped her face in his palm, traced her lips with his thumb. 'I saw you,' he murmured, 'and I knew.'

'What?' she said wearily. 'What did you know? What could you possibly know?'

'That . . .' *You belong to me*, he thought, but didn't dare say the words aloud. 'That I felt something. An energy, an attraction. A craving. This morning, and again in there just now.' *And inside you.* It had never been like that before. But he didn't think she'd believe him. 'Your music. Why didn't you tell me?'

'Because this . . . This is the one place I come to be . . . me.' She hesitated, then shrugged. 'To be bad.'

His body instantly went hard and he had to take a deep breath to keep from grabbing her again. 'But?'

'I can't have this 24/7. I let myself be me here only. My daily life has to be stable.'

'Boring?'

She looked relieved. 'Yes. I hope you'll just accept that.'

'All right, but why am I not good for you?'

The relief disappeared, giving way to pain. 'Because you're not boring.'

'You mean the helmet? I don't race anymore, Lucy. I don't take risks.'

'Of course you do. You're a cop. Your life is one big risk. But this isn't about *you*,' she added with quiet desperation.

He frowned down at her. 'You? You're worried about you?'

'I said I was a lot of trouble. You should have listened to me.' She handed him his coat. 'I have to redo my makeup. I left it in Thorne's car.'

She walked out of the alley and toward the line of cars in front of the club. For a few seconds he watched her, too numb to react, then his brain kicked in. He scooped up her choker and the remnants of her panties, shoving them in his pocket as he took off at a jog to catch up to her. 'Lucy, wait. Stop.'

She stopped, but didn't turn around. 'Make it about the case, JD.'

Okay. Just keep her talking. 'Bennett and Edwards had their bank accounts drained after their deaths. They are connected and Mr Bennett somehow knew that.'

Slowly she looked over her shoulder. 'But what does that have to do with me?'

'Other than that they knew your brother, I don't know. Yet.' He fell into step beside her when she began walking. 'But it does. So you need to go somewhere safe until . . .'

She walked to Thorne's Mercedes, then stopped abruptly. 'No,' she whispered.

He followed her between the parked cars. 'Lucy, don't be stubborn.'

'Oh, God.' She looked up at him and he could see horror in her eyes. 'Look.'

He bent around her so that his line of sight was identical to hers. And his gut turned inside out. There was someone in the car. Sitting in the passenger seat.

It was a woman, slumped against the window which was streaked with blood. The woman was dead, her face slashed but still recognizable. Her head had been beaten until it was bloody. JD swallowed hard. Her eyes were gone. Something white was in her mouth, just like Bennett that morning.

'Number two,' Lucy whispered, pale and stunned.

He thought of Malcolm Edwards, *lost at sea*. 'No. She's number three.'

Monday, May 3, 11.25 p.m.

'Damn,' Stevie muttered. JD had called her with the news. 'Does Lucy know her?'

He stood next to Thorne's Mercedes, while Lucy studied the victim through the window. 'She doesn't think so, but it's hard to see. There's a lot of blood smeared on the window. The victim appears to be about sixty. Her head is shaved.'

'Just like Bennett,' Stevie said. 'Who else knows you've found her?'

'I called for backup, CSU and the ME. Then I called you. There's a valet around here somewhere, but I don't see him. Everyone else is in the club.'

'Where Lucy plays an electric violin wearing leather,' she said in wry disbelief.

'Yes,' he said. Lucy was staring at the victim with a combination of horror and clinical focus. He trapped his phone between his shoulder and ear and put his coat over her shoulders again. She shot him a grateful look and pulled the coat around her.

'Hey, my reaction is mild compared to what some will say. Especially Hyatt, who's been suspicious of the doc all day. And who, I should add, you have not yet called.'

'No, not yet. I will when we're done.'

'I'll call him on my way. Hey, wait a minute. Did you say "valet"?'

The thought immediately struck him. 'Yeah. He'd have keys. Lots of keys. Hold on a minute. Hey, Lucy, did you self-park your car, or did you use the valet?'

She turned slowly, understanding in her eyes. 'Valet. It's a perk of ownership. That's how he got my car key to put Russ's heart there. I didn't think of that today. I would have told you if I had, even if it meant telling you about this place. I'm not lying.'

He believed her, but he didn't want to say so with Stevie listening. So he nodded, gently brushing a stray lock of hair from her cheek. 'Yeah, she used the valet.'

'I heard,' Stevie said.

'Looks like the valet parks cars for a lot of clubs. Do you employ him, Lucy?'

'No,' she said. 'It's an independent contractor. They're a chain all over town. But I know the guy on duty tonight. He's a good kid.'

'I heard,' Stevie said again. 'I'm on my way. Hyatt will probably get there first.'

It was a warning, he knew. 'The squad cars are here. I'll secure the perimeter.' He hung up and turned back to Lucy. 'Hyatt will probably come. He's been suspicious of you since this morning.'

'Why?'

'Because you hide things,' he said.

She lifted her chin. 'It's my life. My right.'

JD might have criticized her defiant tone, but her misery-filled eyes told a different story. 'Stay here until I get the uniforms set up. Then I'll walk you inside.' He looked around, but saw nothing that looked out of place except that the valet wasn't back. Cars were starting to line up on the street. 'Don't go anywhere alone. Even the bathroom. He may still be here. Watching us. Watching you.'

'JD, he could have left this body for me to find tomorrow, but he picked here and now. And he knew I'd be driving Thorne's car. I only knew that myself a few hours ago.'

'I know. We'll make a list of everyone who knew. He could have been waiting here for you, too.' He waved to the cops getting out of their squad cars. 'Over here.'

He put one uniform next to the car, sent two others to cover the

209

exits in the side and rear of the building, then sent the fourth to string the crime-scene tape. 'Keep your eye out for the valet, too,' he told them. 'College kid, dark hair, five ten, one-seventy, wearing a purple vest. He was out here when I got here. He may be a witness.'

'Or the perp?' one of the cops asked.

'Maybe. Window of opportunity was less than thirty minutes. I've got more backup coming. I want them to canvass the neighborhood for anyone who saw a person being put in this car. Come get me when they arrive. I'm going inside to find anyone who might have seen anything.' He took Lucy's elbow. 'Let's go.'

Lucy stood outside the club's door, hesitating. 'It's eleven-thirty. Gwyn might be on.'

'That's good. I finally get to meet Gwyn.'

She pulled Fitzpatrick's coat tighter around her, thinking of what he was about to see. 'We'll see about that. Come on.'

She slipped inside the door and was stopped by Ming, the Samoan-born bouncer who was every bit as big as Thorne. 'No entry,' he boomed over the roar of the crowd, then faltered. 'Miss Lucinda. I didn't realize it was you.' His eyes narrowed at Fitzpatrick, focusing on the gun in his shoulder holster. 'Is this guy bothering you?'

Yes. 'No. This is Detective Fitzpatrick, Homicide. Detective, this is Ming.'

Ming's mouth dropped open. 'Homicide. What homicide?'

'The one outside,' Fitzpatrick said. 'I'm going to need to take your statement. Where have you been for the last half-hour?'

'Here.' Ming's eyes flashed to Lucy's, panicked. 'I swear it.'

She laid her hand on Ming's arm. 'Just answer what he asks. You'll be fine.'

'But who died?'

'We don't know. But Detective Fitzpatrick will find out. Ming's been with us for two years, Detective. He keeps good track of who comes and goes. Can you remember who came in or left after Thorne and I arrived?'

'Nobody left. Only a dozen came in. Including you, sir,' he said to Fitzpatrick.

'I'll need you to point them out when we bring up the house lights,' Fitzpatrick said. 'But that doesn't seem a lot of people. Not for a crowd this size.'

'Because it's Monday,' Ming said and Lucy's cheeks heated, 'and everyone knew Miss Lucinda would be coming back from her vacation, so everyone came early.'

Fitzpatrick cast her a curious glance. 'I see. Anybody here ever start anything before? Any rowdiness or fights? Anyone threaten Miss Lucinda?'

'Nah, they're mostly regulars,' Ming said. 'None of them would kill anyone.' Then he seemed to reconsider. 'Well, maybe—'

'Ming,' Lucy said sharply, cutting him off. 'Don't speculate.'

Ming looked sorry and Fitzpatrick looked both surprised and very annoyed as he led her away from the front door, along the curtain that kept the outside light outside.

'What the hell was that?' he hissed.

She deliberately misunderstood. 'That was Ming. His name is really Clive, but he feels like Ming makes him sound scarier.' She shrugged. 'Go figure.'

'That's not what I meant and you know it. What did you mean, "don't speculate"?'

She readied herself for an argument. 'If you catch them fair and square, have at 'em. But if Ming tells you people he thinks might be capable of murder, it's not based on anything more than his imagination. Still, you'll write the names in your little book. You'll check them out and likely clear them. But the next time something happens here and you need names, you'll go back to those. Even though they didn't do anything wrong.'

His dark eyes snapped in irritation. 'I wouldn't do that. So next time, please be quiet or I'll have to have you removed.'

It was what she'd expected him to say. Still, it rankled. 'This is my place, and—'

'Not when you have a dead body outside. Look, when you're . . .' He leaned close to say the words in her ear. 'When you're cutting up dead people, I don't tell you what to do. This is my investigation. I don't want to have you removed, but Hyatt would in a heartbeat.

211

So don't do that again.' He backed away to search her face. 'Please.'

Grudgingly she nodded. 'Fine. We need to tell Thorne.'

A cheer rose on the other side of the curtain. Dammit. Gwyn had started her act.

'What's that?' He started to push through the curtain, but she grabbed his arm.

'No. Not here. You can't enter here. You'll let in the light and you might distract Gwyn. Somebody could get hurt. Come. We may be able to stop her before she starts.'

Hurriedly, she led him to the end of the curtain and slipped around it, holding the edge so he could follow. The roar of the place dramatically dipped, the crowd gone eerily quiet. Gwyn was about to do her thing. There was no time to safely stop her.

Lucy signaled Fitzpatrick to remain silent. She didn't have to worry. He was staring at the stage where Gwyn, wearing a black bustier and thigh-high boots, held a coiled bullwhip in each hand. At the other end of the stage stood Mowry, their club manager and drummer, with a piece of straw in his mouth. He bent slightly at the waist, the straw being Gwyn's target.

In rapid succession Lucy's tiny best friend cracked each whip five times, alternating right to left, snipping off the straw a fraction of an inch at a time. When it was over Gwyn turned to bow and Mowry held up the now-short straw, pretending to slump in relief. It was an act they'd perfected through countless hours of practice.

The crowd cheered and Gwyn beamed. Lucy looked up at Fitzpatrick, whose expression was a mix of horror, fascination and awe. But mostly horror, she thought.

'Earlier tonight you asked me how we got out of Anderson Ferry,' she said.

'You said you went to college and Gwyn joined a sorority,' he said, still staring.

'That was a lie,' she admitted. 'But only because the truth is so fantastic.'

'What's the truth?'

'You know those kids who threaten to join the circus? Gwyn did. Did high wire and was quite the contortionist. But she got hurt, so she quit, fell for a rocker, and joined a traveling band. She ditched the rocker, kept the band. That's most of them, up there.' Resetting the stage for the next set, unaware that their world was about to change.

That a killer could be here. *Right here*. She shivered, suddenly cold.

Fitzpatrick had recovered from his shock at Gwyn and her act and was checking out their crowd in a clinical way that made her feel a little safer. 'Seems like it would get old, fast. I think I'd want a home that I could come to every night.'

There was a wistful note to his voice that she wondered if he was aware of. 'The band was where she met Thorne, who was smart enough to have a day job and needed a secretary. She's got a hell of a voice, but the bullwhips make more of an impact. Plus, she's kind of a ham. I guess we all are.'

He glanced down at her dryly. 'You know the most interesting people, Lucy.'

'We need to tell Thorne and Gwyn so we can up the lights.'

Gwyn had already seen her and was pushing her way through the crowd, her eyes darting from Fitzpatrick's face to the gun in his shoulder holster. Thorne appeared from behind the curtain, making Fitzpatrick frown.

'Where did you come from?' he asked.

'The office,' Thorne said. 'The door's right behind Ming. What's happened? Ming's babbling about a homicide and there's a cop standing outside the front door.'

'Homicide?' Gwyn gasped. 'Again?'

'Again,' Lucy said. 'There's a body in the passenger seat of your car, Thorne.'

Thorne's expression darkened. 'The Mercedes or the SUV?'

'The Mercedes,' she said.

His face grew darker still. 'That *you* were driving. You found the body? Again?'

She nodded. 'Yes, again. It's a female victim this time. She looks about sixty.'

'The killer knew you'd borrowed my car, Lucy.' He looked at

Fitzpatrick, something just shy of panic in his eyes. 'What are you doing about this, Fitzpatrick?'

'Investigating,' Fitzpatrick replied levelly, 'any and all people who knew she had your car or who could have been here waiting when you two arrived.'

'Do you know her, Luce?' Gwyn asked and Lucy shook her head.

'No. We have a tight window in which the victim could have been put in the car.'

'Between the time you got here and the time the two of you rushed out,' Gwyn said.

'You saw us leave?' Fitzpatrick asked, looking uncomfortable.

'Honey, everybody saw you leave,' Gwyn said seriously. 'I'm Gwyn Weaver, by the way, and I did not kill Russ Bennett. Just in case you still wanna ask.'

'I'm Detective Fitzpatrick,' he said. 'What about the last hour? Where were you?'

Gwyn lifted her chin. 'Right here. Ask anyone.'

'I will,' Fitzpatrick said calmly.

'Wait,' Thorne said, shaking his head. 'If someone put a body in my car, which really pisses me off, then Kevin should have seen them.'

'Kevin's the valet,' Lucy told Fitzpatrick. 'Nobody's seen him,' she told Thorne.

Gwyn bit her red lip. 'That's not good. Kevin wouldn't leave his post.'

'Detective?' An officer poked his head around the corner and gaped at Gwyn.

'What is it, Officer?' Fitzpatrick asked and the officer jerked his gaze away.

'We, uh, found something you need to see.'

Fitzpatrick leaned close to the officer and they whispered back and forth, then Fitzpatrick turned, his expression gone unreadable, and Lucy's stomach pitched.

'No,' she said. Denial rose strong in her chest. 'Not Kevin.'

He nodded. 'I'm sorry.'

'How?' she asked, her mouth forming the word, but her voice

wouldn't cooperate. *Kevin*. He was dead. *People are dying, and I am connected*.

'We can discuss it later,' Fitzpatrick said formally, but his eyes were sad. 'Your ME crew is outside, and they're asking for you. You may want to change first.'

Lucy looked up at Thorne who'd grown very pale. Gwyn had started to cry. Lucy took their hands and held tight. 'We need to up the lights. Detective Fitzpatrick will need to talk to everyone who came in during the time frame in question.'

'Detective, I've known Kevin for years. His parents are friends of mine. I got him this job.' Thorne's throat worked as he tried to swallow. 'Did he suffer, like Bennett?'

'No,' Fitzpatrick said kindly. 'It was quick. I'm sorry, Thorne. I'm sorry to all of you, for your loss. Let's get moving and catch the bastard who did it.'

Thirteen

Monday, May 3, 11.45 P.M.

'It ain't your day, kid,' Ruby said as she and Alan pushed the gurney around the back of the club where Kevin's body lay in a pool of blood, his throat cut ear to ear. 'Discovering three bodies in twenty-four hours. That might be a department record.'

Crouched next to the boy's body, trying to separate her grief and guilt from the job she needed to do, Lucy wanted to scream at Ruby to *shut up*. But Lucy knew it was morgue humor, intended to help Ruby get through a hard night.

'This was Kevin Drummond,' she said quietly. 'Twenty-five. He had a girl named Jen and a dog named Leopold. He wanted to be a rock star but couldn't carry a tune in a bucket.'

'Oh, honey, I'm sorry,' Ruby said, squeezing Lucy's shoulder through the white coveralls she'd pulled over a pair of sweats that she'd borrowed from the drummer. 'You knew him? How?'

They didn't know yet. Didn't know she spent almost as much time here as she did at the morgue. Now, looking down into the boy's lifeless eyes, her secrets were no longer important. *This young man is dead. Because he worked near me.*

'Yes. I knew him.' His blood was everywhere, covering his body, the gravel bed on which he lay, splattered all over the wall behind them. 'He was a nice young man who had the bad luck to be in the wrong place at the wrong time.'

'Which is not your fault,' Fitzpatrick said firmly. He crouched next to her and met her eyes, his grim. 'It looks like he was dragged around the building. From the other side,' he added flatly,

216

pointing away from the alley where they'd . . .

Oh, God. They'd been having sex while Kevin was being murdered. Nauseous guilt surged.

'Don't,' Fitzpatrick said sharply, as if he'd read the direction her mind had gone. 'What can you tell me, Dr Trask?'

'Cause of death is the severing of the jugular,' she said. Kevin hadn't suffered. For that she could be grateful. 'There's a bruise forming on the jaw, pre-mortem.'

'He might have hit him to stun him first,' Fitzpatrick murmured.

'Yes. And there are defensive wounds.' She lifted Kevin's hand in her gloved one, pointing to the abrasions on his knuckles.

'He fought, then,' Fitzpatrick said.

'For his life,' she murmured. 'Alan, be careful to bag this victim's hands.'

'Does he have his heart?' Alan asked and Ruby quickly shushed him.

Lucy frowned up at him. 'What?'

Alan flushed. 'Is he going to be like the guy this morning? I'm sorry. I just wanted to . . . prepare myself better than before.'

When he'd looked like he'd faint. 'The victim has his heart. As for the woman in the car, I don't know. The assailant was taller than the victim. This wound angles up.'

'Okay,' Fitzpatrick murmured. 'Over six feet, then. That's good. The blade?'

'Non-serrated, thin. Very sharp. He finished with a flick of his wrist. The wound curves around the ear.'

'Okay,' he said again. 'We're almost finished taking statements from your staff. Your Ming provided a complete list of people who'd come and gone.'

'What's a Ming?' Ruby asked. 'Luce, what's going on here?'

Lucy rose, drew a breath. 'This is my club.'

Ruby frowned. 'What do you mean, your club?'

'I'm part owner, along with two friends.'

Ruby's mouth fell open, but Alan was strangely unsurprised. Ruby glared at them. 'Why am I the only one who finds this news?'

Alan met Lucy's eyes. 'She's *Lucinda*,' he said and it was Lucy's turn to gape. Alan's smile was dry. 'My friends brought me here for my twenty-first birthday and I've been coming ever since. The bands rock. But you . . .' Something glittered in his eyes, a sexual appraisal she found more disturbing than complimentary. 'I thought you'd recognize me when I interviewed for the morgue job, but you didn't seem to. Or you didn't want to admit it, if you did. My friends are green that I get to work with you.'

'Drew says he's ready to pull the other body from the car,' Fitzpatrick said brusquely, changing the subject. 'If Ruby and Alan can get this victim moved, we'll get started out front.' He took Lucy's elbow and led her toward the club's back door.

Lucy threw a last look at Kevin's body, at Ruby who looked stunned, and at Alan, who'd known. The thought left her uneasy. How secret had her 'secret' really been?

Fitzpatrick escorted her into the club's main room where she soon got her answer.

The club's employees sat in a circle, shaken. Half were crying. The other half looked like they had or would. Hyatt and Stevie were standing by the bar, talking to Thorne and Gwyn, who'd changed into street clothes. The employees looked up when Lucy entered, staring at her like she was a stranger. *They hadn't known.* She was now even more disturbed that Alan had.

Kraemer, the bartender, eyed her up and down. 'Your day job, I take it,' he said.

'You said you worked a desk job for the state,' Jasmine said, clearly hurt. She was Thorne's latest girlfriend and had probably thought herself privy to all their secrets.

'I do,' Lucy said. 'The state medical examiner's office. Where I have a desk.'

'So,' Mowry said, 'to be crystal here, you cut up dead people all day.'

Lucy sighed. Mowry had been with the band since day one and last year Thorne had hired him as their operations manager. He looked the most surprised of them all. 'Yes,' she said.

He gave her a single nod. 'Cool.' The others agreed, with nods and murmurs.

'*No*. Not cool. Not dark. Just . . . necessary. Especially for victims like Kevin.'

Mowry rose and cupped her face between his hands, resting his forehead against hers in a gesture of friendship that made her eyes sting. 'That's why it's cool. For victims like Kevin, who didn't deserve what happened to him. You'll help your cop here catch the sonofabitch that took him from us. So it's cool.'

'Thank you,' she whispered. 'I needed to hear that.'

He kissed her forehead, something he'd never done before. 'I never would have dared to do that to the lady in the leather dress. But like this, you're approachable.'

Fitzpatrick cleared his throat behind her. 'We need to be getting outside. Excuse us.'

Gwyn met them at the door, her eyes swollen from crying. 'Everybody in this place was texting the news. Kevin's parents need to know.'

'We sent two detectives over to tell them, as soon as his body was discovered,' Fitzpatrick said. 'We expected the texting.'

Lucy looked to the bar where Hyatt and Thorne were arguing. 'What's going on?'

'Hyatt demanded a client list,' Gwyn said. 'Thorne told him to get a warrant.'

'Considering one of your own was murdered outside your back door, I'd think Thorne would cooperate,' Fitzpatrick said, annoyed.

'Then you'd be wrong,' Lucy said simply.

'Fitzpatrick and Dr Trask,' Stevie called from the door. 'We're ready outside.'

Gwyn put a key in Lucy's hand. 'My apartment. You've got the place to yourself tonight. I'm staying with Royce. He's coming to pick me up because the cops impounded my car as evidence.' She glared up at Fitzpatrick. 'Why'd they do that?'

'Because your car was next to the Mercedes. We're hoping the bastard touched it. We'll take prints, then return it. Lucy, we need to go.'

Lucy impulsively leaned down and kissed Gwyn's cheek. 'Be careful. Please.'

'You too. Call if you need me. And when you know who that is in Thorne's car.' Gwyn bit at her lip. 'I know this sounds awful, but I just hope she's no one we know.'

Lucy hoped the same, but had a bad feeling they'd be disappointed.

Tuesday, May 4, 12.00 A.M.

He hadn't planned to kill the valet. *Dammit.*

He'd *planned* to knock the guy out from behind and drag him around to the back where he'd eventually be found and revived. But no . . . The idiot had to fight back. *Had to see my face. Note to self: Ski masks only work in the movies.* In real life the victims could tear them off, rendering them less than useless.

Before he'd known it the knife was in his hand and the guy's carotid was history. *I'm getting good at the move. Maybe in my next life I'll be an assassin.* He started to laugh at the thought, then sobered. *Why not?* He was good at it. He could make money at it. And there were definitely people in the world that needed killing.

He'd already started wondering how to advertise such a business when his attention was jerked back to the scene. They were moving the Mercedes.

The better to get the body out, my dear.

Lucy might not recognize Janet Gordon, even though he'd left most of her face intact. She might not recognize Janet's name when they identified the body. Janet had remarried a few times. But when they identified the next of kin . . . Then she would know. Then she'd start to fear for her own life.

Be afraid, Lucy. Because I'm coming. Soon you'll be sorry you took what wasn't yours. Soon you'll know what it's like to lose everything and everyone that matters. Soon you'll belong to me.

'Are you sure, Dr Trask?' Hyatt pressed. 'Are you sure you don't know her?'

To her credit, Lucy remained calm. At least on the outside. JD

220

imagined she was boiling on the inside. Hyatt had asked her the same question three times.

'No, Lieutenant Hyatt,' she replied, not taking her eyes off the techs who were trying to pull the body from the seat as gently as possible. 'I do not. But if you'll give me some time and space, I'll do my best to determine the victim's identity.'

'See if she's got a "II" on her back,' Hyatt said, again for the third time. At least.

'As soon as we get her back to the morgue. I don't think it's wise to examine the body here,' she said quickly, interrupting Hyatt before he could demand exactly that. 'We could lose trace evidence here in the parking lot or, perhaps worse, provide one of the TV cameras with newsworthy footage.'

'I don't want to give those TV vultures a thing,' Hyatt muttered. 'I'll follow you to the morgue, Dr Trask. You'll examine the body the second you arrive.'

'The very second,' Lucy agreed with enviable equanimity.

'She's good,' Stevie whispered. 'You'd almost think she doesn't hate him.'

'Almost,' JD murmured. Except that Lucy leaned away from Hyatt, a cringe in her posture. JD felt relieved that when he'd helped her from Kevin's body back into the building, she'd leaned into him for support. It gave him hope. She hadn't entirely pushed him away. He hadn't entirely ruined things by letting his other head think for him.

Shit, that had been one of the stupidest things he'd ever done. Sex in an alley, for God's sake. And if given the opportunity, he'd do it again in a heartbeat.

'There's a hat in here,' Ruby said. 'Must've rolled under her foot. It's godawful ugly, but would have hidden her face if she was wearing it when he put her in the car.'

'That fits,' JD told Hyatt. 'One of the officers talked to a couple coming out of the bar across the street. They saw a man rolling a woman to this car in a wheelchair. She was wearing a big floppy hat that hid her whole head.'

'And the man pushing her?' Hyatt demanded.

'The husband said he was six feet with dark blond hair. The wife said he was shorter than that, with dark brown hair. Neither could describe his face. All they could agree on was the big floppy hat.'

'Wonderful,' Hyatt said grimly. 'The other victim?'

'The valet attendant,' JD said. 'There's evidence of a struggle where the body was found. No physical evidence at this point. Had he not been killed, he may have been a suspect. He had access to Dr Trask's car key. As it stands, it doesn't appear he was involved, but we'll check him out.'

Hyatt's eyes narrowed. 'You were here when it all went down, Fitzpatrick. Why?'

JD had prepared himself for the question. 'I was following Dr Trask, sir. She'd already been targeted twice today. I felt she was in danger.'

'We both did,' Stevie inserted. 'And we agreed that this killer has made a study of Dr Trask's routine. If we stay close to her, we'll intersect paths with the killer sooner versus later. JD offered to take the first watch. I was planning to relieve him at four A.M.'

It was a total fabrication, of course. JD fought the urge to meet Stevie's eyes to thank her. Hyatt would see the exchange and know Stevie was covering for him.

Fortunately they were spared any more of Hyatt's questioning by Ruby and Alan's removal of the body from the front seat of Thorne's Mercedes. Together they laid the body on its side on the unzipped body bag spread over the gurney. The victim wore a long-sleeved dark dress that covered her from knee to neck. She wore no shoes.

'She's in rigor,' Lucy said, crouching next to the gurney. 'The victim is female, Caucasian, between fifty and sixty. She's had a facelift. Her fingers have been broken, but not severed. Her eyes are gone.' With gloved fingers, she probed the dark fabric covering the victim's chest, then looked up again. 'So is her heart.'

'Shit,' Hyatt muttered.

'Indeed,' Lucy said quietly. 'Lividity visible in the lower legs indicates she was lying on her side at the time of death or shortly thereafter. She was struck repeatedly in the head by a blunt object. Her face has been sliced by a thin, non-serrated blade.'

'The same blade used to kill the valet?' Hyatt asked.

'If not the same, then similar. There is an object wrapped in a handkerchief in her mouth. Time of death between two and five this afternoon. She does not appear to have been frozen, but I'll take core temps at the lab.' She stood up, stepped back. 'Zip her up, please, and transport.'

Drew joined them. 'The key to the Mercedes is missing from the valet station. Thorne had an extra that we used to unlock the car just now. We'll take the cars on all sides into the lab and dust for prints. We might get lucky.'

Somehow JD doubted it.

Tuesday, May 4, 12.45 A.M.

It had taken Clay a little while to lose Sherman's tail. He'd found the Pussycat Lounge and had barely been seated when he saw a cobra tattoo up on the stage.

Hello. He imagined Mrs Klein would be extremely displeased with her granddaughter, working in a place like this. In his misspent youth, Clay might have found the women on stage hot. Now, not. He wasn't dead, so he was affected. But the thought of touching them . . . No way.

Cobra Girl had noticed him watching her and gave him a practiced leer. Nicki's notes had said that 'Margo' had called the woman 'Linda'. He was about to find out if they'd both used fake names.

He ordered the mandatory overpriced drink, set it aside and waited for Cobra Girl to finish her set. When she had, she slithered by. 'You like?' she asked.

He fought the urge to cringe, keeping his smile bland. 'What's your name, honey?'

'Cleo. Short for Cleopatra, you know, on account of the snake.' She flexed her bicep, making the coiled cobra appear to strike.

Lovely. 'Makes sense,' Clay said. 'How much for a private?'

'A hundred. Fifteen minutes. No hands, big guy.'

'I wouldn't dream of it.' He followed her to a private room and let her close the door. She pointed at an old chair. 'Sit. Relax.'

Clay didn't want to think about what was soaked into the chair's upholstery. Neither sitting nor relaxing was going to happen. 'Let's cut to the chase, *Linda*. I'm not a cop. I'm a PI, and interested in the woman you let use your grandma's condo two months ago. She went by the name of Margo Winchester.'

Linda took a step back. 'I don't know where she is.'

'I know *where* she is,' Clay said. 'I want to know *who* she is.'

Linda frowned. 'Then where is she? She hasn't shown up to work in a week.'

'She's in the morgue. She's been dead for a week.'

Linda's hand flew up to cover her mouth. 'How?'

'She was murdered. What was her real name?'

'Mary Stubbs,' she whispered. 'Oh, my God.'

'I need to know why she lied to my partner two months ago. Why she said her name was Margo Winchester.'

Tears began rolling down Linda's face. 'She got hired by this guy to act out a role, to be this crazy woman, Margo. I told her not to, but she needed the money. She can't be dead.'

'How did this guy pick her?'

'He knew her boyfriend. They went to school together.'

Clay's heart sank. 'And the boyfriend's name?'

'Ken Pullman. He's a cop. Are you sure Mary's dead?'

'Very sure. Who knew they were together, Ken and Mary?'

'Hardly anyone. It was a secret. Ken's married. Does he know?'

Clay ignored her question. 'Did she have any recent contact with the guy who hired her?'

Linda nodded miserably. 'She called him, said she wanted more money, that she'd tell everyone that he was a liar. I told her not to, but she said Ken would protect her.'

And that ended well. 'When was this?'

'Last week.'

It fit. It all fit. *Goddammit*. 'Did the guy who hired her know about you?'

224

Terror filled her eyes. 'I don't think so. I never met him. Did he kill her?'

'I don't know. You let her use your grandma's condo. What did you get out of it?'

'Ten per cent of her fee. And she put in a good word for me here. I needed a job.'

Clay thought of the body at the morgue, slashed ear to ear. It didn't seem likely that Mary had snitched on her friend, because Linda was still breathing. 'I'm going to have to give the cops information on your friend. They'll probably come to the lounge, ask questions.'

Her expression hardened. 'I don't like cops.'

Which in this case was a good thing. 'They'll be insistent,' he said.

'Why?'

'Because Mary's cop boyfriend, Ken, is also dead.'

Linda swayed. 'Oh, God. She thought Ken would protect her.'

'He didn't.'

Panic flared in her eyes. 'I have to get out of here. I can't let him kill me too.'

'Can you go to your grandmother's condo?'

Her lips twisted. 'No. She still hasn't forgiven me for the last time I got in trouble. I got some money put away. I'll go tonight. As soon as my shift's done and I get paid.'

He might have felt sorrier for the woman, but she'd knowingly participated in a scheme to defraud and deceive, not that he was in any hurry to report the crime. Escape was probably her best option. *You just don't want her talking to the cops.*

Well, yeah, that too. But as far as Clay was concerned, it all worked out, leaving him free to catch Reardon. And find Nicki. When he did, he'd give Sherman all the details he could.

'Good luck,' Clay said. 'And be careful.' He left the club feeling the need for a shower. He'd hit his hotel, grab a few hours' sleep, then drive to Ocean City to find Nic.

He'd driven a few miles when his phone rang. Alyssa's cell. Dread lay heavy on his chest.

'Did you find her?' he asked tautly.

'No.' She sounded stilted. Upset. 'I tried to call you, but you didn't answer.'

'I was in a noisy place. What's wrong?'

'I got a hit on the Ted Gamble card. It was used tonight at the Orion Hotel.'

'There?' he demanded. 'In Baltimore?'

'Yes. And . . . and I was tired, so I started for my place. I pass Nicki's apartment on my way. I drove through her parking lot. Clay, her car is there.'

Clay's heart stopped. 'What? Are you sure?'

'Yes. It's her car. It's not in Ocean City.'

But the tracking device was in Ocean City, which meant someone had taken it off her car. Probably Nicki, since her car was there. A thief would have stolen it. Clay's hands were shaking. 'I'm going to get my files from the hotel safe, then I'm coming home. Where are you?'

'In my apartment.'

Clay thought of Mary Stubbs and Ken Pullman, their throats slit. 'Stay there until I contact you,' he said hoarsely. 'Lock your door. Do you have a gun?'

'Yes,' she whispered. 'I know how to use it. My dad taught me.'

'Good. Load it, and if you see Evan come through your door, shoot him.'

Tuesday, May 4, 1.00 A.M.

Lucy had an entourage as she entered the morgue. In front of her, Alan pushed the gurney bearing the unidentified woman. Behind were Hyatt, Fitzpatrick and Stevie. Ruby brought up the rear, pushing the gurney that held Kevin's body, while staring at Lucy as if she were an alien.

Craig Mulhauser was waiting. 'Let's see what's what,' he said.

Lucy unzipped the bag and took a moment to study the body again.

'Well?' Hyatt snapped, stepping next to her at the table. 'Take off her dress so we can see if she's got a "II".'

Lucy ground her teeth, but kept her voice cordial. 'Lieutenant Hyatt, we need to examine this body properly. I'll see things in this light that I couldn't see under the street lamps in the parking lot. Please take a step back. It's procedure, sir.' She looked up at him, her brows lifted in mild challenge. 'I'm sure you understand about procedure.'

His eyes flashed but he took a step back. 'Just hurry.'

She and Craig examined the body, cataloguing the cuts and bruises on the victim's face and legs. Then Lucy focused on the dark dress that buttoned all the way to the victim's neck.

'This doesn't appear to be her dress,' Lucy said as she unfastened buttons. 'It's too big in the bodice—' She stopped, then grimaced. Not only was there a hole in the victim's torso, her breasts had been mutilated. Most of the tissue was gone. 'Oh, hell.'

Fitzpatrick leaned over her shoulder. 'Please tell me that was post-mortem.'

'It wasn't,' Lucy said grimly. 'She'd had a breast augmentation. He left behind part of the implant.'

Stevie took a place next to Craig on the other side of the table. 'I bet we'll find the serial number on the piece he left in her,' she said. 'Like he left the ring on Bennett.'

'But does she have a "II" on her back?' Hyatt demanded.

Lucy pulled the sleeves from the victim's arms and, with Craig's help, peeled the dress away from her torso. And even though she'd been expecting it, the sight of the evenly spaced burns on the victim's back made her stomach churn.

Hyatt bent sideways to get a closer look. And frowned. 'The bottom part looks like a "2",' he said. 'What the hell's that on top?'

It was a curlicued figure, grotesque in its precision.

'Looks like two "2"s connected in the middle,' Mulhauser said.

'No.' Lucy had seen the figure before. She'd drawn it before. In fact, she drew it every time she signed her name. 'Not "2"s. It's a cursive "L".'

'She's right,' Stevie said grimly. '"L" for "Lucy"?'

Hyatt was looking at Lucy even more suspiciously. 'Or "Lu*cinda*"?'

Lucy closed her eyes for a brief moment, wishing Hyatt to perdition even as her cheeks burned fire. She opened them to find Craig glaring at Hyatt balefully.

'Does it matter?' Craig asked tightly. 'You cannot blame her for this. Dr Trask has done nothing wrong.'

'Except that she has kept secrets from us since this began,' Hyatt said snidely.

Craig's jaw tightened. 'She has kept her private life *private*. It's not your business or my business what she does after she leaves here, as long as it's legal. Not. Your. Business.'

Lucy touched his gloved hand with hers. 'It's okay, Craig. Really.'

'It matters,' Fitzpatrick said, his voice even and soothing without being patronizing. 'But only because whoever killed this woman knew about the club. He may have had access to the keys at the valet station, which explains how he gained access to her car. It matters because of how it connects. But that's all, Dr Mulhauser.'

'Then find the goddamn connection,' Craig snapped.

'Finding this victim's identity would be a good start,' Stevie said quietly.

'We'll suit up and remove the remaining fragment of breast implant,' Lucy said. 'He left it there for a reason. Let's find out why.'

Tuesday, May 4, 2.30 A.M.

'Her name is Janet Gordon,' JD said, putting the woman's driver's license photo on his desk. He and Stevie were at their desks and had Hyatt on the speaker phone. The lieutenant had gone home for the night. *Thank God.* 'She's sixty, currently unmarried, divorced three times, and lived downtown about five blocks from Russ Bennett's condo on the Harbor. So far the proximity is the only similarity we've found.'

'Other than that she and Bennett are both dead,' Hyatt said dryly. 'Is Gordon one of Bennett's women?'

228

'She's not on the list we got from the courier,' JD said. 'Doesn't mean she's not one of his women, but she's a bit out of the age bracket.'

'Wouldn't be the first time a guy slept with a woman old enough to be his mother,' Hyatt said. 'Is she from Anderson Ferry?'

'That we don't know,' Stevie said. 'Yet.'

'She doesn't have a Facebook account?' Hyatt asked sarcastically.

Across the desk, Stevie rolled her eyes. 'No, sir, she does not. We've got warrants in progress for her home, her phone records and her financials. If the pattern holds, her bank account will either be wiped already or will become wiped. If her account hasn't yet been wiped, we may be able to track where the funds go if there's an attempt.'

JD's cell phone buzzed. It was Lucy. Excusing himself, he walked away from their desks so that Hyatt couldn't hear him. 'Hi,' he said quietly.

'Hi,' she said briskly. Professionally. 'I got confirmation from the silicon manufacturer on the surgeon who did Janet Gordon's plastic surgery.'

'Let me guess. Dr Russell Bennett.'

'Yes.'

'Well I can't say that I'm surprised. Are you two done with her cut?'

'We just finished. I'm typing the prelim now. Cause of death appears to be the blunt force trauma to her skull. As with the first victim, removal of tongue and eyes was pre-mortem, removal of the heart was post. The burn marks on her back are of smaller diameter.'

'Made with a different cigarette.'

'Yes. I sent Ruby out to buy a variety of brands. The first victim could have been burned with any one of several brands. Janet Gordon was burned with Virginia Slims.'

'I wonder why.'

'He may have chosen a small diameter so he wouldn't run out of room for the "L".'

'That's very premeditated.'

'So is cutting out her heart. There was another difference.

229

This victim didn't have nearly as much blood in the thoracic cavity as the first victim.'

'Meaning?' he asked. 'In layman's terms, please.'

'He sucked out her blood. With the first victim, there was more blood in the chest. He'd sopped up some of it with the towel he put in the cavity. This victim was relatively clean.'

'What could he have used to suck her blood?'

'Considering the use of a Sawzall to do the actual cut, I'm thinking Shop-Vac.'

JD grimaced. 'So the same device was used to remove the heart of this victim?'

'Maybe not the exact same one, but one of similar make and model. We did find some bruising that you're going to want to see later. I've sent digital photos to your email, so you can take a look now. When we turned her over, there were two very crisply defined semicircular bruises. Both appear to be part of a wheel tire, one much larger than the other.'

'Like on a wheelchair?' he asked.

'Exactly. It's post-mortem, so Craig and I thought she'd been laid against it at close quarters. Maybe in the trunk of a car. We pulled fibers from her hair and sent them and her dress to Drew. The fibers are short and stiff, like carpet fibers, but he can tell you more. Her fingernails have been severely clipped, back past the quick. This looks like a woman who would have had an expensive manicure, so it follows that her killer clipped her nails.'

'She fought back, then. How do you know she'd have a manicure?'

'Because she has well-tended feet with a fresh pedicure. I told you yesterday morning, in my business I see a lot of feet.'

There was a brief pause and JD could picture her studying her notes with that intensity that he now knew was so much more.

'Her stomach was empty, her blood alcohol zero. That's all I'll put in the preliminary report. We'll be looking at tissue and tox reports as they become available.' She hesitated. 'Craig said he'd assist Dr Bellamy with Kevin Drummond's procedure tomorrow. I'll be here, but in another room. I can listen and ask questions.'

It would be hard for her to do, he knew. 'Thank you.'

'It's all right. His parents, are they all right?'

'As all right as they can possibly be. Morton and Skinner went to tell them earlier.'

'They were in the conference room with Hyatt yesterday,' she said, her tone grown cool.

'They didn't know what Hyatt had planned. They knew the facts, knew you weren't found guilty.' She said nothing, quiet for so long he finally said, 'Lucy?'

'I really need to go,' she said, sounding defeated.

'Wait.' He wanted to snarl it, but kept his voice merely urgent. 'What did I say?'

'Good night, Detective. Don't worry about me. I'm going home with Craig. He and his wife have a spare room. He'll bring me in tomorrow and I'll rent my own car. I won't take any unnecessary chances. You'll let me know when I can return to my apartment?'

'Don't do this.' Now he did snarl.

'What? Don't go back to my apartment? You mean ever?' Her tone was now artificially pleasant, which grated even more.

'You know what I mean. Don't push me away, Lucy.'

'Good night, Detective,' she said again and hung up, leaving him to pinch the bridge of his nose in frustration.

He turned to find Stevie watching him. She pointed meaningfully to the speaker phone, her brows lifted. 'Fitzpatrick just got off the phone, sir. JD?'

JD returned to his desk. 'Bennett did Janet Gordon's plastic surgery.'

Stevie frowned. 'Her facelift, too?'

'That I don't know. This came from the breast implant manufacturer. They wouldn't know about her facelift. Why?'

'Because Brandi said Russ Bennett did breasts and his partner did faces.'

'Regardless,' Hyatt said, 'this should give Miss Montgomery ammo to get a warrant for the practice's medical records. What else, Detective?'

JD gave them the autopsy information. 'We need to get more info on Janet Gordon's background. Find out how she connects to the others. Besides being dead.'

'When can you get into her apartment?' Hyatt asked.

'Daphne said we'd need to wait until morning.' Stevie checked her watch. 'Which is only five hours away.'

'Then go home,' Hyatt said. 'Get some rest and be in my office at oh-nine. I'll have Morton and Skinner there too.'

'Oh,' Stevie said. 'I almost forgot. I contacted Dr Berman this afternoon, after we left the first Mrs Bennett's house. I asked him to consult with us on this case. He's a psychologist,' she said to JD. 'Excellent profiler.'

'I've heard of him,' JD said, 'but never met him.'

'Then you're in for a treat. He's a little off the beaten path.'

'Speaking of off the beaten path,' Hyatt said, 'we'll talk about the employees of that club of Dr Trask's tomorrow. That defense attorney, Thorne, would not cooperate.'

'No, he wouldn't. He refused to give us the client list,' Stevie said to JD. 'Told us to get a warrant. Daphne's working on that, too.'

'I heard,' JD said, his tone guarded.

'So while you are *sleeping*,' Hyatt said, innuendo dripping from every word, 'get Dr Trask to give you that list.'

JD's face heated, both in embarrassment and anger. 'I won't see her until the next time we go to the morgue, which will be tomorrow. I'll ask her then.'

'Don't *ask* her, Fitzpatrick. *Tell* her. And if she refuses, tell her that I'll put a squad car out in front of her place every night with its lights flashing until she or Thorne cooperates.'

'She won't agree, even if you put ten squad cars in front of her club.'

'Make her agree. Sweet-talk her.' Hyatt paused. 'Or whatever.'

JD opened his mouth to respond but Stevie cut in quickly, probably saving his career. 'We'll see you tomorrow morning, sir,' she said. 'Now we're *all* going to get some sleep.' She hit the speaker button and the line went dead. 'JD, don't let him draw you into an argument. He likes to do that.'

'Why?' JD asked, annoyed.

'I don't know. It's always worse when he's between wives. Once he gets married again, he'll argue with his wife and leave us alone.' She shrugged. 'It's like he has to argue a certain amount every day or he goes into withdrawal.'

JD smiled, as she'd intended. 'Okay. Tomorrow then.' He stood up, suddenly so weary that his vision frayed around the edges. 'I think I'll hit the crib upstairs versus driving home. If I'm not at my desk when you get here tomorrow, wake me up, okay?'

'Will do.' Stevie rose, a frown on her face. 'You know we're going to have to check out every person that works at Lucy's club, right?'

JD nodded. 'Yes. The only person I know isn't involved is Lucy herself. She was either on stage or with me, the entire time.'

'But her friends weren't.'

'No,' JD said, not relishing the prospect of questioning Lucy's friends.

'We'll worry about it tomorrow,' Stevie said. 'I'm going home.' She stopped at the elevator as he headed to the crib. 'By the way, you do know what you said, right?'

JD looked back with a puzzled frown. 'What?'

'When you were on the phone with her. You said something and she got mad, right? Then you said, "What did I say?" You *do* know what you said, don't you?'

JD shook his head. 'I have no idea. Do you?'

'Oh, yeah. You said that Morton and Skinner knew she'd been "found not guilty".'

JD closed his eyes. 'Instead of saying she was innocent.'

'I imagine if you've sat through an entire trial, having been unjustly accused, that would be an important distinction,' Stevie said quietly. 'Think about it.'

The stupidity of his words hit him full force. 'As if I'll be able to do anything but.'

Tuesday, May 4, 6.30 A.M.

Clay crept into Nicki's apartment building unseen, his step heavy with dread. It was still early and the neighbors had not yet ventured

233

outside. Not that they'd be coming out any time soon anyway. Most were creatures of the night, loners, like Nic.

It was a hovel of a building that probably should have been condemned. But Nicki liked it, or said she did. Clay thought it gave her an excuse to be solitary.

He forced himself up the stairs, his heart heavier than his feet. *Please. Please.* With every mile he'd driven, he'd worried, his fear growing. Now that he was here, he could barely put one foot in front of the other. *Move it, Maynard,* he barked in his mind.

He stood outside her door and closed his eyes. *No.* But he knew the smell. *Please. Please, let it be anything but this.* Maybe she hadn't taken out the trash. Maybe . . . But he knew.

His hands shaking, he pulled on gloves, then let himself in with the key he'd taken from the emergency ring at the office. *Please, please.* He flinched as he entered and closed the door behind him. *She's dead.* Years of being a soldier and a cop had taught him to view death stoically. *She's dead.* But Nic was his friend. His partner.

Move. He tied a handkerchief over his mouth and, gritting his teeth, forced his feet to walk the fifty feet to her bedroom. Her door was open. She was on the bed. She . . . Her insides . . . on the sheets. *Can't breathe.* He stared, horror making his limbs inoperable. *God. No.*

Nicki. Tears rolled down his face and he couldn't move. Couldn't breathe. *Oh God, Nic. What did he do to you?* Gutted. The SOB had gutted her.

Goddammit. It was a whimper in his mind.

Move. Again he forced his feet to move until he stood next to her bed, his breath now coming in labored pants. Her bed had once been white. No more. It was red. *Red.*

His teeth clenched, he looked down, blocking out all the red. Ignoring the flies, Clay focused on her right ear, where the sonofabitch's blade had curved up and around. He wasn't sure how long he stood there, staring at her ear, his own heartbeat the only thing he could hear.

Then something within him snapped and he backed out of her room, on autopilot now. Nic kept no client files out in the open – her neighborhood was too bad. Mechanically Clay went to her kitchen and moved aside all the cans of soup in the pantry, revealing the safe he'd installed for her himself. His hand steady, he dialed the combination and popped it open.

Her laptop was inside, along with six file folders. He took them and closed the safe, replacing the soup cans. He locked her front door behind him and placed her things in his trunk. He rapidly cleaned out Nicki's car of all receipts and loose papers.

Then he got in his own car, drove a mile, then stopped.

He got out, walked to the grass shoulder, sank to his knees and threw up.

Fourteen

He stood at the mirror, frowning at his reflection. He tilted his head to better see his neck where two red scratches stood out like beacons. The valet had got him but good. Luckily they were low enough that his collar covered them. He buttoned his shirt, knotted his tie, and nodded at the result. Nobody would see. Nobody would know. Soon it wouldn't matter anyway.

Soon he'd be sailing the seas in the *Satisfaction* because soon all the names on his list would be in Lucy Trask's morgue.

He had to hand it to the woman. She'd maintained her double life like a CIA pro. That she'd cut up dead people all day had been a revelation to all those freaks at the club. Nobody knew the other secrets she held, but they would soon.

Soon everyone would know what kind of person Lucy Trask really was. Soon everyone would know what she was willing to do to get her way. What lies she was willing to tell. In due time he'd expose every part of her life for everyone to see. *And then she'll be mine.* Soon.

But today he had a different fish to fillet. He put on his jacket, tugged his shirt cuffs into place. Janet Gordon's son should be here soon. His flight was due in an hour.

From his pocket he withdrew one of the business cards he'd made on the printer in James Cannon's condo. *Biddle and Light, Attorneys at Law.* After seeing his mother's remains, there would be few people Ryan would trust. His mother's attorney would be one of them.

Because Ryan didn't really have a choice. If he wanted Mommy's money, he'd have to talk to Mommy's lawyer. *We'll have a nice little chat. And then he'll die.*

Killing Ryan wouldn't take quite as long as the others, he didn't think. Ryan hadn't profited from his sin like the others. Not like Edwards or Bennett or Janet Gordon.

Certainly not like Lucy Trask.

If he played his cards right, he could be finished with Ryan by dinnertime and onto the next name. *I might just make it to Anderson Ferry by nightfall.* Lucy had taken the detective there last night, which displeased him. They'd gone straight to the Bennetts' house, presumably to notify the parents of their son's unfortunate demise.

His device was accurate to fifteen feet, so he was sure they'd gone nowhere else, which was good. He wanted to control the Trask family reunion. She was getting very chummy with that cop, though. He wondered what trouble she was stirring up. Or trying to silence.

Tuesday, May 4, 7.50 A.M.

JD pulled up behind Stevie's car, already parked on the curb in front of Janet Gordon's apartment building. Stevie waited on the front stoop.

He'd slept poorly, tossing and turning and wondering if Lucy would speak to him again. And, of course, reliving the alley. The little sleep he had gotten had been filled with dreams of dark rooms and swirling music and a naked Lucy in his bed.

The last might never become a reality if he couldn't convince her to talk to him again. Which would never happen if he didn't catch whoever was taunting her with mutilated bodies.

'Daphne got the warrant?' JD asked Stevie when he got to the stoop.

'In my pocket,' she said. 'Covers the apartment, phone and financials. The super is upstairs with a key. The officer we put at her door says nobody approached all night.'

'What about the warrant for Thorne's client list?' JD asked.

'The judge said he'd take that one under advisement.' Stevie shrugged and opened the apartment building's door. 'Try to sweet-talk Lucy, okay, JD?'

'I don't think anything I have to say has a lot of currency with her just now.'

'She's a logical woman. Just apologize for saying she wasn't found guilty versus she was innocent. Blame fatigue, male stupidity, or anything you want. Flash your dimple. That would sure as hell sway me.'

Except it was more than that. *She said I'm not good for her.* 'I'll try,' he said.

The super was waiting by Janet Gordon's door, his hand out for the warrant. The exchange made, JD and Stevie pulled on gloves while the super unlocked the door.

'Nice,' JD murmured. There were expensive paintings on every wall and a baby grand piano in one corner. 'When was the last time you saw Mrs Gordon?'

'A few days ago,' the super said.

'Did she have a husband or boyfriend?'

'She's a widow. She has "gentlemen callers", but no regular boyfriend. Not unless you count that doctor fella, which I don't, no matter what the gossipers say.'

'What doctor?' JD asked, even though he was sure he knew.

'Young fella. Hey, don't touch that!' he exclaimed when Stevie began going through the desk drawers. 'Mrs Gordon will have my head.'

Stevie looked up, annoyed. 'Sir, were you listening when I introduced myself?'

'Yeah. Of course.' The super frowned. 'Not really. It was early.'

JD wanted to roll his eyes. 'Fitzpatrick and Mazzetti. We're Homicide.'

The super's mouth fell open. 'Homicide? Then she's dead?'

'Yes, sir,' Stevie said. 'Now, tell us about the doctor she hung around with.'

'I don't remember his name, but he was young enough to be her son. I never thought there was anything between them, but my wife, she said more power to Mrs Gordon if she can snag a younger man and hold him.'

'What did the young doctor look like?' JD asked impatiently.

'Five eleven, dark hair. I don't think they were a couple. I don't think he liked her.'

The description matched Russ Bennett. 'Then why was he with her?' JD asked.

'I assumed it was for her money. She was loaded. Her last husband was in oil.'

'Why didn't you think he liked her?' Stevie asked.

'I don't know. It was just his attitude. Like he'd kill her if he could.'

'Who was her next of kin?' JD asked.

'It's on her lease. I'd have to go get a copy.'

JD smiled mildly. 'Please do that. Now.'

Grumbling, the super went to do as he was told.

'He's probably telling every tenant in the building that she's dead,' Stevie said.

'I know. This kitchen is immaculate.' JD opened the refrigerator. 'No food.' He opened a drawer. 'Menus for all the expensive places. She must've spent a fortune on restaurants.'

'She was loaded.' Stevie walked back to the bedroom. 'JD. *Come see.*'

It was a bedroom decorated for a teenage boy. Trophies lined the shelves and banners hung on the walls. All bore the initials AFHS.

'Anderson Ferry High School,' JD murmured, unsurprised. He picked up a trophy. 'Ryan Agar, Most Yards Rushed.'

'Football player,' Stevie said.

'Not just any football player.' JD picked up a framed photo from the top of a highboy. 'His team picture, senior year. This team won the regional championship that year. Look at the names.' He held the photo so she could see. 'There's Ryan Agar and Malcolm Edwards, aka Butch, and Linus Trask, aka Buck.'

'Brother of Lucy, aka Lucinda.'

JD held the photo closer, studying the jersey numbers. 'Malcolm was a defensive tackle and Linus was the quarterback. MVP.'

'How do you know he was MVP from the picture?'

'I don't. Lucy told me on the drive back from Anderson Ferry last night.'

'So the boy was golden, died in a motorcycle accident a few weeks after graduation and twenty-one years later Lucy isn't speaking to her parents. About right?'

'Yes.' He bagged the photo. 'You take the closet, I'll take the drawers.'

They searched in silence until Stevie called, 'Box of yearbooks. I'll grab 'em.'

JD was sorting through pictures and letters shoved into the highboy's top drawer. 'Ryan was accepted to college on a football scholarship, but he flunked out. Here are letters warning him of academic probation. And one dismissing him from the university.'

'Seems odd for a boy to keep letters like that,' Stevie said.

'He's never lived here.' The super was back. 'Her son, I mean. He's her contact.'

'Ryan Agar?' Stevie asked.

'Yeah. He visits, but only at Christmas. I got the impression there was no love lost there. Here's her lease application. The son lives on a ranch in the middle of nowhere in Colorado.'

'It'll take him at least a day to get here,' Stevie said. 'Let's get CSU here to fingerprint.'

'I can go down to the morgue and ID her,' the super said, sounding a little too excited.

'That won't be necessary,' JD said. He walked the super out the door. 'Can you wait downstairs for the crime-scene unit? They'll need to be shown which apartment.'

The super did not look fooled. 'If you want me to leave, just say so.'

'Not at all,' JD lied. 'But every moment we talk is a moment we're not investigating Mrs Gordon's death. We would like a list of Mrs Gordon's "gentlemen callers" if you know their names, plus anyone in the building she was friendly with.'

The super snorted as he walked away. 'Janet Gordon wasn't

friendly with nobody. Not unless you could do something for her. But I'll make you a list.'

'Why would she make this room up for her son if he never lived here?' Stevie asked. 'It's not like he grew up here and moved away. This is kind of creepy.'

'I don't know. We should ask that shrink you invited to morning meeting.'

'Lennie Berman,' Stevie said. 'Let's do that. I'm going to check out her bedroom and bath. Why don't you finish checking the desk and see if there's anything on the computer in the living room?'

A search of Gordon's desk turned up various invitations to charity functions, bills, and bank statements. The bank statements were a month old. On a hunch, JD touched the computer mouse and the screen lit up. He brought up an Internet browser and scrolled through Gordon's favorites until he came to her bank's website.

Her user name and password fields were filled, the password a series of asterisks. 'Stevie, can you come here?' he called, waiting until she was watching before clicking the log-on button.

'Why do people save their settings?' Stevie asked. 'On bank websites, especially.'

'I guess because they don't expect to be murdered and have a cop sitting at their PC snooping around,' JD said, staring at the screen. What had been nearly a two-hundred-thousand-dollar balance just days before was now a big zero. 'He wiped her out, just like the others.'

'Looks like it was the night before last. Did she have any appointments then?'

JD opened Gordon's calendar. 'Nothing scheduled. Lucy was right. She'd had a manicure and a pedicure that afternoon. The damage to her nails was done by her killer.'

Stevie looked over his shoulder. 'Janet had a date that night, JD. Look, she has a regularly scheduled appointment with her manicurist every other Tuesday. She had one last Tuesday, but went again less than a week later this past Sunday.'

'The same day she was probably snatched.'

'Exactly. This time she lists a place and a manicurist's name.

On all the other appointments she just has 'Mani/Pedi'. This last appointment was an emergency job. Not her usual place and on a Sunday. Not many nail places open on Sunday.'

'So she had a date, but it wasn't listed on her calendar. Why?'

'I don't know. But I'm betting whoever she met for dinner is our guy.'

JD was about to agree when Stevie's cell phone rang.

'Mazzetti.' She listened a minute, then her eyes widened abruptly. 'That's not possible. How did he get here so fast?' She looked at JD with a perplexed frown. 'Guess who just showed up in Hyatt's office? Ryan Agar.'

'No way,' JD said in disbelief.

Stevie held her phone flat and hit the speaker button. 'We're both here, sir.'

'He is here,' Hyatt said, 'and upset over the death of his mother. He's demanding to see her body. I asked him to wait until you arrived.'

'Then he didn't come from Colorado,' JD said. 'He had to have been local. Where did he come from and how did he know his mother was dead?'

'He came from Colorado,' Hyatt said. 'He showed me his plane ticket. He left Denver on the midnight red-eye.'

'How?' JD asked harshly, having the feeling that Hyatt was drawing this out.

'He got a call to his cell at eight P.M. Mountain Time last night from the Baltimore PD saying his mother had been murdered and could he please come and identify the body.'

JD clenched his jaw. 'Sonofabitch. The killer called him. There's no other way.'

Stevie's frown had deepened. 'Who from Baltimore PD called him?'

'The "detective" ID'd himself as JD Fitzpatrick,' Hyatt said flatly.

JD blinked, stunned. 'Me?'

'You, Detective. This killer obviously knows you're on the case.'

JD's temper was bubbling. *Sonofabitch killer is mocking us*. With an effort he tamped it down. 'Where did the call to his cell come from?'

'I don't know yet. Both of you need to get in here right away and deal with the son.'

'We will,' Stevie said. 'Before we hang up, you need to know that Mr Agar went to high school with Bennett, Edwards, and Dr Trask's brother.'

Hyatt sighed irritably. 'Of course he did.'

'And Janet Gordon's bank account has already been wiped,' JD added.

'Dammit,' Hyatt hissed. 'Of course it has. I'll see you both in my office, forthwith.'

Stevie hung up and shook her head furiously. 'This perp's fuckin' with us, JD.'

JD reined in his own fury. 'Then let's fuck with him.'

Tuesday, May 4, 8.10 A.M.

'Rhoda.' Lucy sat at Craig Mulhauser's kitchen table as a plate of eggs and bacon was placed before her. 'I wish you hadn't gone to so much trouble.'

Craig's wife bustled around her kitchen, making Lucy think of her own mother. Rarely had she bustled around a kitchen, but there had been a breakfast table and a smile over cornflakes.

But those days were long gone. *Now she just peeks at me through window blinds.* And that hurt, far more than Lucy wanted to admit. She'd managed to block it from her mind until she'd woken to the luxurious aroma of Rhoda's homemade bread. Her mother had made bread, once upon a time. It had been their special treat.

Going back yesterday had been more painful than Fitzpatrick could ever have guessed. *At least I don't have to go back again.* Her native guide duty was done.

'It was no trouble at all,' Rhoda said. 'I always cook for Craig before work.'

From the stunned look on Craig's face as he sat down to his own plate, that was an utter falsehood and Lucy had to smile, just a little.

'Eat up,' Rhoda chirped. 'You two have a busy day.'

'That's for sure,' Craig muttered. 'Damn bodies keep piling up.'

'I'll work on the backlog,' Lucy promised between mouthfuls. 'Delicious, Rhoda.'

Rhoda beamed. 'I can make more.'

'No, no,' Lucy said. 'I won't be able to finish this. Although I am hungry. It was a long time since my last meal.' It was the drive-thru burger she'd shared with Fitzpatrick, eons ago. But it hadn't been eons. It hadn't even been twelve hours.

She'd tossed and turned most of the few hours she'd spent on the Mulhausers' guest bed, her mind churning. Thinking about poor Kevin and the dead woman, Janet Gordon, wondering who she was. *And how I connect to her.*

But mostly she'd thought of JD Fitzpatrick, replaying the alley in her mind. It had been . . . mind-blowing. *God.* It had also been the stupidest thing she'd ever done, and she'd done some truly stupid things. *Really, Lucy. In an* alley? *God.* Even Gwyn had never done that.

What was I thinking? She hadn't been. The long day and the night and the going home and the music and the way he'd looked as he'd watched her play . . . *Like he could gobble me up.* And suddenly she'd had to have him. *Then.* And when he'd put his hands on her . . . *God.*

She shivered. It had been amazing. *And it can never happen again.*

'Lucy?' Craig asked.

Lucy looked up, saw both Craig and Rhoda watching her, concerned, and realized she'd been staring at her nearly empty plate. 'I'm sorry?'

'Your cell phone, dear,' Rhoda said. 'It's buzzing.'

It was. Flustered, Lucy grabbed it and hit the green button. 'Hello?'

'Where the hell are you?' Gwyn demanded.

'I'm at Dr Mulhauser's house. Where are you?'

'At my place, standing on my doormat because you have my key.'

Lucy winced. 'I'm sorry. Why are you there? I thought you were at Royce's.'

'I was, but I forgot my pills. I figured you'd be here. Why are you there?'

'I didn't want to stay by myself last night.'

'Oh,' Gwyn said, deflated. 'I guess I can understand that. I just assumed that big hot cop would stay with you.'

Lucy's cheeks flamed. 'That isn't going to happen.' *Ever again.* She cupped the phone, looked at Craig. 'I have my friend's key. Can you drop me there on the way in?'

'Of course,' Craig said.

'Okay, Gwyn, I'll be there in twenty.'

'Oh, wait. Hold on.' There was muted conversation, then Gwyn was back. 'My neighbor found the key I gave her last year when she took care of my plants.' There were sounds of a door opening. 'Good thing she had my spare . . .'

The phone went silent.

'Gwyn?' Lucy strained to hear. 'Are you there?'

'Oh, God,' Gwyn whispered. 'Lucy, there's a box on my coffee table.'

Lucy's stomach dropped. 'Is it wrapped?'

'Yes. With red, purple and pink hearts.'

'And a big red bow,' Lucy said grimly. Across the table, Craig's face paled as he understood what had happened. 'Get out of there, now.'

'I closed the door. I'm calling 911.'

'Can you go to that neighbor's place?'

'Yes.' Gwyn's voice shook. 'Do you think he's still here?'

'I don't know, but we're taking no chances. Is Royce there?'

'He's waiting in the car.' Gwyn sounded small and frightened, and Lucy's jaw clenched. How *dare* he involve her friends?

It was supposed to be you, Lucy. You were supposed to be there. The thought made her sick. What if Gwyn had been there alone?

'Okay,' Lucy said, staying calm, 'I want you to call 911, then call Royce to come up and wait with you.'

'Okay.' Gwyn was crying and Lucy had to swallow her fury.

'I'll call Fitzpatrick, then Thorne. I'll be there as soon as I can.' Fingers trembling, Lucy dialed Fitzpatrick's number from memory. 'JD, it's Lucy. We have another box.'

'*What?* Where?'

245

'Gwyn's place. I stayed with the Mulhausers last night, but I was supposed to be there. She's calling 911. Can you meet us there? It's my apartment complex, across the green.'

'I'll be there as soon as I can. I have to go into the office first.'

Lucy frowned. 'What's happened?'

He hesitated a moment, then swore softly. 'Janet Gordon's son is Ryan Agar.'

'I don't know that name, but let me guess. He graduated with my brother.'

'Yes. He played on that same championship team.'

She sighed. 'So did you call him? Do I need to do an ID with him today?'

'Yes on the ID, no on the call. Not exactly, anyway. Somebody called Agar at ten our time last night. Told him his mother was dead.'

'That's impossible. Unless . . .' Lucy's jaw went tight as understanding dawned. 'That motherfucker.' She winced. 'Sorry, Rhoda.'

Rhoda Mulhauser looked concerned and fascinated all at once. 'That's okay.'

'It gets better,' Fitzpatrick said. 'The caller said he was me.'

Lucy bit back another curse. 'He's playing with us. Where is the son?'

'In Hyatt's office. I have to go check him out. I'll let Hyatt and Drew know about the box. We'll have someone there as soon as possible. Do not go into Gwyn's apartment yourself.'

'I'm not stupid, JD,' she snapped.

'I know,' he said quietly. 'I'm sorry. I wanted to . . . Never mind. I'll be there as soon as I can. I'll send one of the others out right away.'

Never mind. What had he wanted to say? Or do? Lucy stood up, putting him out of her mind as best she could. 'Thanks for breakfast, Rhoda. Craig, we need to hurry.'

'I'll stay with you at your friend's place until Fitzpatrick arrives,' Craig said.

'Actually, you'll be needed in the morgue to do an ID. Next of kin of last night's victim has come from out of town. There'll be lots of cops at Gwyn's. I'll be fine.' She softened her refusal with a smile. 'But thank you.'

Tuesday, May 4, 8.40 A.M.

Ryan Agar was a big, quiet man. His face was tanned, and even though he was only about forty, he looked much older. It was his eyes, JD thought. They were desolate.

He sat at a table in one of the interview rooms, an untouched cup of coffee in front of his folded hands. 'I'd like to see my mother.'

'We're making the arrangements,' JD said. 'We weren't expecting you this early.'

Agar met his eyes. 'So I hear. You're not the man who called me.'

'No, sir,' JD said. 'We're tracing that call now. How did that other man sound?'

'I don't know. His voice wasn't as deep. Had more of an accent.'

'What kind of accent, Mr Agar?' Stevie asked.

'Not southern, but not northern. Definitely not Midwest. Why would he pretend to be you?'

'We don't know,' JD said. 'Do you know anyone who'd want to hurt your mother?'

'My mother was not a milk-and-cookies kind of woman. Not many people liked her unless they wanted something from her. But to murder her? That I don't know.'

'When was the last time you saw her?' Stevie asked.

'Last Christmas. I make a yearly pilgrimage.' His voice had grown sardonic. 'We have dinner at a fancy restaurant. She gives me a gift which I cannot use and tells me how well I'm looking. We exchange pleasantries that mean nothing and then I go home.' His eyes unexpectedly filled with tears. 'Please tell me she didn't suffer.'

JD and Stevie exchanged a glance and Agar's face crumpled. He bowed his head as silent sobs shook his massive shoulders. JD placed a box of tissues at his elbow and he and Stevie patiently waited for the initial storm to pass.

'We're sorry for your loss,' Stevie said softly when Agar's

shoulders finally stilled. 'We know this is a hard time for you, but we need to ask you some questions.'

Agar lifted his head, his glare harsh. 'Do you have any leads?'

'We do,' Stevie said, 'but only because your mother isn't the first victim. Mr Agar, do you know a man named Russell Bennett?'

For a moment Agar froze. Then he swallowed. 'The name sounds familiar.'

'He was found dead yesterday morning,' Stevie said. 'Many of his injuries are similar to those we found on your mother. Do you know if they knew each other?'

Agar frowned, his confusion feigned. 'It's possible. She knew a lot of people.'

'Mr Agar,' Stevie said, 'you went to high school with a Russell Bennett.'

He swallowed again, harder this time. 'Oh. That Russell Bennett? I kind of remember him. We lost touch after high school.'

'What about Malcolm Edwards?' JD asked softly. 'Do you kind of remember him?'

Agar's eyes flickered wildly. 'Why?'

'Because he disappeared two months ago. He's thought to have been lost at sea.'

'I don't see what that has to do with my mother or me.'

'Edwards and Bennett both had their bank accounts wiped the day they were last seen.' JD let the statement hang and watched as realization dawned in Agar's eyes.

What color remained behind his tanned face slid away. 'My mother's accounts were wiped? All of them?'

'At least one,' Stevie said. 'These men and your mother are connected. They all came from your hometown, they all had their accounts wiped, and they're all dead.'

Agar moistened his lips. 'Why?'

'That's what we want to know,' Stevie said, her voice dropping to a menacing murmur.

'There's one more connection, Mr Agar,' JD said coldly, when Agar didn't reply. 'Bennett was a plastic surgeon. He did at least one procedure for your mother. And if we're not mistaken, he visited her apartment on more than one occasion.'

Agar flinched. 'Bennett operated on my mother? No, that's not possible.'

'Why would you say that's not possible?' Stevie asked.

'B-because,' Agar stammered. 'Mother was beautiful. She didn't need surgery.'

Stevie sat back, her expression annoyed. 'Mr Agar, I have three bodies in the morgue. Please don't bullshit me.'

His eyes widened. 'Three? I thought you said Edwards was lost at sea.'

'He was,' Stevie said. 'A young man was murdered last night at the scene where we found your mother's body. Something is going on here, something that has to do with your hometown. What happened in Anderson Ferry, Mr Agar?'

'I said I don't know,' Agar said, his teeth clenched. 'I need to go. You have my cell number. Please call me when I can identify my mother's body.'

'What about Buck Trask?' JD asked, as he and Stevie had prearranged he would if Agar had gone the bullshit route, which he had.

Agar paused, halfway out of his chair. Slowly he sat back down. 'He died more than twenty years ago,' he said carefully. 'It was a tragic accident. What about him?'

'He's connected too,' JD said coldly. 'Or at least his family is.'

'I don't understand.'

'The bodies of both Bennett and your mother were discovered by Lucy Trask,' JD said. 'They were left for her to find.'

Agar shook his head. 'I don't understand what you mean. I don't remember her.'

'Buck's younger sister,' Stevie said.

Again he shook his head, a little more desperately. 'I don't know her. I don't know why she found my mother's body. Are we finished now?' He stood up. 'You can't keep me here.'

'You're right,' JD said levelly, 'but before you walk out of here, I want you to remember that somebody drew you here. There has to be a reason for that.'

'Are you saying I'm next?' he asked, fear in his voice.

JD shrugged. 'I'm saying I'd be careful,' he said, then rose to look Agar straight in the eye. 'I'm saying I think you know a lot more than you're telling. And I'm saying that if anyone else gets hurt, I'm holding you personally responsible.'

Agar's eyes closed and his throat worked nervously. JD hoped he'd talk, but then he opened his eyes and JD knew he would not. 'I need to go.'

'I'll take you to someone who can get you a list of hotels,' Stevie said, 'and get an officer to drive you to whichever you pick. My partner is right, Mr Agar. You were brought here for a reason. We'd hate to see anything happen to you.'

Agar nodded once but said no more.

JD watched the man go, irritated as hell. He picked up the phone on the table and called Hyatt. 'It's Fitzpatrick. Ryan Agar knows what this is all about and won't tell us. Stevie's helping him find a hotel room. We need to put a tail on him. My money says he's going to run.'

'I'll take care of the tail. You and Mazzetti get over here for morning meeting.'

'We will.' He hesitated. 'Have you heard from Drew about the newest box?'

'Not yet. Call him on your way. We're waiting for you.'

JD hung up, then dialed Drew, waiting several rings before he picked up. 'It's Fitzpatrick. You got the box?'

'Yes,' Drew said. 'X-ray says it's fist-sized. The blood on the resident's coffee table says we've probably got another heart and that it wasn't frozen.'

JD grimaced. 'It leaked?'

'All over the damn place. We've taken prints off the door and the knob and the table. Nothing else looks like it was disturbed. Morton and Skinner canvassed the building. Nobody saw anything. No cameras in this building, just like in Dr Trask's. Same development, different building. Shitty security.'

'Any sign of forced entry?'

'No. Appears they had a key.'

'Is Dr Trask still there?'

'Yes, standing outside in the hall with her friend. You want to talk to her?'

Tuesday, May 4, 8.50 A.M.

'We're never going to get that black fingerprint powder off the walls,' Gwyn said wearily. 'And that blood will never come out of the carpet.'

'It'll be okay,' Royce said, his arm around Gwyn's shoulders. 'I'll help you scrub.'

'And we'll get new carpet,' Lucy said. 'I'm sorry.'

Gwyn sighed. 'It's not your fault. I'm just glad we weren't here at the time.'

'Amen,' Thorne said. He'd come right away, just as he always did when they called. He stood behind them, feet spread, arms crossed. Like a bad-ass bodyguard, prepared for anything. 'From here on out, you two do not go anywhere alone.'

Royce nodded. 'Gwyn will stay with me tonight.'

Gwyn frowned up at him. 'I thought you had to go out of town tonight. You've got that sales review in Atlanta.'

'I'll move some things around, put my trip off for a few days. My client will understand. This is a lot more important.' Royce's expression was stern. 'What are the cops doing about this, Lucy? This has to stop.'

'I know,' Lucy said. 'Believe me, they know, too.'

'You should stay with us tonight,' Royce said. 'We have room.' His jaw tightened. 'And I have a gun. I'd like to see that prick try terrorizing someone his own size.'

Lucy thought of Gwyn's often graphic descriptions of the nights she spent with Royce. She wasn't sure if she could listen to the two of them . . . together. Especially when the memory of that damn alley was never far from her mind.

'Thanks, but I think I'll stay with Thorne tonight.' She glanced over her shoulder. 'If that's okay with you.'

'You know it is,' Thorne said simply. 'As long as you need it.'

They turned when Drew came through the door, holding his cell. 'It's for you, Dr Trask.'

A little puzzled, she took the phone. 'This is Dr Trask.'

'It's JD. I wanted to tell you that I won't be able to get over there. Hyatt's got a meeting scheduled and . . . well, I'm sorry.'

Lucy was conscious of Gwyn's and Thorne's worried expressions. 'Nothing's wrong,' she told them, then stepped to the edge of the landing for privacy. 'Is there? I mean, anything new?'

'Probably not. We just finished talking to Ryan Agar. When we mentioned your brother's name, we got a reaction. We told him you'd found the bodies, hoping he'd tell us the connection, but he insisted he didn't know.'

'But you think he's lying.'

'Yeah, I do. I want you to be careful, keep your eyes open in case he approaches you. He's about six four with reddish hair and a tanned face.'

'If he does, I'll call for help.'

'Good. Then call me. Where will you be today?'

'At the morgue. We've got a backload of bodies. Craig went in to do Janet Gordon's ID.'

'Oh. We thought you'd do it. We sent Agar to find a hotel until you were ready.'

'Craig's probably waiting for your call. When he's done with the ID, he'll start on . . .' She bit her lip, watching Thorne and Gwyn watching her. 'The other autopsy,' she said, not wanting to say Kevin's name. Thorne had spent most of the night grieving with the Drummond family.

'I understand. Lucy, I need to talk to you. Later. Alone.'

She closed her eyes, a shiver racing across her skin at the thought of the last time they were alone. They hadn't done much talking. 'Not a good idea.'

'I have a lot of questions. I'd like some answers. *Please*.'

It was the *please* that moved her. Or maybe she just wanted to say yes. 'All right. I get off at five. I'm probably staying with Thorne tonight.'

'All right. I'll try to break for dinner. Lucy, one more thing. Hyatt wants the list of your regular customers at the club. He says he'll put a squad car out front until you hand it over.'

Lucy's jaw tightened. 'I really don't like that man. Do you think he will?'

'Honestly, no. But someone there knew you were staying with Gwyn last night.'

'Or the killer assumed it. He might have stopped by my place first and seen the crime-scene label on the door. My staying with Gwyn would be an obvious leap.'

'He had a key.'

That stopped her cold. 'And if Gwyn had been home . . .' That left her colder.

'Will you try to get the list?'

'I'll ask him. He'll say no. But I'll try.'

'We'll be talking to your employees, too. We hope you'll encourage them to cooperate.'

'I will. I need to go. Drew wants his phone.'

'I'll call you when I get a break. Be careful.'

Yeah, she thought, hanging up. Easier said than done when Fitzpatrick got too close. She handed Drew his phone. 'Thank you.'

'No problem. Look, we'll be here a while. We've got your statements, so you can go. Do you need an escort?'

'No, I'll catch a ride with my friends.' *I need them. Especially now*, she thought as she rejoined the others. 'He says we can go. Thorne, can you drive me to work?'

Thorne checked his watch. 'I'm almost late to court, but if we hurry—'

'You go to court,' Royce interrupted. 'I'll drive and walk them both in. Don't worry.'

But Thorne clearly was. 'You know how to use that gun, Royce?' he murmured.

'Yeah.' Royce looked back at the CSU team, still working in Gwyn's apartment. 'I hope Lucy's cop figures this out quickly. My trigger finger's feeling damn twitchy.'

Lucy's cheeks heated. 'He's not my cop. Let's just all go to work.'

253

Fifteen

Tuesday, May 4, 9.10 A.M.

JD assumed that the man in Hyatt's guest chair was the shrink. He was about sixty and wore a tweed suit. Daphne had kicked convention to the curb and dragged a chair from someone else's desk into Hyatt's office. She sat on it like it was a throne. Hyatt glared at her from time to time.

It made JD want to buy her lunch.

'Is Agar gone?' Hyatt asked.

'He is,' Stevie said. 'He got a room at the Peabody. Tory Reading is driving him. She's his first shift tail, too.' She gestured to the man in the chair. 'Lennie, this is my new partner, JD Fitzpatrick. JD, meet Dr Lennie Berman.'

JD took the hand he offered. 'Dr Berman,' he said.

Berman nodded once. 'So who is Agar and why is he being tailed?'

JD and Stevie brought the group up to date. 'He knows something,' JD said firmly.

'I'd have to agree,' Berman said. 'But it sounds like Mr. Agar is more afraid of what he knows than he is of you. Is there another way to get to this information?'

'Yes,' Hyatt snapped. 'Make Agar more afraid of us.'

'Or,' JD said, 'we go back to Anderson Ferry and ask questions. Something ties these men together. I think Russell Bennett's father knows what it is.'

'Why kill Agar's mother, though?' Daphne asked. 'Why cut out her heart?'

254

'Maybe because he's a sick SOB?' Stevie said. 'We're pretty sure he used her death to draw the son back – and quickly. He could have waited for us to make the ID and notify next of kin. But then Agar wouldn't have made it here until this evening.'

'He's in a hurry,' Berman mused.

'He lost two weeks,' JD said. 'He killed Bennett, but Dr Trask was out of town.'

'So he froze the victim,' Berman said. 'He went to a lot of trouble to put the bodies where Dr Trask would find them, then he left her their hearts. You can't get much more symbolic than that. She's definitely at the center. Her brother died after high school?'

'Yes,' JD said. 'Motorcycle accident. He was eighteen. Dr Trask was only fourteen.'

'And she has no clue what the connection could be?'

'Not that she's aware of,' Stevie said. 'We know Bennett hated her and kept a file on her adult life. We also know Bennett had dozens of extramarital affairs. So far, twelve have had ties to his hometown. What gives with that?'

'I'd guess he had a sexual event occur back in that town. Something that he'd been trying to either re-create or forget. Given the sheer number of women, I'd say the second one, although I'd imagine he'd claim it was the first. He was trying to prove something to himself, one way or the other. We definitely need to go to that town.'

'We?' JD asked. 'You're going?'

'Oh, yes. If this killer is leaving no evidence, we have to find his motive. That is correct, isn't it? He's left no real evidence?'

JD nodded. 'So far. We're hoping the ME will get some skin scrapings from under the valet's nails, because it seems that's the only death he didn't execute off site.'

'What do we have on possible locations for his kills?' Hyatt asked.

'Somewhere near the water,' JD said. 'Bennett's first ex-wife remembers hearing seagulls when he called her. We think his killer had him by then.'

'We know he has access to a big-ass freezer, too,' Stevie said.

'Morton and Skinner made a list.' Hyatt gave them a copy. 'Morton said these are the facilities within fifty miles with a flash freezer big enough to handle a human body.'

Stevie skimmed the list. 'All of them run twenty-four-hour operations. It would have been hard for anyone to slip a body in there when nobody was looking.'

'But we know he did it,' Hyatt said. 'So keep looking. What else do we know?'

'He steals their money,' JD said. 'Edwards, Bennett and now Janet Gordon have had their bank accounts wiped. Gordon had close to two hundred grand taken.'

'We need IT to trace the transfers,' Stevie said. 'Hopefully the detectives working the Edwards case have some leads.'

Hyatt nodded. 'Find out. Who was the last person to see Janet Gordon alive?'

'Her manicurist saw her that afternoon,' JD said. 'Assuming she went out for a date, somebody would have seen her there.'

'What about the victims?' Berman asked. 'What kind of people were they?'

'Bennett was an asshole,' Stevie said. 'Womanizer, abusive. Real piece of work. From the two people we've talked to about Janet, she didn't seem too sweet either.'

'The Edwardses were socialites,' JD said, 'until recently when he became a philanthropist.'

'Why?' Berman asked.

'He got cancer,' JD said, 'became involved in a church, left them his estate.'

'Interesting,' Berman said thoughtfully. 'He was searching for absolution.'

'My money says Buck Trask has something to do with it,' Stevie said. 'The look on Agar's face when JD said his name was all fear and guilt.'

Berman's eyes gleamed. 'I think a field trip is definitely in order.'

'Okay,' Hyatt said. 'Stevie, you and Fitzpatrick take the doc to Anderson Ferry. Find out what the hell happened to connect these victims. Hell, take both docs. Maybe Dr Trask will remember something. I'll put Morton and Skinner back on finding that flash freezer.' He glanced at Daphne who'd been sitting quietly. 'Why are you here?'

Her lips twitched. 'You charmer. You asked for a warrant for Bennett's medical files.'

'Because Janet Gordon got her breast work done by Bennett,' JD said.

'That's disturbing,' Stevie countered with a shudder. 'She knew Bennett when he was a kid. Her son grew up with him.'

'Agar did say his mother wasn't the milk-and-cookies type,' JD said. 'The super's wife thought Bennett and Gordon had a thing. The super thought Bennett hated her.'

'Yet she trusted him to cut her open,' Berman said. 'I find that very interesting.'

'So what about Dr Bennett's office?' Daphne asked. 'Because if you want access to his records, getting a warrant's gonna take a long time and a lot of peach cobbler.'

'I want them,' Hyatt said. 'Financial and patient. Maybe he worked on other women from Anderson Ferry. Hell, maybe he worked on the hot doc who wears black leather.'

JD frowned at Hyatt's familiarity even as he bit back a denial. Lucy's breasts were definitely natural. That much he could guarantee. 'That doesn't explain the death of Edwards or the luring of Agar,' he said levelly and thought Hyatt looked amused.

'True. Still, we need to find out all the details. What about the doc's friend's apartment?'

'CSU's still there,' Stevie said. 'There doesn't appear to be anything missing and there's no evidence of forced entry.'

'Which means he has a key,' JD said. 'All the staff at Dr Trask's club saw Gwyn give her a key last night. So they all thought she'd be there. We need whereabouts of the staff.'

'I'll put Morton on it,' Hyatt said grouchily. 'Skinner can run down the freezer. What about cameras at the club? What did they pick up last night?'

'Nothing,' JD said. 'There was a camera in the rear alley, but all it caught was the blood splattering on the wall. The actual murder was out of camera range.'

'Damn.' Hyatt pointed at Daphne. 'I want a warrant to make that arrogant SOB Thorne give me his client list. Somebody there saw something.'

Daphne's brows went up. 'Yes, sir,' she said sarcastically.

Hyatt rolled his eyes. 'Go. Get information. Report by five.'

Tuesday, May 4, 9.45 A.M.

There he was. Ryan Agar. The man was in an unmarked police car, taxied to his hotel courtesy of the Baltimore PD. The car stopped under the hotel's overhang and Agar got out, taking his small suitcase with him.

The unmarked car left, then doubled back to sit a half-block away, watching the entrance. Luckily there were two entrances. He'd take Agar out via the elevator to the parking garage.

But first, the set-up. He dialed the cell phone number Janet had screamed under torture. Agar answered on the third ring. 'Hello?'

'Mr Ryan Agar?'

'Yes,' Agar said cautiously. 'Who is this?'

'This is Joseph Biddle, from Biddle and Light. I'm your mother's attorney. First, please let me offer my condolences on the untimely death of your mother.'

'Thank you. How did you know she . . . ?'

'I got a call from her housekeeper this morning and called the police to be sure. They said you were here and looking for a hotel. Do you need my assistance?'

'No, that's okay. I found a place.'

'Good. I'm sure you're tired from your trip. Before you sleep, though, I'd like to meet with you. Your mother left me an envelope to give you. Also, I'm aware that the trip east was costly. I have access to an emergency fund your mother set up for you.'

'She did? When?'

'Last year. She wanted to give it to you, but she didn't think you'd take it.'

'I probably wouldn't have. But the cost of the last-minute airline ticket stretched my finances. I don't know how long I'll need to be here, so an advance would be helpful.'

'Excellent, excellent. If you tell me where you're staying, I can meet you.'

'The Peabody.'

'They have a nice restaurant.' Whose door he was staring at right now. 'I'll meet you in, say, twenty minutes. We can have breakfast and I can get you your funds.'

'Thank you, Mr Biddle. I appreciate it.'

He hung up and smiled. *So do I.*

Tuesday, May 4, 9.45 A.M.

Lucy needed to do at least two exams today, maybe three. It would help Craig get caught up and would keep her mind off things. And off people, she thought, thinking of Fitzpatrick and her promise to see him later. Whatever had possessed her to say yes?

'Narcotic,' she muttered.

'Excuse me, Dr Trask? You talking to me?' Ralph, one of the ME techs, had looked up from checking a toe tag against the clipboard he held in his hand.

'No, just to myself. I'm here for . . . let's see.' She pulled the printout from her pocket and read the ID number. 'He's an African-American male, aged fifty-two. Suspected heart attack.'

'I can wheel him out of here for you.' He handed her his clipboard. 'If you could just hold this for a minute.'

'Thank you.' She glanced at the clipboard, then frowned. *Cause of Death* seemed to leap off the page. 'We have another victim with a slit throat?'

Ralph looked up from the gurney he was pulling from the row. 'Another?'

'Yes. This says the victim is female. We have one who's male. He died last night.' And she could still see Kevin's blood splattered across the brick wall.

'This victim was just brought in a few hours ago. She's definitely

259

female. Jane Doe, killed last night. Garbage man found her behind a dumpster this morning.'

The bad feeling that had been hovering intensified. 'I need to see her.'

'Anything you say.' He wheeled out the gurney holding the newer victim.

Lucy pulled back the sheet and drew in a sharp breath. The slice was exactly the same as Kevin's. She tilted the woman's head, knowing what she'd see. Still, her blood went cold.

It was exactly the same, down to the way the wound wrapped around the deceased's right ear. Lucy draped the sheet over the victim's face and stepped back.

'Please wheel the deceased into exam room two,' she said quietly.

Ralph regarded her with unveiled curiosity. 'She's last in the queue.'

Lucy thought of Bennett and Gordon and poor Kevin. 'Not anymore.'

Tuesday, May 4, 9.45 A.M.

'Thank you,' Stevie said, on the phone with Delaware PD. 'We'll have our IT guys call your IT guys about money transfers from the victims' accounts.' She hung up with a frustrated sigh. 'Delaware traced the Edwards transfer to an offshore account, then hit a wall. They're waiting on a Federal warrant to trace the account holder.'

'What about the church?' JD asked. 'Could they have cleaned out his account?'

'There's no evidence that they did. Yet, anyway. We're back to Anderson Ferry.'

'Where nothing of note happened twenty-one years ago,' JD said. 'At least nothing that's available online. Their archives only go back ten years.'

'Then let's collect Lennie and Lucy and get out there. It's going to take us all day to do this field trip, so let's take two cars in case we need to split up or I need to get Lennie back. Did you ask Lucy to come?'

'I called, but she didn't answer.' Which he hoped was because she was busy and not because she was avoiding him. 'I left her a voicemail. I left Agar a voicemail, too. Mulhauser's waiting to do his mother's ID.'

'Agar's probably sleeping. I'll give his tail a heads-up that she needs to take him in for the ID. We'll grab Lucy on the way to Lennie's. I want to take another look at the "L" on Janet's back. I'm wondering if we have an "I" and an "L" as in letters, or if they're still numerals.'

'"IL" would be what, in Roman numerals? Forty-nine? What's the significance?'

'Could be an age or an address. Or the number on a football jersey.'

JD pointed to her briefcase, impressed. 'You've got the team picture. Check it.'

She checked the photo and frowned. 'Damn. No forty-nine on this team.'

'It was a good try,' he said. 'What if it's just letters? Why an "I" and an "L"?'

'Part of a word?' she mused as they walked to the elevator. 'A place? Maybe a name? What starts with IL? Illegal? Illogical? Just plain ill?'

'That would be my word for him,' JD said grimly.

'I'm serious. Help me out here. Places, names. Illinois? Ilene?'

'Eileen starts with an "E".'

'Maybe he spells it differently. You're not helping.'

JD hit the elevator down button. 'Whatever it is he's spelling, I hope it's short.'

Tuesday, May 4, 10.15 A.M.

'You're right.' Craig met Lucy's eyes over Jane Doe's body. 'The neck slash is the same as Kevin Drummond's. This was made by the same style knife.'

'Look at the ear,' Lucy said, tilting the deceased's head a few degrees.

'Exactly the same little curve,' Craig said. 'Good catch, Lucy.'

'Thanks. But why? Who is this woman and why did he kill her?'

'You say she was found behind a dumpster?'

'This morning. Time of death was between eight and ten last night. The bruising on her back and face is post-mortem. She'd had intercourse shortly before death.'

Craig's eyes narrowed. 'Semen?'

'Yes. I took samples and submitted it for DNA. We'll compare it to what we took from under Kevin's nails last night.'

'Did you call the detectives?'

'Not yet. I wanted to show you first.'

Craig's eyes narrowed further. 'Or you wanted me to make the call for you.'

Lucy dropped her gaze back down to Jane Doe. 'That, too.'

'Coward,' Craig murmured. 'Call Fitzpatrick yourself.' As if conjured by evil genies, the man appeared with Stevie. Craig looked surprised but satisfied. 'Or you could tell him now.'

Fitzpatrick wore the same suit as the night before, but somehow remained wrinkle free. He moved gracefully, sending the now-familiar tingles of awareness skittering across Lucy's skin.

His blue eyes were sharp, focusing on her as he walked through the doors to the autopsy suite. She couldn't look away, even though she tried. She couldn't get the memory of the alley out of her mind, even though she tried. *Why did I agree to see him later? Alone, for God's sake?*

'Tell him what?' Fitzpatrick asked.

'This.' Lucy gathered her composure and gestured them closer, pointing to Jane Doe's throat. 'Look at her ear.' Immediately she saw they understood.

'What the hell?' Fitzpatrick murmured intensely. 'When did you find this woman?'

'*Where* did you find this woman?' Stevie added. 'Who is she?'

'She came in as a Jane Doe,' Lucy said. 'Just this morning. I saw her throat and knew she was killed by the same person that killed Kevin.'

'No ID?' Fitzpatrick asked.

'None. She was found behind a dumpster. She was dressed like she was going or had been clubbing. She had had sex, but there appears to have been no force used. I took semen samples.'

'Do you recognize her?' Fitzpatrick asked.

'Noooo,' Lucy said, overly patiently. 'That's why we call her a Jane Doe.'

Fitzpatrick's eyes flashed. 'I mean, could she be from Anderson Ferry?'

'I'm sorry,' Lucy said, contrite. She'd been condescending and rude and he didn't deserve that. 'I've never seen her before, but I didn't remember knowing Brandi Bennett either. I sent this victim's prints to Latent. Maybe the system knows who she is. I took some face shots for you to show around, ones that don't show her throat.'

Fitzpatrick nodded once, his ire dissipated. 'All right.'

'I was getting ready to start the cut. I'll call you when I know something.' *Now go away.*

She watched Fitzpatrick and Mazzetti exchange a glance. 'Can somebody else do the autopsy?' Stevie asked. 'We're headed to Anderson Ferry and want you to come.'

Lucy thought of the eyes at the window. Watching her. *I don't want to go back and I don't want to spend another day wanting Fitzpatrick.* 'I'm sorry. I'm needed here.'

'Why do you want her to go?' Craig asked.

'Our victims are connected through Anderson Ferry and Lucy herself,' Stevie said. 'Our boss wants her to come. We're taking a profiler with us as well.'

'Then go, Lucy,' Craig said. 'I'll do this exam as soon as I'm finished with Kevin Drummond's. I'll call you with whatever I find as soon as I find it.'

Lucy shook her head. 'I would really prefer not to go back.'

'We need you to come, Lucy,' Fitzpatrick said quietly. 'Please. It's important.'

She blew out a sigh, feeling churlish. 'Fine. I'll ride with Stevie.'

'Sorry,' Stevie said with a shrug. 'Dr Berman already called shotgun with me.'

Fitzpatrick looked a little grim. 'Looks like you're stuck with me, Dr Trask.'

'I don't have any clothes,' she said, sounding desperate even to herself. 'Just scrubs.'

'We'll drive by your place so you can change,' Fitzpatrick said.

She gritted her teeth. 'All right. Let me get my things.'

Tuesday, May 4, 10.25 A.M.

What do they feed cowboys anyway? he thought as he supported a staggering Ryan Agar the final few steps to the car he'd parked in the underground parking garage.

Ryan was a big man. Soon he'd be a dead man. He shoved him in the backseat, covering him with a blanket. He wasn't sure how long it would take the pills he'd slipped into Agar's coffee to wear off, but it should be a while. He'd given him enough to take down an elephant.

He needed to get him out of the garage. Once he'd cleared the traffic of downtown, he'd pull over and restrain the cowboy. Trussed, he thought, pleased. *A fitting end.*

He got behind the wheel and lit a cigarette, inhaling deeply, feeling the stress ebb a bit. He took a look in the rearview mirror, smoothing down his fake moustache with his thumb and forefinger. His wig had come askew and he tugged it back into place.

His own mother wouldn't know him. Of course, he thought bitterly, she'd never get the chance. His mother was dead, because of Ryan Agar and the assholes just like him.

Prepared to be stopped, he had ID in his shirt pocket. People were a lot more likely to allow a cop to pass, and rarely did anyone check to see if the name was real or not.

If he was stopped, he was Officer Ken Pullman, up from Virginia on vacation, and his friend in the back was sleeping off one hell of a hangover. But no one stopped him. No one noticed as he exited the garage, feeding a crisp bill into the self-serve pay machine. With good winds he should have Ryan out on the Bay by noon and then the party would begin again.

A beep caught his attention and he pulled his cell phone from his jacket pocket. The bouncing blue ball on the tracking website had left the morgue. Little Lucy was on the move. He frowned. She was supposed to stay put in the morgue all day today.

Maybe she's running away. He'd honestly thought she'd run at the first sight of Bennett yesterday and again at Bennett's heart in her car, but she hadn't taken his warning seriously. Instead she'd stayed, sticking close to the detective.

They'd been hot and heavy in that alley, which had been good for him. Had they finished any faster, they might have interrupted his delivery of Janet Gordon's body.

Of all people, he hadn't thought Lucinda would fall for a cop – or pretend to, which was more likely. He wondered in what direction she was steering the investigation.

Away from herself, without a doubt. He wondered whose name she was whispering in the cop's ear, who she was blaming. He wondered what the cop would say when he learned the truth.

I'll have to keep a close eye on Lucy. He might need to change his plans for the afternoon, depending on where she was going. If she was going back to Anderson Ferry, this time he'd have to go along too. He couldn't let her talk to her parents, not just yet. Not until he was ready for their family reunion. He had a few more letters to burn first.

Tuesday, May 4, 10.30 A.M.

Clay stopped outside the Orion Hotel, taking a moment to compose himself. He'd ensured that all of Nic's files had been relocated to his house before going back to her apartment and calling 911. By the time he'd done all of that he was numb, and behaving just like the detectives would have expected him to behave, having stumbled on a scene like . . . *that*.

Before, he had been reacting. Now, it was time to act. He squared his shoulders and walked into the Orion as if he hadn't discovered the mutilated corpse of his partner four hours before.

He stopped at the concierge's desk. 'I'd like the head of security, please.'

'Can I ask what this is in reference to?' the concierge asked.

'My name's Maynard. I'm a PI, searching for a man owing thousands in child support. I got a tip that he checked in here last night. I'd like to look at your tapes.'

The concierge was annoyed, but not with Clay. Citing the search for a deadbeat dad was the best way of viewing tapes in privately owned buildings, especially if the person behind the desk was female. It was no lie. Evan was behind in his support payments, having faked his own death. And having murdered three others.

'I'll see what I can do.' The concierge waved over a man in a suit. The two talked and then the man in the suit took him to the security office. Within ten minutes the security chief had the footage. He turned his screen so that Clay could see it.

'This your man?'

Evan Reardon. Pure hate bubbled up within Clay and he let it simmer as he watched the tape. Standing with a scantily clad woman, Evan gave his credit card to a guy behind the counter. The woman clung to him like ivy. When the two practically ran for the elevator, Clay shook his head. Once he'd dealt with Evan, Ted Gamble's name would not be heard again. No need to leave a loose end for anyone to trip over.

'No,' he lied. 'That's not him. But thank you.' Clay left the hotel, grimly determined. Reardon was here, in Baltimore. *When I find you, you will wish you'd never been born.*

Sixteen

Tuesday, May 4, 10.55 A.M.

'Lucy.' JD slammed the door of his car and jogged to catch up with the long-legged stride that had her almost to her apartment door already. 'Wait.' He tugged at the duffle bag on her shoulder and she jerked away.

'I'll carry it,' she said curtly, then drew a breath. 'But thank you.'

She was trembling. 'Lucy, what's wrong?'

'I don't want to go back there,' she said tightly. 'That's what's wrong.'

'You mean to Anderson Ferry?'

'No, I meant the seventh ring of hell,' she snapped. 'Yes, Anderson Ferry.'

'Why not?'

She gave him a look of consternation. 'Why not?' she repeated incredulously.

'Yeah. Westcott's a bitch and Bennett threw you under a bus. I can cut Bennett some slack because he'd just found out about his son, but he does know something. Their opinion of you doesn't carry any weight with me. So, why not?'

For a moment she stared at him. 'Never mind.' She started walking again.

JD stood still. 'Is it because your parents still live next door?'

She stopped abruptly. 'Yes,' she hissed.

'Talk to me, Lucy. Please.' *Please* seemed to work when nothing else made a dent.

'I know I have to go. I get that, Fitzpatrick. But it doesn't mean I have to relish the trip.'

'You wanted to go yesterday. You asked several times.'

'No, I never *wanted* to go. I felt I owed something to the Bennetts.'

He closed the distance between them. 'And yet they threw you out.'

'They're grieving. We can't blame them. Let's just . . . get this day over with.'

She still wouldn't look at him. He tried to tip up her chin, but she looked away. 'And then there's me,' he murmured. 'I know we didn't plan what happened last night, but we have to talk about it sometime. Please, don't shut me out.'

She sighed wearily. 'I don't blame you, okay?'

'But?'

She closed her eyes. 'The truth is that most of me is embarrassed. Mortified, even. The other part is . . . thrilled and would do it again in a heartbeat. And that's not okay. You are not good for me. I wish you'd accept that.'

He opened his mouth, but no words came out. All the blood had rushed out of his head when she said 'thrilled'. By 'heartbeat' he was hard as a rock.

'Lucy!' The voice came from above their heads and as one they looked up. There was an older woman standing on one of the second-story balconies looking upset.

'What is it, Barb?' Lucy called.

Barb was wringing her hands. 'He's bad today. I almost called you.'

'I'll be right up,' Lucy said. JD had no choice but to follow her into the building and up the stairs, still speechless and wincing. But the blood started pumping back to his brain as she unzipped the duffle bag and pulled out a violin case. Barb was standing by an open door.

'I tried the recording but he broke the recorder. Threw it at the mirror on the wall.'

Shards of broken mirror littered the floor and an old man wearing orthopedic shoes paced and muttered angrily. A tape recorder lay smashed at his feet.

'I can't get close enough to the glass to clean it up,' Barb said in a loud whisper.

Lucy handed the mostly empty duffle to JD. 'Hold this, please.' She cautiously approached the old man. 'Mr Pugh, it's Lucy.' She touched his shoulder. 'You sound worried. Can I help?'

'Can't find it,' he muttered. 'Can't find it.'

'What can't you find?' she asked him, so sweetly it made JD's heart ache.

The old man shook his head. 'Can't find it.'

'Come,' Lucy said, tugging the man's arm. 'Sit with me for a while.'

Bewildered, Mr Pugh let himself be led to a sofa with big blue flowers. 'Can't find it,' he said plaintively and Lucy smiled at him.

'I know. We'll find it. Don't worry.' She took the violin and bow from the case, positioning the instrument under her chin as if she'd done so a million times.

Maybe she had. JD realized he held his breath, waiting for her to begin.

'No!' the old man shouted and jumping up, grabbed Lucy's arm.

JD had reflexively stepped closer, but Lucy stopped him with a glance. 'It's okay,' she said. 'There's a little box inside the duffle. Can you give it to Barb?'

Apparently Barb knew what to expect because she shook a silver charm bracelet from the box and fastened it to Lucy's wrist. Lucy showed it to Mr Pugh.

'See, here it is. Now let's sit down.' The old man sat and Lucy stood, the bracelet dangling from the wrist that curved around the instrument's neck. A moment later the music flowed and JD simply listened, speechless once more.

It was nothing like the music she'd made the night before. That had been pounding energy. Searingly hot. *This* . . . this was sheer beauty. Rich and full and pure, he knew he'd heard the piece played a hundred different times. But never like this.

It was haunting and lovely and stirred something deep within him.

Mr Pugh's eyes closed, a contentment settling his features where there had been agitation before. A tear slid down his wrinkled face as he clasped his hands together. Lucy's gaze became unfixed and JD knew she'd gone somewhere else in her mind.

His own eyes stung. She stood there wearing no makeup and a pair of scrubs, her red-gold hair pulled back in a plain ponytail. She was as beautiful as the music she created. *I want her.* The thought hit him like a brick. He wanted her, of course. That was an already established fact. But this was different. *I want her for myself.*

You don't know her. She won't let you. That would have to change.

'It's Albinoni's *Adagio*,' Barb whispered beside him. 'She performed this for her senior recital, the last time she played as his student.'

'It's . . .' He gave up. There wasn't a word.

'I know.' Barb patted his arm. 'She has a gift.'

A movement at the edge of his vision caught his eye and he looked over his shoulder. Doors in the apartment building were opening on every floor, residents coming out of their units to stand in the halls, listening. He imagined the look on his face mirrored theirs. Sheer bliss.

Too soon the piece was finished and Mr Pugh lifted his face expectantly. Lucy seamlessly launched into another piece, equally haunting and moody. Broody. Wonderful.

Barb Pugh started to kneel on the floor to pick up the shards of mirror, but JD shook his head and did the task himself. Lucy had nearly completed her third piece by the time he finished and had carted the now-empty frame into the hall.

'Thank you,' Barb whispered. 'She's almost done. You are the detective from yesterday morning, aren't you? The one who called me at my sister's.'

'Yes, ma'am.' JD motioned her into the hall so they could talk undisturbed. 'I'm Detective Fitzpatrick. Did you and Mr Pugh live in Anderson Ferry?'

'Oh no. We've always lived here in Baltimore,' Barb said.

JD frowned. 'I thought your husband was Lucy's music teacher in high school.'

'He was. He taught at a residential school for girls here in town.'

'Residential? You mean a boarding school?'

'For some, yes. Lucy lived too far away to commute so she lived in the dorm.'

'Was it a music school?' he asked and she hesitated, then nodded.

'Yes, among other things. There was painting and chorus and dance and music.'

'So it was a school for the arts.'

She hesitated again, longer this time. 'Among other things. You should ask Lucy.'

Among other things? Like what? 'I'll try. She's not big on sharing.'

'Give her time. I think you'll find the key to unlocking those secrets of hers.'

'But why does she keep so many secrets?'

Barb's smile was sad. 'Sometimes our secrets are all we *can* keep, Detective.'

In the living room Lucy had finished the third piece and was putting her violin back in its case when Mr Pugh rose again to grab her arm. 'Please,' he said and she patted his hand.

'Do we have time for one more, Detective?' Lucy asked.

'Please,' JD said simply, now understanding the power of that one word.

She was startled, then resigned, as if he'd peeled away one of the layers she'd held onto for dear life. She fitted the violin under her chin and played the first piece again. Once again Mr Pugh's cheeks were wet. This time JD's were too.

For a long moment she held his gaze and JD could hear every beat of his own heart. Then she looked away and put the violin in its case.

'Will he be all right now?' JD asked Barb as Lucy knelt at the old man's feet and took off his shoes. Barb shook her head.

'No. He'll have another few episodes today, but that was probably the worst one.'

271

'You know what you're going to have to do,' JD murmured and Barb nodded.

'I know.' Suddenly she looked so weary. 'I know.'

'I'm sorry. I know the expense is—'

'Not a factor,' Barb interrupted. 'Lucy's taken care of it. She started putting money away as soon as I called to tell her Jerry had been diagnosed. She quit her job and came right back, no questions asked.'

'Where was she before?'

'California. She's a good person, our Lucy.' Who had persuaded Mr Pugh to lie down and was covering him with an afghan. 'She's got a nice place picked out. She's just waiting on me to . . .' Barb swallowed hard. 'To be ready to lose him. But she doesn't push, not hard anyway. She knows what it's like to be put somewhere against her will.' She pressed her lips together. 'And I've said too much.'

'No, ma'am. You've said just enough.' He gave her one of his cards. 'If you need anything, just call.'

Barb took the card. 'Why did this killer do this?' she asked, her voice low and urgent. 'Set up a dead man to look like my Jerry?'

'To frighten Lucy,' JD said. 'If you have any reason to be afraid, do not hesitate to call 911. Don't call one of us first. Call 911, and then call me.'

Barb paled. 'I understand. You'll take care of her, won't you?'

'Yes,' he said without hesitation. 'Can you answer one more question?'

'Maybe.'

'Did her parents come to her final recital, when she played the *Adagio*?'

Barb frowned, anger flashing in her eyes. 'No, they never came. Not once. It was like they threw her away. It broke our hearts.' She drew a breath. 'And hers.'

Tuesday, May 4, 11.25 A.M.

Fitzpatrick was uncharacteristically quiet as he opened the door to her apartment. CSU had put their own lock on the door, so Lucy's key no longer worked.

'Maybe that's why he put the heart in Gwyn's place,' she murmured. 'He doesn't have the key to my place anymore.'

'Maybe. But I don't think so anymore than you do. He knew you were there, Lucy. And whether you want to admit it or not, the people who knew were there in your club.'

'I know.' He was right on both counts. The club's staff had known. And she didn't want to admit it. She went to her bedroom, thinking about the last piece she'd played for Mr Pugh.

Fitzpatrick had cried. Mr Pugh had cried, of course. But he always had, even before the Alzheimer's. He'd cried the first time she'd played the piece in high school. But Mr Pugh's tears were different – he'd been an artist. A musician.

And more of a father than the one who'd borne her.

But Fitzpatrick . . . his tears had given her a jolt, just as they had that day in the autopsy suite. *And the way he looked at me*. Like he'd been trying to see . . . *me*.

She opened her bedroom door tentatively, but her room looked exactly as she'd left it. 'I'll be quick,' she said, proceeding to pack yet another suitcase.

Fitzpatrick's gaze roamed the room, coming to rest on Lucy for a long moment before sliding toward the bed against the wall. It was as if all the air had been sucked out of the room and her heart suddenly pounded in her throat.

'I didn't expect pink . . . or lace,' he said gruffly.

Her bedspread was frothy, lacy and very girly. It was the bed she'd always dreamed of having all those nights she'd slept in a plain dorm bed.

'Not everything can be black leather,' she said, intending for the words to come out light and airy. Instead they were as deep and gruff as Fitzpatrick's had been. His dark eyes flashed dangerously, his hands flexing before curling into fists at his sides.

With a great effort she made herself turn around and march into the closet.

Her closet was nearly empty. 'I can't have any more clothes become part of a crime scene,' she grumbled. She gathered the few work outfits she had left and stood staring at the black dresses that remained. 'How long will our club stay closed?' she called.

'Another day at least,' he said from right behind her.

Startled, she spun around. He stood inches away in the closet doorway. His face had taken on a sharp edge. Stubble already dusted his jaw. He looked like a pirate eyeing his booty. *Which would be me.* She should tell him to step back. *I should.*

'Maybe more than a day,' he added, leaning closer until the lapels of his coat brushed her breasts. He stretched, reaching his arm over her head to her closet shelf and she had to concentrate on not ducking. But she stood her ground and when he straightened, he held a pair of stiletto heels in his hand. 'Better take a dress or two,' he said. 'Just to be sure.'

She closed her eyes, her body pulsing in all the places it shouldn't. 'You are so bad for me,' she whispered.

His chuckle was dark, sending shivers down her back. 'I think you were bad long before I arrived.' Reaching over her shoulder, he pushed at hangers. 'Hm. A shame.'

When she opened her eyes, he had several leather dresses hanging from his crooked finger. 'What's a shame?'

He grinned wickedly, his dimple coming into full view, making her want to reach up and touch it. 'No outfits like the one Gwyn had on last night.'

Gwyn's bustiers were the stuff of legend. 'There's only so far my bad goes.'

His brows rose. 'And how far is that?'

She looked away, remembering his motorcycle helmet. And the alley. *Can't forget about that. As if.* 'Let me change my clothes. I'll meet you in the living room.'

With a frown he laid the black dresses and the shoes across her bed. 'All right.'

She changed from the scrubs into a plain navy sheath and jacket, then packed the rest of the clothes into a suitcase. Pausing, she stared at the black dresses on the bed and swore before putting them on top. 'Just in case,' she muttered. In case of what, she wasn't sure.

Tuesday, May 4, 11.40 A.M.

He looked up from the photo he'd been studying when Lucy dragged her suitcase into her living room, the duffle that he now knew held her violin over one shoulder. She'd changed into a dress with another skinny skirt. He eyed the suitcase, hoping she'd packed the black dresses.

Her eyes narrowed slightly at the frame in his hand. She was annoyed that he'd intruded into her personal life, but he didn't care. This case revolved around Lucy. The more he understood about her and the faster he understood it, the better. They needed to catch a killer before he could burn letters into any more backs or slit any more throats.

Especially Lucy's. The very thought made his blood run cold.

He turned the frame so she could see. 'It's you and Mr Pugh.'

She took it, brushing at non-existent dust. In the photo was a young Lucy wearing a school uniform. She sat in a chair, a violin under her chin, her bow at her side. Her very serious eyes were fixed on Mr Pugh who was playing his own violin, his expression one of great joy.

'I remember this day,' she said wistfully. 'It's hard to remember him like he was, then see him like he is today.'

'You love him.'

Her eyes flashed up to his, filled with pain. 'He's been . . . like a father to me.'

While hers peeked at her from behind window blinds. 'You were young in this picture.'

'Fifteen.'

'Barb said it was a residential school.'

Lucy's cheeks flushed. 'Barb sometimes talks too much.'

'Why were you in a residential school?' he asked intently. 'Please tell me.'

She lifted her chin. 'You could ask Mrs Westcott. She'd be happy to tell you.'

'I'm not asking Mrs Westcott. I'm asking you.'

'Fine.' She squared her shoulders, as if facing a firing squad. 'I got into trouble and got sent to a home for "troubled girls".'

His brows crunched slightly. 'How did you get into trouble?'

'I broke into Mrs Westcott's house. Then she accused me of stealing from her.'

His brows crunched more. 'Why did you break into her house?'

'There was something there I wanted.'

He closed his eyes. 'Lucy, are you going to tell me the whole story or do I have to dig it out of you with a grapefruit spoon?'

She put the frame back on the shelf with a weary sigh. 'Westcott's got a son.'

JD rocked back on his heels, crossing his arms over his chest. 'Let me guess. He knew your brother and Edwards and Bennett and Agar.'

She frowned. 'Yes. Sonny's the same age, played on the team with my brother.'

'Linus.'

One side of her mouth lifted sadly. 'He hated that name. My mother's maiden name is Buckland, and that was his middle name. Everyone called him Buck.'

'You loved your brother.'

'Yes. Buck was . . . bigger than life. My parents' living room is filled with his trophies, all sports. I sat in the bleachers for every game. He got all the cheers. Everyone loved Buck.'

'But?' he asked.

'When he was gone, everything . . . stopped.'

'What stopped?'

'My m—' She caught herself and shrugged. 'Life. My parents worked their important jobs and when they came home, it was all about Buck. My father watched videos of his games and my mother polished his trophies. His room became a shrine. Nobody was allowed in there.'

'Even you?'

She let out a breath. 'Especially me.'

'Why?'

'Because my mother said so. But I'd go in his room when my mother was . . . not home. I missed him, so much. I'd sneak into his

276

room to be near his things. Weeks became months and suddenly a year had passed. His funeral had been a few days before my fourteenth birthday, so it was my birthday again and I snuck into his room and found this.' She jangled the bracelet on her arm. 'It was in a cigar box under some baseball cards. He must have gotten it for my birthday right before the accident.'

JD lifted her hand so that he could read the charm. '"Number one sister".' When he lowered her hand, he held it loosely so she could pull away. Instead she held on tighter.

'Buck probably got it out of a Cracker Jack box, but for a girl missing her brother, it was like a gift sent down from heaven. I never took it off except to shower.'

'What did your parents say?'

'Nothing. They didn't notice it. They weren't noticing much of anything by then.'

'So what did Mrs Westcott have that you wanted back?'

Her smile was sardonic. 'I knew you'd come back to that. My bracelet disappeared, just a few days after I'd found it. I'd taken a shower and came back to my room to find it missing – and a boy climbing out of my window.'

'Mrs Westcott's son?' he asked and she nodded.

'I threw on clothes and went to the Westcotts' to get it back. Old lady Westcott wasn't home, so I opened the door and went in. Sonny was there along with Russ Bennett. I demanded my bracelet back and Sonny bald-faced lied and said he didn't have it. I got so angry.'

JD lifted his brows. 'You broke his nose?'

Lucy winced. 'More like I bruised it. But it bled an awful lot. Russ was dragging me off him and that's when Mrs Westcott came home, saw her baby bleeding and went ballistic. Called the cops and everything. My father was very unhappy.'

'But Westcott's "baby" was your brother's age.'

'Nineteen by then. And none too happy that a girl had bloodied his face.'

'He was a football player,' JD said incredulously.

'Yes, he was. Which, I imagine, made it worse. The boys taunted him. I heard that even after he went back to college the story followed him and he was always getting into fights because people called him a wuss.'

'How did you get your bracelet back?'

'Like I said, I broke into Mrs Westcott's house. The time before the door was unlocked and I walked in. After the bloody nose brouhaha died down, I broke Sonny's window and snuck in after Westcott had gone to sleep. By this point Sonny had gone back to college, so I figured it was safe. I found the bracelet under his skin magazine collection. Unfortunately, Mrs Westcott caught me climbing out of the window and called the cops again. I dropped the bracelet behind a bush. If the cops caught me with it they'd have taken it.'

'What did you do?'

'Took the Fifth, got a stern talking-to by my father, hysterics from my mother. I waited till it all died down and went back to get my bracelet. After that, I kept it hidden. I couldn't wear it anymore anyway. Sonny had pulled it apart. The chain was broken and the clasp was crushed.'

'So . . . why were you sent away?'

'Because Sonny came home for Thanksgiving. He must have heard that I'd broken in, and he came over and threatened me. I told him I didn't know where the bracelet was and all of a sudden he smiled and said, "Okay".'

'That doesn't sound good,' JD murmured.

'Because it wasn't. The next morning – Thanksgiving – a deputy showed up at our house. Mrs Westcott had filed a complaint. She was missing a ring and some cash. Since I'd broken in before, she accused me. The deputy found both the ring and cash in my underwear drawer.'

'Sonny had planted it.'

Fury had her eyes flashing again. 'Yes.'

'Is that when you were sent away?'

'Yes. To St Anne's School for Troubled Girls. For three years.'

'For a first offense?' he asked, shocked.

'I'd had some trouble in school, too. Lots of detentions the year after Buck died. A few fights. Let's just say I had a little practice before I bloodied Sonny's nose.'

'When did you meet Mr Pugh?'

'After school one day. I was scrubbing a floor because I'd gotten in trouble again, and I heard this horrible music coming from one of the rooms. The screeching had been a girl getting a music lesson, but then Mr Pugh played, showing her what to do. I hid, listening. I didn't think anyone could see me, but after the lesson he walked straight to where I was hiding. Turns out he knew I'd been in trouble. I was apparently the topic of lunchroom teacher conversations.'

'What did he do?'

'He asked if I liked music. My mother had always forced me to take lessons, but all of a sudden I wanted to play. I started lessons the next afternoon.' She swallowed hard. 'My parents were asked to pay for my lessons but my father wouldn't. Mr Pugh taught me for free, for three years. Later he told me it was a joy to teach someone who was so thirsty to learn.'

'That was kind of him. And explains a lot. Did you come home during the three years?'

'The first summer I went home supposedly to stay, but my parents didn't really want me there. Plus, the first week at Anderson Ferry High was harsh. Everyone knew I'd been away and the kids looked at me as an oddity, like a caged animal they could poke with sticks.'

'They tried to get you to fight.'

She nodded. 'Finally they succeeded and it was one dilly of a fight. One of the kids filed charges and I got hauled before a judge. I was so miserable at home. I wanted to go back to St Anne's and I told her so.' She shrugged. 'The teachers were kind to me there. The judge said the school was expensive, but if my parents would continue to pay, she'd send me back. My father said he would, so I packed up what little I had and went back.'

'Wait. What do you mean your parents *continued* to pay?'

She met his confused eyes, realization dawning in hers. 'It wasn't juvie, JD. It was a private facility for kids with behavior problems. My parents paid for my years there.'

JD was angry. 'Barb said they never came to visit you.'

She flinched and pulled her hand away. 'That's true. That's one of the many reasons I no longer visit them.' She hiked the duffle bag onto her shoulder and headed for the door. 'Time's passing, Detective. If we're going to Anderson Ferry, let's go.'

He needed a moment to calm his voice. He'd made her painful memory worse without meaning to. 'Lucy. I didn't expect you'd tell me what happened. Thank you.'

She shrugged. 'You were going to hear most of the story from Sonny Westcott sooner or later. I just wanted to give you my side first.'

'Wait a minute.' He gently grabbed her arm to stop her when she opened the door to leave. 'I'm going to meet Sonny Westcott?'

'I imagine so. You do plan to visit the Anderson Ferry sheriff's office, don't you?'

'Sonny Westcott works for the sheriff's office?' he asked, surprised.

'Sonny *is* the sheriff.' She tugged free, leaving him open-mouthed. 'Let's go.'

Tuesday, May 4, 12.25 P.M.

Breathing hard, he stepped back from Ryan Agar who now sat slumped in the wheelchair, passed out cold. Getting him from the car to the chair had been a pain. *Guy weighs a freaking ton*. He needed to rest before pushing Ryan up the ramp and onto the *Satisfaction*.

Pulling his cell from his pocket, he checked the tracking website and frowned. Lucy was on the move again. She'd left her apartment and was headed east, back to Anderson Ferry – which troubled him. She could mess everything up. He needed to know what she was doing.

Ryan would have to be stored for a little while. Now that he was in the chair, it would be easy to dump him down the stairs into the hold. He'd leave him trussed up like a Christmas turkey and when Ryan woke up, he'd have time to stew a bit. Apparently the police hadn't told him specifically what had been done to his mother.

No matter. He'd find out for himself soon enough.

Seventeen

JD was relieved to find the highway in the direction of Anderson Ferry to be fairly empty, allowing him to catch up to Stevie and Berman who were miles ahead of them.

It was a fine day for a drive. The sun was shining, the sky a cloudless blue. But the mood in JD's car was dark and tense. Lucy sat in the passenger seat, her duffle at her feet. She stared out the window, having said nothing since leaving her apartment.

He'd been on the phone with Sloane and Kaminski, the detectives who'd picked up the Jane Doe case. The pair had searched for leads as to where Jane Doe had been before her throat was slit. So far they had nothing. They were waiting on Latent to run her prints, hoping she'd be in the system.

He'd then checked in with Tory Reading, the cop staked out in front of the Peabody Hotel. So far Ryan Agar had not emerged. He'd not called for room service nor to the morgue to arrange to ID his mother. JD thought the man might run. Agar was definitely terrified and had every right to be. He'd asked Reading to make sure Agar was still in his room, because if this field trip to Anderson Ferry was a bust, Janet's son was their only link to real answers.

Thirty hours after finding Russ Bennett's body, they had six victims and so far nothing more than connections and a lot of unanswered questions. And Lucy Trask, who for some reason was the center of it all. Something had happened in her town.

'Lucy, I need to—' His question was cut off by his cell phone. 'Fitzpatrick.'

'It's Debbie.' Hyatt's clerk. 'I have those LUDs you've been waiting for.'

'Russ Bennett's?'

'Home and cell. They came last night, but they were sent to the fax in Narcotics. Somebody had your old fax number in their file. What do you want done with these?'

JD glanced at the clock. Even if everything went well it would be hours before they returned to the city. 'Can you email them to Mazzetti and me? She has her laptop.'

'Yeah. It'll take a little while to scan them,' she said. 'I'll call you when it's sent.'

'Thanks,' he said and started to hang up.

'I'm not finished yet,' Debbie said. 'You asked for a trace on the number that called the victim's son last night. It came from a pay phone.' She gave him the address and JD frowned.

'That's just a mile from the dumpster where Jane Doe was found. Can you send a request to Latent to take prints from that phone?'

'Will do. I'll call you when those LUDs are on their way.'

'Thanks.' He hung up and glanced at Lucy who was checking her messages. 'Any news?'

'A bit. Craig just finished Jane Doe's exam and checked the lab results on the samples we submitted yesterday. Both Janet Gordon and Russ Bennett's urine tox screens came back positive for pentobarbital and chlorohydrate.'

'Old-fashioned Mickey Finn,' JD said. 'They would have been highly suggestible, but for a little while able to walk on their own.'

'Stagger, anyway. Eventually it would have knocked them out. No news on Jane Doe's prints, but she'd had intercourse with two different men the night she died.'

'A prostitute?'

'Maybe, except most higher-class prostitutes that I see use condoms.'

That was true. 'How do you know she was higher class?'

'Her blouse was designer, probably ran her at least one-fifty. Her hair was well tended in a salon and her perfume was expensive, too.'

'Her body was behind a dumpster. How could you smell her perfume?'

'You learn to discern the smells you need to pay attention to,' she said and he decided to leave it at that. 'Few street hookers are going to be able to afford niceties like that. She also had no visible evidence of drug use, no track marks. We'll need her tox report to confirm or deny.'

'Anything else in the messages?'

'The heart is the same blood type as Janet Gordon, just as we expected. That's it.'

He said nothing for a minute, wondering how to phrase the rest of his questions, none of which she was likely to appreciate. She huffed an irritated sigh at his silence.

'You want to ask me more questions. Go ahead. Get it over with.'

'Okay. How long have you been partners with Thorne and Gwyn in the club?'

'Four and a half years. The club's been open a little more than three years. The first year and a half was planning and raising money.'

'How long have you known Gwyn?'

Her glance was sharp. 'She has nothing to do with this.'

'I'm pretty sure I believe that, too. So how long?'

'I told you yesterday, we knew each other as kids, before Buck died. We met again when I broke Russ Bennett's nose.'

A detail fell into place. 'You said you and Gwyn had become separated by life. That's when you were sent to St Anne's.'

'Give the man a Kewpie doll,' she said sarcastically.

He let her sarcasm roll off his back. 'So she introduced you to Thorne.'

'Yes, because I needed an attorney when Russ brought charges against me.'

'And the three of you hit it off.'

'What are you getting at?' she snapped.

'Nothing yet,' he said, frustrated. 'You won't tell me enough to get *at* anything. I'm not the enemy, Lucy. My questions might just save your life or the lives of your friends. It's too late for Kevin.' She flinched, but he didn't back off. 'Somebody knew enough about you to know you'd be at the club last night. Somebody with a key to Gwyn's place – who thought you'd be there – left you a heart. How did they get a key?'

'I don't know,' she said, frustrated also. 'Gwyn insists that the only person who had an extra key was her neighbor. Gwyn couldn't get into her place this morning because she'd given her own to me last night.'

'She has a boyfriend. Does he have a key?'

'No, they're still in the sleepover phase. She doesn't usually hold onto them long enough to get to the key-exchange phase.'

'Tell me about him anyway.'

'Royce is in Sales. Office printers, I think. I only know him from the club. We never spend much time together on the outside.'

'Why?'

She shrugged. 'I didn't want him to know I was an ME, plus . . .' She hesitated. 'Gwyn's last boyfriend tried to pick me up behind her back. She knew I had nothing to do with it, but it still hurt her. She's kind of kept Royce at a distance until recently.'

'What does Thorne do at the club?'

'For a while he did the books and paid the bills. Now Gwyn does all that, along with keeping his schedule at the law office. We hired Mowry to be the club's manager when the job got too big. He orders the booze and pretzels, takes care of the day to day stuff. Now Thorne scouts new talent and plays a mean bass.'

'Thorne told me that the two of you shared a common past.'

She frowned. 'Oh. Our trials. I suppose you want to know about that, too.'

'I do.'

'Then answer me something,' she said, her jaw cocked belligerently.

'If I can.'

'Why did you come to the autopsy of a little girl you didn't know and weren't responsible for? And don't say because you found her. She was the only autopsy you ever came to witness. I checked the sign-in records last night, after you dropped me off at the morgue. Before you followed me. I'd like to know. Please.'

He supposed she was entitled to some quid pro quo so he sucked it up and made himself tell it. 'My mother was . . . is a drunk. Not bad enough so that I got taken away, but bad enough that my childhood sucked. I was lucky enough to have an aunt take me in and give me some consistency in high school. I graduated, but not by much. I ended up going in the army.'

'What did you do?'

'Killed a lot of people,' he said evenly. 'Which messes you up. I was a loner before the army, but when I came home I was more so. Alone even in a crowd. I didn't dislike people, I just didn't know how to connect. And then I met Paul Mazzetti, Stevie's husband. He was the first friend I ever had.'

'But he died,' she said softly and he nodded.

'And so did Paulie, their son. I loved that boy, and when he was killed . . .'

'It's okay,' she murmured, placing her hand over his. 'You don't have to say any more. I get it now.'

He turned his hand so that their fingers laced. 'No, I don't think you do. My wife died a few years later and I went a little crazy, took some risks I shouldn't have. Then one day I came upon that little girl. She was dead when I got to her. Something happened as I stood there looking at her lying there dead in the grass. Something happened to me when I stood over her autopsy. I realized I was pissing my life away on grief and selfishness. I knew I needed help, so I joined Stevie's group.'

'She set you straight,' Lucy said, using the same words he'd used the day before.

'Yes. I can't tell you why I was there that day, Lucy. I just knew I needed to be.'

She was quiet for a moment. 'What happened to your mother?'

'She's still around. I would have thought she'd have drunk herself to death by this point, but she keeps on tickin'. She must have a liver of iron.'

'Only the good die young,' she murmured.

'Well, I've met my share of bad that've died young too,' he said pragmatically. 'It's just a lot less fair when it's the good ones.'

'But life is not fair,' she said.

'No, it often is not. Then other times, you win.' Hesitantly he lifted their hands and pressed a kiss to her wrist. She didn't pull away and he was encouraged. And then he noticed her bracelet, dangling from her wrist. 'Lucy. This charm is a heart.'

'That it is,' she said, her voice strained. 'I'd say it's a coincidence, but . . .'

'But it seemed awfully important to Sonny Westcott all those years ago,' JD said. 'Did you say Russ Bennett was with him the day he stole it from your house?'

'Yes,' she said, very softly. 'Oh God, JD. Russ asked me about this bracelet, when I was seeing him. He was in my apartment and saw that picture of me and Mr Pugh.'

'You're wearing it in the picture,' he said, suddenly remembering the detail. 'What did Bennett ask you?'

'He asked me about the violin, and did I still play.'

'Did you tell him about the club?'

'No. I told him that I sometimes still played for my old teacher and that I gave lessons at my old high school.'

His brows went up. 'St Anne's?'

'Yes, on Wednesdays during my lunch hour. The girls need role models.'

His respect for her soared higher. 'That they do. So what did Bennett say then?'

'He pointed to my bracelet in the picture and said it was pretty. I got irritated and told him that his friend stole it from me when I was fifteen years old. He said he didn't know that Sonny had really done that, that had he known, he would have made him give it back that day.'

'Did you believe him?'

'I didn't *not* believe him. But then he asked where it was and I told him I'd lost it.'

'So you lied to him.'

'Yes,' she said, troubled. 'I felt bad about it at the time, but

I didn't want him to know I still had it.'

Which was telling, JD thought. 'I thought you said Westcott broke it that day.'

'He did. I also said I hid it. The priest gave me a prayer book when Buck died. I hid the bracelet in it.'

'How?'

'I watched a lot of TV then and saw someone carve a hole in a book and hide something in there. I did the same thing. When I got to St Anne's I thought they'd let me keep the prayer book, but they found the bracelet. I had to earn it back, just like all my other privileges. I did and one of the teachers helped me fix it. After that I wore it all the time. That's why Mr Pugh likes me to wear it when I play for him now.'

'What about when you went home, that one summer?'

'I hid it again,' she said in an odd voice. 'I don't know why.'

'You trusted your instincts. What do your instincts tell you now?'

'That this bracelet is somehow very important. What do yours tell you?'

His jaw flexed as he considered. 'Depends. Did your brother give you gifts often?'

She sucked in her cheeks, annoyed, and he knew she understood the question behind his question. 'No. This was the first.'

'Then my instincts tell me you weren't supposed to have it.'

He thought she'd protest, but she didn't and his opinion of her ratcheted even higher. 'I wonder what Sheriff Westcott would say if he saw me wearing it,' she mused.

'Let's find out.' JD released her hand to call Stevie on his cell. 'We need a plan.'

Tuesday, May 4, 12.50 P.M.

How sweet, he thought, disgusted. Kissing her hand. Fitzpatrick had achieved what no man had in a whole lot of years. It was a shame. He had nothing against the detective, but if the man got too close to Lucy then he'd be in the way. Which meant he'd need to die too.

Right now the two were engaged in what appeared to be serious conversation. He wished he knew what they were saying. In hindsight he should have gone for the more deluxe tracker that broadcasted sound. Live and learn. He could order the more deluxe model, but by the time it was delivered she'd be dead.

So there didn't seem to be much point.

It was enough to know that they were going to Anderson Ferry. Whatever she was telling the detective would be lies and half-truths anyway. She wasn't wired to tell the whole truth and nothing but the truth. No Trask was.

He dropped back several car lengths so that his presence would continue to go undetected. He'd been riding too close. He didn't need to do that. He knew exactly where Lucy was and where she'd go. It didn't matter if he lost them. He patted his right jacket pocket, felt his cell phone with its tracking website. He then patted his left pocket. Felt his pistol.

Well, Ken Pullman's pistol, anyway, but Ken wouldn't mind if he used it. Wasn't like Ken needed it anymore. *Asshole*. He'd got what he deserved. He should have been ashamed of himself. A cop, extorting a civilian. Greedy sonofabitch.

Now a dead sonofabitch. Exactly what he deserved.

Lucy's car sped up, putting distance between them and changing lanes. She and Fitzpatrick were headed for the next exit. *Let them go. I'll keep going and get there first.* He was pretty sure he knew where she'd go. *And like the big bad wolf, I'll be waiting.*

Tuesday, May 4, 1.20 P.M.

'Where are you going?' Lucy whispered.

'Wait,' Fitzpatrick mouthed. He'd been on the phone with Stevie for a long time, telling her all the details Lucy had shared, but he'd just whipped over to the right lane and was now exiting off the highway, several exits early.

She remembered what he'd done the last time he'd exited early. Part of her wished he'd do it again. Quite a bit of her wished he'd do it again, if she were honest. She caught him watching her as he pulled to a stop at the end of the exit. He looked like he wanted to say something, but he was listening to Stevie who'd received Russ Bennett's LUDs on her laptop and had pulled over several miles ahead to review them.

He turned at the exit and pulled into a gas station. 'I've got Janet's cell phone bill in my briefcase. Wait one.'

Lucy leaned back toward her window to give him room as he twisted to grab his briefcase from the backseat. He brushed his lips against her cheek as he resettled himself into his seat and gave her a wink.

'Later,' he mouthed and Lucy felt her face heat. That she'd wanted him to kiss her again was so plain on her face it was embarrassing. But it was what it was. She couldn't change what she wanted. Last night in the alley shouldn't have happened. It shouldn't happen again. But it would. She knew it would.

Fitzpatrick's eyes grew darker. Either he could read her mind or she was still broadcasting her desires, loud and clear. She looked away and he dropped his gaze to his briefcase, which he balanced precariously on the gearshift. Lucy took the briefcase and held it open on her lap so that he could find the papers he sought.

'Here they are,' he said, his voice gone husky. He cleared his throat. 'What was the number that called Bennett the afternoon he disappeared?' He ran his finger down the list of calls on Janet's bill. 'Janet got a call from that same number the day after Bennett disappeared. But no calls before that. We'd need her most recent statement for any calls she got the day she disappeared. I wonder how this guy lured them both to meet him.'

He listened. 'You're right. There's no way this guy bought a cell phone in his own name. He had to know we'd be looking at LUDs.' He frowned. 'Wait. When was the first time Bennett got a call from that number?'

He rummaged in the briefcase and came up with a folder with a familiar scribble on the tab. When he opened it, Lucy recognized the papers Hyatt had shown her yesterday – the file Russ Bennett had collected. 'All of these newspaper clippings on Lucy's trial are stamped as having been copied by the newspaper office the day after Bennett first got a call from that number. The byline of the trial articles is—'

'Milo Davidoff,' Lucy said.

'Milo Davidoff,' Fitzpatrick told Stevie. 'If Bennett requested these the day after he got a phone call from the guy who lured him out and killed him, the newspaper office might know why. Let's start with the sheriff, then talk to Davidoff. I'll meet you in front of the sheriff's office.'

'We can't talk to Davidoff,' Lucy said when he'd hung up. 'He's dead.'

'How do you know?'

'Same way I know that Sonny is the sheriff. I keep up with the news that's published online. Kind of like when you get fired from a job and go back to see your boss from hell is dead.'

'I've done that,' he confessed, and tossed his briefcase to the backseat, then pulled his cell phone from his pocket and hit a few keys. 'Stevie, it's me. I forgot to tell you that we were being followed by a black Lexus. I hoped it would pass me when I pulled off the exit, but it hung back. It could just be someone on their way to the beach, but I'm betting a reporter. Keep your eyes open for him. I'll see you soon.'

After hanging up again, he put them back on the road toward the highway and Lucy found herself disappointed. 'I'm on the clock,' he said. 'I shouldn't have kissed you yesterday afternoon. Although I'm not the least bit sorry.' He hesitated. 'Are you?'

'No.' He put his hand on the console palm up and she aligned her fingers with his. 'I'm sure I'll be later, but I'm not now. What do you need to know about my trial? Most of it was covered in the Davidoff articles.'

'Which I read after we hung up last night. I'm sorry, by the way. I should have said you were innocent, not "not guilty". I wasn't thinking.'

'It's okay. I'm sensitive about it.'

'Understandable. I guess I also understand now why Mrs Westcott testified against you. She thought you'd stolen from her, so you had history. How were the Bennetts involved?'

'Mr Bennett put up my bail and hired my attorney,' she said. 'I was poor, putting myself though college, living with the Pughs. My fiancé and I weren't married yet, so I wasn't entitled to any of his life insurance, not that his parents would have let me have a penny. Heath did leave me a little in his will and they fought that, saying I'd murdered him. After my acquittal I eventually got that money. I used it all for med school.'

'Mr Bennett hired your attorney?' JD said, surprised.

'He did. I had a public defender who sucked. I thought I was going to prison and then Mr Bennett showed up with an attorney. It didn't take the guy more than a day to get the evidence to show I couldn't have been in the vehicle when it crashed.'

'How did he prove it?'

'Hired an expert witness, again at Mr Bennett's expense. This guy measured skid marks, damage to the other car, and all the accident markers. If I'd been driving, my ribs and sternum would have been crushed and I never could have run a mile for help.'

'Most people didn't have cell phones then,' he said.

'Rich kids had them, but I didn't. You don't know how many nights I wake up wishing I'd had one. I can still hear that baby's cries.'

'The baby and her mother in the other car lived.'

'Yes. The baby was in a car seat and was terrified but fine. The mother was a mess. Huge gash to her femoral artery. I applied first aid and stopped the bleeding.'

'You saved her life.'

'Yeah,' she said bitterly. 'After I almost took it.'

'I don't understand,' he said. 'You weren't driving.'

'No, my fiancé was. Heath was . . . kind of like Buck. Bigger than life.' She looked at Fitzpatrick from the corner of her eye. 'He raced motorcycles. Motocross.'

Cognition dawned. 'Oh.'

'And so did I.'

He jerked around to stare at her before returning his gaze to the road. 'You?'

291

'Yes. Which sounds utterly preposterous now, with me spouting statistics for every dangerous activity known to man.'

'But it explains a lot.'

'I guess.'

'You said you were too poor to afford a cell phone back then. How did you afford motocross? It's not a cheap sport.'

'Heath paid the bills for racing. His parents had money, lots of it.'

'How long were you engaged to him?'

'Four years. I met him my first semester in college. I was waiting tables to help pay tuition and he . . . swept me off my feet. I was twenty-one when he died.'

'Did you love him?'

She drew a quiet breath, remembering. 'Yes, very much. But I was young and so was he and it was quite possible that I loved loving him more, if you know what I mean.'

He nodded grimly and she wondered about the wife he'd lost. 'I do.'

'I did love him, though, and I loved to race. Loved the speed and the thrill and all the danger. And to be honest, loved knowing that it drove my parents crazy that I was on a motorcycle after what happened to Buck.'

'They knew?'

'I made sure they did. I'd send them clippings of my race stats, which I suppose was childish of me, but I was angry with them for, well, abandoning me.'

'You should have been angry. They did abandon you.'

His fierceness was sweet. 'When I finally got out of St Anne's and went to college, I was mad at them and the world in general. I thumbed my nose at them, and then disaster struck.'

'What happened that night, Lucy?'

'Things were getting out of hand. Heath had gone from this sweet, reckless boy to a mean, spiteful person. He started driving too fast everywhere we went. At first I egged him on, because I loved speed. Then he started drinking and popping pills and I couldn't stop him.'

'You testified that you tried to take his keys that night.'

'I did, but he was strong. I had one glass of wine but he'd had two bottles. He found this road to race that went down to one lane over an old bridge. I tried to grab his keys from the ignition, but he hit me and threw me out of the car.'

'That's how your face got bruised.'

'Yes. The prosecutor claimed the bruises were from the accident, but the expert witness proved that false quickly. Heath revved his engine and took the road at about eighty. The limit was twenty. The woman was coming over the bridge and there was nowhere for either of them to go. Heath was in a convertible. He was thrown from the car, dead before I got to him.'

She squared her shoulders to finish the story. 'Because I had alcohol on my breath, I was charged. Because Heath died, it was vehicular homicide. Because I'd had a "troubled past", people were all too happy to believe that I'd done it.'

'What about your parents?'

Lucy laughed bitterly. 'They came to court every day, sat behind me looking so ashamed of me. The only character references I had were Mr Pugh and Barb.'

'Your parents didn't stand up for you?'

'No,' she said flatly. 'Heath's parents called me a liar, said their son never would have gotten behind the wheel of a car while drunk. What turned the tide in my favor was when my lawyer got hold of the autopsy report.'

Fitzpatrick frowned. 'I don't understand.'

'Heath had cancer,' she said, 'a brain tumor that was affecting his behavior. He'd been having awful headaches and had started drinking to self-medicate. His family knew, but hadn't told me. They said I was a bad influence, and at that stage of my life, I was. But I didn't cause him to drink and drive. When the jury heard about the tumor, it made a difference. They looked at me with sympathy and not revulsion.'

'So an autopsy report saved you.'

'That and a good defense attorney who knew to ask for it. I thought I knew what it was to be scared. I was terrified the first few nights at St Anne's. But to sit in a courtroom like that and know I could be truly locked up and that I was *innocent* . . .' The memory still had the power to make her queasy. 'That was fear.'

'That makes a lot of things clearer. When was the last time you saw your parents?'

'The day I walked out of court. My mother looked like she wanted to say something, you know, nice. But my father pulled her out of the courtroom. I didn't want to hear it anyway. When I graduated, I went as far away as possible.'

'California,' he said. 'Barb told me that's where you'd come from.'

'When I finished my residency I took a pathologist's position there. I came back for holidays with the Pughs. And then Mr Pugh was diagnosed with Alzheimer's.'

'So you came home for good,' he said and she nodded.

'I was lucky to find a position with the state. I'd kept in touch with the Bennetts, holiday cards and such. I owed them so much for hiring that attorney. I tried to pay them back, but they wouldn't let me. So I'd take them to lunch when they came into the city.'

'Then you went back to a place you hated to give them the news about their son.'

'That pretty well sums it up.'

'Not entirely,' he said and she frowned.

'What else do you want to know?'

He cast a sideways glance. 'After your fiancé died, was there anyone else?'

Lucy looked away, too tired to even go there. 'We're almost in town.'

'I guess that means you don't want to answer my question.'

'You tell me about your buddies and I'll tell you about mine.'

He made an annoyed sound. 'How many "buddies" did you have?'

The *Welcome to Anderson Ferry* sign approached, then disappeared behind her. 'After Heath, two. You met one of them yesterday morning, slumped over a chess table. Where did you want to go first? Sheriff, Mr Bennett, or newspaper?'

'Sheriff's office,' he said, much more calmly.

She pointed ahead, the bracelet dangling. 'Then turn right at this intersection.'

'All right. Do me a favor, change the bracelet to your right arm.'

'Because I'll shake Sonny's hand with my right,' she said, bracing herself to see him again. And to see her parents again. Deep down, she'd known she'd have to.

Tuesday, May 4, 1.30 P.M.

Sitting on the edge of the sofa in his living room, Clay was slowly bringing his fury under control. No longer boiling, he felt ice cold inside. *Nicki.* Stabbed, gutted, throat slit. Left to rot.

'Evan was here in Baltimore last week and as recently as last night,' he said.

'In Nicki's apartment,' Alyssa murmured. He'd brought Alyssa here, not wanting to risk leaving her alone at the office. Not until he'd found Evan. 'I'm sorry. I know you were close.'

'She was my first partner in DCPD. We rode patrol together. She was smart, and good at her job. I don't understand how Evan caught her sleeping like that.'

Alyssa hesitated, then drew a sheet of paper from her purse. It was a photograph printed on a computer and Clay sighed. It was Evan, sleeping in a bed. Clay recognized the coffee mug on Nicki's nightstand – he'd given it to her himself. 'Goddammit,' he said wearily. 'When did you find this?'

'While you were resting. I was reviewing the files on the laptop you took from her safe. She sent it to herself two months ago.'

'Two months?' Clay felt sick. 'Dammit.'

'I thought you'd want to know,' Alyssa said tentatively.

Clay rubbed his eyes again. 'This explains a lot, especially the missed clues. She didn't want to see them. So we know how he got into her place. Why that night?'

'Maybe she started to suspect him. That he'd lied to her.'

'Maybe. How could she have been so fucking stupid?'

'Because he's a good liar,' Alyssa said softly. 'Even you believed his story about not being able to go to the cops. That the woman who was stalking him had a powerful daddy on the force.' She bit her lip, hesitating, then shrugged. 'He could have picked you and Nicki because he thought you'd be sympathetic to his situation.'

Clay nodded, unable to speak. She was right. He closed his eyes, bile rising to burn his throat. *God help me.* 'I let my own bias blind me. Now three people are dead.'

He stood, began to pace. 'We know he was in Newport News a week ago. That's when he killed the cop and the pole dancer because they got greedy. Then he came back and . . .' He drew a breath, pushed the image of Nicki from his mind, focusing instead on the man who'd slept in her bed before he'd killed her. 'We know he was at the Orion Hotel last night.'

'He could be at his Ted Gamble apartment.'

'He never claimed his key, but that doesn't mean he's not there.' Clay stopped to stare out the window. *Why is he doing this? Why the scam?* 'He wanted the identity.'

'A new start,' Alyssa murmured.

'He's here in the city for a reason. I doubt he'd stick around a whole week after killing Nicki for softshell crabs,' Clay said. 'He didn't go to his Gamble apartment. That's over an hour's drive. He's here, somewhere.'

'Why? Why not take the new identity and run?'

'Maybe Nicki knew why.' He turned to find Alyssa's eyes trained on him. 'Evan could be anywhere in the city. Without a reason for him staying, we're looking for a needle in a haystack. Let's find where Nicki went in the days before he killed her.'

Eighteen

Tuesday, May 4, 1.50 P.M.

Stevie and Dr Berman were waiting for them in front of the sheriff's office. The older man shielded his eyes as JD and Lucy approached, she with the duffle bag slung over her shoulder. She'd put her purse inside it to consolidate what she carried, but had refused to leave it in the car, afraid it would get tied up in another crime scene. JD couldn't blame her.

'So this is Dr Trask. I've heard much about you,' Berman said with a smile.

'It's nice to meet you. I'm sure Stevie passed on what Detective Fitzpatrick told her in the car. What do you think?'

'I think you are our key, my dear. I think your brother and his friends knew or did something for which they are being hunted. You could merely be a substitute for your brother or you could be involved, albeit unwittingly.' Berman brought her hand close to his face and examined the bracelet's charm. 'Was your brother the type to give you gifts?'

Her cheeks flushed as she glanced at JD. 'You don't think this was supposed to be mine.'

'I didn't say that,' Berman averred.

'But you think it and so does Detective Fitzpatrick.' She drew a deep breath. 'I guess we'll find out.'

Stevie tapped JD's shoulder as Lucy and Berman started up the stairs to the police station. 'We have other problems.'

JD looked down at her, forcing his focus away from Lucy. 'Like what?'

'Like Tory Reading just called me. She's in Ryan Agar's room, but he's not.'

'*Shit*. Where was she doing her surveillance?'

'Outside in her car like she was told to do. She said one of the waiters remembered Agar. He met with another man for breakfast, but didn't look well. The other man helped him to the elevators. In the Peabody those elevators can go up to the rooms or down to the parking garage.'

'Shit,' JD snapped again. 'We never should have let him out of our sight.'

'In hindsight, you're right. At the time, he wasn't a suspect. We couldn't hold him.'

'So what's Tory doing now?'

'Checking the security tapes to see if any of them show Ryan. She'll get back to us.' Stevie pointed to Berman and Lucy, who were just climbing the last stair. 'Let's meet Sheriff Westcott and hope he grew out of his asshole-ishness.'

JD snorted. 'Having met his mama, I don't think you'll get your wish.' He took the stairs in a jog and opened the heavy door for Lucy and Berman. Lucy gave him a look that was both thanks and a plea. 'It'll be fine,' he murmured. JD hoped he hadn't lied.

Behind the counter was an older woman whose nameplate said *Gladys Strough, Clerk*. 'Can I help you?'

'I hope so,' JD said. 'I'm Detective Fitzpatrick, Baltimore Homicide. This is my partner, Detective Mazzetti. Is Sheriff Westcott in?'

'Oh, you're here about the Bennett boy. Tragic,' Strough said. 'The sheriff is in. I'll tell him you're here and see if he's got time to see you.'

A few moments later a wide-shouldered, barrel-chested man in a uniform emerged from a back office. He looked older than his thirty-nine years, his face jowly and his hair thinning. He scanned their faces, lingering longest on Lucy's, his eyes narrowing.

JD watched placidly, although he seethed on the inside. From the corner of his eye he saw Berman cover the hand with which Lucy gripped his arm. Now no one could see Lucy's white knuckles nor the bracelet around her wrist. *Good for Lennie B.*

'I heard you'd come back,' Westcott said to Lucy a little too softly, then turned to JD with a brusque nod. 'I understand you've had a murder in the city. Russ Bennett.'

JD nodded, still placidly. 'Yes. Malcolm Edwards is dead too.'

'We heard about that weeks ago. Old news, Detective. Edwards was lost at sea.'

'About midnight we found another body, left much like Dr Bennett's had been,' JD said evenly. 'This morning we identified the remains as belonging to Janet Gordon.'

Gladys Strough sucked in a startled breath. 'Dear Lord.'

Westcott frowned down at her. 'Who?'

'Janet Agar,' she whispered. 'Dan Gordon was her third husband.'

There had been a moment, right after Strough had said Agar's name, that Westcott stiffened. But his reaction only lasted a split second and he went back to the guarded nonchalance with which he'd greeted them. 'Why?' he asked.

'We're not sure,' Stevie said. 'We think one of the reasons was to lure her son from his home in Colorado. Ryan arrived in Baltimore this morning.'

JD could see the wheels turning in Westcott's eyes. 'How did he know?' Westcott asked. 'If you didn't ID her until this morning, how did Ryan know to come?'

'We believe Janet's killer called him,' JD said. 'And now Ryan is missing too.'

Lucy's head swung so that she stared at him wide-eyed, but she said nothing.

Westcott paled, but didn't flinch. 'Maybe he made the ID and went home. Ryan and his mama didn't get along.' He glanced at Lucy. 'You know how that is, *Dr* Trask.'

'I do indeed,' she murmured. 'Times two. I don't get along with my mama or yours.'

'Some of us just aren't sociable,' Westcott said, making JD want to hit him. Or wish Lucy would. That would be entertaining. Westcott turned back to JD. 'I'm sorry for your rash of murders, son, but they're out of my jurisdiction. As you are out of yours.'

'This is a courtesy call,' JD said. 'We're going to be talking to various folks around town and we wanted you to know we were here.' He caught Lucy's eye and gave her a tiny nod.

Like a pro, she smiled and extended her hand to Westcott. 'It's been a pleasure to see you again, Sonny.' Westcott took her hand and she shook firmly, making the bracelet jangle. 'I guess sometimes you can go home again,' she added softly.

Westcott stiffened, his eyes dropping to her wrist. He looked back up, his cheeks a dark, unattractive red. 'Do you have an alibi for Bennett's murder, Lucy?'

'I do,' she said, not breaking eye contact with him. 'Do you?'

Westcott's jaw tightened and he carefully dropped her hand before taking a step back. 'I have business to attend to, if you'll excuse me.'

'Not yet,' Lucy said quietly. 'Something happened here, in this town, Sonny. Something that involved Bennett, Edwards, Agar, quite possibly you, quite possibly my brother, and somehow, most definitely, me. What happened?'

Westcott's eyes glittered with undisguised malice. 'I could sue you for slander.'

'I have a good lawyer,' she said. 'Go right ahead. But first answer my question.'

'I'm sure I don't know,' he said and headed to his office.

'I'd be careful, were I you, Sheriff Westcott,' she called softly after him. 'Or you might end up on my table too.'

He shot her one last very threatening look, then slammed his office door.

Lucy led them out, not exhaling until she was at the foot of the stairs. The look she shot JD was miserable and now that it was over, she was trembling. 'I hate this place,' she whispered fiercely.

He took her hands in his, unsurprised to find them freezing cold. 'I know,' he said gently. 'But you did great, Lucy. Really, really great.'

'Indeed,' Berman said, puffing a little from the stairs. 'Well played, my dear. We got a reaction. He definitely knows something.'

'But he's not going to say. Yet anyway,' Stevie said. 'What next, Lucy?'

She straightened her spine. 'We talk to the old sheriff. Come with me.'

Tuesday, May 4, 2.20 P.M.

They followed Lucy down Main Street. Quickly buildings became farther apart, revealing the Bay. With Stevie, Berman and JD behind her, Lucy turned into a marina with a dozen docks. The smallest boat was at the end of the boardwalk. A man stood on the deck, hands on his hips. Watching them.

A very bad feeling skittered down JD's spine. A glance at Berman and Stevie showed that they too felt the tension in the air.

No, JD thought. *Just . . . no. Don't let it be what I think this is.*

JD followed her until she stopped, halfway down the dock. She slid the duffle bag to the dock and waited, her hands at her sides. The man stared at her for a very long minute before mounting the steps from his boat to the dock which rumbled under his feet as he approached.

He was a big man, with broad shoulders and ice-blue eyes that could have drilled through steel. He said nothing as he and Lucy locked gazes and then JD knew for sure.

Oh, Lucy. Honey.

'These people are from the city,' she said to the man, bypassing any greeting. 'They want to talk to you. They are Detectives Fitzpatrick and Mazzetti and Dr Berman, their profiler.' Her tone became lightly mocking. 'Everyone, meet Anderson Ferry's retired sheriff, Ron Trask.'

JD thought of the story she'd told him. Mrs Westcott had called the police. *And my father gave me a stern talking-to.* Her father was the police. JD felt the fury surge and shoved it away. She didn't need his anger. She had plenty of her own. It was coming off her in palpable waves.

'Your father,' JD murmured. 'Why didn't you tell me?'

But Lucy said nothing, keeping her gaze fixed on her father's face.

'Why are you here?' Trask asked harshly.

301

'We're investigating a homicide,' Stevie said. 'We'd like your cooperation.'

Ron Trask didn't look away from Lucy. 'Russ Bennett?' he asked. Lucy nodded.

Trask's jaw hardened. 'Are you involved?'

She nodded again and said not a word in her own defense.

JD stepped to her side, put his hand lightly at the small of her back. 'Bennett is dead along with Malcolm Edwards. Ryan Agar has been abducted.'

Something flickered in Trask's cold eyes, but it was quickly extinguished. 'Of course I knew Bennett and I remember Edwards and Agar. They played ball with my son.' He said *my son* in an exclusionary way that pissed JD off.

'Whoever's doing the killing is leaving the bodies for *your daughter* to find,' JD said. 'He's killed two other people that we know of.'

Trask's eyes narrowed as he stared at his daughter. 'What have you done now?'

JD's vision went red around the edges. 'She has done nothing,' he snapped. 'What do you know, sir? And I'm not taking "I don't know" for a goddamned answer.'

'Then you'll get no answer at all,' Trask snapped back. 'This has nothing to do with me.' He started to walk away when Lucy surprised them all by springing forward and grabbing handfuls of her father's shirt.

'*Tell me*,' she growled. 'Tell me what happened or I swear I will make you pay.'

Stunned, Trask's hands came up to push Lucy away, but she held firm. 'I don't know,' he gritted. 'Let go of me or I'll throw your ass in jail where it belongs.'

Lucy gripped his shirt, lifting herself on her toes. 'An innocent young man was murdered last night. His throat was slit *ear* to *ear*. He did *nothing wrong*. He was working a job, that's all, when some *asshole* with a vendetta *slit . . . his . . . throat*.' A sob barreled out of her. 'Buck's friends are dying. So tell me *now*. What. Did. Buck. Do?'

Trask ripped Lucy's hands from his shirt, holding her by her wrists. 'Nothing. Your brother did nothing. *You* were the bad kid, always the one in trouble. Always the embarrassment.' His hands tightened, his thumbs digging into her wrists as he forced her arms backward. With a flinch and a gasp of pain she rose higher on her toes and from the look in her eyes, JD knew this wasn't the first time her father had hurt her.

JD's fury erupted and he'd twisted a handful of Trask's collar in his fist, digging his knuckles into her father's throat before he even knew he'd planned to do so. 'Let her go,' he said deliberately and quietly. 'Now.'

He had the satisfaction of seeing Trask's eyes flash in fear before he let go. JD shoved Trask away so hard that the man stumbled. From the corner of his eye he saw Lucy rub her arms with a grimace of pain and JD's fury bubbled over again.

He followed Trask step for step, invading his space, satisfied that even though they were the same height Lucy's father had to look up because he was cowering. 'Touch her again,' JD whispered, 'and I'll see *your* ass in jail where it belongs.'

Trask flashed his daughter a look of hate before stomping away, sending the dock shaking under his feet. He climbed aboard his boat and disappeared below deck.

The dock stopped shaking, but Lucy didn't. JD pulled her against him and to his surprise she didn't fight him. Instead she turned into him, pressing her clenched fists into his chest. Meeting Stevie's sad eyes over Lucy's head, JD wrapped her in his arms and let her tremble. And cry. 'Did he hurt you?' he murmured.

'No. Nothing my mother couldn't patch up anyway,' she said, then stiffened when JD went rigid, his fury bubbling up all over again. She cleared her throat roughly. 'But you meant just now, didn't you? No, he didn't hurt me.'

'You should have told me,' he whispered.

Berman slipped a handkerchief into her clenched fist, reminding them that they were not alone. 'Your father didn't notice your bracelet or he didn't think anything about it if he did. When you're ready, I suggest we go to a place that will delight in spreading gossip our way.'

'The beauty parlor?' Stevie asked, tongue in cheek and Berman's lips twitched.

'My lovely wife says the beauty parlor, although a perfect microcosm of social networking, is off limits for my observation.' He sobered. 'I was talking about the newspaper office.'

Lucy drew a deep breath and released her hold on JD. She used Berman's handkerchief to swipe at her face, shuddering out a sigh. 'I'm okay. This way.'

Tuesday, May 4, 2.35 P.M.

Well. That had been fascinating on several counts. Old man Trask still had some piss and vinegar in him. *We'll see how brave he is once he's on my turf.*

Had he not known the truth about Lucy Trask, he might have felt sorry for her. But he did know, and even if he'd been one iota unsure, he now knew without a shadow of a doubt. He'd seen it just now with his own eyes. She had it. *Wore it.*

Like it *belonged* to her. *The bitch.*

It had been all he could do not to leap from his hiding place and rip the bracelet off her arm. But he'd restrained himself. Barely. It was only the mental image of what he'd do to her when he finally got her in his hands that kept him calm. Mostly.

He'd planned how he'd take the next names on his list, but that was before she'd brought detectives to Anderson Ferry. Now it would be harder to steal one, then another. People would become suspicious and less easily manipulated.

He could remedy that easily. *I'll just take them all.* He'd keep them in the plant until he was ready to deal with them. Then he'd be back to his own timeline, unrushed by Lucy Trask's continuing presence.

She was smarter than he'd realized. She came back here, head high, hiding what she'd done in plain sight. She'd led the search, so no one would suspect her now.

Except for me. Because I know what a lying, conniving bitch she really is.

He watched as Lucy led the detectives back to Main Street, then slipped from between the buildings where he'd been waiting. His step light, he made his way aboard Trask's boat, then below, where the sound of cheers came from a small television. It was a video of a football game, made with an old camcorder. The print was lousy, the picture worn, as if it had been viewed a thousand times. It probably had.

Ron sat with his back to the stairs. A glass of vodka in one hand, he stared broodingly at the picture on his shelf. Boys in football jerseys stared back, championship grins on their faces.

He knew the picture, remembered the first time he'd seen it. *I thought those guys walked on water. If I'd only known, I would have killed them then.* But he sure as hell could now, and he would. He withdrew his gun from his pocket and approached, the sounds of the cheers muffling his footsteps. Ironic, that.

The old man sensed his presence and turned in the chair. 'What the hell? Who—'

It was all he got out before slumping to the ground. The butt of a gun was still a damn good way to knock someone out. He hog-tied Ron and shoved a gag in his mouth.

Then he put on one of the old man's shirts and chose a hat from the closet.

'Sheriff' was embroidered on the brim. It would do nicely. When he sailed the boat from the dock, nobody would guess that it wasn't Ron Trask at the wheel.

Tuesday, May 4, 2.50 P.M.

Fitzpatrick and the others had given her space as they walked to the newspaper office, and for that Lucy was grateful. The outburst was embarrassing enough, but she hated crying in front of people. Seeing her father again had been a shock. And then to be accused . . . again. *What have you done now?* he'd asked. Cold sonofabitch.

She'd snapped. She'd seen Kevin Drummond's lifeless body with that obscene, gaping wound across his throat and she'd snapped. *What did Buck do?*

She'd lied. Her wrists did hurt. Her father had always known how to cause the most pain the fastest way. But Fitzpatrick had stopped him. *He took up for me. Protected me*. Then he'd held her, the way she'd always wanted to be held.

He could be good for you. Foolishly, she let herself hope. Just a little. But the hope skittered away as the larger question hit her hard again.

What did Buck do? She'd racked her brain on the drive down, trying to think of anything, anything he could have done. Anything that could have driven a killer to such rage that he'd beaten and mutilated Russ Bennett and Janet Gordon. That he could so callously slit the throats of Kevin Drummond and the still unidentified woman in her morgue.

Her feet slowed to a stop at the corner of Main and Church, a memory pressing her mind. It had cut through the turmoil raging through her as she'd grabbed her father's shirt. As the words had spewed from her mouth. *What did Buck do?*

And she realized they were not her words.

'Lucy?' Warmth radiated against her back, making her shudder. Fitzpatrick's hands gently covered her shoulders. 'What is it?'

'What did Buck do?' she whispered. 'It's what *she* said. My mother.'

'When?' he murmured.

'The morning of Buck's funeral. She was sitting on his bed, crying. My father had gone into Buck's room to tell her it was time to leave. For the church. He was so angry. He was always angry, but that day . . . There was something in his voice. I was scared.'

'Of what?'

She closed her eyes. 'I left my room and stood in the hall, just in case.'

'Of what?' he asked again.

'In case he hurt her. He did sometimes. Never where anyone could see. When Buck got old enough . . . and big enough . . . it stopped.' She swallowed. 'I knew Buck had made it stop.'

'Your brother saved you from your father's abuse,' he said softly.

'Yes. But then he was gone. All of a sudden, he was gone.'

'What happened the morning of the funeral?'

'She was crying and my father grabbed her arms and yanked her to her feet. Shook her. Hard. He was so angry. I thought he'd hit her then, but she grabbed his shirt and screamed at him, "What did Buck do?"'

There was a moment of tense silence. 'What did he say?' Fitzpatrick asked.

She clenched her closed eyes tighter. 'I don't know. He lifted her off her feet and got in her face. I couldn't hear what he said, but she went white and just nodded. He let her go and I ran back to my room. I wanted to hide when he walked by, but he stopped in the doorway and said, "Two minutes." I knew better than to say a word.'

'What did you think she meant, "What did Buck do?"'

'At the time I guess I thought it was about driving his motorcycle and drinking.'

'He'd been drinking?' Fitzpatrick asked, surprised.

'Yeah. A lot. He was so drunk he shouldn't have been able to walk.' Her voice flattened, went bitter, making her wince at the sound of it.

'How do you know that, Lucy?' Dr Berman asked softly from in front of her and she started, opening her eyes. She hadn't realized that he and Stevie weren't still behind her. They'd been watching her and she shrank away from their scrutiny.

'He'd gone to see his ex-girlfriend that night and she said he was drunk. Then, I looked up the autopsy report,' she admitted, 'after I started with the ME's office. His blood alcohol was three times the legal limit. I'm not sure why I looked. I just needed to know.'

'He left you,' Stevie said. 'He'd been your protector and he left you. You needed to understand why. That's perfectly natural.'

That should have made her feel better. But it didn't. Because another memory had intruded, this one worse than the first. The letters 'I' and 'L' had been burned into the backs of the victims. Now Lucy knew where she'd seen them before. Her stomach churning, she looked over her shoulder, meeting Fitzpatrick's concerned stare. 'I need to go to church, JD.'

Questions filled his eyes, but he only nodded. 'Take us there.'

*

It was four blocks to the little church that stood at the edge of the town. JD held her hand, and with every block her grip became tighter. By the time they stood in front of Our Lady of Mercy she was squeezing his hand so hard he had to fight not to wince.

'I haven't been in the church since the funeral,' she said quietly. 'My father would make us come every week, but after Buck died, he stopped coming. I used to sit on the pew when I was really little and try not to squirm. Usually he hit us on the back of our legs and those hard pews hurt. I'd pray that God would kill my father.' Her lips twisted. 'Then I'd cower, thinking lightning was going to strike me where I sat.'

Before JD could think of a response, she released his hand and started walking again, going around to the back where there was a fenced-in cemetery. She paused, her hands gripping the gate. Then she drew a breath and pushed it open. Silently JD, Stevie, and Berman followed.

Lucy stopped at a headstone that read *Linus Trask, Beloved Son.* For a moment she stared down at it. Then she looked up and around to get her bearings. 'I haven't been in the church, but I came to the cemetery several times that summer I came home from St Anne's. It was quiet here and I could be near Buck. Creepy as that sounds.'

'We all process grief differently,' Stevie said.

'I suppose so. It's over here.' Lucy led them to the far side of the cemetery, stopping at a plain marker set into the ground, and JD sucked in a breath. A glance at Stevie and Berman told him they were also stunned.

'Ileanna Bryan,' JD said, reading the marker. *I and L.* Born the same year as Buck Trask, she'd also died the same year. Just two weeks before Buck. 'Who was she?'

'She was assaulted the night of their senior prom. Raped and beaten by her ex-boyfriend, who killed himself later that night. Apparently he was jealous because she'd gone to the prom with someone else. I don't remember the boy's name, only hearing that he'd gotten high on something and went berserk. She died of her injuries before the sun came up. It was all the talk until Buck died. Then he was all the talk.'

'How does this connect to Buck?' JD asked.

'He was her prom date.'

'Oh, wow,' Stevie murmured. 'Did this happen at the prom? Was your brother there?'

'No. He'd taken her home early and gone out with his friends. She was kind of a substitute date, I think. He'd broken up with the girl he'd been seeing for two years and ended up taking Ileanna. I'd forgotten about her until this afternoon.'

'What made you remember today?' Berman asked.

'Like I said, I came here a lot that summer break from St Anne's. By then it had been two years since Buck died, but I still missed him. I haunted this cemetery that summer. Knew all the headstones and made up stories about how they'd lived. Anything was better than going home. I'd get sad when I came to this marker. She had her life stolen and it wasn't her fault.'

'Unlike your brother, who carelessly threw his life away?' Berman asked softly.

'I did resent him, then. But as I got older I realized how miserable he really was. I always wondered if he'd had an accident on purpose, to get away from home. But then that didn't make sense – he had a football scholarship. He was getting away. I thought that's what my mother meant that night. "What did Buck do?" I thought she meant he'd wrecked his motorcycle on purpose. Now, I'm not so sure.'

'Was he ever suspected of involvement in Ileanna's death?' Stevie asked.

'No. He said he took her home, dropped her off, then went back out. My father backed him up, said he'd seen Buck come in, change out of his tux and take off again. My father was the sheriff, so nobody asked Buck a second time. The girl's ex-boyfriend was found the next morning. He'd shot himself in the head. The case was closed.'

'Except that now somebody thinks Buck was involved,' JD said quietly. 'Or you wouldn't be finding bodies. Did Ileanna have family?'

'She had a dad who was angry.' Lucy frowned. 'There was something that she'd been wearing when she died that wasn't on her body. They accused my father of stealing it. But that was

309

ridiculous.' She said it hollowly, like she might have believed it ridiculous then, but was no longer certain now. 'It was a diamond necklace. They made a big deal about it.'

'Where is the family now?' JD asked.

'I'm not sure. I think they moved away. By then things were really bad at home and I don't remember much of anything.'

'What was happening at home?' Berman asked and Lucy shrugged tightly.

'My mother had a nervous breakdown and had to go away for a while.'

JD's heart sank. 'Leaving you alone with your father.'

'Yeah,' she said curtly. 'I kind of checked out the rest of that year.'

'And then you found the bracelet,' Stevie said.

Startled, Lucy stared at her wrist. She seemed to have forgotten about the bracelet. 'Yes. And Sonny Westcott took it from me. Why?'

'I don't think he's going to tell us,' Berman said practically.

Lucy's lips firmed. 'Then let's find someone who will.'

Tuesday, May 4, 3.30 P.M.

'Hold on,' Fitzpatrick said, stopping her before she could walk into the newspaper office. She'd been a woman on a mission, leading them from the cemetery back to Main Street while Fitzpatrick, Stevie and Berman had murmured behind her. 'We've got a motive, Ileanna Bryan. We know Russ, Ryan and Malcolm were involved, or perceived to be. We know Sonny reacted to your bracelet. How many other people might be involved?'

Stevie took the team photo from her briefcase. 'There are twenty-five boys in this picture. I checked names against the yearbook I found in Janet's closet and had Hyatt's clerk run whereabouts on the four other seniors on this team – George Cuzman, Marty Swenson, Randy Richards, James Cannon. Two have moved from the area, one died several years ago in a car wreck and the fourth lives in downtown Baltimore. We're trying to contact the three still alive.'

310

'Bennett didn't play on the team,' Lucy said and Stevie nodded.

'True, so we could have other potential targets. I want the police and coroner reports on Ileanna, but since we're here, let's get anything the newspaper has on the night of that prom, both the dance and her assault.' Stevie opened the door to the newspaper office. 'Hello?'

A man nearing forty came out from the back room, polishing his eyeglasses. 'Can I help you?' His eyes widened when he saw Lucy. 'Lucy Trask.'

Taken aback, Lucy searched his face for clues to who he was. 'You know me?'

'Oh, yes. I'm Bart Higgins. You broke my friend's nose the first week of the tenth grade.'

Lucy saw Fitzpatrick's brows raise. 'I'm sorry,' she said to Higgins. 'I really am.'

'It's okay,' Higgins said. 'He deserved it for taunting you when you came home from that girls' school that summer.' He leaned his elbows on the counter. 'Why did you come back?'

She introduced the others and let Stevie take the lead.

'We're interested in the death of Ileanna Bryan,' Stevie said.

Again his eyes widened. He went to a file cabinet and was back in less than a minute with a folder. 'Ileanna Bryan.'

Fitzpatrick and Stevie leafed through the papers in the file, Fitzpatrick looking up with a frown. 'Why did you have this at your fingertips?'

'Nobody asks about the Bryan girl for twenty years, then two of you do. A PI came in asking questions and this was what I pulled. Her name's on the request form on the back.'

'Nicki Fields,' Fitzpatrick read. 'I think we'd like to talk to her.'

'Shouldn't be too hard,' Higgins said. 'She lives in Baltimore.'

Stevie flipped the folder over, jotted the address down. 'Thanks.'

'When did you give this to the PI?' Fitzpatrick asked.

'About a week ago. Maybe a little less.'

Stevie checked her cell phone, read a message, then frowned. 'I need to make a call. Can we get copies of this file?'

'Of course,' Higgins said. 'I'll be right back.'

Higgins disappeared in the back and Fitzpatrick and Stevie went outside, Berman following. Lucy was right behind them when her phone buzzed in her pocket. It was a text from Craig. *Tried to call, keep getting your v/m. CALL ME. It's critical.*

Her phone was getting only one reception bar in the office. Apparently all her calls were going to voicemail, but luckily texts came through. She continued reading Craig's messages and her stomach rose to clog her throat. She rushed outside to where Stevie was having some trouble with her cell phone too.

'Stevie's talking to the detective looking for Ryan Agar,' Fitzpatrick told Lucy before she could speak. 'He was on the hotel's security video from this morning, leaning on another man who took him to the elevator, and looking kind of sick. They went to the parking garage where Ryan got pushed in a wheelchair to a black Lexus.'

'Like the one following us before,' Lucy said. He'd been close. *So close.* A shiver ran down her back. *He was following us. Me.*

'Is the man pushing him identifiable?' Berman asked.

'No,' Fitzpatrick said. 'He's wearing a tweed hat that covers part of his face.'

'Like the one he left on Russ Bennett's head,' Lucy said.

'Exactly,' Fitzpatrick said. 'The Lexus exited from the self-pay lane. The camera caught a mustache on the driver's face, but that's it.'

'The license plate?' Lucy asked, but Fitzpatrick shook his head.

'Stolen. We put a BOLO out anyway, but it's likely he's changed the plates.'

In which case the be-on-the-lookout wouldn't help at all, Lucy thought.

Stevie hung up her cell. 'We need to find that PI. I'll get Debbie looking.'

Lucy held up one hand. 'Don't bother. I know exactly where she is.'

Fitzpatrick's face fell. 'No way. Don't even say it.'

'She's dead,' Lucy said. 'Craig finished the cut on the Jane Doe and was reviewing the new cases. Nicki Fields was brought in this morning. Her throat was slit with that little curve around the ear, just like Kevin and Jane Doe.'

'Shit,' Fitzpatrick hissed.

'Oh, dear,' Berman murmured.

'Craig says it appeared she'd been dead in her apartment for several days.'

'I wonder if the file was what got her killed,' Stevie said. 'And I wonder why she was looking for this information to begin with. What else did Dr Mulhauser say, Lucy?'

Lucy scrolled through the text messages. 'She was found in an apartment in Laurel. The call was put in to 911 by one of her co-workers who was worried when she didn't check in. Two Laurel detectives are assigned to the case. Wenzel and Graham.'

'I'll call them,' Stevie said. 'We need to talk to the person who made the 911 call.'

'What was in the file?' Lucy asked.

'Mostly what you already told us,' Fitzpatrick said. 'The suicide was an eighteen year old named Ricky Joyner.'

'Who'd gotten into it with Buck Trask after a football game earlier that season,' Higgins said from behind them and all four of them jumped. In his hand he held an envelope that he extended to Stevie. 'The copies you asked for. I'm sorry. I didn't mean to sneak up on you.'

Stevie glared at him. 'Yes you did,' she said.

Higgins shrugged. 'Okay, I did. Call me curious. There are events that have an impact on a kid's life. Ileanna Bryan's murder was one of those for me. Buck's accident was another. Every kid I knew had wanted to be him. Including me.'

'What did you mean?' Fitzpatrick asked. 'About Ricky Joyner and Buck?'

'Joyner played for another team. Rival school. He'd sacked Buck with a dirty hit in one of their games. Afterward, some of Buck's pals worked him over. Lots of folks thought that's what made him lose it, finding out his girl dumped him to go to the prom with Buck of all people. Of course, all the crack he'd smoked sure didn't help.'

'What about Ileanna?' Berman asked. 'What do you remember about her?'

Higgins sighed. 'You have to remember, this was years ago. I remember people saying that girls who "dressed like that Bryan girl" were asking for trouble.'

'Asking to be raped,' Stevie said flatly.

'I know,' Higgins said, holding up his hands in surrender. 'And I agree with you.'

'What happened to Ileanna's family?' Fitzpatrick asked.

'They moved away somewhere,' Higgins said. 'I didn't know any of them. Ileanna was older than me and her brother was younger.'

Lucy's blood went cold. 'Younger brother? She had a younger brother?'

'His name was Evan. That's who the PI was originally checking on when she requested the articles.'

#1 Sister. Lucy stared at the bracelet on her wrist, her stomach beginning to churn. She looked up and saw that Fitzpatrick had come to the same conclusion. She slipped her hand into her pocket, hoping her action was subtle and knowing it was not.

'I heard Ileanna was missing some jewelry,' Fitzpatrick said.

'A diamond necklace, shaped like a heart,' Higgins said. 'It was supposedly an heirloom.'

'Supposedly?' Stevie asked.

'Nobody had ever seen it before that night. Mr Bryan was a hard-working waterman. He worked the channels for crabs and whatever else he could pull from the Bay. People said that if they'd really owned a diamond necklace they would have sold it long ago to have a better life. The Bryans said they kept it in the mother's jewelry box, that nobody wore it.'

'But Ileanna was wearing the necklace that night,' Fitzpatrick said.

'Yes. That's a fact. It was in the prom picture and it's heart-shaped. Whether it was diamond is anybody's guess, because it never turned up. Apparently Ileanna had wanted to wear it to the prom, her mother had refused, and Ileanna snuck it out anyway. Her family made a big fuss about it.' He glanced at Lucy uneasily. 'They even went as far as to accuse the police and coroner of stealing it.'

'What was the response?' Berman asked and Higgins shrugged.

'The police said the guy who'd killed her and then himself had probably taken it and who knew where it had gone? Then Buck crashed and died and people were happy not to focus on the murder of a girl from the wrong side of the tracks anymore.'

'Do you have a copy of the prom pictures?' Berman asked.

'Yes. My uncle took the pictures for the paper. He took homecoming and graduation photos too. They're stored in the basement, but I can find that year's box.'

'How long will it take you to get it?' Fitzpatrick asked. 'We need to get back to the city.'

'An hour, tops. If I can get it faster, I will.'

Fitzpatrick gave Higgins his card. 'One more question. A few weeks ago Russ Bennett requested copies of the articles on Lucy's trial. Do you know why?'

Again Higgins glanced at Lucy uneasily. 'It wasn't Russ. It was Jason Bennett.'

Lucy flinched, feeling like she'd been punched in the gut. 'Russ's father? Why?'

'He didn't say. I didn't ask. I'll call you when I've found the pictures.'

Lucy stared after him, barely breathing, and when Fitzpatrick put his arm around her she leaned into him without hesitation. Shoving furious tears back down, she fumbled with the clasp on the bracelet, bile burning her throat. 'I want this *off*. *Now*.'

'Whoa,' Stevie said quietly. 'Let me help you.' She took it off Lucy's wrist and placed it in a plastic evidence bag. 'Number One Sister,' she said grimly.

'Which was not me.' And it hurt, a lot more than she'd thought possible. 'I think we have a more specific question to ask my father now. What did Buck do *to Ileanna Bryan*?'

'We have questions for a lot of people,' Stevie said. 'I want to go back to the sheriff's office and get the official report on Ileanna's death.'

'I want to ask Jason Bennett why Russ asked for those articles,'

Fitzpatrick said. 'They're probably connected to the "client" he was meeting the day he disappeared.'

'And I want to talk to my mother,' Lucy said grimly. 'I want to know what she meant by "What did Buck do?"'

Tuesday, May 4, 3.55 P.M.

Ah. They were here. It paid to have a good memory. He'd played on this section of beach once upon a time. Before his world was smashed to oblivion by the Trasks. He tied Ron Trask's boat to the dock and went below.

Trask had come to, muffled grunts coming from his mouth. He shoved in more of the gag. If the old man fought, he'd throw up. Then he'd choke on it and die. Which was too good for him. Taking the cell phone from Trask's pocket, he scrolled through the contacts until he found the one he wanted, then dialed.

'Hello?' a woman asked.

'Hi, I'm trying to reach Mrs Kathy Trask.'

'This is she. Who is this and why are you calling from my husband's cell phone?'

Because I'm going to kill you. 'I was fishing when your husband's boat hit my dock. He kind of staggered out of the bridge and collapsed on the deck. At first I thought he was drunk, but he doesn't look so good. I'm no doctor, but I think he's sick.'

'Oh, dear God. Oh no. Did you call 911?'

'I was going to but he asked me not to. He got really upset and asked me to call you first. He said you'd know what to do.'

'Of course. He hates hospitals. Where did you say you were again?'

He smiled down at Ron, who seemed to have just caught on to what was going on. The man's eyes were almost bugging out of his head. 'I'm renting a place about two miles up the shore. It's a little cottage with blue shutters. The mailbox says "Turlington".'

'I know the place. Tell Ron I'll be there as fast as I can.'

'I will. And I won't leave him until you get here.'

'Thank you so much,' she said, her voice shaking. 'You can't know how much I appreciate this.' A car started, then screeched out of the driveway. 'I'm on my way.'

He hung up and smiled at Ron. 'She's going to meet us. Then the fun will begin.'

Tuesday, May 4, 4.15 P.M.

'Clay,' Alyssa said.

Clay looked up from the stack of Nicki's client files he'd removed from her office. They'd spread the files out on his dining room table and had been searching for clues for hours. 'Did you find something in her credit card statements?'

'Maybe. I've been through her statements for the last four months and haven't seen any changes in her spending patterns. Any place she went coincided with her case log, except for a day about two weeks ago. She had no purchases, not even Starbucks.'

'A cash-only day,' Clay murmured. 'She went under, but where did she go?'

'I'll start looking through her receipts. Maybe she kept something.'

Clay put the box client files aside. 'If she went on a cash-only day, she probably didn't keep anything. Not on purpose anyway.'

'What are you doing?'

He found the box of trash he'd taken from her car. 'Check the toll tickets. I'll go through the receipts. I want to know where she went that day.'

Alyssa frowned. 'Wait. Didn't you say you could track her car?'

Clay closed his eyes. He'd been so preoccupied with where she was that he hadn't thought to use the tracker to find where she'd been. 'Yes.' He opened his eyes to find Alyssa giving him a sympathetic look.

'You're still in shock,' she said. 'Don't beat yourself up.'

He nodded, logging into the tracking website he and Nicki had used. 'I can see the last fourteen days.' He immediately saw what he'd been looking for. 'She went to Ocean City that day, but the long way. The really long way. She went to a place called Anderson Ferry first. It added about two hours to her drive.'

'What's in Anderson Ferry?' Alyssa asked.

'I don't know. I have to pick up Nicki's parents from the airport. I promised them I'd go with them to the morgue to do the ID. When I'm done with that, I'll drive out to Anderson Ferry and find out.'

'I'll go with you.'

'No, you don't have to. I'd rather you stay here until we find Mr Reardon.'

'I'll see what I can find on Anderson Ferry while you're gone.'

'Lock the door behind me.'

318

Nineteen

Tuesday, May 4, 4.25 P.M.

'Which one first?' JD asked. The four of them stood on the sidewalk between the Trask and Bennett houses. Lucy stared anxiously at her childhood home while Stevie finished texting DA Grayson Smith for a little assistance in getting the Bryan case file from the Anderson Ferry police. Sheriff Westcott's clerk had informed them of the twenty-four-hour response time on archival requests.

Ryan Agar had been taken by a killer and twenty-four hours might be too late.

They'd also been unsuccessful in talking to Lucy's father again – his boat had been gone when they'd returned to the dock. Lucy had looked both frustrated and relieved. And lost. The look on her face when she'd really accepted that the bracelet had not been bought for her, that she was not the '#1 Sister' . . . It had broken JD's heart.

'My mother,' Lucy said. 'If she'll speak with me. Dr Berman, I may need your help.'

'You know I will,' Berman said, 'but I have to ask how and why?'

'I told you my mother had a nervous breakdown.'

'From the grief. Because your brother died,' Berman said.

'Yes,' Lucy said, but she didn't sound convinced. 'My mother was once a sharp woman with an important job. She was always busy, always going somewhere, helping someone. Then Buck died and she . . . wound down like a clock. She'd spend hours polishing his trophies while my father watched Buck's games on videotape over and over. One day I found her sitting on his bed, staring into space. She was unresponsive and I got scared. I called my father, who called her doctor. I didn't know she'd been seeing a psychiatrist. They took her away.'

'What about when she came back from the mental hospital?' Berman asked softly.

'She was different. She'd been afraid of my father, but after she wasn't. If you mentioned Buck, you got a response and you could never be sure which one it would be. Sometimes weepy, sometimes angry. Sometimes she'd shut down again.'

'So why are you afraid she won't speak to you, Lucy?' Stevie asked.

'I don't think I understood how very fragile she'd become and I pushed her buttons. I talked about Buck as often as I could. I was getting in trouble a lot and then I got caught by Mrs Westcott and I think that was the final straw. She contacted St Anne's and they took me away.'

'Your mother sent you away?' JD asked, stunned. He'd assumed it had been her father.

'Yes. Asking about Buck may upset her. I'd like you to be there, Dr Berman. Just in case.'

'It's been twenty years,' Stevie said. 'Surely she'll be better now.'

'Not according to the Bennetts. They update me whenever we have lunch. My mother is still fragile. She's never gone back to work. She rarely leaves the house.'

'Do you think your father still hits her?' Stevie asked carefully.

'I don't think so. Like I said, she was different when she came back. She'd defy him and he'd back off. So I don't think he does.' A sad yearning filled her eyes. 'Although she wouldn't leave him, even if he did.'

JD thought of the mixed feelings he got when his mother came around. Mostly hate, but always that kernel of hope. Of wishful thinking. He hoped Lucy's mother didn't turn her away.

Lucy squared her shoulders. 'Let's get this over with.'

The four of them walked up to the Trasks' front door and JD started to knock.

'She's not there.'

JD's fist froze an inch away from the door and the four of them looked to the right. Two doors down Mrs Westcott stood on her doorstep, her arms crossed over her sizeable bosom, a formidable frown on her face.

'Where is she?' JD asked.

'I don't know. I saw her rush out about a half-hour ago with her medical bag.'

It was JD's turn to frown. 'Medical bag? Why?'

'Because she's a doctor,' Lucy murmured.

'Because she's a doctor,' Mrs Westcott said at the same time, with some importance.

'Your mother is a doctor?' JD asked, surprised. *A sharp woman with an important job.*

'Was,' Lucy said, so softly he had to strain to hear.

'She was.' Mrs Westcott cast a scowl at Lucy. 'Until her daughter drove her crazy.'

Lucy stiffened and once again JD wanted to strike Mrs Westcott.

Mrs Westcott must have sensed she'd hit a nerve because she smiled with satisfaction. 'Now all she does is see hypochondriacs and people crazier than she is.'

Lucy's fists tightened. 'Don't,' JD murmured. 'She's not worth it.'

Stevie cleared her throat. 'Let me and Lennie talk to her.' She and Berman crossed the front yards until they looked up at Westcott on her stoop. Stevie introduced herself and the doctor.

Westcott looked at them suspiciously. 'Are you with *her*?'

'More like she's with us,' Stevie said. 'How did she drive her mother crazy?'

'She was wild, that's how.' Mrs Westcott descended her front steps, standing inches from Stevie. 'You know she did time,' she said loudly, ensuring that Lucy heard.

Stevie feigned shock. 'Really? Dr Trask?'

'No,' Westcott said, then blinked. 'Yes. The daughter, not the mother. She's a bad seed, that's all. She stole from me.' Again Westcott scowled at Lucy. 'I bet she didn't bother to tell you that. Stole my ring and a hundred dollars in cash. Found it in her unmentionable drawer. She got sent away. Then she killed a man and nearly killed two others. She sat in jail for that.'

'We understand she was found innocent,' Stevie said.

Westcott sniffed. 'What she *found* was a fancy-pants lawyer who got her off. Lots of excuses, half-baked explanations and what-have-you. No justice in this world.'

'It's a shame,' Berman said quietly. 'Sometimes people can have the truth stare them in the face and yet they won't accept it.'

'That is so true,' Westcott said, aggrieved.

'If I needed to reach Mrs Trask, would you have her cell phone number?' Stevie asked.

'Of course. I'm the Neighborhood Watch coordinator. I have everyone's number. I'll be right back.' Quickly she returned with the list. 'Why do you need to talk to Kathy Trask?'

'Very complete,' Stevie pronounced, ignoring the woman's question. 'If all Neighborhood Watch coordinators were this prepared, our job would be so much easier. We stopped by the sheriff's office to ask a question, but your son had been called away. Might I also have his cell?'

'I'm sure he wouldn't mind,' Mrs Westcott said, still preening at Stevie's compliment. 'Anything to help a fellow officer.' She rattled the number off and Stevie wrote it down.

'Thanks. If you'll excuse us, we need to check on the Bennetts before we leave.'

'You missed them,' Mrs Westcott said. 'They left this morning.'

'Do you know where they went?' Stevie asked.

'Into the city,' she said. 'To make arrangements for Russ's burial. Sad to have to bury your own child. Not the way it's supposed to be.'

'No, ma'am,' Stevie said. 'It's not. Thank you for your time.'

Tuesday, May 4, 4.25 P.M.

'Hello? Where are you? Ron?'

He peeked out the cabin window. All was ready for Mrs Trask, who was now rushing up the dock, her medical bag in her hand.

'Down here,' he called. He'd hoisted Ron to the bed, covering him with a blanket so that his bonds remained unseen. 'I thought he should rest.'

Mrs Trask hurried down the steps, whisking past him to where her husband lay. 'Ron.' Too late she saw the gag. Then she saw the gun in Evan's hand and grew deathly pale. 'Please don't hurt us. I'll give you anything you want. Cash, credit cards . . . I have a few narcotics in my bag. You can take it all.'

'That's not what I want, but thank you for the offer,' he said politely.

'Then what do you want?' she asked in a small voice.

'I want what you stole from me.' He shoved her face down on the bed, easily overpowering her. He taped her hands and feet together, then gagged her, all in plain view of her husband who had to lie there helplessly and watch. 'I want my sister back. I want my parents back. I want the life that you ruined.' He leaned forward, watched her eyes go wide with horror. 'I want my mother's necklace. But you can't give me any of those things, can you? All you can give me now is my satisfaction.'

He also wanted his damn bracelet, but he knew exactly where to get that. 'We need to pick up one more passenger. I need you to make a call for me, Sheriff.' He loosened the gag from Ron's mouth.

'Go to hell,' Ron spat.

'You know, Malcolm Edwards didn't want to do what I asked the first time either. So I cut off his wife's finger, right in front of him. Then I slit her throat.'

A terrified mewling sound came from Mrs Trask's throat and Ron was barely able to contain his fury. 'You're sick,' Ron spat.

'I'm sure many would say so. I really don't care.'

'She's old and ill. She's no threat to you. Let her go.'

His brows lifted. 'Such tenderness. My mother was old and ill, too. I was with her when she died, and you know what the last things were that she asked for? Her mother's necklace and her dead daughter. She didn't get what she wanted and neither will you.'

Using Ron's phone, he found the other number he desired. 'Now you're going to tell Sonny Westcott to get his ass up here. That those

Baltimore detectives have come asking questions and the two of you need to talk. And you're going to be convincing or your wife will start losing important body parts.'

'We've seen your face. You can't let us live. Why should I do what you say?'

'I guess this is going to dictate how you die. Malcolm's wife died relatively painlessly.' He shrugged. 'If you don't count the finger. Last week I killed a PI who crossed me. Gutted her like a pig and she felt everything. So it's up to you. I'll have my revenge. Whether Mrs T here goes nicely or very painfully is entirely up to you.'

He put his knife to Mrs Trask's throat. 'I'm dialing now. Think carefully about what you say. I can have her gutted before you utter my sister's name. I promise you she'll feel every slice. Okay, here he is. Make it good, *Sheriff.*'

He put the phone far enough from Ron's ear so that he could hear too. Ron sent him a glare full of hate. *Right back atcha, boy.*

'Sheriff Westcott. Who is this?'

'It's Trask. I need to meet.'

'Not a good idea.'

'Don't make me push you,' Trask snapped. 'Meet me at the Turlington place. Now. Or else I start saying things nobody's gonna want to hear.'

'Sonofabitch,' Sonny hissed. 'You and that daughter of yours can't leave it be.'

Evan pressed the knife a little harder to the old lady's throat and Trask's jaw tightened. 'Look,' Trask said. 'If you don't come, I'll tell the detectives what they want to know.'

There was a small pause. 'Fine. I'll be there.'

He closed the phone and nodded to Trask. 'Very good.'

'Now let her go,' Trask said, somehow still holding onto his arrogance.

'No.' He took out their phone batteries, then leaned closer, so he could feel their terror. Smell it. 'You ruined my life. Your son killed my sister.'

'No. He didn't,' Trask said, desperately. 'He didn't touch her.'

'And you're a fool. You knew what your son did and you knew

324

what he'd stolen from us. Knowing that, you actually stood in my father's house and threatened him.'

Trask could say nothing. He lay there, a muscle twitching in his cheek. Mrs Trask had turned her head to stare at her husband.

She didn't know. He'd assumed she had. 'She didn't know you went to my parents' house and threatened to have them arrested because they wouldn't "shut up about that damn necklace". You ran us out of town. Made us move. We lost *everything*. I was there, hiding in my room, so scared of you. I'm not afraid of you now, old man.'

'She didn't know,' Trask said. 'Let her go.'

'No. Even if she didn't know that, she knew plenty.' He sheathed his knife. 'Even if she knew nothing, she lived a life my mother never got to have. When you ran us off, we lost our business, our house. We had nothing, no money. When my father killed himself, it got even worse. You destroyed my family. Now yours belongs to me.'

Tuesday, May 4, 4.40 P.M.

Higgins was waiting for them in the newspaper office. 'I found the photos from the year Ileanna Bryan died,' he said. 'We've got homecoming, prom and graduation.' He glanced at Lucy. 'Plus some photos of Buck's memorial service. I didn't know if you'd want them or not.'

Lucy swallowed. 'Thanks,' she said and Fitzpatrick rested his hand on her back.

'We'll take everything you could find,' he said. 'Can we see Ileanna's prom picture?'

Higgins took a folder from the top of the box. 'This is their formal photo.'

The four of them crowded the counter to see. Lucy meant to go straight to Ileanna's wrist, but was stopped by the handsome face of the brother she'd adored. That everyone had adored. In a few weeks he'd be dead, all their lives forever changed.

She forced her eyes to Ileanna, a pretty brunette with a smile just a shade naughty. Around her neck was a sparkling heart. But her wrist was bare. Lucy wasn't sure if she was relieved or disappointed. 'It's not there,' she murmured.

'No, it isn't,' Fitzpatrick murmured back and Higgins cleared his throat.

'That,' he said, 'was the formal portrait.' Lucy watched his gaze drop to her own wrist, now also bare. 'My brother took some candid shots, too. Because Buck was Prom King, he and Ileanna are in a lot of the candids.' He put them on the counter and spread them out.

And there it was. For a moment, Lucy couldn't breathe. 'Oh, God.'

Buck and Ileanna were slow-dancing, her hand on his shoulder. From her wrist dangled a silver heart on a bracelet.

Fitzpatrick's hand slid from her back to the curve of her waist. 'Nobody ever asked about the bracelet? Ever?' he asked.

'Not to my knowledge.' Higgins said. 'It wasn't in the police report.'

Fitzpatrick's brows went up. 'You have the police report?'

'A copy's in the box. My grandfather kept it after he wrote the articles about Ileanna.'

Lucy's eyes were drawn back to the prom photos, while Fitzpatrick and Stevie viewed the old police report.

Berman pulled the photos closer. 'Your brother seems . . . large.'

'He was large,' Lucy said. 'He was six three before his fifteenth birthday.'

'I mean his presence. He eats up the frame. He had "it", whatever it was. Look at the expressions of the other boys. At least one of every two doesn't like him. Look at the animosity in their faces and body language.'

Lucy frowned at him. 'Everybody loved Buck.'

'Everybody wanted to *be* Buck,' he corrected. 'Not the same thing. Look at this boy, his jaw. He's tighter than a wound watch. And his fists are clenched. Eyebrows lowered, head slightly bent. If he were a mountain goat, head-butting would have commenced.'

Lucy gave a small smile as she suspected he'd intended. 'That's Russ Bennett.'

'Ah. See? What about this guy?' He pointed to an equally disgruntled-looking boy.

'Malcolm Edwards,' she said. 'Where's Ryan Agar?'

'Not in this picture,' Higgins said, looking until he found one. 'That's him.'

Agar appeared completely uncomfortable, standing alone by the wall.

'He doesn't look angry,' Lucy said. 'More like he wants to be anywhere else.'

'His feet hurt,' Berman said. 'See how he holds his back? His shoes are probably too small. And he's shy.'

She could see it when he described it for her. 'Look at Buck in this picture. Ileanna is looking up at him like he hung the moon, but he's not looking at her.'

'Very good,' Berman praised. 'Who is he looking at?'

She traced his line of sight and a piece of puzzle settled. 'He's looking at Sara, the girl he'd just broken up with.' Lucy tilted her head, looking at her brother with the eyes of an adult. 'That's an eff-you look. He took Ileanna to get back at Sara. I wonder why.' She looked at Higgins. 'What happened to Sara Derringer?'

'Her family moved after high school. She lives in DC and has six kids. I can give you her contact info.' He started spinning his Rolodex before she could say a word. 'Here's her card.'

Lucy slipped it in her pocket. 'Thank you.'

Fitzpatrick and Stevie looked up from their conversation. 'Lucy,' he said, 'your mother was the first responder. Ileanna wasn't dead when she got there. She died about fifteen minutes later, but she was conscious for the first few minutes.'

They'd had to learn her mother was the town doctor from Mrs Westcott. Why Lucy hadn't just told them herself, she didn't know. 'She took calls all hours of the day and night back then. That she was the doctor at the scene makes sense. But Ileanna's body would have been sent to the state morgue, even then. I'll look it up. What about Ricky Joyner, the suicide?'

'Him I don't know about,' Higgins said. 'You might check with the state police.'

'I'll do that,' Fitzpatrick said, taking the box of photos. He and Lucy thanked Higgins, then went out to the car. On their way out of town they drove past the marina, just to see if her father's boat was back, but it wasn't.

'I know we need to talk to him for this case, but I'm relieved,' Lucy said. 'I'm filled up and washed out, all at once. I know that makes no sense.'

'It makes a lot of sense. What I did wonder was how you knew he'd be there.'

'I saw his truck parked in his driveway last night when we visited the Bennetts, then in front of the marina when we drove into town today. I knew before we got here that I'd have to see him, but I just couldn't make myself do it right away.'

'Having met him, I understand.' He squeezed her hand. 'I've got to call into Hyatt's office for our status meeting now. Just relax for a while. You've had kind of a busy day.'

Tuesday, May 4, 5.05 P.M.

'I've got a press conference in less than an hour,' Hyatt said when JD and Stevie phoned into the status meeting from their cars. 'Morton, Skinner and Miss Montgomery are here with me and Drew is on the line from his office. The press knows about Bennett, Gordon, and the valet. I'm expecting one of them will have figured out that the dumpster woman is connected. So please tell me this little "field trip" of yours gave me something I can use.'

'It did,' Stevie said and she and JD debriefed everything they'd found that day. 'We've got motive. Ileanna Bryan was murdered and somehow this group of boys was involved.'

'And Dr Trask's brother is at the middle of it, thus putting the doctor in it too – by what, association?' Hyatt asked, but for the first time he didn't sound suspicious of Lucy.

'And by the bracelet,' JD said. 'Whether Buck put it where she found it or not, we don't know. If he took it off the dead girl or obtained it another way, we don't know.'

'And there's the missing diamond,' Stevie added. 'The family moved away a few months after the murder, but nobody we talked to knows where they went. It's like they disappeared.'

'Nobody just disappears,' Hyatt said. 'Why now? It's been twenty-one years.'

'We don't know yet,' Stevie admitted.

'So what do we know?' Hyatt snapped.

'That the current sheriff of Anderson Ferry is involved,' JD said. 'His name is Sonny Westcott. He definitely reacted when he saw the bracelet. But he's avoiding us. We got the original police report and Dr Trask will search for the girl's autopsy report.'

Lucy held up her phone. 'I already requested Ileanna and Ricky Joyner's autopsy reports.'

'I heard her,' Hyatt said. 'Tell her thank you.'

'I will,' JD said. 'Have we ID'd Jane Doe yet?'

'Yes,' Drew said. 'Her prints were in the system. Her name is Sue Ellen Lamont. She was arrested three years ago, credit card scam.'

'So far,' Elizabeth Morton said, 'nobody's reported her missing. She's got a closet full of condoms in her apartment. I think high-class call girl is a good guess. We can give her driver's license photo to the news and see if anyone's seen her around town.'

'What kind of car does she drive?' JD asked, thinking of the black Lexus.

'Ford Focus,' Elizabeth said. 'And we haven't found it yet. We've also been unable to track the black Lexus that took Ryan, if that's what you were thinking, JD.'

'I wish I hadn't lost the guy tailing me earlier,' JD said, annoyed with himself. 'It was probably him and I let him get away.'

'You didn't know,' Hyatt said grudgingly, surprising him. 'Elizabeth, get the woman's picture ready for me to give to the press at six. We'll get some extra staff to man the phone lines. I'd rather announce it than make it look like we're hiding something.'

'What about the PI?' Stevie asked. She'd already updated Hyatt with the news of Nicki Fields's death. 'Will you include her in the press conference?'

'No, I won't include the PI,' Hyatt said. 'Not yet. Laurel PD's handed the investigation over to us. I debriefed the two detectives assigned the case. They've tried to track the PI's movements, but hit a roadblock. Her cell was prepaid. There are no files anywhere in her apartment or office and somebody took her computer.'

'Could have been our guy,' Stevie said.

'Or her own co-workers,' Hyatt said. 'The Laurel detectives said her partner who called 911 was very non-specific about everything. They also talked to the secretary who says she just answered phones and got coffee. Laurel PD thinks they're both lying, but they don't know why. Could be nerves or could be that they're covering up. I'll have Debbie send you their info, Stevie. Check them out. The partner is Clay Maynard and the secretary is Alyssa Moore.'

'Will do.'

'Skinner, what do we have on the big-ass flash freezer?' Hyatt asked.

'Nothing yet,' Detective Skinner said. 'I've got a list of places that have gone out of business in the last few years that might have one. I'll start on those tomorrow.'

'We've spent most of the day on the alibis for the club personnel,' Elizabeth Morton said. 'Unfortunately, only two people don't have alibis for all the murders. Both are women, and Ryan Agar was definitely abducted by a man.'

'Any progress on getting the club's client list from Thorne?' JD asked.

Lucy looked up, a frown on her face. JD shrugged.

'I've got the warrant written,' Daphne said. 'Grayson is reviewing it. I do have news, though. I talked to Russ Bennett's partner. I mentioned the American Medical Association might have some issues with that cheek implant switcheroo. You know, his implanting Bennett with that other guy's cheeks. I told him a little cooperation with me certainly couldn't hurt him if he gets investigated. He was . . . persuaded to give me Bennett's financials for one patient – Janet Gordon.'

'And?' JD asked, wishing he could have witnessed Daphne's 'persuasion'.

'Janet got two procedures from Bennett. A facelift and a breast augmentation. She was scheduled for a tummy tuck next month. She didn't pay him a single dime.'

'Bennett did Gordon's surgery for free?' JD asked, astonished.

'That doesn't sound like the Russ Bennett we've heard about,' Stevie said. 'Why?'

'The super said Bennett didn't like her, so it wasn't altruism. Could have been blackmail,' JD said. 'I wonder what Janet knew?'

'Same thing her son knows, I'm betting,' Stevie said.

'It'll be "knew" if we don't figure out who's got him before he ends up slumped over a chess table,' Hyatt said grouchily. 'Drew?'

'We processed prints on the cars parked around the Mercedes where Janet Gordon was found. The prints on Thorne's vehicles belong to him, Dr Trask, and the dead valet. There are at least twenty individual prints on Gwyn Weaver's car. Still processing. So far nothing's popped. Her apartment was also clean.'

'There's a boyfriend,' JD said. 'He's probably one set of prints. I'll get his name.'

'Royce Kendall,' Lucy said and JD passed it on.

'Get him in to give elimination prints,' Hyatt said. 'Fitzpatrick, keep digging. Find out what happened to the Bryan family. Especially the son. Stevie, you take the PI and the secretary. I want to know what they're hiding. Elizabeth, you get the hooker. Find out where she's been and her client list. Somewhere the hooker, the PI and Ileanna intersect. And Skinner, I want that freezer. Yesterday.' He paused. 'And I still want the warrant for Thorne's client list.'

'Why?' Daphne drawled. 'Because Thorne's a prick or because you think one of his clients is guilty?'

'Yes,' Hyatt snapped. 'Both. Just do it. Keep me updated day or night. I want updates from everyone by eleven P.M. and everyone back here at oh-eight tomorrow. Agar's life depends on how fast we move.'

Lucy tapped JD's sleeve. 'Can you ask when I can go back into my apartment?'

He asked and there was murmuring. 'Drew says she can go back tonight,' Hyatt said. 'The suitcase from last night's scene is still being processed, as is her car.'

'I can deal with that. At least I'll have some routine back. Thank you,' Lucy said.

'She says thanks,' JD said. 'Are we done?'

'No,' Stevie said, and something in the slow way she said it had the hair raising on the back of JD's neck. 'Look, this guy has killed five people in Baltimore alone. Seven if we assume Edwards and his wife are victims too, and eight if we don't find Agar in time. I think we need to draw him out.'

'No,' JD said, knowing now where she was going.

'Say more,' Hyatt said and JD ground his teeth.

Lucy turned to study him warily, but said nothing.

'He wants Lucy,' Stevie said. 'We need him to come out of hiding and try to get her.'

'No,' JD said, more forcefully.

'Detective, that's enough,' Hyatt snapped. 'What did you have in mind, Stevie?'

'First, we make sure she's protected at all times. But this guy knows her routine. He has access to personal details. She's going back to her apartment, a part of that routine. Let's make sure she does everything she did before. The morning run, the club, driving herself to work. All of it. JD, we knew right away that this was all about Lucy.'

He glanced at Lucy from the corner of his eye. She'd turned in her seat, her arms crossed over her chest, watching him. 'What?' she asked. 'What do they want?'

'They want to make you bait,' he said flatly and watched her eyes narrow.

'Protected bait,' Stevie insisted.

'I don't like this, Peter,' Daphne said forcefully. 'She's a civilian.'

'She's a state employee,' Hyatt returned. 'Still, it would have to be completely voluntary. We'd provide her with a security detail. What does she say, Fitzpatrick?'

'Protected bait,' JD told her, jaw clenched. 'Hyatt wants to know what you say.'

She nodded once. 'Tell him I say okay.'

'I heard her,' Hyatt said grimly. 'Tell her I said thank you.'

'Tell her she's going to need to wear the bracelet,' Stevie added.

'You have to wear the bracelet,' JD told her and watched her flinch.

But she nodded again. 'Okay.' She straightened in her seat. 'Let's do it.'

'Bring her in,' Hyatt said. 'Drew, get a wire together. We want to know where she is at all times. Now I've got to get ready for the damn press. Meeting adjourned.'

Tuesday, May 4, 5.40 P.M.

Lucy was on the move. He stood on the deck of Trask's boat, shading his eyes to better see the tracking screen on his cell phone. She was about to hit the Bay Bridge. That meant she'd be back in Baltimore in an hour. Ron Trask's boat was fine and the winds were good, so Evan, Sonny and the Trasks should arrive at their destination an hour or two after that.

Then it was Ryan Agar's turn at bat. So to speak. How painful it would be for Ryan would depend on the man himself. Edwards had made it very hard on himself by taking the moral high road and refusing to reveal the list. Hypocrite. Fucking hypocrite.

If Edwards had taken the high road when it really mattered, everything would be different. *Ileanna would be alive and my life would have been . . . not shit.*

James Cannon had fought back, stupidly. He'd been tied up. *And I had a bat. And a knife.* Like shooting fish in a barrel, except the fish got the last laugh that day. What was left of Cannon must have made them a nice snack.

Now, Bennett . . . He had to laugh. Bennett had tried to negotiate. *Negotiate.*

Bennett had nothing that would counterbalance what he'd done, anyway. He did provide information on Lucy, so he was useful. Plus he'd delivered the goods on Janet Gordon and several of the other parents who'd known what had happened – including Bennett's own father.

Russ Bennett had thought he could buy his freedom, but he had thought wrong. He'd simply added another few names to the list.

The body slumped at his feet stirred. Westcott was regaining consciousness.

'What?' Westcott moaned. 'What happened?'

'You've been abducted,' he said helpfully.

Westcott made a feeble attempt to roll over, only to find he'd been securely bound. 'What the hell?' he gritted through teeth clenched in what had to be agony.

'You got hit in the head, Sonny.'

'By what?'

'By me. Technically, by my bat. I love hi tech, but often low tech is the best weapon. And the most satisfying.'

'Why?' he moaned.

He squatted next to Westcott so that he could clearly see his face. 'Because you're a stinkin' prick, Sonny, and twenty-one years ago you did a very bad thing.'

Westcott struggled briefly, but gave up, closing his eyes. 'I didn't do anything.'

He stood and delivered a vicious kick to Westcott's ribs, making the man cough convulsively. 'Yeah, you did. I wouldn't recommend trying to convince me otherwise. Your fate is in my hands, just like my sister's fate was in yours. If you piss me off, you'll pay the price. Did you read what happened to Russ Bennett?'

Westcott nodded, a small movement. 'You're going to kill me?'

'Absolutely.' He squatted again, glad to see Westcott coughing up blood. 'See, I know what happened that night. I know what you did.'

'Wait,' Westcott said harshly. 'I'll pay you. I have money.'

Evan stood. 'I'm listening.'

'I can get a hundred thousand. But it'll take me a few days.'

'You don't have a few days, Sonny.'

'I'm serious.' Westcott managed to move his head for emphasis, then moaned again. 'I have investments, but I'll have to sell some stock.'

'When we get to where we're going, you can tell me where those investments are. You know, account numbers. Passwords. That kind of thing.'

Westcott slumped. 'I don't know them.'

'You were going to buy me off with stolen money? What kind of sheriff are you?'

'They belong to my mother,' he muttered.

'Oh, now that's just plain mean. Stealing from your mama. Shame on you. Bad, bad sheriff. So, did your mama know?'

'About what?'

'About what you and the others did not do?'

Sonny closed his eyes. 'Have you seen it on CNN?'

Evan almost smiled. If Myrna Westcott had known, she never could have kept it to herself. 'No.'

'Then she didn't know. You killed Ryan Agar's mother. Why?'

'I killed her because she did know. And like you, she did nothing. I tortured her because she profited from my loss. As, I suspect, did you.'

Westcott's eyes flew open. 'I don't know what you're talking about.'

'Yes you do. I was wondering how you got to be sheriff. I kept thinking, Sonny? *Really?* And then I thought the old sheriff would have a lot of say in who followed him.'

'I got elected.'

'That's not what Ron Trask said. He said you threatened to spill the beans on Buck unless he threw his hat into your ring. You want to ask him? He's in the hold.'

Westcott's eyes flickered wildly. 'You have Trask? Here?'

'And his wife.' He had to chuckle at the panicked expression on Westcott's face. 'You thought Trask could save you? Because he's the only one that knew where you went? That's priceless. Nobody knows where you are or who has you. Nobody's going to do anything to help you. Which is justice, don't you agree?'

Twenty

Fitzpatrick gripped his steering wheel until his knuckles were white. 'This is the stupidest thing I've ever heard. Bait. Goddammit.'

'I don't know what you're so upset about,' she said, feeling a calm that rather surprised her. 'I was his target anyway. Now I'm a protected target.'

'You're bait,' he ground out.

'You say tomato. He's coming after me. That's why I'm here, in this car. You feel a need to protect me. Which is nice,' she allowed. 'I'm not going to take unnecessary chances. If they want me to go on TV, shake the bracelet and say "come and get me, big boy", well, then we'll have a conversation. But this isn't that. This is me, living my normal life. With bodyguards.'

Some of the whiteness faded from his knuckles. '"Come and get me, big boy"?'

'Gwyn's the comic. Look, I'm not thrilled about wearing the bracelet again, but there are worse things. Kevin's dead, as are two other people who had nothing to do with whatever happened to Ileanna Bryan. They deserve justice. Ileanna deserves justice.'

'Her murderer's dead, by his own hand.'

'And her bracelet was under my brother's bed in an old cigar box.'

'Could he have killed her and not Ricky Joyner?'

'I've been asking myself that. I want to say no, but nothing is what I thought it was. If Buck had any part at all in her death, that needs to come out.'

He shot her a sideways glance. 'Even if it makes your mother more "fragile"?'

'Yes.'

'If I tell you that you weren't responsible for your mother, would you believe me?'

She shrugged. 'Probably not. She did take care of me, before Buck died. But then she had her breakdown and went away. I guess I never knew how much she protected me until she was gone. And I was mad at her for leaving.'

'What did he do?' Fitzpatrick asked softly. Menacingly, even, and she remembered the look on his face when he'd grabbed her father by the throat.

'Nothing sexual, if that's what you're asking.' She watched his shoulders slump in relief. 'But he did hit. Hard. So I went to school and hit other people hard.' She smiled ruefully. 'It never seemed fair that I got in trouble for it and he never did.' More guilt hit her for being so wrapped in her own woes. 'But my childhood wasn't awful until Buck died, just lonely. You had a bad time, too. Your mother didn't take care of you either.'

'No, she didn't,' he said. 'Although sometimes she did try. Not well, but I hang onto that. Then again, this isn't about me and my mother because I didn't have to see her today.'

'You still see her?'

He shifted his shoulders. 'Occasionally. Seeing your dad today wasn't easy. And being angry with your mom is understandable. But while believing you caused her mental breakdown may be understandable at fourteen, at thirty-five it's not.'

She looked at the phone in her hand and changed the subject. 'I was getting lousy reception in Anderson Ferry. I couldn't download anything but texts until we hit the main road. I just got the autopsy reports on the PI, Nicki Fields and Jane Doe.'

'The Jane Doe's name was Sue Ellen Lamont. Drew found her in AFIS.'

'Well, Sue Ellen ate steak before she died, probably fillet. Her blood alcohol was just a little elevated, so maybe a glass of wine. No drugs in her system. Nicki had an empty stomach and it

337

appeared she was alive when he gutted her.'

Fitzpatrick flinched. 'Oh, God.'

'Yeah. No drugs in her system either. She was still alive when he cut her throat. His first knife wound missed her heart by an inch. I have to wonder why. He's been so precise with his other victims. I have to wonder if he wanted her to suffer.'

'Which would make her different than Kevin, who was wrong place, wrong time.'

'Exactly. Craig didn't send photos of the Fields scene, but the description was horrific. He stabbed her, slid the knife down her abdomen, then turned her and slit her throat. She would have been in excruciating pain. This seems personal.'

'I'll tell Stevie. She's going to dig into the PI's case tonight and I'm going to find out what happened to Ileanna's family when they left Anderson Ferry – after I take you to be fitted for surveillance. Hyatt will assign you security for tonight.'

She turned her gaze out the window, pondering her next statement carefully. Below them was nothing but miles of water. They'd reached the midpoint on the Bay Bridge, which seemed too symbolic to ignore. 'You could just stay,' she said and felt him tense beside her.

'As a bodyguard or . . .' He exhaled. 'Do you want me to stay because you want me?'

There was a carefulness to his phrasing. 'Yes, JD. That's why I asked. Well?'

'I'd like to stay,' he said simply.

She forged forward, still looking out the window. 'About last night.'

His laugh was a little shaky. 'Last night was . . . unforgettable. But not me. Amazing sex in alleys . . . I have to tell you that I'm not normally that exciting.'

She turned to glare at him. 'You think I am? That I have sex in alleys on a routine basis?'

'No,' he murmured. 'Am I in trouble?'

'Probably,' she said, irritated. 'Good God. That was the first sex I'd had in years.'

He glanced at her, surprised. 'Really? How many years?'

'Why do guys always want to know that?'

'Because guys have egos that need stroking,' he said. 'How many?'

She rolled her eyes. 'Seven. And he was my fiancé.'

'Your fiancé died more than seven years ago.'

'The first one did, that's true.'

He blinked. 'The *first* one? How many fiancés have you had?'

'Two,' she muttered, embarrassed as hell. 'And before you ask me any more, be prepared to dish a little quid pro quo.'

'Like what?'

'Like, how many years had it been for you? And what about your wife, whose car still sits in your garage after three years?' She began ticking off her fingers. 'And what about *your* mother, for God's sake? And what the hell does JD stand for anyway?'

His jaw went tight as he stared straight ahead at the road. She didn't think he'd answer, but then he did. 'Three years. Jack Daniel, which should also answer the question about my mother.' He went still. 'And I killed her.'

Lucy's mouth fell open, at first thinking she'd heard him wrong. 'Your mother?'

'No, my wife. Now if you'll excuse me, I have to make a few phone calls. Would you mind handing me my phone?'

Unable to think of what to say, Lucy complied.

Tuesday, May 4, 6.45 P.M.

'Oh, my God,' Gwyn said as soon as Lucy's call connected. 'I thought you were dead.'

Sliding her duffle to the shiny counter of the police station's cafeteria, Lucy trapped her phone between her ear and shoulder as she searched for her wallet. 'Why the hell would you think that? Dammit. Where is it?'

'Where is what?' Gwyn asked.

'My wallet. Here it is. Hold on.' She gave a twenty to the lady behind the counter. 'Two coffees, please.' Hefting the bag to her shoulder, she carried the tray to the condiment table. 'Okay, I'm back.'

'Why didn't you call me earlier? I've been worried sick.'

'I texted you that I was fine,' Lucy said, downing a bracing gulp of her coffee. 'You didn't have to leave me ten messages. I didn't have enough bars to make a call where I was. And don't yell at me. I've had a long day.'

'I'm sorry,' Gwyn said more calmly, 'but a text isn't good enough. Anybody could have stolen your phone and been texting that you were fine, and not been you.'

Lucy sighed. 'You read too many suspense novels. This is me. I am fine.'

'Given that somebody's leaving you hearts in baggies, I think I have reason to fret. But I'll let it go. You sound whipped. What's wrong and where are you?'

'I'm in the police department.' She stared at the second cup of coffee. *I've had sex with the man and I don't even know how he takes his coffee.*

'Why are you at the police department? Did they arrest you?'

'No, no. I'm fine. I'm being tagged. Like a polar bear.'

'You're making no sense.'

'I know. I'm tired.' And still thrown for a loop at the statement Fitzpatrick had so casually flung. He'd spent the rest of the drive making calls. They hadn't shared another word. She knew he hadn't killed his wife, really. That was ludicrous. Still . . . 'The cops are concerned, so they're rigging my purse with a tracking device.' It was best not to mention that she was bait. 'They let me take my phone and wallet and come to the cafeteria, as long as I promised not to leave the building. Where are you now?'

'At Thorne's,' Gwyn sighed. 'Royce is working late and my place is still a crime scene.'

'I thought Royce was taking time off to stay with you.'

'He is, but he had to wrap up some business so that he didn't have to go out of town. He's been texting me every hour, though, which is kind of sweet, right?'

There was a hopefulness in Gwyn's voice that Lucy instantly

recognized. She'd felt it herself when Fitzpatrick had nearly taken her father's head off to keep him from hurting her. She and Gwyn could care for themselves – they'd proved it for years.

But it was so nice to have someone else care, every so often.

'Yes, very sweet,' Lucy said quietly.

'When are you coming over? Right now it's just me and Ming. And Jasmine,' she added with a hint of annoyance. Jasmine was the latest employee from the club to attach herself to Thorne's side. He'd tolerate them for a while, then send them on their way. 'Ming isn't much of a conversationalist and all Jasmine wants to talk about is Thorne. She's driving me crazy.'

Lucy frowned. 'Why is Ming there? Where is Thorne?'

'Thorne had to meet a client after court, so he sent Ming to drive me here and stay with me till either he gets home or Royce picks me up. Don't worry.' Gwyn lowered her voice. 'Ming's carrying tonight. He'll make sure nobody gets through the door.'

'Okay,' Lucy said grudgingly. 'As long as you're not alone.' Their bouncer could defend against a small army, so Gwyn was safe.

'So when will the police be finished with the polar bear tagging? I got us a DVD, ice cream, and even some of that healthy shit you pretend to like.'

Damn. Lucy had forgotten she'd told Thorne she was staying there tonight. 'I'm actually going back to my apartment. They let me back in.'

'Thorne won't like that,' Gwyn warned. 'Neither do I.'

'It's okay. JD's going to stay with me.' *I think.*

'Really, Miss "That's-not-going-to-happen"? Are you going to sleep with him?'

Lucy controlled the urge to spill the truth about the alley. 'I've considered it.'

'Finally some sense out of you, girl.' Gwyn paused. 'So where did you go today, Lucy, that you didn't have enough bars for a phone call?'

She sighed. 'I went back again, with the detectives. And I saw my father.'

Gwyn drew in a sharp breath. 'I wish that sonofabitch would just die.'

'Well, he's alive and kickin'. And still blaming me for everything.'

'Sweetie . . .' Her voice gentled. 'Your father's a dick. Don't listen to him.'

'It was kind of hard not to. We were yelling at each other.' Lucy told her what had happened and Gwyn went silent.

'Did your father hurt you, Lucy?'

'He tried. JD grabbed him by the throat and pulled him off me.'

'Wow. That's really hot. If you want my advice, I'd do more than consider tonight. You don't want to let him get away.'

Lucy frowned. 'That's not a good reason to have sex.' *Again.*

'It's also not a bad reason to have sex.' Gwyn tsked. 'You did it already, didn't you?'

Lucy sighed. Sometimes Gwyn was a little too empathic. 'Yes.'

'Where? When?'

'Never mind.'

'Oh, no. I want details.'

Lucy looked around the cafeteria. 'No way, not here. I'll tell you later.'

'That good?'

'Better. I really need to go.'

'Then call me when you get to your place. With your voice.' Her swallow was audible. 'I really was scared today when I couldn't reach you. I kept thinking of Kevin. And then I kept seeing you . . . the same way.'

'I'm sorry I scared you. I'll do better next time. This coffee's getting cold. I gotta go.' Lucy pocketed her phone and went to find out what the hell was wrong with JD Fitzpatrick.

Tuesday, May 4, 7.10 P.M.

JD was so tired, all the numbers on his screen were blurring together. Then he smelled coffee. Lucy put a cup in front of him, followed by cream and sugar packets.

'I didn't know how you liked it,' she said. 'Your coffee, I mean,' she added wryly.

He looked up to find her studying him. 'I thought I'd scared you away.'

'No. Stevie wouldn't leave me alone with a crazed killer.'

He dumped the sugar in the coffee, then tossed the cream packets to Stevie's empty desk. 'Stevie likes a little coffee with her cream.'

'Good to know. Can I sit?'

He pulled a chair from another empty desk. 'Please.'

'So, what the hell, JD? What happened back there? I know you didn't kill anyone.'

'But I have. I was a sniper. A good one.' He waited for her reaction.

'You want me to be upset?' she asked. 'Are you trying to scare me away?'

'Maybe,' he admitted.

'Well, I'm still here. What gives with the drama? What happened to your wife?'

'She died. Stupid accident that didn't have to happen.'

'What kind of accident?'

'Diving. Maya was into extreme sports. Skydiving, rock-climbing, stuff like that.'

'I knew it,' she said, narrowing her eyes. 'I knew you were dangerous.'

'I'm *not* dangerous,' he insisted. 'Which is why she's dead.'

'That makes no sense. Back up and start at the beginning. How did you meet?'

'In the army and we hit it off. I got out first and came back here. The aunt who took me in was still living. She was sick, though, and I was able to help take care of her in her last months. I never knew her that well, but the years I spent with her were the most stable of my life. I wanted to, you know, repay her a little of what she'd given me. Like you and the Pughs.'

'I understand.'

He knew she did. 'Then Maya got out, but she had no family, so she came here, to me. I'd joined the department, she became a firefighter. A year later we got married.'

343

'Did you love her?'

'Yes, but not the way Paul and Stevie loved each other. Maya and I were more like friends with benefits who filed our taxes jointly. When the fun was done there wasn't much to say.'

'So how did you kill her?' she asked.

'I did a little of the extreme stuff with her at the beginning, but it wasn't my thing. I'd had enough. Plus, I'd met Paul and Stevie by then and wanted what they had. I wanted to have kids.'

'But Maya wasn't a kid kind of person,' she murmured.

'No, she was not. She accused me of making her give up her fun and I guess I was, so she spent less time at home, more time doing whatever gave her a rush. More time away from me.'

'She went diving without you one day and didn't come home?'

He nodded. 'She dived too deep and didn't have an adequate ascent plan.'

'And you blamed yourself.'

'We'd had a bad argument right before she stomped out.'

She was studying him. 'Did she say you weren't exciting enough for her?'

He flinched in surprise. 'Yes. How did you know that?'

'Before you kissed me yesterday, I'd said that whether I got involved with you would depend on how exciting you were. I've been wondering why that made you so intense.'

'I guess it's still a sore spot.'

'I'm sorry. I'm sure she didn't mean it.'

'Yeah, she did. That's the problem. She was furious when she left that day and I didn't calm her down. I pushed her buttons and if I hadn't, she'd still be alive.'

'So let me get this straight. Your wife, a mostly rational adult, got angry, took a foolish risk and died. JD, that's nowhere close to killing her.'

He met her eyes directly. 'So let me get this straight. Your mother, a doctor, a seemingly rational adult, endured a terrible tragedy that you did not cause, after which she had a mental breakdown. You, her child, desperately vying for her attention, gave her additional

344

anxiety, so she sent you away. That's nowhere close to driving her literally crazy.'

Her eyes narrowed. 'You set me up.'

'But was I right?'

She stewed a few seconds. 'Yes. Don't do it again, please.'

'Fair enough. I learned the technique from Stevie, so you can blame her.'

She cocked her jaw. 'I just might.'

'Are you mad?'

'No,' she said. 'You're right. I've always known it in my head.'

'But the heart's another thing.'

She nodded. 'So you went to Stevie's group after your wife died.'

'Not right away. I got a little crazy first, taking chances to take down any badass that crossed my path. Nearly got myself and my Narcotics partner killed. My CO at the time told me to get help or get a transfer. Eventually I did both.'

'And here you are,' she said simply.

He smiled. 'Here I am.'

'And here I am,' Drew said from behind them, his expression furious as he put her purse on JD's desk. 'I was testing the tracking device I hid.' He took a compact out and opened it, revealing a transmitter the size of a key fob. 'But I kept getting false readings and didn't know why. Then I found this.' Opening her purse, he pulled on the lining. 'It's sliced. This was hidden inside.' On his palm he held a transmitter nearly identical to the one in the compact.

JD came to his feet. 'What the hell?'

Lucy stared at it, the color draining from her face. 'Somebody bugged my purse?'

'It's not a bug,' Drew said. 'It's a tracking device.'

'Somebody's been watching me?' she whispered. 'Listening?'

What the hell? JD let out a relieved breath when Drew shook his head.

'No,' Drew said. 'Some of these devices come with a listening feature. The one I was planting did, in fact. This one doesn't. But he knows where you are at all times.'

'He didn't have to be physically near you to know your schedule,' JD said.

She nodded, considering. 'He knew I *wasn't* at Gwyn's last night when he left Janet's heart. Oddly enough, that makes me feel better. So what do we do with it?'

'Leave it,' Drew said and she blinked in surprise.

'This guy has to think he's a step ahead,' JD said. 'Can we track it to him?'

'It goes through a website, which means IP addresses, and warrants. So for all intents, no.'

'How long has it been there?' Lucy asked.

'The manufacturer's website says the battery provides up to ten days' coverage in standby mode,' Drew said. 'It's motion-activated and you've been on the move, so less than ten.'

'Ten days ago I was in LA and I bought this purse there,' Lucy said. 'Unless he followed me to California, it had to have been when I came back.'

'Who's had access to your purse?' JD asked.

'I keep it in my desk drawer at the morgue and no, I don't lock it up like I should. When I'm at the club it's locked in the office. I left it in your car when we went to the Bennetts' house. After last night, I've kept it and my duffle with me everywhere. I don't want to have them sucked into another crime scene.'

Two possibilities jumped out at JD, and he knew Lucy would like neither of them. There was Alan, the ME tech who already knew more than everyone else at the morgue about her personal life. And Thorne, her friend. For now he'd keep both to himself.

'Our window of opportunity is yesterday,' JD said. 'Can we check for prints?'

'We can,' Drew said. 'Don't expect any. I haven't found a useable print yet.'

Lucy's eyes widened. 'He couldn't have known my routine from this. He's only been tracking me for two days. Either there are other devices, or he was physically following me.'

'You're right,' Drew said. 'We'll go over your car again and check your other purses.'

'They're in my closet,' she said wearily. 'Your lock is still on my door.'

'I'll check your wallet and cell phone, too. You could have tracking software installed on your cell that you don't even know about.'

'How on earth could I have gotten that software on my phone?'

'It could have come through a text, an attachment, something that looked like a photo link. It could be running all the time in the background and you would never know. Your phone?'

She gave it to him. 'That's just . . . squicky.'

'Maybe, but better safe and squicked out than sorry and dead. I'll be in touch.'

He'd started to walk away when she tugged his sleeve. 'Wait, Drew. Did you say the device you were planting in my purse has listening capabilities? I don't like that.'

JD's mind immediately went to the night ahead in her apartment. *Neither do I.*

'It's not broadcasting all the time. It's remotely activated. I can call it from my cell if you get in trouble or go somewhere you haven't told us you're going. I can hear what's going on.'

The look of horror on her face would have been funny had it not been so appropriate. *And shared.* 'I really, really don't like that,' she said.

Drew shrugged. 'If he gets you, you'll want us to know you're in trouble.'

Her eyes flicked to JD's. 'I don't like this, JD. I can take being tracked and guarded and being bait, but I don't like the idea of people listening to my private conversations. That puts me and everyone else I know in jeopardy.'

'I know,' he said. After hearing about her trial, he understood. 'It's just until you're safe.'

'No. Use the other kind of device, Drew. I'm giving up enough of my privacy rights.'

JD grasped her shoulder gently. 'Lucy, listen to me. He cuts out their hearts. He tortures them. He burns a letter into their backs. Slits their throats.'

She'd grown paler with each sentence. 'I know.'

'This man we're looking for is a monster. I'm going to make sure he never puts his hands on you, but if he gets close, don't you want to be able to communicate with us?'

She looked away. 'Yes.' Then squared her shoulders in a gesture with which he was becoming all too familiar. 'Is there a way for me to block it when I want privacy?'

'Yes,' Drew said. 'But that puts you in danger of not having it available when you need it. JD is right, Lucy. This is a dangerous man. You've seen what he can do.'

She swallowed hard. 'Who will have the number to call this thing?'

'Me,' Drew said. 'JD and Stevie. And Hyatt.'

She grimaced. 'Hyatt, too? Does he have to?' she asked in a whine.

One corner of Drew's mouth lifted. 'He signed off on the security, so yes.'

She sighed. 'Okay. I don't like this at all, but I'll do it so we can catch this man before he kills anyone else. Me included. Fine. I'm in, just not happy about it.'

Drew nodded soberly. 'Good. I'll bring your purse back when I'm done with it.'

When Drew was gone, Lucy sank back into the chair. 'I hate this, JD.'

'Which part?' he asked. 'The being stalked part or the privacy disaster part?'

'Both, but it doesn't really matter. The only important thing is making this stop. What were you doing when I came in?'

'Trying to track down the Bryans after they left Anderson Ferry. I have the father's social security number from the police report and I located his death certificate. He died in North Carolina a year after Ileanna's murder.'

Lucy rolled her chair to look at his screen. 'Oh,' she said sadly. 'Suicide.'

'Gunshot wound to the head. I found the police report for his suicide scene which says the body was discovered by his son, Evan Bryan.'

348

'It's looking like Evan has plenty of reasons to be angry. Where is he now?'

'Can't find him yet, and my eyes are crossing.' But he'd keep looking because Evan's only sister had worn a bracelet that had brought Lucy a lot of trouble. The boy was a link, if not their man. And until they ID'd him, Lucy was living in the cross hairs.

'Mine too,' she said. 'Craig found the autopsy reports on Ileanna and Ricky Joyner. He sent them to my email, but my eyes can't focus on the small print on my phone anymore. Is there a computer I can use here to check my email?'

'Use mine,' he said, then tortured himself with the feel of her against him as she leaned closer to input her user name and password. 'Lucy?' he murmured.

The skin on her arms pebbled as a shiver shook her. 'Hm?'

'Can I still stay?'

She turned her head to look at him, putting her mouth within inches of his. 'Yes.'

'Then let's hurry so we can get some food and a few hours' sleep.'

Her mouth slowly curved and it took all the discipline he possessed not to kiss her right here in the bullpen. But as Stevie had said, Hyatt was watching – and less than happy that twice JD had told him no over Lucy's being bait. He'd watch himself, for now. And hope like hell Hyatt was too honorable to listen in where he shouldn't, because later . . .

'Food and sleep are good.' She turned back to the screen, her focus immediately redirected. 'Ileanna, what happened to you, honey?' she whispered.

It was a gruesome report. The photos of the body were stark and grim, something they'd both seen way too many times before. 'She was beaten severely.'

'With fists, probably. The ME concluded that one of the head wounds was the cause of death. She was also raped, brutally. There's bruising here, and tearing. This was a vicious assault.' She enlarged the photo. 'Look. This welt on her neck.'

'Where the chain of a necklace might have been yanked off,' he said.

'Exactly. But there's no similar welt on her wrist. When I found the bracelet in Buck's room, it wasn't broken. That didn't happen until Sonny stole it from me.'

'So the bracelet was taken off. But by whom?'

She bit at her lip thoughtfully. 'Do you have the bracelet?'

'Yeah.' He took the evidence bag from his pocket. 'Stevie gave it to me.'

She looked at the bracelet through the plastic. 'Could you manage this clasp?'

'Not easily. It's really small and I'm not used to doing it.'

'A boy Buck's age wouldn't have been, either. Did Ileanna have a purse?'

JD looked through the box until he found the candid prom photos. 'Yes.' He showed her the picture. 'But there was no purse found with her body according to the police report. Initially they called it a robbery.'

'Until they discovered the suicide – Ricky Joyner. Do we have a police report on his death?'

'I requested his police report be faxed from the state police. Wait,' he said. Luckily the state police were a lot faster than Gladys Strough and the report was sitting on the fax machine. He read it as he walked back to Lucy. 'No purse found with his body.'

She was staring at Ileanna's autopsy photo. 'My mother saw these injuries. She treated babies with sniffles and boys who'd fallen out of trees. She didn't have experience with anything like this. I see this a lot . . . It doesn't get easy, but the shock tends to wear off. She must have been blown away. And then to lose Buck right after.'

He rubbed her back comfortingly and said nothing, letting her talk it out.

'I guess I never realized how much I wished things were different until I stood on that dock today. I kept thinking, maybe he'll hug me. Maybe he'll let my mother talk to me. Maybe it'll be okay and there's a damn good reason that my brother had a dead girl's bracelet in his room.'

She scrolled past the pictures to the report. 'The ME back then took semen samples.'

She was done talking about her personal life, but it was more than she'd offered before without his asking. 'Ileanna's report doesn't mention a DNA test,' he said.

'They didn't do one. Probably because no one was prosecuted. It took weeks to get DNAs done back then, when they were done at all. But they did do blood type.' Abruptly she switched to Ricky Joyner's autopsy report. 'Which was consistent with that of the suicide victim. And not Buck.'

She'd been thinking Buck had raped Ileanna. Which had also crossed JD's mind more than once. 'Not conclusive,' he said.

'No. But add to it that the bruising on Joyner's knuckles was also consistent with the injuries on Ileanna's face and body, and you have a stronger case. Plus there was some anger that goes to motive. She'd broken up with Joyner to go to the prom with Buck.'

He read more of the report. 'Joyner had scratches on his face and chest.'

'And she had skin under her nails.'

'Seems like a slam dunk,' he mused. 'Why does it feel wrong?'

She opened Joyner's autopsy photo and JD had to swallow hard. It, too, was grim. Joyner had eaten his gun and there wasn't much face left. But Lucy didn't flinch, just stared at the screen with that instant concentration he found so fascinating.

'Because it is wrong,' she said. 'Look at his face.'

JD grimaced. 'How? There's nothing left.'

She shook her head and zoomed the photo on Joyner's right jaw. 'It's a bruise.'

'He shot himself in the face, Lucy,' JD said flatly. 'He's gonna be dinged up.'

'This isn't from the shot. He was hit in the face, hard. Premortem.' Quickly she clicked on the victim's arms. 'These are defensive wounds, and this,' she clicked on his torso where there was a dark bruise over the rib cage, 'is a boot kick.'

JD frowned. She was right. His eyes had immediately been drawn to the victim's lack of face and he'd missed the other injuries. 'Why didn't the ME catch that twenty-one years ago?'

'Could have been any number of reasons. The cops said Joyner did it. The victim and killer were both dead, so the cases were closed. Maybe he had a huge caseload and cut a corner.'

'So did he kill himself?'

'Maybe. But he had one dilly of a fight before he did.' She clicked to the next photo and went still. 'Or not. Not before he died, anyway.' She zoomed in. 'See this bruise on his back? Post-mortem. Also looks like a boot kick.'

It certainly did, he thought grimly. 'Somebody either killed him or came along and kicked him right after he was dead.' He paged through the police report and knew she was right. 'He did have gunshot residue on his hand. Which still held the gun. If he'd shot himself, the gun probably wouldn't have been in his hand. This was staged.'

'Serial number of the gun?' she asked.

'Filed off. We might be able to raise it today – if the state boys still have the gun.'

Her stomach growled loudly. 'Can you print these reports? Then maybe get an escort to go with me to get some dinner? I can bring you back something. The cafeteria was out of almost everything that wasn't junk food. That stuff'll kill you.'

He hit PRINT, then stood. 'I'll go with you.'

'Okay. Then I have to go to the morgue, check for some blood work I ran on Russ Bennett.' But she hadn't moved. Her eyes had moved back to Joyner's autopsy photo.

'What's wrong?'

'I was just remembering how my mother would scold Buck for scuffing her floors.'

He understood. 'He wore boots?'

She nodded, troubled. 'Pointy-toed ones, everywhere except the football field.'

'He couldn't have been the only one to wear pointy-toed boots, Lucy.'

'Yeah, but he's the only one who hid a dead girl's bracelet under his baseball cards.'

He tugged her arm. 'Come, let's take a break, get dinner. Worry about this later.'

She closed the file and logged off. 'All right.'

Twenty-one

Tuesday, May 4, 7.30 P.M.

Clay was so damn tired. Nicki's parents had been weeping when he met them. They wept as he drove them to their hotel. He was sure they were weeping now. Part of him wished he could weep too. But once he started, he wouldn't stop.

He pushed open his front door and flinched. Alyssa was standing in his dining room, a gun in her hand. She lowered the gun when she saw it was him, her shoulders slumping.

'What the hell?' he asked, exhaustion making him monotone.

'I kept hearing noises. I kept thinking that Evan's out there. I'm sorry, I was just scared.'

'I can't blame you.' He watched her put the gun in his china cabinet drawer, already filled with Nicki's files. 'Why are there files in my china cabinet?'

'Because June got a visit from a BPD homicide detective asking about me.'

Clay wanted to groan. June was Alyssa's roommate and not the sharpest crayon in the box. 'What did she tell them?' His eyes narrowed. 'What *could* she tell them?'

'Just that I'm here. I called her to let her know I was okay, so she wouldn't worry. And I told her to lock the door. Just in case Evan decides to get rid of everyone who knew him.'

His annoyance dissipated. She was right. As long as Evan was free, there was danger. 'What else did June say?'

'The cop told her to lock her door, too. Because there were three more murders last night. Two of the victims' throats were slit.' She met Clay's eyes and he could see her fear. 'Like Nicki.'

Clay's mouth dropped open. 'What? Who?'

'I checked the news. One looked like the woman you saw with Evan on the hotel's video.'

He swallowed hard, his stomach churning. 'Who was the other?'

'A parking valet working a club downtown where a second woman's body was found. She'd been left in one of the cars in front of a club named Sheidalin. She'd been murdered too. The news didn't give specifics on that one. What are we going to do?'

Clay closed his eyes. 'I don't know.'

'Well you need to decide fast, because that cop, Mazzetti, is probably coming here next.' Outside a car door slammed and Alyssa jumped. 'That's probably her right now.'

'Go back to my room,' Clay said. 'Do not come out.' For once, Alyssa obeyed.

There was a knock at the door. 'Baltimore PD,' a woman said. 'Detective Mazzetti, Baltimore Homicide. Can I come in?'

Clay opened the door, a little surprised. The woman's body did not match her voice. She'd sounded large, but Mazzetti was petite, with dark eyes that tried to see right through him. 'How can I help you, Detective?'

'I'm here to talk to you about Nicki Fields. Laurel PD transferred the case to us.'

Because of the other murders. Evan Reardon had killed at least two more, maybe three. The need to do the right thing and tell her what he knew battled with the need to do the right thing and see Reardon breathe his last. 'Do you have any leads?'

'Yes,' Mazzetti said. 'Do you?'

'No,' he murmured. 'I wish I did. I'd give them to you.' Which was true. If he had Evan, he'd hand him over so fast. Evan would be dead, but Mazzetti would get her man.

'Where is Miss Moore?' she asked.

'She's not here,' Clay said.

'Her roommate says she is.' Mazzetti lifted a dark brow. 'Her car's parked on your curb. I ran the plates. The Laurel police found very few files in Ms Field's office or apartment, Mr Maynard. Are they here?'

'Why would they be?' Clay asked and Mazzetti's smile was razor sharp.

'I can think of a number of reasons, none of them positive. What are you and Miss Moore looking for in your partner's files?'

'My assistant is not—'

'Clay? Baby?' The bedroom door opened and Alyssa came out wearing one of Clay's shirts, her long legs bare. Stretching her arms over her head, she yawned. 'I heard voi—' She stopped abruptly, her eyes widening at the sight of Mazzetti. She took a step back and Clay had to struggle to hide his shock and annoyance.

'So she *is* here,' Mazzetti said. 'The two of you are . . .' She let the thought trail.

Alyssa tugged at the hem of Clay's shirt. 'Yes. Not that it's any of your business.'

Which it really wasn't. Except Mazzetti looked at Clay with such disappointment. He felt dirty and wanted to leap to his own defense.

'You're a little young, Miss Moore,' Mazzetti said.

Alyssa lifted her chin. 'I'm eighteen.'

Mazzetti's smile was brittle. 'So says your driver's license. Okay, this is how it's going to work. I could haul both your asses in for questioning. Maybe you'd break and maybe you wouldn't. I don't believe anything you've said, Mr Maynard. Your partner's files went somewhere. I could search this room and not find them, so don't worry, I won't try.'

'You'd need a warrant first anyway,' Alyssa said coldly.

'That I would. I don't know what you're hiding, but I've got a bunch of bodies in the morgue and my patience is pretty damn thin. One more time.' She stared directly at Clay. 'What do you know?'

'That my friend is dead,' Clay said wearily. 'And that I want whoever gutted her and left her to rot to pay. But I'm no vigilante.' At least he hadn't been before this morning. Now, he was. After seeing Nicki's savaged body, he totally was.

'I hope not. Because you're impeding an investigation and that's a felony. I'd hate to add vigilantism to that.'

She had nothing and they both knew it. 'I have to pick up Nicki's parents from their hotel and take them to identify her body,' he said quietly. 'So if you're finished, you can go.'

'All right. For now, please accept my condolences on the death of your colleague.'

'She was my friend,' Clay said sharply, more so than he'd intended.

'Then I'm sorry for your loss,' Mazzetti murmured. She put her card on an end table. 'If you think of anything you'd like to tell me, it'll go easier on you than if I have to dig it up myself. I want this killer behind bars. I want him badly.' She turned for the door, then changed her mind and turned back. 'Does the name Ileanna Bryan mean anything to you?'

'No,' he answered honestly. 'Should it?'

She seemed to believe him this time. 'Probably. I'll see myself out.'

Clay closed the door behind her, then turned to Alyssa, his fury bubbling to the surface. 'What the hell is this?' He pointed to the shirt she wore.

'Jesus, Mary, and Joseph.' Alyssa flopped in the chair. 'You're supposed to be training *me*, for God's sake. She knew we had files. She knew I was here. Why *else* would I be here? You want to give her probable cause for a warrant on a goddamn silver platter?'

She was right, and it grated. 'Fine. Stay here until I get back from the morgue.'

'No way. Evan's out there somewhere. I'm staying with you.'

Tuesday, May 4, 8.40 P.M.

Evan upended the wheelchair so that Ron Trask landed on the concrete floor of his factory with a *whump*, his feet still handcuffed to the chair. The old sheriff's face had taken a major beating. Only a little was from his contact with the floor. The rest, to give credit where due, *was done by me*.

Mrs Trask already lay on the floor, huddled in the fetal position, largely because that's how he'd left her tied when he'd brought her in from the boat. He re-tied the old man again, not trusting him as far as he could throw him. Crouching next to Trask, he smiled. 'That's a hell of a sweet boat, Sheriff. I might just add her to my fleet.'

Trask glared, then glanced out of the corner of his eye at his wife. The sounds he made behind the tape on his mouth sounded concerned. Evan lifted the tape enough for the old man to speak, ready to slap it down again if he screamed. 'Is she all right?' Trask rasped.

'She's not dead,' Evan said flatly.

'She needs her medicine.'

'All she'll need is a coroner. Oh, wait. You have one of those in the family. I'm sure you're so proud of your daughter, following in your footsteps. She's got the look-at-me-I'm-so-upstanding gig down pat, but then again she learned at the feet of the master.'

'She has nothing to do with me,' Trask said furiously. 'I disowned her years ago.'

'Then the family reunion should be tons of fun. Sit tight, I'll be back later. I get to play with Ryan and Sonny now. But don't worry. Soon enough it'll be your turn.'

Tuesday, May 4, 8.45 P.M.

A baggie full of cookies slid across JD's desk and he looked up from the screen on which he'd been focused for too long. Stevie sat behind her desk. 'Cookies for me?' he asked.

'Cordelia made them to thank you for the locket. I popped home for a minute to tuck her in and she and my sister were just taking them out of the oven. Don't worry, Izzy makes sure she washes her hands. So where's Lucy?' she asked.

'At the morgue. The PI's parents arrived to do the ID while we were at dinner.'

'I thought they only did IDs during the daytime.'

'Normally, but the tech on duty called and said the parents showed up and were distraught, so Lucy went in. We need to go over to talk to the parents, too, but I thought we should go together. Lucy said she'd call when they were ready for us.'

'She's there alone?'

'Hell, no. Hyatt assigned Phil Skinner as her shadow for tonight.'

She studied him across their desks. 'Until you take over as body-guard?'

JD shrugged and redirected the topic. 'We've been getting tips on the hotline from people who claim to have seen Sue Ellen Lamont, the hooker. Hyatt's got people following up, but mostly the reports are from the usual nutjobs. What did you find out about the PI agency?'

'That the PI and his assistant are lying and I don't know why. They'd set it up to look like they were having an affair. She was in his shirt, all rumpled and sleepy-looking.'

'But?'

'But he didn't look at her the way a man looks at a woman he's just had sex with.'

JD's eyes skittered away, then back to Stevie's face. 'Which is how?'

'Like you looked at Lucy last night and most of today.' She propped her feet up on her desk and scratched one knee. 'There was something about the partner. He was sad.'

'His partner was just murdered. He's entitled.'

'He did seem devastated by her death, but there was more. Guilt, maybe. I don't know. I gave them Ileanna Bryan's name before I left.'

His brows lifted. 'Why?'

'Because they didn't kill Nicki Fields, I'm sure of that, but I'm just as sure they know who did. They didn't know Ileanna's name, though. I figure I'll give them through the night to connect some dots for us, then we can put them under surveillance. I wouldn't be surprised to see them headed to Anderson Ferry tomorrow.'

'I know just how to track them now,' JD said. He told Stevie about the device planted in Lucy's purse and watched her eyes grow wider than saucers. 'Drew just called to say he'd found three more devices, all hidden in the lining of her purses.'

'Sonofafuckingbitch,' Stevie said. 'Now I gotta wonder if he's tracking all of us.'

'Drew's going to give our vehicles the once-over. He already checked my briefcase and said he'd check yours, and your purse, too. And our phones.' He then told her about the autopsy results and Lucy's conclusions about Ricky Joyner's 'suicide'.

'She thinks Buck killed Ricky Joyner,' Stevie said and JD nodded.

'She thinks it's very possible. Her logic is sound. The theory answers a few questions and sets up a host of others.'

'One of the big ones is, why now?' Stevie said. 'Ileanna was murdered twenty-one years ago, so why start all this killing now?'

'Malcolm Edwards was the first death. The killing started two months ago. Whatever happened to trigger this happened then.'

'I'm putting a lot of my eggs in the Ileanna's-little-brother basket, but learning that Ricky Joyner might have been murdered means we have to look at anyone out to get vengeance for his death, too. How've you done tracking the Bryan family?'

'I found the dad. He ate his gun the year after Ileanna died. Little brother Evan found his body. He and his mother seem to have fallen off the grid after that. When I search on Evan Bryan I get over twenty hits nationwide but none are the right age, and six are women.'

'He changed his name somewhere along the line. Or maybe his mother did.'

'Yes. I ran Yvette Bryan through the system. Came up with nothing.'

Stevie thought a moment. 'What about her maiden name?'

'She was a widow, not divorced.'

'Maybe she was going to leave him before the suicide. Sixteen per cent of marriages fail after the loss of a child. A violent loss puts a huge strain on a family.'

'Her maiden name is Smith.'

She groaned. 'Even with Yvette as a first name, she's gonna be a bitch to find.'

'And I'm running on less than six hours' sleep for two nights. I used to be able to handle no sleep better. I'm having trouble thinking straight.'

'Me too. I got tired watching Lucy drag herself through her past. Poor thing.'

'She'll hold,' JD said. 'I wanted to beat the shit out of her father, though. SOB.'

'I'm glad you controlled yourself because I'm not sure I would have stopped you. Lennie Berman was impressed, by the way.'

'What, that I didn't kill Trask?'

'Pretty much. He wanted to, too. We did a lot of talking on the drive back. Lennie thinks the killer's trigger has to be something specific. That it's likely not a gradual build of rage that just overflows one day. The rage was like a pressure cooker and then something made our guy snap. It has to do with the jewelry, with the hearts.'

'So we're back to finding Evan,' he said. 'If we find the mother, she might be able to point us to the son, even if it's only through a call she makes to warn him after we confront her. Evan could have changed his name, but his mother will probably know where he is.' *Mine does. Unfortunately.* 'I say we make finding Yvette a priority.'

'You're right,' she agreed. 'How many can there be?'

'Whittling by birth year . . .' He frowned at his screen. 'Ileanna would have been thirty-eight, so Yvette could be anywhere from fifty-five to seventy-five. Still over five hundred nationwide. We need the mom's birth date and social. I'll get Records to run the check.'

Stevie rubbed the back of her neck. 'He's had Ryan Agar for nearly a day.'

'I'm betting Ryan's dead by now,' JD said.

Stevie sighed. 'I should feel . . . sorrier. But the dumb fuck should have listened to us, told us what was going on and let us protect him. His mother had her heart cut out, for God's sake. He should have told us. He'd be safe.'

'I agree, but he didn't. I'm thinking this could let us be proactive for a change. This guy's tracking Lucy, so he knows she's back in the city. If we assume Ryan's dead, we have to assume his killer will leave him where Lucy can find him.'

Stevie sat up straighter. 'Makes sense to me. Keep talking.'

'He's already used her apartment and her club. He's left hearts in her car at work and her best friend's home. So where next?'

'Thorne's place?'

'Maybe. She stayed with Mulhauser last night. Maybe his place. We really need to know more about her schedule. Restaurants, shops. Wherever she frequents.'

'Wherever she feels safe,' Stevie said quietly.

Safe. A thought hit him and made him angry. 'Depending on how much he knows about her background, I have an idea of where that might be.' He checked his watch. 'Hyatt wanted status by eleven, but I think we need to call him now.'

Tuesday, May 4, 8.45 P.M.

Lucy put her duffle on her desk, then found her wallet and locked it in a drawer, the first time she'd done so in a long time. *He's tracking me. He knows where I am. Right now.*

The phone on her desk rang shrilly, making her jump. *Relax. You're not alone.* A detective named Skinner had been pressed into guard duty and stood outside her office door.

'This is Dr Trask.'

'It's me,' Gwyn said furiously, sounding like she'd been crying. 'I tried your cell and you didn't answer. I've been calling every number for you I know. Dammit, do not *do* this to me.'

'I'm sorry.' Lucy sank into her chair, feeling awful. 'The cops have my phone now.'

'Why?' Gwyn bit off the word.

'Because . . .' She hesitated and lowered her voice. 'Because they're checking it for a tracking device. This guy slipped one in my purse, Gwyn.'

'Oh, my *God*. Lucy, you need to go to a safe house. Why isn't that Fitzpatrick putting you somewhere *safe*?'

'I've got a bodyguard. And later JD will be with me. I'm safe. Just . . . scared.'

Gwyn shuddered out a breath. 'This is a nightmare, Lucy.'

'I know. Believe me, I know.'

'Why are you there, at the morgue?'

'The family of a deceased came in from out of town.' The PI's parents. 'They're here to ID the body.'

361

'Let somebody else do it,' Gwyn said tightly.

Lucy wished she could. 'There is no one else for this one. I can't say more.'

'He's killed someone else,' Gwyn said dully. 'Like Kevin.'

'Yes,' Lucy whispered.

'Lucy.' Ruby stuck her head into Lucy's office. 'Oh, sorry.'

'It's okay, Ruby, I'm almost done. I gotta go, Gwyn.'

'You call me,' Gwyn said. 'When you get home. Promise me.'

'I promise.' Lucy hung up, turned to Ruby. 'The family's here?'

'Yes. They insisted on talking to the ME that did the autopsy, but Mulhauser's asleep. I was tempted to go to his house and wake him up, but I'm on duty by myself tonight.'

'Let him rest. I'm here and I've read the report. Why are you on duty by yourself?'

'Alan quit.'

Lucy gaped. 'He did what?'

'He up and quit. Called in an hour before his shift. Said he didn't want to mess with dead people anymore. Personally, I think his little weenie thrills of watching you when you thought he didn't know about your bad-ass leather-dress club went fizzle when everyone found out. Putting up with the dead wasn't worth it anymore.'

'You could be right,' Lucy said, both relieved and creeped out. 'Where are the parents?'

'In the waiting room.'

'Make sure there's double sheeting over the torso.' Where the victim had been gutted. 'Make sure it extends up to cover her throat, then put another sheet over that.'

'Already done,' Ruby said. 'She's the best I can make her.'

'Good. The report said she has a tattoo on her left ankle. Show that first, then wait for my signal. We may be able to avoid showing them her face.'

'I doubt,' Ruby said glumly. 'They always gotta see the face.'

It was closure, Lucy knew. But incredibly painful for the families. *And for me and Ruby.* 'Then wheel the deceased into the viewing room. I'll go talk to the parents.'

'Thanks, Luce. Look, there were two other doctors on call before you, so I'm sorry to drag you in here. But you have all the facts in this case.'

'I was nearby, so it's okay.' She turned to Detective Skinner, who'd been waiting in the hall. He appeared to be bracing himself. 'You okay?'

He nodded. 'I've done them before. Identifications, that is. Never liked them.'

'Me either,' she said grimly, then made her way to the front entrance where four people waited. An older man paced, agitated, and an older woman sat, pale and numb with shock. Next to the woman sat a man, tall, dark, about forty years old. A few seats down sat a young woman who looked more afraid than grief-stricken.

The receptionist had gone home for the day, so the security guard sat behind the receiving desk. 'Dr Trask, these are the parents of Nicki Fields, Mr and Mrs Fields.'

The pacing man abruptly stopped, turning to glare at her, a reaction to which she was accustomed. The woman looked up, dazed, her eyes filled with pain.

'Mr and Mrs Fields?' Lucy said softly. 'I'm Dr Trask. Please come with me.'

Mrs Fields stood unsteadily and the dark-haired man rose to hold her arm. 'Can he come with us?' Mrs Fields asked.

'Of course.' It was Lucy's experience that families who had support were better able to endure the often excruciating identification process. She paused at the desk and scrawled Fitzpatrick's number on a pad. 'Can you call Detective Fitzpatrick?' she asked the guard. 'Tell him we're ready for him and Detective Mazzetti as soon as they can get here.'

She turned to the man and the young woman. 'You are?'

The man spoke. 'I'm Clay Maynard. I'm a friend of the family. This is my assistant. Can she stay here?'

'Of course.'

'Is that the detective on the case?' Maynard pointed to Skinner.

'No, sir. This is Detective Skinner. He's doing some training tonight,' she said. She led them to the family side of the viewing room where a curtain was pulled across a large window. Skinner stood near the door while she stood with the parents and Maynard at the window.

'I'm very sorry we have to ask you to do this,' Lucy began and Mrs Fields began to cry. Normally Lucy was uncomfortable with the families, rarely touching them because her hands were always so cold. But the touch of JD's hands had given her immense comfort over the last few days. And this mother had lost her child. Lucy couldn't help but think of her own mother.

Her mother had been the coroner. She would have done the comforting. Lucy wondered who'd comforted her mother when Buck died. As she took Mrs Field's hand in hers, Lucy wondered why she'd never wondered it before. 'Your daughter won't look like herself. I'm so sorry. Are there any special scars or marks you can remember?'

'She had a tattoo,' Mr Fields ground out. 'On her ankle. Left ankle. A rose.'

'All right.' Still holding Mrs Field's hand, she tapped the intercom button. 'We're ready, Miss Gomez.' Then she pushed the button to open the curtain. Mrs Fields was holding so tightly to her hand, it was a wonder her bones didn't crumble.

At the first sight of her daughter on the table, Mrs Fields began to weep. When Ruby showed them her ankle tattoo, Mr Fields sucked in a pained breath.

'Yes. That's her tattoo.' He clenched his jaw. 'Show me her face.'

Lucy met Ruby's eyes through the glass and nodded. Ruby pulled the top sheet back. Mrs Fields dropped Lucy's hand and turned into her husband's arms, her sobs filling the room.

Lucy pressed the intercom button. 'That's all. Thank you.' She closed the curtain.

Maynard lifted devastated eyes to meet hers. 'Is it possible for them to speak with the detectives tomorrow? I don't think they can do it now.'

'Of course.' She led them to the front and gave Mr Fields her card. 'We should be releasing your daughter's body soon. We'll need to know your wishes. If you're working with a local mortuary, please give them my name. And please call me if you have any questions later.'

Mr Fields nodded unsteadily. His face was very gray. 'Thank you.'

She put her hand on his sleeve. 'Do you need a doctor, Mr Fields?'

'I'm fine.' Holding his wife, he left, followed by Maynard and his assistant.

Lucy knew the Fieldses weren't fine. She knew it would be a very long time before they'd be fine again. *Any of us.* Squaring her shoulders, she turned back to her office.

Tuesday, May 4, 9.40 P.M.

It was a twofer he hadn't anticipated, but one he'd thoroughly enjoy – the Ryan/Sonny throwdown. Once the *Satisfaction* was far enough out on the Bay so their screams would go unheard, he dragged Ryan up from the hold to the deck and dumped him next to Sonny, who had one hell of a headache. He imagined Ryan wasn't feeling much better. The big cowboy apparently got seasick. Being left on the boat all day had been akin to torture. Or so Ryan thought. He'd soon find out what torture really felt like, just like his mama had.

Sonny's eyes narrowed when he saw Ryan. '*You.* I should have known.'

It took Ryan a few seconds longer to recognize Sonny, but when he did, he stared at the patch on Sonny's sleeve in disbelief. 'You're a sheriff?'

Sonny ignored him. 'You lily-livered coward. Why the fuck would you squeal now?'

'I didn't. I didn't say a word. He already knew. Whoever the hell *he* is.'

Both men looked up at him with hate. How much was for him versus each other was hard to say, although he suspected he scored the most. If he didn't, he soon would.

'I'm Ileanna's brother,' he said mildly. 'You do remember Ileanna, don't you?'

Both men went silent. Sonny looked scared. Ryan looked . . . guilty.

'Don't you?' he repeated, more threateningly.

Ryan closed his eyes. 'The detectives said my mother suffered. You did that.'

'I did. I hadn't actually planned to, but I learned something that changed my mind.'

'Which was?' Sonny demanded.

Arrogant prick. 'She made a deal with Russ Bennett,' Evan said.

Ryan opened his eyes. 'What kind of deal?'

'She traded secrecy for a nip/tuck and a boob job. Put it all in a letter that when she died would be mailed to the DA. I'm guessing the letter will arrive within a day or two.'

Sonny shook his head in disgust. 'Bitch.'

Ryan said nothing, but it appeared he agreed with Sonny on that one.

'How did you get the letter?' Sonny asked.

'I didn't,' Evan said. 'Not her letter anyway.'

Ryan struggled to sit up, then gave up. 'Who told?' he asked simply.

'Malcolm. He was dying and sent an anonymous letter to my mother, begging her forgiveness.'

'Brave of him,' Ryan murmured. 'Sending it unsigned.'

'Considering you wanted your mother to tell the cops for you, you shouldn't talk.'

Sonny flashed Ryan a glare. 'You told your mother. You idiot.'

'You're right,' Ryan said quietly, then looked up, meeting his eyes. 'And so are you. I wanted to tell back then, but I was scared. I ran away. I am a coward.'

'You're a coward now,' Sonny said in furious frustration, 'telling him this just so he won't gut you like he did your bitch mother. I got news for you. He's gonna do it anyway.'

Ryan paled, looking like he was going to throw up.

Evan squatted next to Sonny. 'That was downright insensitive.'

Sonny spat at him, his spittle falling a few inches short. 'You can go fuck yourself.'

He smiled and had the satisfaction of seeing Sonny cringe. 'I'm really going to enjoy you. I thought Bennett was fun, but you . . . I have to say, the badge puts you right up there with Trask and his daughter.' He turned to Ryan. 'Tell me what happened that night. I'm making a scrapbook of your varying accounts.'

'All right,' Ryan said calmly. As if it really didn't matter.

'Shut. Up,' Sonny gritted.

'No,' Ryan said. 'I know how Malcolm felt. I need to say it. Just once so that it matters. Besides, if my mother wrote a letter – and I have no doubt that she did – it'll surface. If Little Brother here doesn't kill you, everyone will know. Even if you don't go to jail, your career will be ruined. Can I at least sit up?'

'No,' Evan said. 'Just talk. I want to know what you did and what Buck Trask did.'

'All right. It was prom and Buck had had a big fight with his girl. He'd caught her cheating and he was pissed, so he dumped her and invited the one girl that would humiliate his old girlfriend the most. I'm sorry to say it, but that was Ileanna. She had a reputation for . . . putting out. I don't know if it was earned or not. It didn't matter then and it doesn't matter now. She didn't deserve any of what happened to her.'

Evan was seething now, just hearing the words. 'What happened?'

'Buck took her to the dance,' Ryan continued, 'but he was determined to make his old girlfriend feel like shit. After the dance he and Ileanna snuck under the bleachers on the football field. We knew they were going. The others thought it would be fun to watch. I wasn't going to go. I don't know why I did. I've regretted it my whole life. By the time I got there, the others were there and Buck was standing off to the side. Another guy was beating up your sister. He'd already raped her once, but he did it again.'

'Ricky Joyner?' Evan asked, his stomach queasy.

'Yes. Buck had told us that the girl he was taking to the prom dumped some other guy for him. That would have been Ricky. He and Buck had had a run-in, months before, during the season. Ricky was mad. And high on crack. I think he must've seen Buck and Ileanna either doing it or ready to and just . . . exploded. Buck had this dazed look, like he couldn't believe it.'

'Why did you let it happen?' Evan asked. The question he'd always wanted to ask.

'I don't know. I wish to God I'd stopped it, but I didn't know how. So many times now when I make a call on my cell, I wonder if it would have been different back then if we'd had cell phones. But I doubt it. We probably would have taken pictures,' he said bitterly. 'It was a mob mentality. Bennett, Edwards and Cannon egged Joyner on.'

'Did Sonny?' he asked.

Sonny struggled against his bonds. 'No,' he said desperately. 'I didn't.'

Ryan shrugged one shoulder, which said it all. 'When Ricky staggered away, we got scared. Buck said we should make it look like a robbery. He took her purse and the necklace. He said he knew how to get rid of them, since his dad was sheriff. It sounded like a plan. We hadn't actually done anything. Or so we told ourselves. We ran.'

'And left her there to die,' Evan said with contempt.

'Yes,' Ryan said quietly. 'I'm sorry.'

'Your "sorry" means nothing now.'

'I know. The next day we heard Ricky had shot himself in the head. We figured he'd sobered up, realized what he'd done and couldn't live with it. The necklace never showed up.'

'What about the bracelet?' he asked and Ryan looked genuinely confused.

'I don't know about a bracelet. I saw a necklace. That's it.'

He turned to Sonny. 'You know about the bracelet?'

'No,' Sonny said, but he was lying. *I can tell.*

He delivered a vicious kick to the same place he'd kicked Sonny before. 'Tell me.' Sonny was silent, so Evan brought out his bat and watched Sonny's eyes flicker in fear. 'Tell me.'

'Yes, I saw it,' Sonny ground out. 'It was in her purse. Your sister's purse. But Lucy Trask took it. I saw her wearing it, back then and again today.'

As did I. 'And the necklace?'

'I don't know.'

He brought the bat down hard on Sonny's hip, hearing the crunch of bone followed by Sonny's scream of pain. 'Not a good answer, Sheriff.'

'I don't know,' Sonny repeated harder, sobbing. 'Buck was supposed to get rid of the stuff, but we saw Lucy wearing the bracelet the next summer and we panicked. We didn't want anyone tracing the stuff back to us.'

'So?'

'I got the bracelet back from her, but I couldn't find the necklace. Then she stole the bracelet back and wouldn't tell me where it was. I wanted the necklace, so I put some of my mother's things in her room and said Lucy stole them. I thought I'd get her in trouble with her dad, make her so scared that she'd tell me where she'd hidden them so I wouldn't plant more things and get her sent to juvie.'

Hell of a sheriff, he thought. 'Did she tell?'

'No. I didn't know her parents would send her away the first time. Three years she was gone. I couldn't find the necklace. I looked a thousand times.'

'Well you didn't look hard enough,' Evan snapped. 'She's had the bracelet and the necklace all along. She *sold* my necklace, knowing full well it belonged to *me*. Her father ran me and my parents out of town. Bankrupted us. My father killed himself.'

'Not our fault,' Sonny said, still sobbing and writhing in pain.

'I know. You didn't *do* anything.' He brought the bat down on Sonny's skull, heard his yelp, saw Ryan flinch as warm blood sprayed his pale cheeks. 'So I will.'

Twenty-two

Tuesday, May 4, 9.20 P.M.

'They changed their mind,' Lucy said as she walked through the morgue's parking garage with Stevie, Fitzpatrick and Detective Skinner. 'The victim's parents looked sick.'

'Me too,' Skinner muttered.

'It was a hard ID to do,' Lucy said kindly. 'We have the cell phone numbers for the parents so you can call them tomorrow and talk to them about their daughter.'

'I'll take over your shift,' Fitzpatrick said to Skinner when they'd reached their cars.

'If you're sure. My wife would appreciate it.' Skinner looked at Lucy. 'We have a new baby and I know she needs a break.'

'Go,' Lucy said. 'I'm fine here.'

Stevie looked exhausted. 'I'm going home to eat dinner and catch up on paperwork while Records does their thing.' With a wave she was gone, leaving Lucy and Fitzpatrick alone.

His expression was suddenly so hungry that her cheeks heated. But his words were all business. 'I got your purse and phone back from Drew. You're set up as bait.'

'Good to know.' He took the duffle from her shoulder and put it in the backseat. Then kissed her. It was sweet, yet restrained, hinting of what was to come. 'Feels like you haven't done that in forever,' she said when he lifted his head. 'But it's only been a day.'

'One hell of a day,' he said. 'Let me take you home.'

For the first time, that phrase sounded lovely.

370

'What is Records checking?' she asked when they were on the road.

'Same thing I was checking before. Still looking for the Bryans. It'll take awhile to track Ileanna's mother, especially if she remarried. Some of those records are kept at town level, especially from twenty years ago.' He glanced at her. 'Didn't you say you gave music lessons to the kids at your old boarding school? St Anne's?'

Lucy smacked her forehead lightly. 'On Wednesdays. I should cancel this week.'

'No, I don't want you to cancel. I want you to keep your routine.'

She lifted her brows. 'My routine is to go home alone.'

His smile was guarded, putting her on alert. '*That* routine can change,' he said.

'Tomorrow's Wednesday. You think that's where he'll leave Ryan's body, don't you?'

'Yes, so the school's going to have a bug infestation tomorrow. Students get a vacation day and our officers will patrol, dressed as exterminators. It'll be last minute, so hopefully it'll catch him off guard.'

She rubbed her forehead. 'All right. The kids will be ecstatic for a day off.'

He hesitated. 'I don't want you to mention this to anyone. Not even your friends.'

Her eyes narrowed. 'Just who are you accusing, JD?'

'Everyone,' he said. 'Until we put this guy away, everyone.'

'No. I won't suspect them. Not my friends.'

'Fine, but don't tell them. Not yet. Can you promise me?'

'I don't know,' she said honestly. 'You're asking a lot. They could be in danger.'

He sighed. 'Look at it this way. Somebody has been tracking you, watching you. It could be someone you know or someone your friends know. They make a mistake and trust the wrong person, or let a detail slip . . . they could get hurt. He killed the PI. She must've gotten in his way. There was no sign of forced entry in her apartment. He had a key. Just like with your car.'

Her stomach twisted. 'And Gwyn's apartment. Okay, okay. I get it. I promise.'

'Thank you.'

'Oh, I meant to tell you. Alan quit. You know, one of the techs?'

His jaw hardened. 'You mean that little prick that knew about the club and thought he was such hot shit? The one that had access to your purse?'

She blinked. 'Yeah, him. So what do you really think about him?'

'I think we need to check out his alibi for every second of the last forty-eight hours.'

'He was on duty for a lot of it.'

'Yeah, but he could have left for a little while.'

'True. What are you doing?'

He was dialing his cell. 'Getting his address. I need to pay the little prick a visit.'

'He was with Ruby when Janet's body was left last night,' she said. 'I checked. But you can check yourself if you want to.'

He hung up, annoyed. 'I wish he didn't have an alibi, just because I didn't like him.'

He was jealous, which was a little nice, especially since he'd backed off. 'Can we not talk about any of this for a while? Nothing about work or crazy killers or my family or yours?'

He smiled. 'What's left?'

'Music.'

'The last time we talked about music we ended up in an alley,' he said, his voice silky and suggestive. He lifted her hand to his lips.

A shiver ran straight through her body, remembering. 'We never settled it, did we?'

He turned to give her another hungry look. 'Actually, you conceded my point. But I'm a fair man. I'd be willing to go for best two out of three.'

She laughed breathlessly, the mood suddenly urgent. 'Drive faster.'

Tuesday, May 4, 9.30 P.M.

Clay dropped into a chair in his living room and closed his eyes.

He heard Alyssa sit in the chair next to him. 'Are you okay?' she asked, very quietly.

'No.' He swallowed hard. 'No, I'm not okay. I'm not sure I ever will be.'

'That was hard,' she whispered, 'hearing her cry like that and having no words to say.'

In the car, Nicki's mother had wept. Cursed. Wailed her anguish. 'You held her hand, Alyssa,' Clay said heavily. 'That's all you could have done.'

'I wish I could do something. I feel so helpless.'

'You can. I need you to look something up for me,' he said, his eyes still closed. Hatred for Evan Reardon coldly burned and he was holding onto his control by a thread. 'Dr Lucy Trask. I want to know why she had a bodyguard at the morgue.'

'You mean the detective she said was in training?'

'Yes. His hand never strayed more than a few inches from his gun.'

He waited while Alyssa opened her laptop and searched. Finally she muttered a curse. 'I found it. She's a part owner of Sheidalin. That's the club where the valet was killed and the woman was found dead in her car.'

The bodyguard made sense. Someone was gunning for the doctor. 'Cross-reference Anderson Ferry,' he ordered softly.

'I get a hit on a Ronald Trask, the retired sheriff. But nothing on Lucy.'

'Cross Ileanna Bryan.'

'Nothing.'

'Cross Evan Reardon.'

'Nothing again.'

'Mazzetti's expecting us to dig. Nicki found something that got her killed. So let's keep looking.' But all he could see was Nicki's brutalized body. *Grieve later. Find Reardon.* And when he did? Clay's fury bubbled up and over. *Evan Reardon belongs to me.*

Tuesday, May 4, 9.50 P.M.

There was, JD thought ruefully, a difference between talking about sex and actually doing it. Lucy had grown quiet after telling him to drive faster and by the time they'd reached her apartment she was palpably nervous.

He wanted to grind his teeth in frustration, but did not. Last night had been an explosion. Tonight . . . well, if she needed time and space, he'd give it to her. She had a sofa. *I can sleep there.* Even if it killed him. Which it just might.

He parked in front of her apartment and glanced up at the balcony where Mrs Pugh had greeted them earlier in the day. 'Have you heard from her?'

Lucy looked up, startled. Then she relaxed. A little. 'Barb? Yes. She left a voicemail while we were in Anderson Ferry to say he'd had another minor episode but that he'd quieted down. She's going to have to move him soon. She knows it.'

'She said you'd made the arrangements. Including financial. Very generous.'

Her cheeks flushed. 'He saved me once. Nobody wanted me. My parents didn't. But he and Barb did. It's only money. Mr Pugh and Barb gave me much more.'

JD's eyes stung. 'You're a good person, Lucy. Never let anyone tell you otherwise.'

He got out of the car and opened her door, unsurprised when she wouldn't meet his eyes. But he could see that what he'd said had touched her. Hopefully pleased her. Hopefully she'd let him please her a great deal more. He got her duffle and two small suitcases from the backseat – his and hers – and she frowned slightly.

'When did you pack that?' she asked, pointing to his bag.

'When I handed you off to Skinner at the morgue. I swung home and grabbed a shower and my bag.' He hesitated. 'Since you'd asked me to stay.'

She swallowed hard. 'Yes. I did.'

He tried not to sigh, but a little one escaped. 'Lucy, it's okay.

We'll do whatever you want. I'll sleep on the sofa. Or if you want me to get Skinner back here, I will.'

She looked up at him, startled again. 'Oh, no. That's not what I want. I'm just . . . scared.'

'Of me?'

She glanced away. 'This is embarrassing and I'm sorry. I want you to stay. I really do. It's just . . . Well, it was a lot easier last night. This me isn't used to being . . . you know.'

And suddenly he did. 'Come on,' he said softly. 'It'll be fine. You'll see.' He let them into her apartment and put the bags down.

'I need to call Gwyn,' she said quickly. 'She'll be worried.'

He waited as she did, watched as she hung up, then lifted her chin and took her mouth in what he'd intended to be an uncomplicated kiss. But she surprised him, rising on her toes and sliding her hands into his hair. Meeting him more than halfway.

His control slipped a notch and he kissed her until they were both breathless. He abruptly ended it, darkly satisfied at the yearning he saw in her eyes when she opened them. He slipped her jacket off and laid it on the table.

She lifted her hands to the back of her dress, but he stopped her before she could slide the zipper down. 'No,' he said, pulling her hands back to her sides. 'Not yet.'

Confusion collided with the heat in her eyes. 'But—'

'Trust me,' he murmured. 'It'll be fine.' Better than fine. She deserved that.

Her eyes widened when he opened her duffle and put her violin case on the table.

'What are you doing?'

He removed the violin and bow and handed them to her. 'Play for me.'

She shook her head. 'It's late. I'll wake everyone up.'

'Don't you play for Mr Pugh this late sometimes?'

'Yes, but . . . That's for him, to calm him. The neighbors put up with that.'

'They love your music, Lucy. They came out from their apartments to hear you play today. Think of it as giving them a lullaby.

But play for me.' He put the instrument in her hands. 'I want you to play for only me.'

'You're crazy,' she said, but tucked the violin under her chin. 'What should I play?'

'You choose. I'll like anything you pick. I promise.'

She faltered a moment and he thought she'd refuse. But then she began to play, and as before he was . . . enchanted. It was quiet and pure. And then he recognized the piece. It was what she'd played at the club the night before, but slower, measured. Not frantic. Not at all. It had been blatantly sexual last night.

Now it beckoned. As did she. She watched him as she played, her eyes widening when he took off his jacket and laid it over hers, then narrowing when he pulled his tie free and unsnapped his holster. When he unbuttoned his shirt, she sucked in a breath, bit at her lip.

But she didn't stop playing. When he'd shrugged out of his shirt he was again darkly satisfied, this time with the undisguised glitter of greed in her eyes. She'd looked at him like this the day before, when he'd come into CSU all sweaty. Like she wanted to devour him whole.

It was all he could do to keep from grabbing her and taking her up against a wall again. But he didn't, instead walking behind her and kissing the side of her neck. Her bow skittered, sending the chord sour. For a moment there was quiet, the only sound her rapid breathing and the beat of his own heart, heavy in his ears.

'Don't stop,' he whispered in her ear. 'Play for me. Please.'

Shakily she resumed, going rigid when he slid her zipper down her back, revealing beautiful skin. 'I didn't get to see you like this last night,' he said, kissing his way from one shoulder to the other, smiling fiercely when she shivered again, violently. 'You're beautiful.'

He unsnapped her bra and trailed his fingertips down her spine. He slipped his hands around her to cup her warm, round breasts in his palms and her violin went silent, the hand holding the bow falling to her side.

'What do you want?' he whispered against her neck, lightly

tugging on her nipples. She leaned into him, her head against his shoulder, her violin resting along her hip. She gave him free access and he made the most of it, caressing her breasts, running his hand down her front, teasing the band of her panties until she hummed in response. 'What do you want?' he asked again.

'You. I want you.' Lucy stepped away from him, her hand trembling as she returned her violin and bow to its case. Then she turned slowly, although every nerve in her body was urging her to throw herself onto him. He was perfectly formed, beautifully honed.

He was what she wanted. *Right now*. She licked her lips, wondering where to start.

The muscle in his jaw twitched as he waited. He'd set the stage. *The next move is mine*. She pushed her dress and bra from her shoulders and let them slip to the floor. His eyes dropped to her breasts and his mouth opened as if he'd say something, but he was totally silent.

He took a step forward and she took a step back, turning for the bedroom, keeping her pace slow. He followed her, closely enough that she felt the heat from his body. But she wasn't cold.

She closed her door behind them, then gasped when he swung her into his arms. His mouth closed over her breast and she let the moan she'd been holding back roll free. He yanked her panties down then pushed her to the bed.

Lying flat on her back, she stared up at him, her body pulsing and so ready. His expression ferocious, he pushed his pants to the floor, leaving him standing in a pair of briefs that didn't begin to contain him. 'You're sure this is what you want?' he asked.

She stared at his erection, knowing how it felt inside her. Needing to feel it inside her again. She sat up and traced her finger down his length, watched him twitch, then forced herself to look away long enough to meet his eyes. 'Yes. This is what I want. You're what I want. Who I want. Now.'

It was all he'd needed to hear. He shoved the briefs down, searched his pocket for a condom, then smacked it in her palm. 'Do it.'

Her hands suddenly steady, she did, thrilled with how he watched her every move. Then like a whip he moved, tossing her back to the bed and following her down, kissing her until she had no breath in her lungs. He thrust inside her and she cried out.

He kissed her neck hard. 'Last night was fast,' he said in her ear. 'Tonight might be, too. But I'll make it up to you. I promise.'

'Fast or slow, I don't care,' she gasped, thrusting against him. 'Just do it.'

He laughed, plunging hard and fast until she thought her heart would burst out of her chest. She dug her fingers into his shoulders and her heels into her frothy pink bedspread and met him thrust for thrust. 'Next time you play, think of this,' he said, panting. 'Think of me.'

She couldn't think of playing, couldn't think of anything. She was close. So close. Then he reached between them and touched her and she snapped. Her scream was muffled by his mouth as white lights danced behind her eyelids and pleasure exploded.

He buried his face against her neck, his body going taut as he followed. The minutes ticked by as he lay heavily on her, unmoving. She kissed his shoulder, welcoming his weight. This was good. He was good. *He is good for me. Please let it be true.* She'd been so alone for so long. 'Thank you,' she whispered and he forced himself to his elbows, studying her.

'For what?' he asked seriously.

'For this. And for knowing what I needed. How did you know?'

'Last night, watching you on that stage . . . you were so hot. Like fire. You were like fire when I had you. And fire is good, don't get me wrong. But I wanted . . . warmth, not flame. I think I can sustain warmth. I figured the music was your gateway. But I wanted you to think of me, not all those people screaming your name.' He smiled and his dimple winked. 'Lucinda.'

I think I can sustain warmth. Was that exciting enough for you? JD's wife had done a number on him. 'You have no problem with warmth,' she said. 'In any way. And last night when I saw you at the club, there was nobody else. All I could see was you.'

He chuckled, the movement sending tingles through her body. 'You were angry.'

She lifted her hips against him and felt him grow hard again. 'I had a right to be.'

His eyes darkened as new need filled them. 'Are you sure you can again?'

She closed her eyes as he began to move. 'You said best two out of three.'

Tuesday, May 4, 10.55 P.M.

'I think we should make it best three out of five,' Lucy murmured and JD laughed, amazed he had the energy to do so.

'I think I'd die.' They lay on their backs, breathing hard. 'But it'd be a helluva way to go.'

'I don't think I can move.'

'Then don't.'

'But I'm freezing,' she said. With a groan he forced himself to move, covering her with a blanket. 'Where are you going?' she asked when he went toward the door.

'To get my gun,' he said, regretting the reality that returned to her eyes. He got his gun and their clothes, checked the lock on the door, then returned to find her nearly asleep. For a moment he let himself look. And hope.

Her eyes fluttered open with difficulty. 'Why are you staring at me?'

Because you're mine, he thought. 'Because you're beautiful,' he said.

She smiled at him and for that instant the world was right. 'Come. Sleep.'

He put his gun and cell phone on her nightstand, just in case, then shucked his pants and climbed under the covers, spooning her against him. She hummed happily.

'You're always warm. So warm.'

'I have my uses,' he said wryly and chuckled when she wriggled a little.

'Indeed.'

He switched off the light and they lay in the darkness, but he didn't sleep. Neither did she. Finally she sighed.

'JD? Do you still see your mother?'

'From time to time. Whenever she wants money.'

'Do you give it to her?'

'No. I'll buy her groceries or pay her electric bill sometimes, but money would go straight into some liquor store's cash register.'

'Why? Why do you take care of her? She abandoned you.'

'I didn't for a long time. And I don't often. Usually she doesn't ask. I think she hates to ask. Hates to owe me anything.'

She turned to her back to stare up at him in the darkness. 'But why do you care?'

'I don't know, Lucy. She's my mother. A few times she tried to go sober and straight. It was never good, but it wasn't foster care. I guess I remember the few not-so-bad times when she comes with her hand out.'

'My mother would bake bread,' Lucy said. 'She was always so busy taking care of other people's kids, but on Sundays she'd bake bread. Sometimes she'd bring me a slice in bed, with butter and jam. Every time I smell fresh bread I remember that.'

'And you miss those times.'

'Yes.'

'You know you didn't cause her to become fragile, Lucy.'

'Yes, I know. But I also know I was mean to her when I was in college. I regret sending her all those pictures of me on a motorcycle. I wanted to hurt her and I did.'

Her reaction to his helmet made more sense. It represented a Lucy she didn't want to be again. 'Why don't you just talk to her, honey? Make things right if you can? People can change.'

'My father wouldn't let me. I remembered she'd tried to say something as she passed me in court, but my father dragged her away. I called the house to talk to her and he told me I'd done enough. To leave her alone, that she didn't want to talk to me. Ever again.'

'Maybe he lied.'

'I thought so, so I tried again. I waited till I knew he wouldn't be home and called. She answered and I asked if she was okay. If he was hurting her. She insisted he wasn't. I told her I was going to California, even if I didn't get into med school there. She wished me a good life. Told me it would be best for all of us if I didn't bother her again.'

'I'm sorry.'

'I should be sorry. I'm the one who said we shouldn't talk about family. It's just that going back the last few days makes it all come back. I'll shut up and let you sleep.'

She could keep him awake any day of the week, he thought as she rolled over and snuggled against him. He ran his hand down the silkiness of her arm, physically content. But his mind churned with unanswered questions. She still hadn't gone to sleep, so he ventured to ask.

'Lucy, what happened to your second fiancé?'

'He left me.'

'Why? Although I confess I'm happy he did.'

'I was too, after the fact. Gus was as far from Heath as possible. I met him a few years after I'd moved to LA. I'd been scared straight and decided I'd never have another bad boy. Gus was a good man. And he was a nice man. He just decided I wasn't for him.'

'What did he do?' he asked.

'For his job? He was a carpenter. Once a year he'd go to Mexico and build houses. I went with him, the summer I finished my residency.'

He remembered her story from the day before. 'Oh. The little girl who was injured.'

'Yes. We came up on the accident minutes after it happened. A girl's leg was pinned, bleeding profusely. People had gathered, but nobody could get her out or stop the bleeding.'

'You got her out.'

'Yes.' She went quiet a moment. 'The hospital was hours away by car. They were sending a helicopter for the girl, but she was going to die before they got there. And gas was leaking from both vehicles in the wreck. The other car was burning. People were screaming. Her mother was begging, praying, crying. The girl was going to lose her

381

leg. It was crushed under a truck, for God's sake. So I took the Sawzall from Gus's toolbox and amputated it.'

She drew a breath and shuddered it out. 'I'll never get that child's screams out of my head. It was horrific. After I did it, I pulled her away from the truck and it blew, sky high.'

He was horrified just listening. 'Shit.'

'I kept working on her with whatever tools I could find, trying to stop the bleeding. I went with her to the hospital in the helicopter, praying I'd done the right thing.'

'You saved her from getting blown sky-high.'

'The doctors at the hospital said it was excellent field work. The girl lived. Her parents were grateful. But Gus was horrified. He knew I'd be working in an ER when we got back to LA, but I guess actually seeing me do it was different. He said I was a robot, that I was able to ignore that girl's screams and carve her up like I had no soul. I didn't ignore her screams. They still haunt me. I just did what I thought needed to be done.'

'That's not being a robot,' he said. 'That's being able to focus on what needs to be done.'

She made a small sound of gratitude. 'Even if you don't mean it, thank you.'

'I mean it.' He kissed her temple. 'What happened to fiancé number two?'

'Gus left after we got back home. Engagement broken, fairly amicably.'

'How fairly?' he asked warily. 'Did you break his nose too?'

She laughed. 'No, I just wouldn't give him back the ring. I'd taken a hit on wedding deposits. I figured it was a fair trade. He finally agreed.'

'So where's the ring?'

'I had it made into a necklace, but I couldn't wear it. It reminded me that he hadn't wanted me either. I sold it and put the money toward my share of the down payment on the club.'

'Where nobody calls you a robot.'

'Yes.' She sounded embarrassed. 'I don't expect that to make sense to you.'

He was quiet for a long time, thinking. Remembering. 'It does,' he finally said.

'It does what?' she murmured, almost asleep.

'Make sense to me.'

She rolled over to look up at him. 'I don't understand.'

'The day Maya died, we fought. She said I was cold. Robotic.'

'Why would she say that?'

'She was angry that I wanted to settle down, have a family. I'd never really had one except in the army, and that wasn't the same. Even the time I spent with Paul and Stevie was like being on the outside looking in. They were a unit.'

'Why did Maya say you were cold? And robotic?'

'She said no one with as much blood as I had on my hands should be a father. That anyone who could take out targets like I had was a robot. With no heart. That I couldn't love a child.'

Lucy blanched. 'My God. What a horrible thing to say. She was wrong, JD. You have heart.' She cupped his jaw in her palm. 'I've seen it. You have compassion and you care. And a little girl named Cordelia loves you and you love her. Maya was *wrong*.'

Her words eased his heart. 'I want to think so,' he said.

'Know so. Maybe she thought she couldn't be a parent but didn't want to say it.'

He hadn't considered that. 'It's possible.' Probable even.

'Not everyone should be a parent. But it doesn't mean the cycle has to continue.'

He hesitated. It was too soon to ask it, but he couldn't help himself. He needed to know, before he fell past the point of no return. 'What about you? Do you want kids?'

She met his eyes in the darkness. 'Yes. I'd be a better mom than mine was. I'd never let anyone hurt my child. Any other questions?'

'No. I'm good for now.'

'Then go to sleep.'

Wednesday, May 5, 2.15 A.M.

He'd earned a good night's sleep. Dumping Agar's body had been a breeze. No problems encountered. No one had come, everyone fast asleep in their little beds.

He'd left Sonny Westcott tied up on the floor of his plant, battered but alive. He'd simply run out of time. And energy. He wanted to do the job right versus finishing off Sonny too fast because he had somewhere he needed to be.

His cell rang, startling him. He rolled his eyes at the caller ID. 'What's up, baby?'

'I woke up and you weren't here.'

'I had to run out for cigarettes. I'll be back in a few minutes. Go back to sleep.'

Wednesday, May 5, 5.15 A.M.

JD awoke with a start. The bed was empty, the sheets cold. Lucy was gone.

He rolled over, prepared to swing to his feet, but he stilled abruptly. She was standing by the window, staring down at the deserted street. She wore an oversized T-shirt that left most of her legs bare. Her cheeks were wet and she wiped at them with the back of her left hand, her lips pursed to keep her weeping silent. Her right hand held a hinged frame with two photographs.

Quietly JD rose and put his hands on her shoulders, pressing a kiss to her temple.

She drew a ragged breath and leaned against him. 'I didn't mean to wake you.'

He covered her hand with his, turning the frame so he could see. On one side was her brother Buck, a football helmet under one arm. On the other was a man astride a motorcycle, also with a helmet under one arm. That must be Heath, the first fiancé. He was relieved to find he felt no jealousy. All he felt was concern for her. Her silent weeping broke his heart.

'I was wondering when it would hit you,' he murmured.

'It just did. Today I found out my brother wasn't who I thought he was. I still miss him.' She looked at the picture in her hands. 'This is all I have of him. I don't even have the bracelet anymore. Not that I ever did.'

'Did he love you?'

'I want to believe he did. But I don't know what he *did*.' She said it desperately.

'Which night?' he asked. 'The night Ileanna died or the night Buck died?'

She swallowed hard. 'Both, I guess. I knew something was wrong. I knew my father was angrier and my mother was sadder than normal. And Buck was . . . upset. I thought it was because of what happened with Ileanna – she'd been his date. Naturally he'd be upset, right?'

'Right.'

'The night Buck died, I wasn't home. Gwyn's mom offered to take her and me to the movies, then let us have a sleepover. I always liked going to Gwyn's house.'

'Did you ever tell anyone about your father's abuse?'

'No. Who'd believe me? I mean, he was the sheriff and she was the doctor. Would the doctor let a man hurt her kids? Surely not.'

'But she did.'

'Yeah. Battered wives come in all shapes and sizes, from all walks of life. My mom let him hurt her, and us. I used to wish she'd gather us up and whisk us away in the night.'

'But she didn't.'

'No. She stayed with him. She's still with him. At some point I decided that I had to take care of myself, because she wasn't going to.'

'When was that?'

'My first night at St Anne's.'

His heart broke a little more, but he kept it from his voice. 'You did take care of yourself, and others too. You might have become selfish, Lucy, but you didn't. You love the Pughs and they love you. You've got a career. Two, in fact. And you made your own family with Gwyn.'

'And Thorne. He looks big and mean, but he's had his share of loss too. So has Gwyn. In fact, that's what Sheidalin stands for. When we were choosing the name, we decided we'd each contribute a piece, the name of someone we lost. The "LIN" is for Linus. Now I wonder if I did the right thing in choosing his name. What if he helped kill her, JD? What if he killed Ricky Joyner? What if I never know?'

He cupped her neck in his palm, massaging her taut muscles with his thumb. 'I don't know, honey. Not knowing would be the hardest, but however it turns out, you don't have to face it by yourself.'

'Thank you. Thank you for not telling me it will be okay when you don't know.'

'You're welcome. Now why don't we go back to sleep? We have another hour—' He stopped, narrowing his eyes as he looked away from her reflection in the window and down to his car parked in the lot below. 'What the hell?'

'What?' Lucy leaned forward, straining to see. 'Your trunk is open.'

He grabbed his pants and yanked them on. 'Put some clothes on. You can't stay here alone.' She quickly did so and in minutes they were headed out her front door and down the stairs to his car.

His trunk was slightly ajar, a dent on one side where it had been pried open. He got a pair of latex gloves from the glove box. Pulling them on, he opened the trunk a few inches, peered in, then stepped back, his expression hard.

'Good news, he thinks you feel safe with me. Bad news, we just found Ryan Agar.'

Wednesday, May 5, 5.35 A.M.

They'd both suited up once backup had arrived, JD in a suit and tie and Lucy in her white coveralls. JD was directing the uniforms as to where to string the crime-scene tape when his cell rang. He thought it would be Stevie since he'd left her a message to call, but it was an unknown number. 'This is Detective Fitzpatrick.'

'I'm sorry if I woke you. This is Deputy Sheriff Ashton McHale, Anderson Ferry.'

'Deputy, this is a really bad time. Can I call you back?

'Actually, we're having a bad time too. Our sheriff is missing.'

JD closed his eyes. *Fuck*. Lucy had warned Westcott. 'Since when?'

'He went out yesterday afternoon, soon after your group left our office. We assumed he'd gone home for the day. This morning his mother stopped by to check on him because he hadn't returned any of her phone calls. He hadn't come home, which was not normal. We did a search and found his car parked off the road near a rental property that's been empty for some time.'

JD looked into the trunk of his car where Ryan Agar lay bound and gagged. And beaten. Lucy was bent over the body, starting her preliminary exam with Ruby Gomez at her side, so he stepped back several feet to give them room.

'Were there signs of a struggle around the car?' he asked and Lucy looked over her shoulder. He motioned her to continue with Agar and, though frowning, she complied.

'Yes,' the deputy said. 'We found blood matching the sheriff's type on the ground and signs that he'd been dragged to the dock. We also found another car, registered to Dr Trask.'

JD's brows crunched. 'That's not possible. We have her car in our shop.'

There was a moment of silence. 'Oh. I'm talking about Dr Trask, the mother. You must be talking about the daughter.'

JD's heart sank. Not her mother. He thought of Mrs Westcott's account of her rushing out with her medical bag and had another thought. He stepped much further away, turning so that Lucy couldn't hear. 'Former sheriff Trask's boat. Is it there?'

'No,' the deputy said. 'And he's nowhere to be found either.'

'I understand,' he murmured. 'How many people know about this?'

'Mrs Westcott knows,' the deputy said flatly.

Which meant everyone would soon know. 'Understood.' He made himself think about case logistics and not how this would affect Lucy. The killer had been in Anderson Ferry. *With us.* Again he kicked himself for letting the black Lexus pass him. 'We're going to send a CSU team if that's all right.'

'Fine with us. We don't have the resources for something like this.'

'Thank you. One thing I'd like you to do. These disappearances are related to murders we're investigating here in the city. The killer was last seen driving a black Lexus. Can you do a search around the town? I don't have the plate. When you find it, cordon it off. Don't open it, don't let anyone touch it. It could be our only link right now.'

'Understood. When should we expect your CSU van?'

JD sighed. 'Well, they're processing a scene for me right now.'

'Who?' the deputy asked tightly.

The man had been direct with him and JD respected that. 'Ryan Agar.'

'Oh, my God. I'm sorry. It's just that . . . I grew up with him. I heard his mother was murdered too. Westcott's dead, isn't he?'

'Let's not assume yet. I'll get the van to you as soon as possible.' JD hung up and dialed Stevie again.

'Sorry,' she said. 'I was in the shower and didn't hear my cell. What's happened?' He told her and listened to her creative swearing. 'Lucy warned that SOB Westcott. I'm having trouble feeling sorry for any of them, JD.'

'Agreed. I need to go. I need to tell her.'

'God. Poor kid. I'm on my way in.'

JD hung up but didn't move, dreading this more than anything he'd ever done. Her father was one thing, but she still had feelings for her mother. Bent over the body in his trunk, she went still then looked over her shoulder as if knowing he'd been talking about her. She straightened, her eyes seeking his.

'Who?' she asked.

He crossed to her and started to take her hands, but she held them away and too late he saw that her gloves were bloody. 'Sonny Westcott and your parents are missing.'

She drew a sharp breath. 'When?'

'Probably while we were in Anderson Ferry yesterday.' He wasn't sure what he expected her to do, but it wasn't what she did, which was to nod briskly, square her shoulders and return to her examination of Ryan Agar.

'I checked under his shirt,' she said. 'There's an "E" burned into his back, but it appears to be post-mortem this time, which is different than the others. But his heart's gone and the gag appears to hold his tongue, which is identical to the others.'

'Lucy.' He grasped her shoulder and she shrugged him off.

'Don't, JD. Not now.'

He didn't listen, forcing her to turn to face him. 'I'm taking you off this case.'

Her mouth fell open in outrage. 'You can't do that.'

'Yes, I can.' He leaned close, ignoring the mutilated body behind them. 'I care about you,' he whispered fiercely. 'Besides that, now that your family is involved, anything you touch is subject to dismissal by a judge. You know that.'

She swallowed, her eyes so filled with pain that it broke his heart. 'I have to work.'

'No, baby, you don't.' He removed her gloves and Ruby quietly disposed of them. He drew Lucy into his arms and held her. She was shaking, her hands clutching his shirt.

'I'll call the next doc in rotation,' Ruby said. 'Luce, I'm sorry.'

Lucy nodded and said nothing. She was holding herself so rigidly JD was afraid she'd shatter. He tugged her away from the trunk, his arm around her and she followed numbly.

Drew emerged from the CSU van and took one look at Lucy's face. 'What?'

'Her parents are missing, along with Sheriff Westcott,' JD said. 'There appeared to be a struggle with the sheriff. Can you get someone down there to process the scene?'

'Yeah. I'll get right on it. Lucy, I'm so sorry.'

She nodded, unseeing, and JD walked her to her apartment, tapping a female officer to follow. Lucy sat slowly on her sofa, her face more than pale.

'Stay with her,' he said to the officer. 'She has two friends, Gwyn

Weaver and Thomas Thorne. Call them if you would.' He knelt next to Lucy, taking her hands in his, warming them. 'I have to get back downstairs to the scene.'

'I know,' she whispered, her gaze eerily unfocused. 'He cuts out their hearts, JD. He's going to do that to my mother.'

'We're going to stop him, honey.' He brought her hands to his lips. 'I have to go.'

When she looked at him, her eyes were clear. 'Get him, JD. Please.'

'Try not to worry.' Standing, he glanced out of her front window. In the parking lot Ruby and another tech were zipping Ryan Agar into a body bag and a chill froze JD's blood. *He's out there. Planning. Watching her every move with that damn tracker.*

JD didn't want to leave her, but he knew he had to. To make himself feel better, he found the tracker Drew had hidden in the compact and tucked it into one of the pockets of her coveralls. 'Where's your cell phone?'

'In my other pocket. You can go. I'll be all right.'

'Okay.' He pressed a kiss to her forehead. 'Stay here. Stay safe.'

Wednesday, May 5, 6.00 A.M.

Stevie was buttering a piece of toast when she saw the note her sister had left on the refrigerator. *Cordy has a field trip in day care today. You need to sign the paper. In her backpack. xoxo, Iz.* Stevie sighed. Izzy was always leaving these things till the last minute. Still, Stevie didn't know what she'd do without her.

She searched Cordelia's backpack, conscious of the minutes ticking. JD had things under control, but it wasn't fair to make him shoulder the burden alone. Frustrated, she dumped the contents of the backpack on her kitchen table.

She frowned when a key fob tumbled out. What was Cordelia doing with her car key? She picked it up and squinted at the tiny print on the back. And then the toast she'd eaten rose in her throat to choke her. *Trackamatic GPS.*

'Oh, God. Holy God.' She made herself breathe, even as she was running to Cordelia's room. She shuddered out a panicked sob when she saw her daughter sleeping like an angel, safe. Stevie ran to her sister's room and turned on the light.

Izzy blinked and pulled a pillow over her face. 'Go away, Stevie.'

Stevie shook her hard. 'Wake up. *Izzy*.'

Izzy sat up abruptly. 'What? Is it Cordy? What?'

Stevie held up the device. 'Do you know what this is?'

Izzy squinted. 'My car key?'

'No. Did you put it in Cordelia's backpack?'

'No. Why would I? What's wrong? You're pale as a ghost.'

Stevie nodded over and over, trying to stop her racing heart. 'Okay. Today Cordelia goes nowhere. This is a tracking device. Our ME found one in her purse.'

'I don't understand,' Izzy said.

'A man has killed eight people. He was tracking our ME. Now I find this in my child's . . .' Her voice broke and Izzy wrapped her arms around her.

'Okay, I get it now. Nobody's gonna touch your baby. We won't let them.'

Stevie nodded, but the tears were coming and she couldn't stop them. 'Oh, God.'

'It's okay,' Izzy murmured. 'I'm cancelling everything today. I'll stay here with Cordy and I'll bring over everyone else in the family.'

Stevie pulled away. 'I should stay here.'

'No.' Izzy held Stevie's face. 'You should go find the sonofabitch who just threatened our baby. Now go. I will sit in Cordy's room till Mom and Dad get here.'

Stevie wiped her palms across her wet face. 'You have a key to my gun safe?'

Izzy's jaw was now cocked. 'Oh, yeah. If he tries to come in this house, he'd better be wearing a suit of fucking body armor because otherwise he ain't leaving alive.'

'Good.' Stevie made herself think. Only one name came to mind. '*Clay Maynard*,' she said, her eyes narrowed. 'That man is going to tell me what this is about.'

'I don't know who that is,' Izzy said, 'but I pity the man who fucks with you today.'

'You got that right. But first I'm going to ask Cordelia about this.'

'Calm down first. You're scaring me, and I'm not five years old.'

She was right. Stevie took deep breaths until her chest was no longer tight. 'Now?'

Izzy made a face. 'Not great, but not Monster Mama either.'

The two of them went into Cordelia's room and sat on either side of the bed, flanking her. 'Baby.' Stevie gently shook her awake. 'Mommy needs to talk to you.' Stevie waited until Cordelia blinked her eyes open. 'Has anyone been playing with your backpack? Any grownups?'

'No,' she said sleepily. 'Why?'

'Have you lost it recently and maybe just gotten it back?'

'No. Is it still night?'

'No, baby, it's early in the morning. Has anyone you don't know touched your backpack?'

'No.' Her little forehead bunched. 'Yes. I dropped it and a man picked it up for me.'

Stevie's heart began to pound. 'How did you drop it?'

She shrugged. 'I tripped. The nice man gave it back to me and I said thank you.'

Stevie forced her voice to be gentle. 'Do you remember what he looked like?'

'He was big. Like a tree.'

Stevie made herself smile. 'Dark hair, light hair?'

'Dark. I think. He had a hat.'

'How do you know he was dark, then?'

'He had black eyebrows. Bushy ones, like Grandpa. Can we have waffles for breakfast?'

'You bet,' Izzy said, ruffling her hair. 'You can help me make them. Just like the cookies. But now Mommy has to go to work and catch the bad guys.'

Cordelia tilted her head back to stare up at Stevie. 'Was that man bad, Mommy?'

'I don't know,' Stevie said honestly. 'But you don't need to worry about him. Aunt Izzy and Gramma and Grampa are gonna be here all day.'

Cordelia grabbed Stevie's sleeve. 'Mommy. The bad man had a tattoo.'

Stevie's pounding heart sped up. 'Like?'

Cordelia frowned. 'A heart, but it wasn't pretty. It was squashed.'

'Oh wow, baby. You are amazing,' Stevie breathed. 'Where was it?'

Cordelia pointed to her forearm. 'I don't remember which side.'

Stevie pulled her baby to her in a hard hug. 'It doesn't matter. You are awesome.'

Cordelia's smile lit up her face. 'Can I have chocolate chips in my waffles?'

Stevie's lips twitched. 'You bet. I love you.'

Cordelia bounced on the bed. 'Love you,' she sang, loudly and totally off key.

Music to my ears. Stevie motioned Izzy to the doorway. 'I'm going to get police protection for the house. They may come inside to wait.'

'Then I'll feed them waffles too,' Izzy said. 'You go.'

Stevie had to take another deep breath. 'I love you too, you know.'

Izzy winked. 'What's not to love?'

Stevie called Hyatt as soon as she got to her car and he immediately ordered a squad car to her house. He could be a royal pain in the ass, but he was good about protecting his people and their families. She then dialed JD. 'I have a stop to make before I get to Lucy's.'

'What's wrong, Stevie?' he asked quietly.

'I found one of those tracking devices in Cordelia's backpack.'

'Oh, my God.'

'And I got a description from Cordy.' She told him.

'Tall as a tree and a squashed heart tattoo? That's . . . specific.'

'What are you thinking?'

'That Thomas Thorne is as tall as a tree,' he said.

'Yes, he is. We can't bring him in yet. Not on the word of a five year old.'

'I know. And I just told a policewoman to call him for Lucy. Lucy won't be able to believe it's Thorne. She's loyal.'

'Where's her shadow?'

'Skinner is on his way. Should be here any minute. Where are you going first?'

'To pay a visit to that PI as soon as the squad car Hyatt ordered gets here.'

'I'll give Skinner the heads-up and I'll meet you at the PI's. Hang in there.'

'I will.' She hung up, closed her eyes, and prayed.

Twenty-three

Wednesday, May 5, 6.25 A.M.

JD hung up, so angry his hands shook. First Lucy and now Cordelia. *I want him dead.* It didn't matter why Evan was doing what he was doing or even what he'd endured. It mattered that he needed to be stopped. Permanently.

JD's phone rang again, the call this time from Debbie, Hyatt's clerk. 'JD, I have Detective Sherman from Newport News on the line. Hyatt said to put him through to you, that he has information you'll want to hear. We checked him out. He's legit.'

Before JD could ask a question, he was connected. 'This is Fitzpatrick.'

'Good morning. My name is Detective Sherman. I'm with the homicide department in Newport News. I'll be brief because I can see from the news that you're busy. I hear from your LT that you've met a PI named Maynard.'

'Yeah,' JD said, standing straighter. 'I assume you have too. What did he do?'

'Not sure, but he knows a helluva lot more than he's telling. I got two bodies in my morgue. One's a cop. Both have slit throats with a little curl around the right ear. I understand you have a few of those yourself.'

A cop. This just gets better. 'Physically in my morgue, six,' JD said grimly. This could be the break they'd hoped for. He prayed Sherman knew something they didn't.

Sherman coughed. 'Sonofamotherfuckin' bitch.'

'Maynard's friend was killed by the same person who did the

395

other killings. He found her body yesterday morning.'

'Really. That must be why he went home. How does she connect?'

'We think she stumbled onto something that got her killed. How do your victims connect to Maynard?'

'He came into town on Monday looking for a woman he claimed called herself Margo Winchester. He'd been pestering one of our elderly residents to speak to her granddaughter. We traced the granddaughter to a strip joint but she was already in the wind. Maynard stopped in to talk to her Monday night after he lost our tail.'

'I assume you were tailing him for more than bothering the old lady.'

'Oh, yeah. He stopped by our morgue to ask about a victim of a fire. That was our cop, Pullman. He'd had his throat slit, then his body was burned in the arson of a condemned house. Took us a few days to ID him. In the meantime, a body was pulled out of the Bay – a Jane Doe. Her throat was also slit. She matched the woman Maynard was looking for.'

'Margo Winchester.'

'Yeah, but the Jane Doe was using Margo as an alias. Once we traced the old lady's granddaughter to the strip joint, we passed the Jane Doe sketch around. They knew her as Mary Stubbs. She'd been a dancer there for a year, but hadn't shown up in a week, right about the time she ended up in the Bay. They'd also seen our dead cop hanging around there in the recent past. Pullman was married, and was doing it with the stripper on the QT.'

'Got it. Do you know an Evan Bryan?'

'I don't, but I can check it out. Is he the perp?'

'We don't know, but his name's come up in our investigation. He and his mother were last known to be in North Carolina twenty years ago.'

Sherman waited. 'That's all you got?'

'Plus the six stiffs in my morgue, three more missing, and two victims in Delaware.'

'Shit, Fitzpatrick. What has Maynard told you?'

'A whole lot of nothing, but I was on my way to see him when you called. I'll keep you up to date if you'll see what you can turn up on Evan Bryan.'

'Will do. Good luck.'

'Thanks,' JD said and hung up with a tired sigh. *We're gonna need it.* He'd started to call Stevie with the information when Skinner pulled up in his department car, reminding JD that he had no way to meet Stevie at Maynard's house because his own vehicle was now a crime scene.

'Heard what happened,' Skinner said, jogging over to JD. 'Lucy's parents going missing and now Stevie's kid being tracked. How's the doc?'

'Holding.' She'd been holding for a long time, JD thought. 'Look, I've gotta meet Stevie before she tears that PI Maynard a new one. Can I use your car?'

Skinner held out his keys. 'Good luck. I wouldn't want to be that PI right now.'

'Me either. Tell Lucy I'll be back as soon as I can.' *Tall as a tree.* JD sighed. 'Look, Skinner, Stevie's kid says the guy she saw was tall as a tree and had a tattoo of a squashed heart. I don't know if he has a tattoo, but Thomas Thorne is—'

'Tall as a tree,' Skinner finished. 'Hyatt will get some serious mileage out of that.'

'Thorne is Lucy's friend. He may come, considering her folks are missing.'

Skinner nodded. 'Got it. I'll keep my eyes open.'

Wednesday, May 5, 7.40 A.M.

Clay had another sleepless night, poring over Nicki's records in the hope that he'd find something linking Ileanna Bryan to Evan Reardon and Lucy Trask. But he'd found nothing, so today he and Alyssa were going to Anderson Ferry to get answers so that they could find Evan, who thankfully hadn't seemed to have killed anyone new in the last twenty-four hours.

They should have left already, but he hadn't moved. He stood at his desk, his hands clutching the handle of his briefcase, wondering what had gone so wrong.

Because it was wrong. Nicki was dead because she'd fallen for the wrong man and hadn't seen the truth in front of her. He couldn't change that. But he should have come clean the moment he'd seen Mary Stubbs's autopsy photo in Sherman's office.

But he hadn't and people had died. Innocent people. *And I have to live with that.*

'It's time to go, Clay,' Alyssa said from the doorway of his office.

'I know.' He released a pent-up breath. 'But I can't. Evan has to be stopped and our going to Anderson Ferry will take hours that the cops could be using to catch him. We need to tell Mazzetti what we know. I'll keep you out of it.'

Alyssa's eyes widened. 'Looks like you're about to get your chance.' She'd no sooner said the words when the outside door opened.

'Where. Is. He?' Mazzetti asked coldly from the front.

'Um, he's . . .' Alyssa stammered.

'Look,' Mazzetti said angrily. 'I've already been to his house. That's his car outside and I'm in no fucking mood to play games. Where is Maynard?'

'It's okay, Alyssa,' Clay called. 'Show her in.'

Mazzetti stormed in, followed by a man about Clay's size. The man looked equally grim. Clay wondered if Evan had killed someone else after all.

Mazzetti propped her fists on his desk and leaned in. 'Who is he? Who is the brother?'

'Whose brother?' he asked, although he thought he now knew.

In the blink of his eye she was around his desk, her furious face inches from his. 'I swear to God you'd better not lie to me, Maynard. Tell me who he is. Now.'

'I'd tell her what she wants to know, Mr Maynard,' the other detective said calmly. 'The man who's killed ten people just threatened my partner's five-year-old daughter. I wouldn't stand in your shoes and socks if he touches a hair on her head.'

'Ten?' Clay asked, horrified.

'Ten,' the man said. 'There are two bodies in the Newport News morgue with our guy's signature on them. And three more are missing.'

Clay closed his eyes. 'Dear God,' he murmured.

'You'd better pray,' Mazzetti snarled. 'A name. I know you have one.'

The man sat on the edge of his desk and between the two detectives Clay was boxed in. Both cops were furious. The man simply covered his rage in a veneer of calm that Clay knew would be easily shattered.

'First, no charges against Alyssa,' Clay said.

'I'm not making any promises,' Mazzetti said, a hair more rationally. She backed away, her hands fisted at her sides. 'Talk.'

'Who are you?' Clay asked the man.

'Fitzpatrick. Her partner. A name, please. I'll even give you a first name. Evan.'

This is over. 'Reardon,' he said. 'Alyssa, print them a picture.'

Fitzpatrick looked relieved at the photo, as if he'd thought he might see someone else.

'It could be the guy who took Ryan Agar,' Mazzetti said. 'If we add a fake mustache, it could be the guy in the parking garage photo.' She looked up. 'Does he have any body art?'

Clay thought of the photo Nic had taken of Evan in her bed. 'Yes. A tattoo. A heart that was melted. Like that clock in the Dali painting.'

'How tall is he?' Mazzetti demanded.

'Six three,' Clay said. 'Why?'

'Because my five year old saw him when he dropped a tracking device in her backpack. She can identify him. I don't think he's gonna like that.'

Clay's anger reignited. Until Evan was dead, Mazzetti would always worry that one day he'd come back. Clay could have asked why Evan would threaten her daughter, but he knew. Distract and divide. Grabbing her daughter would be Evan's insurance if they got too close.

'We didn't know about Ileanna Bryan,' Clay said. 'We don't

know how they're connected, but we suspect it has something to do with a town called Anderson Ferry.'

Mazzetti seemed to settle. 'All right. Let's sit down and you tell us what you do know.'

Clay gestured to the chairs, waving Alyssa to one. 'No charges against Alyssa,' he repeated.

Mazzetti studied him sharply. 'When did you know?'

'Definitively, last night. We know Evan met the victim Sue Ellen Lamont. When we heard she was dead, we knew. Until then it was all circumstantial.'

'Who are the bodies in Newport News?' Mazzetti asked.

He crossed his arms over his chest. 'Your word, Detective. She's eighteen. She thought she was doing the right thing. No charges.'

'I'm not promising anything, Mr Maynard. But you did tell us Evan's last name, so I will do my best to see you are not identified.'

For a long moment their gazes locked. 'All right.' He told them almost everything, deleting all references to the fact that Nicki had crafted a new identity for Evan Reardon. 'Evan said he wanted us to make the stalker woman go away,' he finished. 'I don't know why he's doing this. I don't know who Ileanna is or why Nicki went to Anderson Ferry.'

Again a glance passed between the detectives, subtle, but there.

'You do know, though,' Clay said.

'Yes,' Mazzetti said. 'We know Nicki went there. She was given a folder of information by the newspaper office there a few days before she was killed.'

'We didn't find it. I assume we would have known about Ileanna Bryan if we had.'

Mazzetti nodded. 'Reasonable assumption.'

'Something happened two months ago,' Fitzpatrick said. 'Do you know what that was?'

'His mother,' Alyssa said quietly and Clay nodded.

'His mother died, but that was more than three months ago. That I've confirmed.'

'Her name?' Fitzpatrick asked.

'Yvette Reardon,' Clay said. 'Evan told Nicki that she'd gotten sick and he came back to care for her. That's when he said he did it with the pole dancer.'

'Which drove his wife away,' Mazzetti said.

'He said that, but I found she'd run years earlier because he'd hit her and the kids. His mother died, but the rest of what he told Nicki was fiction, I think.'

'How did you know about Sue Ellen Lamont?' Fitzpatrick asked.

'Evan met her in a hotel,' Alyssa said. 'She's a hooker. Was a hooker.'

'We tracked him via his credit card,' Clay said, not intending to mention the Ted Gamble name unless he was forced to. 'I ran a background on Lamont last night and saw she had a record for credit card fraud. I think she may have targeted Evan for a hit. Instead he killed her.'

Fitzpatrick considered it. 'That plays. Ms Fields's apartment had no sign of forced entry. He's also had key entry to other places. How did he get your partner's key?'

Clay sighed. 'Nicki and Evan were having an affair. We didn't know.'

'That would be hard on her family to hear on the CNN loop,' Mazzetti said. 'If we have to tell her parents, we will. But we'll do our best to keep that from the press.'

'Thank you. And when you find him, we'd like to know. If you could.'

'I'll do my best,' she said. 'That's all I can promise.'

'Thank you,' Clay said again. He rose to see them out. 'I'm sorry he threatened your child, Detective Mazzetti.'

She lifted her chin. 'When I catch him, he will be too.' She held up the photo of Evan. 'We need to get this to our boss. Can we use your fax machine?'

Alyssa pulled from her pocket the card Mazzetti had given them the night before. 'I've got your fax on here. I can send it from my computer. Keep that one.'

Fitzpatrick held up his cell. 'I'm getting a call. Stevie, I'll wait for you outside.'

Her partner left and the two of them stood alone by his front door.

'So,' she said, pointing to Alyssa. 'The two of you . . . ?'

The question took Clay by surprise. 'No. God, no.'

'Good.'

He frowned slightly. 'Why?'

'Because I'm a pretty good judge of character and you didn't seem like the kind of man to have an affair with a girl young enough to be your daughter.'

Said that way, he had to wince. 'She was trying to gain us some breathing room. And to be honest, I was hit so hard by Nicki's death that I was numb. We'd been friends a long time and it's still not real yet. Things just kind of happened. I don't know if you can understand that.'

'I actually do understand. So, is Alyssa your daughter?'

'God, no. Every hair in my head would be gray. She's my ex-fiancée's younger sister.'

'The photo's been sent,' Alyssa called from her desk. She brought Mazzetti another copy. 'I printed out one for your partner, too. Just in case.'

'Thank you,' Mazzetti said. 'I'll be in touch.' No sooner was she out the door than she had her cell phone to her ear. She walked to where Fitzpatrick waited, talking on his cell phone too. Getting Reardon's name would be a turning point in their case.

He turned to Alyssa. 'Give me a few minutes, then we'll leave.'

'For where?'

'Anderson Ferry. Mazzetti's not going to tell us anything more, and Nicki's parents need closure. They need to know why she was killed.'

She nodded. 'I can be ready in five.'

'Fine.' Clay went into his office and pulled up his information database. From his own pocket he took the card Mazzetti had given him yesterday. *Detective Ştefania Mazzetti*. Her partner had called her Stevie. Clay personally liked Ştefania better. He typed her name in and pushed *search*. In seconds he had the answer he'd sought.

Marital status: *Widow*. Her daughter was only five. Her loss must be recent. She probably did understand more than he knew. He shut down his laptop. 'Alyssa, let's go.'

Wednesday, May 5, 7.55 A.M.

'I made you some tea,' Skinner said quietly. 'It calms my wife when she's upset.'

Standing at her living room window looking down at the crime scene, Lucy glanced over her shoulder. Skinner was putting a steaming cup on her table, the fragile china cup looking even smaller in his big hands. 'Thank you,' she said. 'I'll let it cool a little.'

Fitzpatrick's car had been loaded onto a flatbed truck and transported back to the department's garage where it would sit next to all the other cars a killer had taken out of commission. Ryan Agar's body had been taken back to the morgue where it would sit in the cold room next to all the other people taken out of commission. Forever.

CSU had processed the scene quickly. There was nothing to see, no evidence to find. Still, a few techs swept the asphalt for anything that might provide a hint. A single squad car remained, ensuring gawkers didn't come too close.

Lucy imagined that the drivers of the cars parked around Fitzpatrick's were feeling very inconvenienced. The lot had been cordoned off. The drivers who'd grumbled at having to park around the side in the overflow lot last night were probably feeling pretty lucky right about now.

'You should step away from the window, Dr Trask,' Skinner said gently.

'He's bold,' Lucy said, ignoring him. 'He wanted me to see. Even when the scene is cleaned up, he wanted me to see it from here, where I'm supposed to feel safe.'

He tugged on the sleeve of her coveralls. 'Come, drink your tea.'

She let herself be led from the window. She sipped at the tea, but didn't sit. She didn't think she could now. *He has my parents. My father might deserve this, but . . .*

No. He doesn't. No one does. My mother nor my father, nor any of his

403

other victims, no matter how bad they were. She checked her phone impatiently. 'Did Detective Fitzpatrick call you yet, Detective Skinner?'

'Not yet. He's only been gone an hour,' Skinner said. 'Not enough time for news.'

Technically it had been an hour and fifteen minutes, but she tried to relax. 'I know. I was also wondering where my friends are. The policewoman left messages on both their cell phones and on Thorne's home phone. I thought they'd have called by now.'

'Maybe they're getting ready for work,' he said. 'I know they'll call soon.'

She narrowed her eyes at him. 'You know, this soothing tone of yours is totally annoying. But you make a decent cup of tea, so thank you.'

He smiled. 'I've had a lot of practice lately. My wife craved the herbals when she was pregnant.' He pulled his own phone out and showed her a photo. 'My kid.'

'He's a beautiful baby, and your wife looks beautiful too.'

'She looks tired mostly. Me too. You got any cure for colic, Doc?'

'My mother swore by strapping a car seat to the washing machine,' she said, then a wave of pain twisted her inside and tears burned her eyes. She hadn't remembered that in years. For years she'd managed not to think about her mother at all.

Now all she could see was her mother with her heart cut out.

'I'm sorry,' Skinner said. 'I didn't mean to . . .'

'It's okay,' Lucy said. Her cell rang, blessedly distracting her. 'It's Gwyn, my friend.' She turned her back to Skinner, needing a second to compose herself. 'Where are you?'

'It's Royce. We got your call. I brought Gwyn over because the cops still have her car.'

He sounded frantic and Lucy's hackles rose. 'What's wrong? Where is she?'

'That's why I'm calling. We're in the overflow lot around the side of your building. You need to come now. Gwyn says to tell you that Mr Pugh's fallen down and his head's bleeding. I've called 911 and they're on their way. Let me give you to Gwyn.'

Lucy was already out the door, Skinner behind her. 'Dr Trask, wait.'

She shook him off. 'Come with me. Hurry.'

'Lucy!' Gwyn yelled a few feet away from Royce's phone, fear in her voice. 'Run!'

'She's putting pressure on his head,' Royce said urgently. 'He's lost a lot of blood. It's everywhere. Where the hell is 911? You need to get down here. We need your help.'

Lucy flew down the stairs and out the door, praying they weren't too late. A sob was building in her chest and she pushed it back. *Please. Not him too. Not yet*.

'Dr Trask, wait.' Skinner was a few feet behind her. '*Stop*.'

But she couldn't. Mr Pugh was lying curled on his side on the grass, motionless, his hat still on his head. She dropped to her knees at his side, but before she could test his pulse, he rolled over and grabbed her and too late she knew.

No. It's a trap. Before she could draw a breath she was yanked to her feet and Skinner jerked forward, falling to his knees. Red started to spread on the detective's white shirt front. *Shot*. Skinner had been shot.

She screamed, but tape was slapped across her mouth and a gun shoved against her temple.

'Move, Dr Trask.'

'*No*.' The tape muted her. She tried to break free but stumbled when the butt of the gun smacked her head. Stunned, she blinked as she was dragged to the trunk of a silver Buick.

'*No*.' She tried to writhe and kick, but he grabbed her around the waist, lifting her off her feet as easily as if she were a child. He threw her into the trunk where she got a glimpse of Gwyn's bound body before hearing a shot, followed by a vicious curse.

He's hit. Hope surged for a split second. And then she felt an excruciating pain crack her head and everything went black.

405

Wednesday, May 5, 8.00 A.M.

'Thank you for this information, Deputy,' JD said. 'We have a CSU van en route. You should see them within an hour, depending on bridge traffic.' He hung up and looked at Stevie, who looked exhausted. 'They found the black Lexus.'

'Didn't take them long.'

'Only so many places to hide a car in Anderson Ferry,' he said. The plates had been stolen, but the vehicle identification number hadn't been removed. 'The car is registered to Malcolm Edwards.'

'That's cold. Kill a guy and steal his car. Then drive it to kill everybody else.'

'I'm wondering if the car's the only thing he stole,' JD said. 'Ron Trask and his boat are gone. The deputy said it looked like Westcott was dragged to the dock. What if Evan abducted Trask on his boat, then sailed it to that rental and lured Lucy's mom and Westcott there?'

'Evan's docked somewhere. Gotta be remote. His kind of torture would be loud.'

'Not necessarily. He cut out their tongues, after all.'

'True. Still, somebody would notice a constant parade of live bodies in and dead bodies out of a commercial marina. I'm betting remote. We know he's got to have access to a flash freezer, too. And he transports his victims in a wheelchair.'

'That narrows it down a great deal. Now if we can only find the damn freezer we'd be in business. What's with Skinner? How hard can it be to find a freezer?'

'Obviously hard,' Stevie said. 'It's hard to function on a few hours' sleep for weeks on end and their baby has been colicky. But he needs to get his head back.'

'And *he's* the one watching Lucy? Great.'

'He can do bodyguard work, JD. Relax.'

'I'd be more relaxed if he'd find the damn freezer. Besides, how can he look for it if he's watching Lucy?'

'He's not looking for it any more. Hyatt gave the task to Elizabeth. I called him while you were talking to the deputy in Anderson Ferry.

He's going to put the BOLO out on Evan Reardon with his photo. I need to stop by my house on my way in, check on Cordelia. Tell Hyatt I'll be there soon.'

'I'm going to stop by Lucy's. Whichever of us gets there first can tell him.'

'Wait. The assistant made you a copy of the SOB's picture.' She gave it to him.

JD studied the man's face. He was wholesome-looking, certainly not a man he would have expected to have killed so many. Then again, evil rarely wore an evil face. 'Handsome guy,' he said. 'I guess that Nicki Fields fell for him isn't too big a leap.'

Stevie shook her head in disgust. 'He probably has women eating out of his hand.'

'Yeah,' JD said bitterly. 'Until he slits their throats. At least he's not Thorne. That will give Lucy some comfort. Let's get back and finish this.'

JD had just pulled out of Maynard's parking lot when he heard it – the words that turned every cop's gut to water, no matter how low the radio murmur.

Officer down. JD's heart started to pound and he jacked up the volume. And his pounding heart stopped. *Lucy's address.* An officer was down at Lucy's address.

Stevie's car pulled beside him, her expression grim. 'I'll meet you there.'

Wednesday, May 5, 8.25 A.M.

She's gone. That was all JD could think as he pulled alongside a row of department vehicles – squad cars, unmarked cars, a rescue squad. No morgue rigs. *Thank God. Where's Lucy?*

He ran from his car to where Hyatt watched Drew's team process the scene. Blood pooled on the asphalt and in the grass next to an empty parking slot.

'Is it hers?' JD asked hoarsely.

'No,' Hyatt said. 'Drew typed it. Not hers. The blood on the asphalt is Skinner's. The medics just left with him. He was

407

unconscious, but alive. Took two bullets, gut and neck, but he fired once. The blood on the grass is the same type as Evan Reardon's. From what he lost there, he's gushing.'

Drew joined them, his expression sober. 'I found Lucy's cell phone in the grass. She'd just received a call from her friend Gwyn Weaver. Gwyn's phone is turned off now, going straight to voicemail. As is Dr Trask's.'

JD tried to control his panic. *He's got her*. 'Reardon used Gwyn to lure her out.'

'We have his face,' Hyatt said coldly. 'He's killed a cop in Virginia and put one here in critical condition. Every cop in the state is looking for him. He won't go far.'

'He may have a boat,' JD said, swallowing the lump in his throat. 'Maybe two. Lucy's father's sailboat and maybe Malcolm Edwards's cruiser. We need to find the place where he keeps them.' He stopped short. 'I put that compact in her pocket. Why aren't we tracking her?'

'We were,' Drew said bitterly. 'Closed in on the tracker's location in minutes. The transmitter had been thrown in the back of a pickup truck and was driving around town. He must have found it on her and tossed it. We can't track her.'

He's going to kill her. JD shoved his fear aside, looking to the edge of the crime-scene tape. Thorne stood alone, his face drawn. 'What's Thorne doing here?'

'He arrived right after it happened,' Hyatt said.

'If Skinner lives,' Drew said, 'it will be because of Thorne. He called 911, made sure we knew an officer was down, did first aid.'

'I want everyone in my office in thirty,' Hyatt said. 'We need to plan. Dismissed.'

'Wait,' JD said. 'Lucy would have needed to recognize whoever it was who called her. To trust them. She trusts Thorne and Gwyn. If it was Gwyn, someone was forcing her.'

'Maybe one of their club friends,' Hyatt sneered. 'Maybe Thorne will cooperate now.'

But JD thought he knew. He could see a sliver of a scene, caught only by the corner of his eye at the time. It had been Monday morning and Stevie had just arrived at the scene at the chess table. Lucy had been walking toward the body when two people stopped her.

One had been Gwyn. The other had been as tall as a tree.

He crossed the parking lot to Thorne, the photo of Evan Reardon in his hand. But he didn't have a chance to say a word before the man turned on him, white-faced with rage.

'*You.*' Thorne grabbed his lapels. 'You were supposed to protect her. Where were you?'

JD had to force the true words to the side for the moment. Lucy was the focus, not his own guilt. 'Look at this picture. Do you know him?'

Thorne's hands dropped to his sides, face immediately changing from terrified and furious to blank with the shock of recognition. 'This is Royce. Gwyn's boyfriend. This is him? This is who has Lucy? Who killed Kevin?'

And at least nine others. 'Yeah,' JD said roughly. *And he has Lucy.*

Shock became terror once again. 'Gwyn's with him,' Thorne said. 'Royce picked her up at my place last night, late. Oh, God. He's got them both. They're all I have.'

Thorne's family, JD realized. *But Lucy is mine. He'll kill her.*

Stay calm. Focus. Be a robot. He called on the calm he'd long ago learned to muster, felt it settle on his shoulders like a mantle. 'We have Reardon's face all over town. Every TV and newspaper will be asking for help. We'll find them.' *We have to.*

Thorne's eyes were desperate. 'What can I do? We have to get them back.'

'Where and when did Royce and Gwyn meet?' JD asked briskly. Tonelessly.

'A few months ago. He came into the club, said a mutual friend had told him to look Gwyn up. Gwyn remembered the name. She'd known Royce's friend from the circus.'

'Who knew Gwyn was in the circus?'

'Everyone. It's part of her résumé.'

'Lucy said Gwyn would sleep at his place. Where was that?'

'I don't know exactly.' Thorne closed his eyes. 'She brings me doughnuts from a place called DoughBoyz, with a z. She said it was near his building. That's all I know.'

'That could help.' But it probably wouldn't. JD knew the place. There were a dozen apartment buildings less than a block away. 'Okay. Stay in touch if you hear or see anything.'

Wednesday, May 5, 9.15 A.M.

Goddammit. Evan leaned against the side of his car when the world began to spin. He'd lost a lot of blood. *Damn cop. I should have aimed a little more to the right, dropped him right there.* Then the cop wouldn't have been able to get off a shot. Evan's second bullet had hit the detective's neck. *I hope I killed the sonofabitch.*

Gingerly he checked the makeshift bandage on his arm. The bleeding had stopped, but the cop's bullet had done some damage. *It'll hurt like a bitch, but I can fix it.* The medical bag he'd taken from Kathy Trask should have what he needed to do the job.

He'd managed to get the car back to the plant with both women in the trunk. Luckily he'd known to check Lucy for a tracking device. Gwyn had imparted that little nugget of information as she'd fallen asleep the night before. *They tagged her like a polar bear.* He'd only had to sleep with Gwyn Weaver a few times to learn that the minutes before she fell completely asleep were the best time to get information.

It was why he'd courted her, why he'd granted her every whim, why he'd made her think he was 'the one'. She knew everything about Lucy Trask, or so she thought. She didn't know that Lucy had abetted a rapist and a killer all those years ago. Gwyn wouldn't have believed it had he told her, which he never would have done anyway. She was too valuable an asset to risk.

The sex hadn't been bad, either. The circus girl knew some moves that he'd surely miss. So had the PI. For a while it had been dicey, doing both Gwyn and Nicki. He'd kept tabs on both women to make sure he would never be seen with the other, planting the tracking devices he'd stolen from Nicki in Gwyn's purse and under Nicki's car. The latter had paid off.

He'd been in Newport News dealing with Ken Pullman and

Mary Stubbs when Nicki made her little trip to Anderson Ferry. How she'd known to go there he didn't know. And it didn't matter. She'd gone, which meant she knew his background, about Ileanna.

She'd checked on him. *Behind my back.* She wouldn't have told. She couldn't have. She'd broken the law, procuring false identification for him, setting him up with a new life. And he hadn't been the first one she'd done it for. If she turned him in, she'd go to prison too. He hadn't killed her to keep her quiet. *I killed her because she pissed me off.*

Afterward he'd regretted it. Not the doing of it, because she'd had it coming. She'd tried to plead with him, promised she understood, that she wouldn't tell anyone about his sister. She'd told him she loved him. Which was a lie. If she loved him, she would have trusted him. She wouldn't have gone behind his back. So she definitely had it coming.

Still, he shouldn't have gone after her that way, in a rage. *I should have brought her here. Killed her here.* Instead he'd had to leave her body behind. Eventually that partner of hers would find her and come looking for him. Luckily he'd left no trail.

He certainly wouldn't make the same mistake again. Pushing himself away from the car, he tested his balance, annoyed when his step was still unsteady. He made his way to the trunk and popped it open. Gwyn was still out cold, but she should be coming out of it soon. He hadn't given her as much of the barbiturate cocktail as he'd given the others. She was so tiny, he didn't want to kill her. He might need her alive to give Lucy incentive to do his bidding.

From what he'd seen on the dock, watching her old man get carved up might not cause Lucy any discomfort. Whether she still had feelings for her mother remained to be seen, but watching little Gwyn getting carved up in front of her would definitely cause her considerable pain.

Lucy had come to. He enjoyed the moment when she realized who had taken her, that little jolt of shock in those cold blue eyes of hers. Her eyes frantically scanned side to side, but he'd placed the two women so that they weren't touching and couldn't see each other.

'Too bad you told Gwyn about finding my tracker in your purse.

411

She went looking in her purse too. She'd found it and was dialing you when I came back from delivering Agar's body.'

It was this that had prompted his risky snatching of Lucy this morning. He'd found Gwyn running from his apartment in her silk pajamas, her cell phone in her hand. She'd figured out who'd planted the tracker and was about to tell. He'd overpowered her easily, but then had to make some choices. If Lucy knew Gwyn had been taken, he'd never be able to use Gwyn as a lure. Lucy's suspicions would soar and he'd never be able to get her alone.

So he'd chosen to act fast. Surgically strike. As it was, he'd had to wait until most of the cops had left the scene to place his call.

'You shouldn't have made her look, Lucy. Now she'll have to die too.'

Twenty-four

Wednesday, May 5, 9.20 A.M.

Stevie hung up her phone. She'd run a background on Evan Reardon as they waited for Hyatt who was late, having been called into another press conference.

'Evan Reardon's last known was in Oxford,' she said. 'Not far from Anderson Ferry. He's a nurse. I just called the hospital where he worked. They said he quit three months ago.'

'When Maynard said Reardon's mother died,' JD said. 'Unwilling to wait idly, he'd been searching the box of photos Higgins had given them.

'We went through that box a dozen times looking for Evan's mother,' Stevie said.

'I'm making it thirteen. Reardon is here. He's got a dock and he's got a damn freezer and he's got an apartment near a damn doughnut shop. He is here, under our noses.' He picked up the team photo. 'There were eight seniors. Buck, Malcolm and Ryan are dead. Sonny is missing. You said one died, two moved away and one lives in Baltimore. Where?'

'I don't know,' Stevie said. 'Debbie was going to check. Let me ask.' She phoned Hyatt's clerk, and when she hung up, her expression was triumphant. 'James Cannon lives in an apartment in Fell's Point. Same neighborhood as the DoughBoyz doughnut shop.'

Yes. 'Let's go.' He was halfway to the door when she stopped him.

'Wait, JD.' Stevie was dialing another number. 'We need a warrant.'

'We need to find Reardon,' JD growled.

'I want him too, but I want it to stick when we find him.'

JD returned to Stevie's desk, trying not to bite her head off as she put Daphne on speaker phone and quickly filled her in. 'Can we search Cannon's apartment?' she asked.

'Not on a doughnut shop, honey. What else you got?'

'Nothing yet,' Stevie said.

'I'm going over there,' JD said. 'If nobody's home, I'll canvass the neighbors, see if anybody's seen Cannon lately and show Reardon's picture. If Reardon's been there, it means James is probably dead too.'

'You call me when you know,' Daphne said. 'I'll have a warrant drafted.'

Stevie hung up and grabbed her jacket. They'd reached the elevator when JD's cell phone rang. It was the morgue.

'It's Craig Mulhauser.'

The doctor had been distraught on hearing Lucy was gone. 'We don't have any news.'

'I know, that's not why I'm calling. I just got a call from Mr Bennett, father of the deceased. He was asking when he could come in and ID the body.'

'What? How are you going to do an ID?'

'I'm not,' Mulhauser said forcefully. 'I told him that we'd made an identification based on X-rays. He became insistent that they'd been called to the city to do an ID.'

JD frowned. 'Did he say who called them?'

'He said it was you.'

'Shit. Not again. He used me to lure Agar, too.'

'I know. I told him to not leave his hotel until he spoke with you.'

'Thanks, Doc. This could be a break.' He hung up, told Stevie what had happened. 'Where do we go first? James Cannon's apartment or to Bennett and maybe get the truth?'

'Bennett,' Stevie said. 'Let's send uniforms to knock on Cannon's door. If Reardon's got Lucy, I doubt he took her there.'

'He took her where he took the others,' JD said, pushing the image of the others from his mind. 'Somewhere remote.'

'Right. If nobody answers the knock, the officers will canvass the apartment building. If Bennett tells us that Cannon was involved, that might be enough for a search warrant.'

Wednesday, May 5, 9.30 A.M.

Lucy's head hurt worse than any headache she'd ever experienced. *Royce. It was Royce all the time.* Except it wasn't Royce. It was Evan. Evan Bryan. *He has me. And Gwyn.*

She was tied, feet and hands, her hands behind her back. The tape he'd slapped over her mouth as he'd shot Detective Skinner was still there. She thought of Skinner, of how proudly he'd shown her the pictures of his new baby. *Please don't be dead.*

Gwyn was lying behind her in the trunk. Now that the car had stopped, Lucy could hear her friend's shallow breaths. They were alive. For now. He had her parents. Had he killed them?

He has my mother. He cuts out their hearts. He'll do that to her. To Gwyn. To me. Panic started to rise in her throat, to choke her. Ruthlessly she shoved it back down.

JD, where are you? He'd put the tracker in her pocket. *He'll be here soon.* But what if he didn't get here in time? She needed a plan. *Like?* Like, Evan was wounded. Just before he'd slammed the trunk, Lucy had seen the bandage around his arm. She remembered the shot she'd heard. Skinner had shot Evan.

Good, she thought fiercely. From the paleness of Evan's face, he'd lost some blood. *Good*, she thought again. She'd watch and wait. And if she had to, if she got the opportunity . . .

You might have to kill him. Can you do that? She thought of Kevin Drummond. Of Nicki Fields. *Oh, yes. I can.*

Wednesday, May 5, 10.00 A.M.

The Bennetts were shaken when JD and Stevie arrived at their hotel room. JD hoped that would make them more forthcoming, but was prepared to deal with them harshly if they lied.

'Now, this is what's going to happen,' JD said acidly. 'You're going to tell us what the hell happened to Ileanna Bryan twenty-one years ago. He has Lucy Trask.'

Bennett sighed. His wife closed her eyes.

'And her parents and your sheriff,' Stevie added and the two grew paler. 'So start talking. What happened and who was involved?'

'We don't know exactly,' Bennett said. 'We knew the Bryan girl was assaulted. And we knew our sons. They all acted . . . squirrely.'

'Guilty, you mean,' JD said. 'Did they rape her? All of them?'

'Russ claimed he didn't,' Bennett said. 'The police closed the case after her old boyfriend killed himself. They said the boyfriend was guilty. Then Buck died and everything changed.'

Mrs Bennett fidgeted with her pearls. 'We parents avoided one another, because I think we knew our boys had done something. Something terrible. We just didn't know what.'

'Who was doing the avoiding?' JD asked impatiently.

'Everyone except Myrna Westcott,' Bennett said. 'She was clueless, or chose to be. If you want a list, it was probably Sonny, Buck, Malcolm Edwards, Ryan Agar and James Cannon.'

JD noted they had not included their own son. 'Will you sign an affidavit stating that?'

Bennett nodded. 'Yes.'

Stevie was already dialing Daphne. 'Got the statement. Get the warrant.'

JD turned to leave, then turned back. 'Why did you request the articles on Lucy's trial from Bart Higgins?'

'Russ needed them,' Bennett said. 'He said a reporter wanted to do a story on Lucy and he wanted them to know the truth.'

JD frowned, confused. 'But you liked Lucy. You had lunch when you came to the city.'

Mrs Bennett spoke up. 'Because her mother asked us to. It was the best way for her to find out how Lucy was doing. I agreed. I don't like to upset the Trasks.'

'Ron can hold a grudge for a long time,' Bennett added.

'And Kathy knows too many secrets,' Mrs Bennett said bitterly.

'What does she know?' Stevie asked. 'Tell us. Now.'

'A little about everybody, I imagine,' Mrs Bennett said. 'But she knew that I had an affair back when the children were younger. I got . . . an infection. I had to tell my husband and he's since forgiven me. But Kathy knew.'

'She threatened to tell?' Stevie asked, unable to hide her surprise.

'Yes,' Mrs Bennett said. 'When Lucy got arrested. Ron refused to help Lucy, so Kathy turned to us. She wanted us to hire a lawyer for Lucy. She would pay for it, but it needed to appear that the money came from us. We refused. We didn't want to make Ron angry. Then she threatened to tell about my . . . condition.'

JD's eyes were wide. 'Her mother paid for her lawyer?'

'Yes,' Bennett said. 'She was too much of a coward to let Ron know, so we had to do it, and Ron has made us pay for years, in all kinds of little ways. It's only that we knew Buck had been involved in that business twenty years ago that kept him from running us out of town too.'

'Too?' Stevie asked and Bennett flushed.

'It's just my guess. The Bryans had been accusing Ron and Kathy of stealing their daughter's necklace. Suddenly the Bryans moved away. We all knew Ron was capable of using his power to further his own agenda. Nobody wanted to make him angry after that.'

What a fucked-up town. 'Why did you get the trial articles for your son?' JD asked again.

Bennett looked away. 'Russ threatened our visitation privileges with our grandchildren.'

Kathy Trask wasn't the only coward. 'Where was Russ going to meet the reporter?'

'I don't know.' Mr Bennett paled further. 'It wasn't a reporter, was it?'

'No,' JD said quietly. 'It was probably Evan Reardon.'

The Bennetts flinched. 'Oh, my God,' Mrs Bennett whispered.

'I didn't know,' Mr Bennett murmured. 'I didn't know. I helped him . . . Oh, God.'

Stevie touched JD's sleeve. 'Detective Fitzpatrick, let's go.'

417

Wednesday, May 5, 10.20 A.M.

He was coming. Lucy could hear his steps echoing as she lay in the car's dark trunk. She had no idea what time it was, but knew enough time had passed that something was wrong. If JD had been able to track her, he'd have been here by now.

The trunk popped open and she closed her eyes, hoping he'd think she was unconscious.

'I know you're awake, Lucy,' he said. 'You might as well open your eyes.'

But she kept them closed, not wanting to give him the satisfaction of seeing her fear. He leaned into the trunk and lifted Gwyn out, and she heard the creak of a wheel. Then a thump.

'I'm going to take you out next,' he said. 'I have a gun in my hand. I will shoot you if you struggle, but not to kill you, just to stop you. I will then gut your friend Gwyn while I make you watch. I guarantee she will feel every slice. Nod if you understand.'

Lucy thought of Nicki Fields, her stomach turning over. Then she let out a startled yelp when he yanked her head off the trunk floor by her hair.

'I said, *nod* if you *understand*,' he snarled.

Lucy nodded and he released her hair. He lifted her out of the trunk with one arm wrapped around her waist. She clenched her body when she was dropped on a cold steel surface.

She smelled rust. She heard the wheels squeak. She opened her eyes to find that she and Gwyn were on a flatbed cart. They were in a large loading dock and from the corner of her eye she saw a garage door, tall enough for an eighteen-wheeler to pass through. But the room was deserted.

It was just Evan, *and us.* Help should have come already. *You'll have to take matters into your own hands.*

Evan loomed over her, large and terrifying, the hand of his uninjured arm clenched into a fist. 'I've waited a lot of years for this moment,' he said. The blow came fast and hard, straight into her face. The pain was blinding and her eyes filled with tears.

Warm blood covered her face. Her nose was bleeding and her

418

mouth was covered. She struggled to breathe, white lights dancing in front of her eyes. Suddenly the tape was ripped from her mouth and she gasped, wheezing.

'That,' he said, 'was for breaking my nose.'

Lucy gagged and had to force herself to take slow breaths as the blood gushing from her nose threatened to choke her. 'I'm sorry. I . . . didn't . . . I don't . . . remember.'

Evan's face grew darker. 'You don't remember?'

'I fought . . . a lot. I'm . . . sorry.'

'You'll be sorrier, I guarantee. Because we aren't even close to being even.'

Wednesday, May 5, 10.30 A.M.

Daphne was waiting for JD and Stevie at James Cannon's apartment where CSU was already searching. 'The warrant is for plain sight and only for any documents you find linked to Cannon's involvement in the Bryan girl's assault. Sorry, it was the best I could do quickly.'

'Let's hope it's good enough,' Stevie said, pulling on a pair of gloves. 'Drew?'

Drew looked up from a pile of paper on the dining room table. 'The neighbors recognized Evan when we showed his picture. They said he moved in about six weeks ago. We've found loads of documents, but so far nothing to tell us where he's gone. Good news is I got a match of a fingerprint to one that my team took from the black Lexus in Anderson Ferry.' He hesitated. 'They also found a knife in his trunk. Long filleting knife, very sharp. Based on the photos they sent to my email, it could be the murder weapon for the valet, the hooker and the PI.'

JD searched Cannon's desk, trying not to picture the knife while Stevie tackled the hall closet. In minutes, JD hit paydirt. 'Daphne?' he asked, his pulse hiking. 'Reardon has no expectation of privacy here, does he? Since he'd be squatting?'

'No, darlin', he most certainly does not.'

'Good,' he said fiercely. 'Stevie, look what I found.' He held it out to her. 'It's a user manual for a flash freezer. He printed it out from his computer. Look at the date.'

'Two weeks ago,' Stevie said. 'The day after Bennett went missing. Nice, JD.'

'Let's find out where the freezer is. Before it's too late.'

JD pulled out another drawer. *Yes.* 'Got something.' He brought out a handful of architectural drawings, spreading them on the table next to the credit card statements. 'It's a factory.' He pointed to one of the pages. 'Right there is the freezer. It's enormous.'

'Big enough for a man?' Stevie asked.

'The manual says it's big enough for six tons of meat in sixty-pound boxes,' Drew said. 'That's damn big.'

'I saw something on that,' Daphne said excitedly, searching through the pile of documents she'd been reading. 'Here it is, dated two years ago. James Cannon applied for a loan to renovate a fish processing plant. It was supposed to go operational a year ago, but the bank withdrew the loan. Credit crisis. James Cannon must have run out of money.'

'So his factory's been sitting abandoned,' Stevie said.

'Until Reardon decided to make himself at home,' JD said, his heart pounding now. *Lucy, we're coming. Hold on a little longer.* 'What's the address?'

Wednesday, May 5, 10.30 A.M.

Lucy lifted her head when the cart shoved two swinging doors open. They'd left the darkened corridor that connected the loading dock to . . . *what?* She blinked back tears and looked around her. It was a factory. A dead one. In the dim light she could see conveyor belts that sat unconnected and unmoving. Big pieces of equipment gathered dust, and, surprise, surprise, there was a big flash freezer. It was the perfect size for about a million frozen peas. Or one man.

She lifted her head a little higher and froze. On the floor beyond were two people. Her father lay on his side, tied and gagged. Several feet away was her mother and Lucy's heart clenched. Kathy Trask sat up, propped against a support post. Her legs were stretched out, her ankles bound. Her hands were tied in front of her. She looked sick, her face gray. But she was alive.

Against the back of her leg, Lucy felt a tiny tap. Gwyn was conscious. Lucy's first thought was to give thanks, but then she reconsidered. If Evan planned to hurt Gwyn, he'd want her to feel it. Lucy wished Gwyn hadn't come to, not yet.

Past the equipment and her parents were two steel tables. On the large table she could make out the form of a man. She blinked again, bringing him into better focus. Sonny Westcott. He was naked and spreadeagled, his wrists and ankles tied to the corners of the table, the rope secured to the table's legs. She couldn't tell if he was still alive.

On the smaller table were . . . tools. Knives, hammers. The Sawzall. Lucy closed her eyes, unable to shake the image of the bodies she'd seen. *He cut out their hearts. He's going to do that to us.*

She heard herself whimper and gritted her teeth. *Stop it. You can't lose it or you won't get out of here alive.*

She forced herself to look up into Evan's eyes. 'You were shot. You'll need stitches.'

One side of his mouth lifted cruelly. 'And you're offering? But first I'd have to untie you, right? Do I look that stupid to you? Don't worry about me. I stitched it up myself.'

She couldn't hide her surprise. 'How?'

'Lots of experience with doing doctors' dirty work.'

She studied him as he stared down at her. He had medical experience, which came as no surprise. The cuts on his victims had been dead on.

His face was still pale and he held his arm against his side gingerly. He was still weak, but gaining back his strength. If she was going to do something, take advantage of his blood loss, she'd need to do it soon.

'Is Sonny alive?' she asked, stalling for time.

He smiled at her, as if guessing her purpose. 'Unfortunately he is. I'm waiting for him to come to so I can finish him off.'

'You realize the police will be looking for you,' she said quietly.

'I realize the police will be looking for *you*,' he countered.

421

'Nobody knows to be looking for me. I'm dead. I paid a lot of money to be dead.'

His being dead made no sense, so she let it go. 'You're Ileanna Bryan's brother. They are definitely looking for you.'

Fury flared in his eyes. 'Don't you even say her name.'

'Wasn't that what you wanted us to do? Guess her name? Isn't that why you burned the letters into their backs? Russ and Janet Gordon and Ryan Agar?'

'Don't you dare try to play me,' Evan snapped. 'I know what you're trying to do.'

'What am I trying to do?' she asked.

He smiled again and Lucy wondered how she'd missed the flashes of madness in his eyes all those weeks she'd thought he'd been Royce. All those weeks he'd been close to Gwyn. *And me. He could have killed me a dozen times.* That he hadn't made her think he had a bigger plan.

'You didn't have to guess her name,' he said. 'You always knew it. You had her things.'

#1 Sister. 'I had her bracelet,' she agreed. 'I thought it was mine. I thought my brother had bought it for me. But I never had the necklace.'

'You are such a liar.' Evan crouched beside her, trailing his fingers over her face in a way that made her shiver in disgust. 'Who did you sell my necklace to? I want it back.'

'I don't know where your necklace is,' she said, then cried out when his fist plowed into her jaw. The impact sent the flatbed cart on which she lay rolling. White stars danced in front of her eyes as he grabbed the cart and stopped it. 'You sold it. You know you did.'

'No, I didn't. I never had— *Ugh.*' He dragged her from the cart to the floor and kicked her ribs. She curled up, feeling like she'd throw up. 'I swear it.'

'You're as big a hypocrite as your father.' He cast a sneer to where her father lay. 'Stealing jewelry off of bodies, throwing families on the street because they want justice.' He crouched beside her, grabbed her chin and got in her face. 'I gave you a chance to make things right but you were just as big a bully as he was. I came to you. I thought you'd help me.'

She thought of what he'd said before he punched her in the face. 'Did I hit you?'

'You know you did. You broke my fucking nose. Looks like I returned the favor.'

'I'm sorry,' she said, unable to keep the desperation from her voice. 'I hit some kids after my brother died. I'm sorry you were one of them.'

'I wasn't just one of them,' he gritted. 'I was the kid whose family was ruined by your father. I was ready to beg you that day. I wanted to save my family.'

She hurt. Her ribs were burning. 'What did my father do?'

'You know what he did.'

'I don't. I was only fourteen,' she cried and something flickered in his eyes. *Belief?*

'He threatened to frame my father,' Evan said. He looked over at her father with such hate. Lucy could understand. She'd hated Ron Trask all of her life.

'How?' she asked softly and Evan turned his hate-filled eyes on her.

'He said he'd make it look like my father stole money.'

'So why did you come to me?'

His eyes narrowed. 'Your father had my mother's property. If you'd just given it to me that day, my parents would have been fine. My father wouldn't have lost everything.'

Her heart sank. *And then Evan's father took his own life.* 'I didn't know what my father had done. I didn't know what my brother had done. If you'd asked me, I would have told you.'

Evan's eyes went cold. 'I tried to ask you. You wouldn't stop to listen.'

Lucy closed her eyes, trying to remember, but she couldn't. 'I'm sorry I hit you. I don't even remember doing it.'

That was the wrong thing to say. Lucy knew it as soon as the words left her mouth.

'You don't even remember?' he whispered. 'My father shot

himself. My mother drank herself to death. You could have stopped it by just giving me the necklace.'

'I never had it,' she said, trying to calm him. 'I never had your necklace.'

He straightened abruptly, his body tense with new rage. 'You lie,' he shouted. He ran over to where Sonny Westcott lay tied on the large table and grabbed a wooden bat. Before Lucy could shrink away, Evan was back, the bat raised high. 'You had it. You had it all along. And you *sold* it. You *sold* it to pay for your damn *club*.' He brought the bat down hard on her thigh and Lucy felt the bone snap. She screamed, unable to hold it back.

My leg. Broken. *Oh, God*. The searing pain took over until it was all she knew.

'Did that hurt, Dr Trask? Let's see what else I can do.' He ran to the steel table, pushed Sonny Westcott to the floor, and ran back to her, his face florid from the exertion. Large beads of sweat covered his forehead. He grabbed her from the floor with one arm, yanking her to her feet and dragging her toward the table. Lucy thrashed and fought and bucked, trying to get away. His steps faltered and he brought his wounded arm around her throat.

Lucy threw her shoulder into his bandaged bicep. With a yelp of pain he staggered and together they fell.

'You bitch,' he snarled. 'You'll pay for that.' He rose to his knees, his good arm around her waist and started to haul her to her feet again. All she could hear was the pounding in her head. All she could feel was the burning in her leg. Like an animal she fought, throwing her body back, crying out when the back of her head connected with his forehead. *Crack*.

The arm around her waist was suddenly gone. Breathing hard, Lucy rolled away, lifting her throbbing head. Evan was lying there, motionless. Out cold. The bandage on his arm was bright red. His stitches had blown and he was bleeding again.

Desperately she looked around, then up – and saw the small table. *Knives*. She'd seen knives. Struggling to one knee, she hooked her chin on the edge of the table and pulled. It toppled, then crashed to the concrete floor, the corner hitting Evan square in the forehead.

Hammers and knives scattered. *Yes.*

She needed to breathe. She didn't have time. *Get away. Get away. Cut the ropes.* But her hands were tied behind her back. She needed help. She looked back over to the flatbed cart. Gwyn was watching numbly.

Lucy twisted her body, maneuvering her hands until she grabbed one of the knives. Then she began to roll toward Gwyn, clenching her teeth against the pain and hoping like hell she didn't stab herself in the back.

Ocean City, Maryland
Wednesday, May 5, 10.30 A.M.

Clay stopped the car. 'Alyssa, we're here. Wake up.'

Alyssa stirred, yawned, then blinked in surprise. 'This isn't Anderson Ferry.'

'No. I was almost there, then I started thinking. We know Nicki went to Anderson Ferry a week ago. Mazzetti said we should have found a package. But we didn't.'

'So either Nicki's got a hiding place you don't know about, or Evan took it.'

Clay nodded. 'I got to wondering why Evan killed her that night. If it was because she got information from Anderson Ferry, how did Evan know she had it?'

'She might have told him.'

'She might have told me,' he murmured. *Why didn't you come to me, Nic?* 'That she didn't meant she didn't want me to know, which meant it was really bad.'

'And if I had something that bad, I wouldn't have let him in my apartment.'

'She didn't let him in. She was in bed when . . .' He had to swallow back the bile that burned his throat every time the images of Nicki's mutilated body filled his mind. 'He caught her sleeping. He knew she knew. He was furious that she knew.'

'So how did he know?' she asked, then let out a breath. 'He hid a tracker in the little girl's backpack. I bet he hid one in Nicki's car too.'

425

'Very good,' Clay said grimly. 'He knew she'd been to Anderson Ferry and he knew she'd gone home. Then I wondered why the tracking device Nicki put under her own car was here, in Ocean City.' He pointed to a motel whose paint had long faded to gray. 'Specifically there.'

'She left you the package.'

'She left me something.' Now that he was here, Clay was afraid to go inside. But he knew he had to. 'Come with me. I don't want you alone until the cops find Reardon.'

'How do you know they'll find him?'

'He shot that cop this morning, the one who was guarding the doc at the morgue last night. Left him in critical condition. And he kidnapped Dr Trask. It's all over the radio.'

'Oh, my God.'

'They will find him, it's just a matter of time.'

'That poor woman,' Alyssa said as she followed him into the motel.

If he kills her, her blood is on my hands too. Clay rang the bell on the desk and an elderly woman came out to greet him. 'My name is Maynard,' he said. 'Nicki Fields sent me.'

'Oh. All right. Can I see ID? Nicki asked me to make sure you showed ID.'

Clay obliged and the old woman hurried away. When she returned, she held a thick manila envelope. 'Thank you,' Clay said, forcing himself to take it.

When they were back in the car, he opened the envelope and pulled out a stack of papers. On top was a note, in Nicki's precise handwriting and Clay's throat closed.

Dear Clay, if you're here, I'm dead and Evan Reardon is responsible. As I write this, I'm hoping I can find him and deal with him myself. I didn't tell you because I didn't want you to know how badly I fucked up. I trusted Evan. I fell for him. I even considered running away with him, becoming Mrs Ted Gamble. Now I just want to take a few days off and fix this.

When Evan first approached me, I did a routine background

check. One of the things I requested was his and his mother's documents from Newport News. The documents came weeks later – after I'd already fallen too hard to see what I should have already seen.

The marriage license listed his mother as Yvette Bryan, not Yvette Smith as Evan told me. Evan had told me his mother's maiden name was Smith and that Timothy Reardon was her first marriage, that she'd had Evan out of wedlock. This was inconsistent and it bothered me.

Timothy died ten years ago, but I located his surviving sister. She said that when Yvette was drunk, she'd cry for her daughter, Ileanna. It's a pretty unusual name and it didn't take me long to find her death certificate. Ileanna Bryan was killed in a town called Anderson Ferry, Maryland. I went there and found her grave. She died when she was only seventeen. I went to the newspaper office and they pulled the articles you'll find in this packet. I'm now worried about why Evan never mentioned this.

That Evan came to me wanting a new identity is now very suspicious. I need time to figure it out, to make this right. If I get to the bottom of things and all is well, I'll come back and get my own package. If not . . . fuck it.

There was no signature. No good-bye. Clay handed the letter to Alyssa and started the car. He didn't need to go to Anderson Ferry now.

Wednesday, May 5, 10.40 A.M.

By the time Lucy reached Gwyn, her friend had pushed herself up to her knees. Lucy rested on her uninjured side, the knife still tightly gripped in her hands. Saying nothing, Gwyn awkwardly maneuvered until her bound hands came in contact with the knife.

Lucy watched Evan's body for any sign of movement, but there was none. Yet. Gwyn's movements seemed painfully slow, but only a few minutes passed before the rope broke and Gwyn was free. She twisted, grabbing the knife and sawing the ropes around Lucy's wrists.

427

'He's got a gun,' Lucy whispered. 'He shot a detective with it.'

'Can we get it?'

Lucy shook her head. 'It was in his waistband and he fell on it.'

'I could try to roll him over and grab it.'

'He's too heavy. I don't think you could move him and I'm afraid to try. He might come to. Just hurry,' Lucy breathed. 'We'll have to get out before he comes to.'

Finally the ropes snapped and Lucy rubbed her aching wrists. 'My leg is broken,' she murmured as Gwyn started on the ropes around her ankles. 'I don't think I can walk out of here, and you're not big enough to move me. You cut my mother loose and get her out of here. I'll free my father. Hopefully he's not too stiff to move. He's been tied like that since yesterday. If he can move, I can lean on him.'

'I have a better idea. We get ourselves out on that flatbed and send the cops for your parents.'

The ropes burst free and Lucy had to bite her tongue to keep from moaning. *Goddamn, it hurts.* 'I'm not leaving her here. He'll kill her. Get my mother out.' She cut through Gwyn's ankle ropes more quickly now that the blood was returning to her hands. 'My father can push me on the cart.'

'I'm not leaving you here for him to kill you,' Gwyn whispered. 'Try to stand.' Lucy did, but her leg buckled, unable to support her weight. Gwyn slid her arms under Lucy's armpits. 'On your butt,' Gwyn directed. 'I'll drag, you push with the other foot.'

Lucy complied, but all she could see were bright lights in front of her eyes by the time she reached her mother. 'Cut her loose,' she said and frowning, Gwyn obeyed. 'Now get her out of here. *Do it,*' she snapped when Gwyn started for the flatbed.

'Leave him here,' Gwyn said. 'I'll get you out and you can send the cops.'

Lucy shook her head again. 'As bad as he is, I can't leave him here either. Get your ass out of here and get her out, too. Get help.'

Lucy grabbed the knife and started sawing the rope tying her father. From the corner of her eye she saw Gwyn lift her mother to her feet and help her to the door, which swung closed behind them.

The door opened again and Gwyn pushed a wheelchair through. It rolled across the floor, coming to a stop midway. Then she was gone again, getting her mother to safety. Getting help. *Please*.

Lucy removed her father's gag. 'Did you take the necklace?' she asked quietly as she sawed at the rope binding his hands.

'No. *Hurry*.'

She grasped the knife tighter, sawed harder until the ropes split. Ron massaged his hands as she started on the ropes at his ankles. When they broke, her father pushed unsteadily to his knees, then his feet. He'd been tied for so many hours, he couldn't stand straight.

Lucy pushed herself up so that all her weight rested on one knee. 'Help me up.'

He took a step back. 'No.'

'What?' Lucy stared up at him in disbelief. 'I helped you.'

'That's your problem,' he said coldly. He turned for the door, leaving Lucy open-mouthed in shock.

'Wait.' She grabbed for him, but grasped only air. 'Why?' she hissed. 'Why do you hate me? Why are you leaving me here to die?'

He turned around, rage contorting his features. 'It's always *you*. *Always you*. She wasn't my *wife*, she was your *mother*. She obeyed me, like a wife should, until it came to *you*. She only defied me because of you,' he spat, then shook his head in disgust. 'The wrong kid died, as far as I'm concerned. Whatever Evan does to you, you have coming.'

He turned again for the door, half-walking and half-stumbling as he made his escape.

'Sonofabitch,' she muttered, recovering. Evan would come to, any minute. *Move*. The wheelchair was closer than the flatbed. *Crawl*. She did, dragging her leg behind her, clenching her teeth against the pain. She was only a few feet from the wheelchair when she heard the clatter of metal behind her. It was the table that had held his tools being shoved aside. Evan was awake. *Dammit*.

'What the hell?' It was a cry of fury. 'Freeze, Trask.'

Ahead, Lucy watched her father stumble to a stop. *Please, Gwyn, be getting help*.

'Get back here, Trask,' Evan ordered. 'Hands behind your head.'

429

Her father looked like he might turn around, then broke into a run. Seconds later he hit his knees, Evan's bullet having struck him square in the middle of his back. Blood was spreading over his shirt and he fell face forward. For a moment Lucy couldn't move. Then she saw her father move slightly – one hand extended to crawl.

'Don't move, Lucy,' Evan snarled when she did exactly that.

'I have to,' Lucy said fiercely. 'I have to stop his bleeding. He's still alive.'

Evan grabbed her arm, dragged her across the floor to where her father lay bleeding. He aimed for her father's head. Lucy closed her eyes and turned her face away as he fired again.

'Now he's dead,' Evan said flatly. 'No worries.'

Oh God, oh God. Breathe. Do not hyperventilate. Do not pass out.

Then the two of them froze as a sound outside grew louder. A helicopter. *JD. Thank you.*

'Fuck,' Evan snarled again. 'Move your ass, now.'

'Reardon!' came a voice from outside and Lucy started to hyperventilate again. *JD. He's here.* 'Police. This place is surrounded. Surrender.'

Evan yanked her to her feet. 'Move,' he barked, then dragged her, making her hop on one foot to keep up. He dragged her down a hallway to the door, shoved it open and put her in front of it, his gun to her head while he stood inside.

'Go to hell,' he yelled. 'I have a hostage. Let me on my boat. Let the two of us leave undisturbed and she'll live. Come a step closer and I'll kill her. I swear it.'

From where Lucy stood she caught a glimpse of JD and Stevie in tactical gear. They were here. *Just hold on*, she told herself. *Just a little longer.*

Wednesday, May 5, 11.00 A.M.

Everything had moved once they knew the address – informing Hyatt, the race to the helipad, the ten-minute flight that would have taken forty to drive. But now, seeing that gun at her head, time seemed to stand still.

'She's alive, JD,' Stevie said in a low voice.

'I know.' But she was hurt. She was pale, her mouth pinched in pain, and she leaned all her weight on one foot. 'He's not getting on that boat, Stevie.'

'I know,' Stevie said evenly. 'We've got two dozen cops surrounding the place and snipers on the way. We need to establish what he's done with the others.' She turned to JD, assessing him. 'Do you need to step down?'

JD had not taken his eyes from Lucy's face. She was terrified, in pain. And staring back at him. Needing him. Trusting him.

'No,' he said. 'He could still have four other hostages, including Gwyn.'

'We need a negotiator.' Stevie grabbed the bullhorn. 'We need to talk, Evan.'

'No. You need to back off,' Evan yelled back. 'Or she dies. You know I will.'

'We know,' Stevie called. 'We're backing away. But we need to talk. Does anyone inside need medical attention?'

There was silence. Then Evan yanked Lucy from view and JD's heart skipped a beat. Minutes later a wheelchair came barreling through the door, a body slumped across the top. The chair hit the end of the sidewalk and pitched forward, the body flying to the ground. The victim was male and had bullet holes in his back and the back of his head.

'Ron Trask,' Stevie said. 'Shit.'

JD's cell rang, the number the one that had lured both Bennett and Gordon to their deaths. 'Fitzpatrick.'

'I don't need any goddamn medical attention,' Evan snarled into his ear. 'Now back off or your girlfriend will end up just like her daddy. You got three minutes.'

The phone clicked. 'He's going to kill her,' JD said in a voice that was both cool and controlled. 'Back everyone away fifty feet and let's figure how we're going to get behind him.'

Stevie gave the order and cars and cops began pulling back. 'You were studying that floorplan of the place on the way here. Which door will get us behind him?'

JD created the picture in his mind. 'We got ten doors and two loading bays. The door where he's standing leads to the main manufacturing room, where all the machinery is. If all the machinery on the plan is still there, he's got lots of places to hide to see us coming, whichever door we use, so we need to keep him in the doorway. Keep him talking.'

'So which door, JD?' Stevie asked quietly.

JD scanned the front of the building, then frowned. 'The one that just opened.'

Gwyn Weaver had slipped from the door at the far end of the building, flattening her body against the outer wall. She rounded the corner so that she now faced the water where both Edwards' cruiser and Trask's sailboat were docked. Her knees buckled and she slid to the ground. Reardon wouldn't be able to see her from the front door.

'Unit on the east,' Stevie said into her radio, 'get the woman away from the building. If she needs no medical attention, keep her there. We don't want to attract Reardon's attention.' To JD she said, 'I wonder if he knows she's gone.'

JD thought Evan probably did. 'You talk to him. Get him to come back to the door. I'm going in the way she just came out.'

'No way. We wait for backup, JD. I want the snipers here before we go in.'

'How long till they get here?'

'Twenty, thirty minutes. He's not going to kill Lucy yet. She's his way out of here.'

Twenty minutes was too long. In twenty minutes she'd be dead.

'But he will kill her, Stevie. It's what he came to do. We need to take advantage of *time* right now. He thinks we'll negotiate. So do that. But we need to get in there.' He stayed calm. 'I've done this before.'

'Keep talking.'

'The size of this place is on our side. He can't watch all the doors. He doesn't have to know the snipers aren't here yet, either. Let him think they are. And let him think you've taken me off the case. He needs to see us argue. You make me leave. I'll double back and go to

432

Gwyn, find out what's going on inside, then I'll go in.'

She paused, then shook her head again stubbornly. 'I want the snipers here, JD.'

He clenched his jaw. 'What do you think I was?' he asked, and she let out her breath.

'This is different. This is Lucy. She's yours, JD.'

'Yes, she is. But he also thinks she's his. She's his revenge. I'm not willing to risk that he values his own freedom over making her die. Make a choice. You know he's watching us.'

She started shaking her head hard but then extended her arm, pointing away from the building as if ordering him away. She looked away from him, hanging her head. 'Hide behind one of the vans. I'll have them bring you a rifle.'

JD pretended to take a desperate step toward her, then ripped off his flak jacket in feigned disgust. He departed in an angry huff, pushing through the crowd of personnel who waited, poised to move. He ducked behind a van and put his jacket back on, then waited until a rifle was thrust into his hands by one of the state cops.

'Your partner says "Don't fuck it up",' he said. 'We'll cover you.'

Twenty-five

Wednesday, May 5, 11.05 A.M.

'They're backing off,' Evan muttered, the end of his gun hard against her temple. She leaned her cheek against the wall, trying to fill her lungs with shallow breaths. He was standing behind her, between her and the door, peeking outside. Lucy braced her hands against the wall, trying to keep the weight off her leg.

He'd dragged Lucy back to the hall, shoved her father's body into the wheelchair and out the door. Then he'd dragged her back. The pain had come in nauseating waves, but now surrounded, unrelenting. She clenched her teeth. She had to stay sharp and watch for whatever opportunity JD created for escape. Because he would. Of that she was certain.

At least Evan was also in bad shape. He weaved slightly on his feet, his skin gone gray. He was sweating bullets from the exertion and the blood loss. But he didn't seem terribly scared and the hand that held the gun to her head was very steady.

'How did he find you?' Evan asked quietly. 'I found the tracker they hid in your compact. Do you have another?'

So that's what took them so long to get here. 'No, there were only two. The one you put in my purse and the one you found.' She lifted her chin. 'Maybe they're just good detectives.'

His jaw tightened. 'Nobody knew about this place.'

'The person it belonged to did. Who did it belong to? Malcolm? Russ?'

'James Cannon,' he said with a sneer.

She recognized the name. Stevie had mentioned him as one of

434

the four other seniors on her brother's football team. 'One of Buck's friends. I assume he's dead too.'

'Very.'

'Why didn't you leave him for me to find?'

'Because when I killed him, I didn't know what you'd done.'

She remembered the words he'd screamed at her, right before he brought his boot down on her thigh. 'You think I sold the necklace. The one your sister was wearing that night.'

He shoved the gun hard against her temple. 'I *know* you did.'

She didn't dare deny it again. It made him too angry and she didn't want any more injuries. She could still crawl if an escape opportunity opened up. And there was the gun in his hand. *With which he killed my father.* She'd seen more bodies during her career than she could count, but before today she'd never actually witnessed a murder. Now she had. Maybe two, if Skinner had died. *Please don't be dead.* Lucy pushed it all from her mind. *I can't think about that now. I have to keep him talking. Distract him.*

'How?' she asked calmly. 'How did you find out about the necklace?'

'Russ Bennett told me, while I was cutting off his fingers. He said he'd seen you wear it.'

Lucy could clearly see Russ's mutilated hands in her mind. She had to grit her teeth to keep the panic from choking her. 'You were torturing him. He would have said anything.'

'I thought the same, *Doctor*, so I got a second opinion from your own BFF.'

Lucy blinked, stunned. 'From Gwyn?'

'You got it, *Doctor*,' he said bitterly. 'Pump the girl full of margaritas and she'll tell you damn near everything. I asked her if you had any diamonds and she said you did once. She said you paid for your share of your precious club by selling a diamond necklace.'

Lucy closed her eyes. *Not your necklace*, she wanted to say. It was the necklace she'd had made from her old engagement ring. But he wouldn't believe her, so she wouldn't even try.

Evan's laugh was sour. 'Nothing to say, Doctor?'

'Nothing you'll believe.'

435

'You could tell me the sky was blue and I wouldn't believe you,' he said with malice. 'You and your family lie easier than you breathe. You walk on people who can't fight back. Steal from people who can't afford it. Just because you can. You laughed at us. Called us "white trash". Your father ruined us. And *you* had it all along.'

Her father had laughed, had called lots of people trash. But Lucy never had. There was no way she'd make Evan believe that, though. 'So you decided to track me.'

'No, I started to track you when I first came here. But you've always been on my list. Since the day you hit me when I came to ask you for help.'

The three minutes he'd given the cops had to be long gone, Lucy thought. But Evan hadn't moved. He leaned against the door jamb, staring outside. From the corner of her eye she could see that the stain on his arm bandage had stopped spreading, but he'd lost a lot more blood. It was a wonder the man still stood. But his gun was still steady.

Keep him standing. Keep him talking. Maybe he'll pass out on his own. And I can escape.

How? You can't run.

Then you'll crawl. 'What list?' she asked.

'My kill list. You were always on it, for years. Long before any of them talked.'

Any of them? Who else talked? *Think.* Malcolm Edwards was first. Malcolm had been dying. Cancer. He'd joined a church. She closed her eyes, trying to remember. Church of the Divine Forgiveness.

'Malcolm asked for forgiveness,' she said and felt Evan stiffen in surprise.

'How did you know that?' he asked.

'I didn't, until right now. I guessed. He was dying. He confessed.'

'With a little help, yes.'

'You tortured him.'

'Oh, yes.' There was a quiet, gleeful pride in his voice that made her stomach turn.

'Then you killed him and his wife.'

'Oh, yes. I did.'

'I get your kill list. But why the hooker? And why the PI?' she asked, knowing that JD would want to know. Because he would get her out of here. He would.

'The hooker stole from me. The PI just pissed me off. Like you do. So shut up.'

He hadn't planned to kill them, she thought. They were mistakes. Kevin Drummond had probably been a mistake, too. Evan had been more than willing to talk about the successes. His kill list. 'When did you put the trackers in my purse?'

'Any time you weren't looking. Women are remarkably careless about their purses. You asked me to hold it while you looked for your jacket in your suitcase on Sunday night.'

When he and Gwyn had picked her up at the airport. She'd been trying to think of who'd had access to her purse since Monday morning. She'd totally forgotten about Sunday night.

Behind her, Evan shifted his balance, watching outside. Lucy could no longer hear the helicopter. Where were they? *Okay, JD. I'm ready to get out of here. Any time would be good.*

'Ileanna had a purse, that night,' Lucy said. 'It was never found.'

The gun jerked against her temple. 'Because your brother *took* it,' he spat, emphasizing the word with a sharp jab of the barrel. 'After he *raped* my sister.'

'I think Buck took her purse,' she said. 'But I don't think he raped her.'

'Because he told you so?' he asked bitterly.

'No. You don't believe me, but he never said a word to me about any of this. I think it because I read Ileanna's autopsy report last night.'

'No, I don't believe you, and who cares about the report? Your mother wrote it.'

Oh. That he would think so made sense. 'Just because she was the doctor on the scene doesn't mean she did the autopsy. Maryland had a state ME even then. The autopsy was done by the state, not my mother. That you can check yourself.' He said nothing but she could sense him listening. 'The man who raped Ileanna had a different blood type than my brother. It matched Ricky Joyner's. Ricky did the rape.'

437

'So Malcolm and the others were telling the truth.' She felt him shrug. 'It doesn't matter if your brother raped her himself. He let it happen. Stood by and watched while it *happened*. That's all I need to know.'

Then she understood. 'They watched. Malcolm, Russ, James, Ryan, Sonny. And Buck.'

'They *watched*. And they *laughed*. And they *cheered* him on. And left her to *die*.' Pain and rage filled his voice, made it shake. 'It's been more than three minutes. Move,' he barked, dragging her to her feet and down the dimly lit hall.

Her leg buckled beneath her and she went down on her knees. Pain radiated, burning, and a sob tore free. 'I can't.'

'Get up.' His fingers grabbed at her hair, yanking her up and all she could see was red.

'No,' she gritted, then twisted, throwing her elbow into his bandage. He stumbled, snapping her head back, but she threw herself forward in desperation. Her scalp burned as her hair pulled, her eyes teared, and his curses filled her ears.

'You bi—'

Suddenly free, Lucy shot forward, scrambling on her hands and one knee as Evan jerked, then slumped to the floor. She stared at his head. Much of which was no longer there.

JD. It was the only thought that penetrated the haze.

Footsteps pounded around her and she let herself slide to the floor.

JD ran the length of the hall, which seemed to stretch forever. Lucy was lying on the floor, not moving. She wasn't moving. *I didn't hit her. I couldn't have hit her*.

One of the state cops who'd come in with him was running from the opposite direction and reached her first. 'She's alive.'

Thank God. JD reached her side and set the rifle on the floor, barely casting a look at Evan Reardon. The man's head looked like a crushed cantaloupe and he deserved far worse.

JD took Lucy's freezing hands between his, rubbing them vigorously. The state guy radioed the all-clear and called for a medic.

'Lucy?' JD leaned closer. '*Lucy?* Open your eyes for me, baby.'

Her eyes opened heavily, filled with pain. 'Did you kill him?'

'Yeah, I did.'

'Good.'

'Other than your leg, what's hurt? Did he shoot you?'

'No,' she said numbly. 'He didn't. Gwyn?'

'She's alive.'

Relief shuddered through her and horror filled her eyes. 'He killed my father.'

'We know, honey.'

'He tried to run. Was going to leave me behind. Evan shot him.'

JD had to fight for control. Gwyn had told him that Lucy had forced her to save her mother while she untied her father. It explained the bullet hole in Trask's back, the coward. JD was fiercely glad Trask was dead, grateful to Reardon for doing what he'd wanted to do himself.

'I'm sorry you had to see it,' he said, his hand trembling as he caressed her cheek.

'My mother?'

'Alive. Gwyn got her most of the way out. One of the other cops carried her the rest of the way, while I came to find you.'

'Skinner?'

He hesitated. 'Still critical.'

A sob choked her. 'Skinner was trying to make me stop running. I should have listened. If he dies . . . I should have listened. He's got a baby.'

'He's still alive and fighting.' *Thanks to Thorne.* 'Try not to worry about him.'

The paramedics burst through the door, followed by Stevie and Hyatt, who'd been minutes away before JD had gone in. He expected Hyatt to be furious, but his CO just stared at Reardon's body and gave a little nod.

The medics splinted Lucy's leg and lifted her to the stretcher, jerking an agonized cry from her throat that made JD want to kill Reardon all over again. Blindly she reached for his hand and squeezed so hard that he grimaced.

439

Hyatt leaned over the stretcher. 'Dr Trask, I need a moment.'

One of the paramedics protested, but she waved him silent. 'Go ahead.'

'Did he tell you anything?' Hyatt asked.

'They watched,' she said hoarsely. 'Those boys watched Ileanna get raped and they laughed. Then they left her there to die. Malcolm confessed.'

'His atonement,' JD said and she nodded.

'He gave Evan a list. All the people who participated. He killed someone else. James Cannon.' She closed her eyes. 'Sonny Westcott's inside. I don't know if he's still alive.'

Stevie ran to check and a minute later shouted for the medics. Another gurney raced by.

'I guess that means he is,' Lucy said. 'You can go to him if you need to.' She said the words, but her grip on JD's hand tightened.

JD pushed her hair away from her face, his hand trembling. He was glad it trembled now and not five minutes before. 'I won't leave you.'

Wednesday, May 5, 5.00 P.M.

The smell of roses tickled her nose and she opened her eyes to JD holding a bouquet of large red blooms. He leaned over the hospital bed's guardrail to place a kiss on her mouth.

'That didn't hurt, did it?' he asked when he'd lifted his head.

'It's the only place that doesn't.' She buried her face in the flowers. 'I haven't had flowers in so long. Thank you.'

He sat in the chair, but he didn't relax. 'Have you seen your mother?'

She plucked at one of the roses. 'Not yet. They won't let me out of bed.' It was a fairly clean break, but her leg still throbbed like hell. Her face hurt and her head ached from her broken nose and her fractured ribs made it hurt to breathe. It might have been unbearable but for the narcotic JD had convinced her to take earlier.

True to his word, he'd sat with her, letting her crush his hand when the doctor had set the bone. He hadn't left her until she'd fallen asleep, still holding his hand.

'But I asked about her and the nurses said she was stable but resting,' she added. JD had told her that her mother was alive, but hadn't mentioned she'd had a mild heart attack as the paramedics had transported her to the hospital. 'They told me about her heart attack, JD.'

'I didn't know about it until I got here with you,' he said. 'I figured you had enough to worry about at the time. She's awake now. Alert. I just came from her room. Stevie was with me. We had to tell her about your father before she heard it on the news or from another patient.'

In her mind she could hear the shots Evan had fired at her father. She could see the blood, smell it. Ruthlessly she pushed the memory aside, just as she'd done dozens of times already. And would likely do many more times until the horror dulled.

'How did she take it?'

'She cried. She didn't ask questions, just thanked us for stopping by.'

Lucy's shoulders sagged. 'I know I'm a coward, but I don't know that I could have been there for that.'

'You're not the coward,' he said roughly. 'He was. We didn't tell her what happened. We didn't think she needed to hear it from us.'

Lucy nodded. On the ambulance ride she'd told JD everything that had happened, including how her father had said, 'That's your problem,' when he'd left her. She'd also forced herself to tell him that Evan had once approached her for help and she'd lashed out, like she'd lashed out at everyone that year. It made her ashamed. And it made her wonder if Evan would have come to hate her had she not hit him.

JD had been quick to point out that had she listened to Evan then, she still would have denied having the necklace, which would have brought about the same end. Evan wouldn't have believed her and still would have blamed her family for the ruination of his.

'I don't plan to tell my mother about my father's last actions,' Lucy said. 'I don't think she needs to hear it. Although I still need to know what she knew about Buck. And about my father running the Bryans out of town.' She told him what Evan had accused.

'The Bennetts told us the same thing. But your mother may have been in the sanitarium by then, so it's hard to say exactly what she knew. There's something else we learned from the Bennetts today. Stevie and I thought you needed to know. They didn't pay for your lawyer. Your mother did.'

Lucy blinked, completely stunned. 'Excuse me?'

He nodded. 'That's what they said. They said your father wouldn't allow her to get you adequate legal help, so she convinced them to do it for her, with her money.'

Lucy was still staring at him. 'You're not kidding. Oh, my God. Why didn't she tell me?'

'I don't know. Maybe she was that afraid of your father.'

'That changes everything.' She sighed. 'And nothing. She wouldn't leave him, even to keep us safe, then she does something like that. I'll go down and talk to her as soon as they let me. I'm more concerned about Gwyn right now.'

He cleared his throat. 'I saw her, before I came here. She's not looking so good.'

'I know. Thorne came by and said the same thing. He took her back to his place and gave her a sleeping pill. He said he'd bring her by tomorrow to see me. All I could think of when we were in there was getting out alive. Now that it's over, all I can think is that for Gwyn, it's not over. I mean, knowing you've slept with a man capable of such violence . . .'

'He fooled a lot of people,' JD said.

'I know. But I keep thinking of how easily she could have been like Nicki Fields.'

'But she wasn't. She'll walk this road and come out stronger, just like you did. She's got good friends to show her the way.' JD took her hand. 'Skinner's awake.'

'Oh, God,' she breathed, relieved. 'Does this mean he's past the worst?'

'The doctor said he's out of the immediate woods. Thorne's first aid made the difference.'

'He'll be so glad to know that. What about Sonny Westcott?'

'Regained consciousness for a few minutes. Stevie questioned him, but she didn't get anything useful. Barring anything unforeseen, he'll survive. He won't have an easy recovery, though. He's missing four fingers and his knees were smashed.'

'With the bat.' Lucy stared down at the cast on her own leg, trying not to remember the sickening crunch of bone when Evan had brought the bat down on her femur. 'I heard the nurses talking about the "A" on his back. I guess my parents would have been the two "N"s. And I would have been the last "A".'

'Has Barb come by?' he asked, changing the subject and she understood that the horror was still fresh in his mind as well.

She sighed, thinking about the Pughs' visit. 'Yes.'

'Why the sigh? I thought that would have been a happy visit.'

'It was, somewhat. I mean, she's happy I'm not dead. But she took one look at my cast and realized it would be a while before I can help her with Mr Pugh. It'll be a while before I can help myself. She can't handle his agitation by herself any longer. We have to place him.' Sadness welled up and she dabbed at her eyes with the tissue JD put in her hand. 'He was so good to me. I hate to do this. But we can't have him wandering in the night and breaking mirrors. It's not safe for either of them.'

He kissed her hand. 'Now when you play for him, the others will hear your music. Maybe it will give them peace, too.'

'That's a nice thought. I'll hold onto that one.' *And to this one*, she thought, gripping JD's hand tightly. JD Fitzpatrick was a good man. Mr Pugh would have approved. 'Is Stevie settled down now?'

'Yeah. But I think poor Cordelia will have an honor guard 24/7 until she's forty.' His mouth flattened. 'When I think that Reardon was watching her too, I get angry all over again.'

'I'm glad he's dead,' Lucy said, an edge creeping into her voice.

'So am I,' he said, but wearily.

She brought his hand to her lips. She'd been selfish, not thinking about how taking a life, even a bad one, had affected him. 'I'm sorry, JD. I'm sorry you had to do it.'

He shrugged. 'Not a problem. Nothing I haven't done before.

I have a briefing in twenty minutes in Hyatt's office. I'll be back after.' He stood, but didn't leave. His hands closed over the rail and his knuckles whitened, his chin dropping to his chest and he shuddered out a breath. 'I was so scared,' he admitted in a whisper, 'knowing he had you. Knowing what he could do.'

Sensing he needed to get it out, Lucy said nothing. She brushed the backs of her fingers over his cheek and he grabbed her hand and held it to his lips. 'I'm glad you fought back,' he said quietly. 'I had my scope trained on Reardon for five minutes, waiting for him to move.' He smiled weakly against her fingers. 'I was hoping you'd punch him in the nose.'

'I was trying to buy you time by talking to him. I knew you'd be coming for me. I knew you'd know what to do.'

Something flickered in his eyes. 'Lucy will know what to do,' he murmured.

'What?'

He shook his head. 'Just something someone said a few days ago.' He released her hand, giving her the TV remote. 'I'll be back later.'

Wednesday, May 5, 5.40 P.M.

'How is she?' Hyatt asked when JD joined them for the meeting. Stevie, Elizabeth and Drew were there along with Daphne and Lennie Berman. To JD's surprise, DA Grayson Smith was also there. Everyone looked as exhausted as JD felt.

'Lucy's much better,' JD said. 'Thank you.'

'Good. Let's begin. Including Ron Trask, the Edwardses, James Cannon, the six victims already in our morgue, and the two victims in Newport News, Evan Reardon murdered twelve people. That we caught him is a testament to your skill, teamwork, and a liberal helping of luck.'

JD couldn't help but wonder if Hyatt was practicing for his press conference.

'We still have casualties,' Hyatt continued. 'Skinner, Sonny Westcott, Mrs Trask, and Dr Trask herself. All will probably survive.'

Add Gwyn Weaver, JD thought. She'd have psychological scars for some time. *Then again, won't we all?*

'I have a press conference at six. With Dr Berman's help, I will paint the psychological profile of this multiple murderer. I'd appreciate anything else we've managed to dig up today.'

JD told them about Lucy's father running the Bryans out of town. 'The Bennetts suspected it, but Evan was there when Ron Trask threatened them. Then a year later, Evan's father commits suicide and Evan finds his body.' He held back the detail of Lucy hitting Evan when they were teenagers. That was something that really helped no one at this point.

'A real reason for him to hate the Trasks,' Berman murmured. 'That's a missing piece. I couldn't account for so much hate, but now I can see it. We'll have a more complete profile for your press conference, Lieutenant.'

Hyatt looked pleased by this. 'Drew?'

'The tracking devices he placed in Lucy's purse and Cordelia's backpack had prints – those of Nicki Fields. We also found devices in Gwyn Weaver's purse and hidden behind the dashboard of Nicki Fields's car. All of the devices had her prints on.'

'Evan stole them from the PI,' Hyatt mused.

'And he killed her,' Stevie said with a thoughtful frown. 'If he was tracking her, he knew she'd gone to Anderson Ferry, knew she had information about him. I guess he figured when the bodies started to pop up that she'd be able to link him.'

'Evan told Lucy that the hooker stole from him,' JD said, 'but the PI "pissed him off".'

'So *that* fits at least,' Stevie said, still frowning.

'What doesn't?' Hyatt asked.

'Oh, just that we never found the file.' Stevie shrugged. 'Evan must have destroyed it.'

'Looking at the website on his phone,' Drew said, 'Evan was tracking several people, Gwyn and Nicki included. I guess it was his way of making sure he knew where they were and that their paths wouldn't intersect, since he was seeing them both at the same time.'

'Cad,' Daphne muttered.

'I found a birth certificate and passport for a Ted Gamble in his firebox,' Drew went on. 'There was a credit card in his wallet with the same name. He'd kept all of his victims' credit cards also. He'd maxed them all out with cash advances on top of wiping their bank accounts.'

'Hell of a guy,' Hyatt said.

'I tracked the hooker, Sue Ellen Lamont,' Elizabeth said. 'We got a call on the hotline late last night from the Orion Hotel. They saw her photo on the news and remembered her. She was something of a regular there. The security tapes show her checking in with Evan and checking out a few hours later. Evan used the Ted Gamble credit card. The card has since been reported stolen and canceled. The PI's partner, Clay Maynard, was also poking around the hotel, trying to find out who the hooker saw.'

'Or who saw the hooker,' JD said. 'He was looking for Evan, too.'

'True,' Elizabeth said. 'When the hotel checked more of their tapes, they found a trend. Sue Ellen Lamont would come in at least twice a night with a different man, but she'd go to the same guy behind the counter – a nerdy-looking guy who was only too happy to spill by the time I got there this afternoon. Remember that Sue Ellen had had sex twice the night she died?'

'With two different clients,' Stevie said.

'No,' Elizabeth said. 'One client – Evan – and one boyfriend – Nerdy Guy. Whose name is Dirk. Dirk concocted the scheme. Sue Ellen would pick up the men, Dirk would steal their credit card info and then send them to a special room which had a video camera.'

'Blackmail?' Stevie asked.

'Oh, yeah.' Elizabeth shrugged. 'They were making some serious money between the credit cards and the blackmail. I checked the tape with Evan's session and he caught her in the bathroom stealing his credit card info. He flashed her a badge and made her think he was a cop.'

'He used the Newport News cop's badge.' Stevie was still frowning.

'Exactly,' Elizabeth said. 'Dirk was pissed, because Sue Ellen was double-crossing him by stealing the cards he'd already stolen. So he didn't say anything when she went missing. When he saw her on the news last night, he was "devastated".'

'Not devastated enough to come forward,' Daphne said dryly.

'Obviously,' Hyatt said. 'Now, you're probably wondering why the DA is here. So Smith, the floor is yours.'

DA Grayson Smith was about JD's age, but seemed years older. He was a serious guy with a reputation for working 24/7 and JD had never seen him smile.

'I got a visit an hour ago from Janet Gordon's attorney,' Smith said. 'She left a sealed letter with instructions that were she to die under "mysterious circumstances" he should mail it to me. He heard the news last night and hand-delivered it instead. In it she details the events of that night twenty-one years ago. It's exactly what we learned from Dr Trask – Ricky Joyner raped and beat his ex-girlfriend, Ileanna Bryan, while a group of boys watched and cheered. The letter names everyone we already know about – except Ryan Agar, her own son. He's conveniently left out of the account. In the letter she swears that when the boys left, Ileanna was alive, and that she died later. The next day, Joyner was discovered dead, by his own hand, which we also now know wasn't true.'

'Why?' Stevie asked. 'Why would she write the letter at all?'

'I would,' Daphne drawled, 'if I were letting a man I'd blackmailed put me under anesthesia and take a knife to my face.'

'Good point,' Stevie conceded. 'I guess she wanted to pressure Russ Bennett without throwing her son under a bus. Except we know he was there.'

Hyatt sighed. 'I think that's everything, unless anyone has anything else.'

JD watched Stevie. She'd stopped frowning, but there was something bugging her. When they'd adjourned, he pulled her aside. 'What gives?'

'Don't know. Something's off. I'm going home to hug Cordelia, then I'll think on it some more. I'll see you tomorrow. Tell Lucy I'm thinking of her and if she decides she needs to talk about her dad, I've got space in the group.'

'I'll tell her. Good night.'

Twenty-six

Wednesday, May 5, 6.40 P.M.

'What's all this?'

Lucy looked up at JD with a small smile. He'd stopped in the door of her hospital room, staring at all the flowers. 'You gave me roses and then everybody jumped in.' She pointed to the bouquets. 'Those are from Craig and Rhoda, those are from the band, those are from Thorne, those are from the morgue. They give nice flowers at the morgue.'

A nurse came in with a wheelchair with an extended leg rest and Lucy's smile dimmed. 'What's wrong?' JD asked.

'They're taking me to see my mother.'

'Do you want me to go with you?'

Lucy looked up at him. 'Would you mind?'

'Not at all.'

The nurse helped her into the chair and Lucy winced. She really should be staying in bed, but her mother was not doing well. The doctor had agreed that a visit now might be the only chance Lucy would have.

It wasn't something she wanted to think about, not that thinking about it made any difference one way or the other. She reached for JD's hand and held on, dread building.

She paid for my lawyer. The news still had Lucy stunned.

What did Buck do? The question still haunted her. *I need to know.*

The nurse pushed her into her mother's room where another nurse was checking her vitals. 'Only a few minutes,' the nurse murmured. 'Try not to upset her.'

Lucy had to swallow back a laugh. Upsetting her mother was pretty much a fait accompli. It always had been. JD gave Lucy's hand a squeeze.

'Mother?' Lucy said quietly. 'It's Lucy.'

'I know.' Her mother didn't open her eyes. 'He hurt you.'

'Who?'

Her mother smiled, bitterly. 'Evan, the brother of that girl.'

'The girl's name was Ileanna,' Lucy said, more caustically than she'd intended.

'Yes, I know. Ileanna. How badly did Evan hurt you?'

'He broke my leg,' Lucy said, since her mother still hadn't opened her eyes. 'And cracked a few ribs. I'll live.' Her voice was harsher than she wanted. 'He hurt you, too,' she said more softly, and her mother opened her eyes.

They were filled with pain. 'He hit you.' She drew a shallow breath. 'You've got bruises.'

'I said I'll live,' Lucy said quietly. 'I know about the lawyer, for my trial.'

Her mother flinched. 'The Bennetts told, I take it?'

'Yes,' she said. 'They told Detective Fitzpatrick this morning.'

'I see. Yes, it's true. Your father wouldn't allow me to help you. I found a way.'

'Why didn't you tell me?'

'Because you got away, Lucy. You made a life. He couldn't touch you anymore.'

Lucy frowned. 'You mean my father?'

'Yes. He didn't want to send you to St Anne's either.' Her chin lifted. 'I did that. I came home from the sanitarium after my breakdown and saw the bruises on your legs. I knew I needed to get you away. I couldn't protect you anymore.'

'Why didn't you just leave and take me with you?' Lucy said, a lump in her throat. Behind her JD rubbed her shoulders.

'I don't know. He wouldn't let me take Buck and I couldn't leave my son. I loved him. I loved your father, too.'

Lucy swallowed back the tears. 'But not me? Didn't you love me?'

'Yes, you. I loved you, always. But I was weak. I still am.' She drew another shallow breath. 'I was weak the night I found that diamond necklace.'

'When?' Lucy asked simply.

'The night Buck died. I found the necklace on top of his baseball cards.'

Lucy frowned. 'Why were you looking?'

'Because I knew Buck. Something was wrong. I stood outside his door, watched him in the mirror. I saw him check the box, then hide it under his bed. Why he kept the necklace I'll never know. But I went in after he was gone and I found it. I sat on his bed, held it in my hand and cried. I remembered so clearly that girl's – Ileanna's wounds. She was brutally attacked. I thought Buck had done it.'

'Did you confront him?'

'Yes, later, when your father came home. He denied the rape, so adamantly that I believed him. Or wanted to. Your father got in his face and screamed at him about screwing trash.' She bit her lip. 'Like Ileanna. I said something and Ron shoved me, hard. Buck got between us, said he'd fixed it. Not that he would, but that he did.'

'He'd killed Ricky Joyner,' Lucy murmured.

'Yes. I knew then. I confronted him with it while your father roared at me. Buck said he didn't do it, that Joyner ate his gun. But he knew what kind of gun it was and your father flinched. Later I checked. That wasn't in any of the information released.'

'What happened to the necklace, Mother?'

'Your father grabbed it from me, said he'd throw it in the Bay. Buck grabbed it back, said it was his mistake, he'd take care of it. He was so angry when he left on his motorcycle. He never came back. That was the last time I saw him.'

'The day of Buck's funeral, you grabbed my father and said "What did Buck do?" What did you think he did?'

Her mother's chin quivered. 'Murder, rape, suicide? Take your pick. I didn't know what he'd done, but your father did.'

JD cleared his throat. 'Where was Lucy? I'd think she'd remember all the yelling.'

'I knew it would be a row, so I asked Gwyn's mother to invite Lucy for a sleepover.'

'A deputy came to get me in the night,' Lucy said. 'You never saw the necklace again?'

'No. I didn't. I assume Buck threw it in the Bay.' She sighed wearily. 'I never knew there was a bracelet too. I don't think I really remember you wearing it. I was medicated fairly heavily back then. Sending you to St Anne's seemed for the best. You were happy there. You had your music. You were safe. But I lost you, too.'

Lucy patted her mother's hand, because she couldn't think of anything else to say. 'What do we do now?'

Her mother looked up at JD. 'Will they press charges against me?'

'I don't know,' JD said honestly. 'It's up to the DA. I doubt it.'

'Then I'll go home, when I'm able. Maybe you can come home too, Lucy. Finally.'

Lucy patted her mother's hand again. 'I am home. Here. But I'll come see you.'

Her mother nodded in a way that said she knew Lucy was lying through her teeth. 'That's good. We can have lunch. You can tell me about your practice.'

'Sleep now. I'll see you tomorrow.'

She waited until JD had pushed her into the hall, then let the tears fall, not caring who saw them. When they got back to her room, he crouched at her side, took her into his arms and let her sob. When she'd cried it all out, he put a cold cloth on her face.

She shuddered. 'I just wanted her to love me.'

'I know, baby. She does, in her own way. It just wasn't enough.'

'Could it be enough? Now that he's gone?'

'Maybe. If you both want it bad enough. And it's okay not to know that tonight. You've got the rest of your lives to figure it out.'

She nodded. 'I'm so tired, JD.'

'Then sleep.'

'Will you stay with me?'

'Until you're asleep. Then I'll see you tomorrow.'

Wednesday, May 5, 7.45 P.M.

JD sat at his desk staring at the stacks of documents Higgins had given them. He'd left them in disarray when he and Stevie had run to meet the Bennetts that morning.

I should pack them in the box. He should do paperwork. But all he could hear was Lucy's pitiful questions. *What about me? Didn't you love me?*

He'd asked those same questions himself, thousands of times. Never found a good answer. *All I've ever wanted was a family. Someone that belongs to me. Someone I belong to.* He'd watched his friends have families. He'd tried with Maya and failed so miserably.

I want it to be Lucy. It was way too soon to hope, but he did anyway. And tried not to feel too pathetic about doing so.

'JD?' a woman asked and he looked up to see Hyatt's clerk studying him from the doorway of the CO's office. 'Why aren't you home sleeping like everyone else?'

'I'm going.' He'd been hesitating, unwilling to return home. To spend another night in that house of his, alone. 'I just have some paperwork to do.'

Debbie's look was sympathetic and JD wondered if he wore a big L for Loser on his forehead. 'Did you listen to your messages?' she asked.

He grimaced. 'No. I've got like a hundred, probably ninety of them from reporters.'

'I doubt there's any room in your voicemail box for reporters after all the messages your realtor left.'

'What are you talking about?'

'You've got your house on the market, right?' Debbie asked.

'Yeah, for a year now.'

'Well, your realtor called, then she stopped by.' She put a stack of pink phone message slips on his desk. 'Said you got an offer and to call her ASAP.'

Stunned, JD dialed and was met by the perky voice of the realtor who hadn't had a single bite on his house in months. 'We have an offer,' she sang.

452

'Are you sure?'

'Of course. You've been in the news, Detective.'

'What does that have to do with my house?'

'Well, I may have dropped your name a few times, got some buzz going. Somebody wants to buy the house that the serial-killer-catching detective lived in.'

'Oh, my God,' JD said, disgust mixing with his surprise.

'Hey, don't knock it, JD. Bird in the hand and all that.'

'That's just . . . gross.'

'Bird in the hand,' she repeated with emphasis. 'They're offering your asking price. You should take it.' She paused, a frown in her voice. 'You do want to sell it, don't you?'

JD thought of Lucy, of the future. *Possibilities*. It was a good omen, not that he believed in such things. *Or maybe I do*. 'Yes, I want to sell it. Draw up the contracts.'

'I already did. Should I bring them tonight? I can meet you at my office.'

JD felt his head spinning. 'Sure. I'll be there soon.'

He hung up and blew out a breath. *Clean your desk and go sign that contract before the buyer changes their mind*. He'd started picking up prom photos and police reports to put in the box when he saw a folder he hadn't opened yet. It was labeled 'Memorial Service'. Bart Higgins had pulled it together for Lucy.

JD opened it now. It wasn't a memorial service, he saw. It was Buck's funeral.

I'm glad Lucy didn't see these. The photos were grainy, like they were taken with a pocket camera with no flash. Someone had chronicled an event that should have been somber. But because of who Buck Trask had been, the town had wanted it captured for posterity.

There were pictures of the priest, of the Trasks. His heart squeezed painfully. Of a fourteen-year-old Lucy huddled in the corner of a pew, looking so incredibly alone and sad.

There were pictures of crying classmates. And one older girl who sat on the front row, staring at the closed casket. She didn't look sad, JD thought. She looked pissed off.

Her fist was clenched tight, but JD could see something resting on top of her hand. He brought the picture closer. It looked like a chain.

I wonder . . . He opened the Anderson Ferry High yearbook Stevie had left on her desk and flipped to the Ds. Yes. The girl looking so pissed off was Sara Derringer, Buck's ex-girlfriend. JD flipped through the photos until he found another shot of Sara standing in the line to pay her last respects. The look on her face as she stared at the casket was utter frustration. And her fist was still clenched. She was holding something in her hand. JD had a damn good idea what it was.

JD quickly boxed up the rest of the files, leaving the funeral folder out. Higgins had given Lucy a card with Sara's current address. He thought he and Stevie needed to pay a visit. But now, he had priorities. He was going to finally sell his house.

Thursday, May 6, 7.55 A.M.

Stevie was relieved to see only one car parked in front of Clay Maynard's office. She wasn't sure she wanted anyone to know she'd come. No one but Maynard, anyway.

She knocked on the glass door and waited. A minute later he appeared, frowning.

'Detective Mazzetti, come in. How is your daughter?'

'She's well, thank you.' Stevie looked up at him. He was a big man, rather gruff. But she didn't feel nervous. Not really. 'I wanted you to know that we found a tracking device hidden underneath the dashboard of your partner's car.'

'I figured that. He planted one in your daughter's backpack and it only makes sense that he'd have kept track of where Nicki was and it was clear he knew she'd gone to Anderson Ferry. She found out Reardon's true background and it got her killed. But thank you for telling me. You didn't have to come all this way for that.'

'You didn't have to give us Reardon's name and photo either.'

'Well, technically I did. Otherwise I think that's called hindering an investigation?'

454

She smiled, unexpectedly. 'Yeah, it is.' She sobered, tilting her head to look up at him. 'We found a few things in the apartment Evan was using. Specifically, the driver's license and passport of Ted Gamble.'

To his credit, Maynard's eyes didn't flicker. 'And?'

She smiled, briefly. 'And . . . you told me you'd found Evan and the prostitute he killed through a credit card search. That would have been at the Orion Hotel. They remember seeing the victim there. And they remember you asking about her.'

Now his eyes flickered. 'And?' he said.

'And . . . Evan's date had a scam running with her partner, the hotel clerk. Credit card fraud and blackmail. But Evan didn't check in under his own name. He used the Ted Gamble card. You weren't looking for Evan, you were looking for Ted. Why?'

His dark eyes studied hers intently. 'You already know. So why do you ask?'

'Those IDs were excellent work. They fooled us all.'

'Should I say thank you or call my attorney?'

'The first one, I think.'

His eyes narrowed. 'Why?'

'You wanted to do the right thing, Mr Maynard. When my child was at risk you did do the right thing. Sometimes I need information. Sometimes it's not always . . . easy to come by.'

'Or legal?'

'Sometimes. Sometimes people need help and the legal way isn't the fast way. I've surprised you.'

'Yes, you have. Your husband was a DA,' he said and she blinked.

'Checking up on me?'

'Yeah. I almost didn't give you that photo. Ultimately it worked out.'

'Mostly. A cop's still in ICU while his wife rocks their baby alone. Knowing who we were looking for sooner might have prevented that. But that would be the past. Wouldn't it?'

'It would. What are you suggesting?'

She smiled. 'Nothing. Until I need some information.'

'What if I need information?'

She thought of Cordelia, safe in bed. She owed him for that. 'You have my card. It's got my cell. Have a good day, Mr Maynard.'

Thursday, May 6, 11.00 A.M.

'Hey.' JD stood in the doorway of Lucy's hospital room, her duffle in one hand and her overnight bag in the other. And a smile on his face.

Lucy couldn't think of a better way to start her day. 'Good morning.'

He came in, kissed her forehead. 'Sleep okay?'

Her eyes narrowed. 'Okay. Why the peck?'

'Because I'm here,' Stevie said, coming in behind him, a big cup of coffee in her hand. 'I got the evil eye from a pack of nurses for bringing in contraband.'

'Thank you,' Lucy said. 'I needed this.'

Stevie stared at the flowers. 'I thought you were kidding, JD. So did you tell her?'

'No, I just got here,' he said, rolling his eyes. 'You have a visitor. I wanted to be sure you were ready before I told her to come back.'

Lucy put her coffee aside. 'Ready for what?' she asked warily.

'Good question,' Stevie said. She went to the door and waved.

A woman entered and Lucy's cup stopped halfway to her lips as her memory churned. She was older, a little heavier, but still beautiful. 'Sara Derringer?'

Sara crossed to Lucy's bed. 'I didn't think you'd remember me.'

'I do. I'm surprised to see you.'

Sara looked down. 'Your detectives came to my house this morning.'

Lucy frowned. 'What?' She looked at JD. 'Why?'

Sara drew a deep breath and pulled a box from her purse. She handed it to Lucy and Lucy stared at it. 'Open it,' Sara said.

There was only one missing puzzle piece, and now that it was in her hands, she was afraid. 'I don't want to.'

'Just do it,' JD said softly. 'You need to. We need to finish this so we can go on.'

Shaking her head, she opened the box. As she thought, it held a heart-shaped diamond necklace. 'You had it, all this time?'

'Yes,' Sara said. 'Buck came to see me the night he died. He'd fought with your parents, about Ileanna Bryan and that necklace. By the time he got to my house, he was drunk. Really drunk, and crying. He told me everything. And I was horrified.'

'What did he say?' Lucy asked, still staring at the necklace.

'We both knew he'd taken Ileanna to the prom to spite me. I'd cheated, just like he had. But he was allowed to have girls on the side and I wasn't. He dumped me, and then he took Ileanna to the prom to hurt me. After the dance, he boasted to the boys that he and Ileanna were going to do it under the bleachers on the football field, kind of daring them to follow. What he didn't know was that Ileanna's ex was following them too.'

'Ricky Joyner. He raped Ileanna.'

'Yeah. And Buck stood there and watched, too shocked or maybe too scared to stop him. Him, the big quarterback, oozing sex appeal, macho man, couldn't defend his date. When the other boys arrived they cheered Ricky on and laughed at Buck. Because he was a coward. And not a man.'

Lucy looked up and met Sara's eyes. 'Buck wouldn't have taken that well.'

'No. He didn't. It was like he'd been knocked off the top of the totem pole. The prom king, dethroned,' she said dramatically, but her voice held tears. 'After Ricky ran away, the boys got scared. Ileanna was really hurt. It was Buck's idea to make it look like a robbery.'

'He stole her necklace and her purse, which had her bracelet in.'

'Yes. He got rid of the purse, but kept the jewelry.'

'Why?' Lucy asked. 'That's the part that didn't make sense.'

'At first he thought he could give it back. He took it home and hid it, then he learned that Ileanna had died. He swore he'd taken her home and dropped her off and because he was Buck Trask and your father was sheriff, nobody questioned it. Sometime during the night he got worried that Ricky would tell, that they'd all go to prison.'

457

'So he killed him.'

'Yes. He and Sonny Westcott.'

Lucy's eyes widened. 'Sonny Westcott helped Buck kill Ricky Joyner?'

'That's what Buck said, and I don't think he was lying. He figured he'd have to restrain Rick, which is why Sonny went too. Sonny hit him, but Ricky was so stoned he didn't fight back. Buck put the gun in Ricky's mouth, wrapped Ricky's hand around it, and pulled the trigger. He used one of your father's throwaway guns.'

Lucy let out a careful breath. 'My father had a throwaway gun?'

'He had a whole stash, according to Buck.'

'My father had a stash of throwaway guns?' Hell. How many times had he needed to plant evidence? Lucy didn't think she really wanted to know.

'Yes, and Buck took one. He said Sonny had made fun of him until he grabbed the gun and just drove. Buck wanted to get back that top-of-the-totem-pole feeling. Except he couldn't live with himself afterward. He couldn't sleep, kept looking in the box to see if anyone had found out he was keeping the jewelry. Finally your mother found it and called him out. They fought, and he came to my place. He asked me to hold the necklace, that he thought it was valuable. He wanted to give it back to the Bryans, to make up for what he'd done.'

'What did you say?'

'I was horrified. I told him that a necklace wouldn't bring Ileanna or Ricky back. He left on the motorcycle and wrecked on his way home. I think it was suicide in its own way.'

It was what she had feared, but still . . . *He wanted to make amends.* Which meant nothing. Sara was right. Nothing would bring Ileanna or Ricky back. 'How did the detectives find you?'

'I saw Sara's picture,' JD said, 'in the file Higgins made for you. She was at Buck's funeral, looking frustrated as she walked by the coffin, holding something with a chain.'

'I wanted to put the necklace in the coffin with him,' Sara said. 'I was eighteen and it seemed very Romeo and Juliet to me, to bury him with what killed him. But it was a closed coffin, because of the accident. I hadn't thought of that. I was young and so upset. So I held onto the necklace, but couldn't hold the secret. I told my parents. My dad was going to go to the authorities, to tell them that Buck and Sonny had killed Ricky. Dad made the mistake of giving your father a courtesy heads-up.'

Lucy closed her eyes, unsurprised by anything now. 'Finish, please.'

'There was a fire "of unknown origin" in our house that night. Dad was able to put it out, but we were scared. There's justice and there's protecting your family. We decided not to tell. We took a Polaroid of the necklace and told your dad that it had Buck's prints all over it, and maybe his too. That we'd keep it as insurance that we'd have no more fires or other calamities. Your father agreed. And we moved away.'

'Now that he's dead, it's safe,' Lucy said.

'Yes. I'm sorry, Lucy. If I had known you were at risk, I would have told you long ago.'

She nodded. 'I understand. It's not okay, but I understand. I'm not sure I would have done things differently.' She held the box out to Sara. 'Take it back. I don't want it.'

Sara flashed a panicked look at JD. 'I don't want it either.'

'We'll hold onto it,' Stevie said, 'as evidence. It's not a real diamond, Lucy. It's only paste. Good paste, good enough to have fooled the Bryans. It's only worth about a thousand dollars twenty years later. Then, not worth a lot.'

'Certainly not the lives it cost,' Lucy murmured.

'We gave the Bryans twice what it was worth back then,' Sara said. 'My dad wrote them a check, said it was an investment in their fishing business. But they ended up moving and we never heard from them again.' She grabbed her purse in both hands. 'Take care, Lucy.'

Stevie sighed when Sara was gone. 'I'm going into the office. You coming, JD?'

'In a few. See you there.' Stevie left and JD pocketed the box.

'I think I'm going back to sleep,' Lucy said glumly. 'Where is Sonny now?'

'Here at the hospital. Daphne says we don't have a prayer of charging him. Since the other two people who might know the truth – Buck and your father – are dead, we won't know what really happened unless Sonny gets a sudden need to pull a Malcolm and confess.'

'I don't see that happening,' Lucy said.

'Me neither. His career could be over, simply on the basis of his injuries. It seems he also has some spinal cord damage and brain swelling. Evan did a number on him with that bat.'

'We may have to be content that he can't be the sheriff anymore,' she said. 'Now I really want to go back to sleep.'

He traced her lip with his thumb. 'How about some good news?'

'Good news. Do I have any? Well, Gwyn called me this morning. She's going apartment hunting. She's can't stay where she is, not after Royce. Evan. Which I understand. Completely. But still.' She shrugged uneasily. 'She's pulled away from me. She's never done that before.'

'She needs time. You knew she would. So where does that leave you, apartment-wise?'

'I don't know. I moved there for the Pughs. Gwyn moved because of me. Our house of cards went *thunk*. I'll start looking for something new when I'm out of this cast. Which will be weeks. Even before that I'm going to need something on the bottom floor, and my place is a walk-up. So other than we're not dead, no good news.'

'When I said "good news", I meant I have some. I sold my house.'

She blinked at him. 'I didn't know you had a house to sell.'

'It was my aunt's. I bought it from her when I came home and lived in it with Maya. It's been on the market for more than a year.'

'But you sold it?'

'The buyer signed the contract this morning. He also bought Maya's car. Apparently catching a multiple murderer makes my stuff worth something.'

'So where will you live?'

He grinned sheepishly, his dimple appearing. 'I was so excited about a new place that I went online and started looking last night.'

She couldn't help but smile back at him. 'And what did you find?'

'I was thinking about an apartment with an elevator.'

Her brows went up. 'Really?'

'Yeah. I called Barb Pugh last night and asked her where the facility you chose for Mr Pugh was located.' Lucy's mouth fell open, her heart squeezing hard. But before she could say a word, he'd forged on. 'I'm taking a vacation day today to check out a place that's closer to work and very near to where Mr Pugh will be, once Barb makes the move.'

Her breath caught in her throat. 'You don't have to do that for me.'

'I'm not. It's for me.' He smiled. 'I'd like to be close so I can come hear you play.'

She took his hand. 'You know, I've been known to give private concerts.'

'Have you now?'

'I have indeed.'

He eyed her cast. 'The stilettos are out for a while, but how about the dress?'

Lucy smiled. 'I think that can be arranged.'

Epilogue

'She's back.'

JD glanced up at the grimly satisfied and very relieved face of Thomas Thorne. Then he turned his eyes back to the stage where Lucy played her electric violin with the band for the first time since that day in May when so many lives had been irrevocably changed.

'Indeed,' JD said. 'She is back.'

And she was. After almost six months' recuperation, Lucy was on the stage looking like nothing had changed. Like she hadn't nearly been killed. Like she hadn't seen her father executed before her eyes. Like she hadn't learned things about her family that she could have lived a lifetime without knowing.

She was up there in black leather and stiletto heels, playing with the same fire and intensity that had made him fall. Irrevocably. And he was so damn glad he had.

'She sounds the same,' Thorne said proudly. 'Not a sour note in the piece.'

'She's been practicing,' JD said. Every night. He much preferred her practicing now that she no longer wore the cast, because it always left him wanting more. Much more.

They'd managed to get creative around the cast, but the day she'd had it removed had been cause for much celebration. Still, it had taken her months more to get back to normal.

Not one of the cheering fans would know that in the last six months she'd worked her ass off in physical therapy to be able to steadily stand for long hours at the table in the autopsy suite or for agonizing minutes next to a grieving family as she did the identifications.

And nobody would know what those identifications took out of her. JD knew, because he was there in the still of the night when the grief she witnessed every day became too much to bear. That's when she turned to him, holding fast until the wave of sadness passed.

And she did the same for him. After six months in Homicide he'd yet to have a case that came close to the one that had brought them together – for which he was very thankful. There was a lot of paper-work, a lot of waiting, a lot of asking the same kinds of questions. The notifications were the worst part – that personal moment with the victims' family in which he was forced to tear apart their world. This he had in common with Lucy and it was the days he had to notify a family that he tended to need her the most.

She'd made him whole and happy and he wasn't sure what he'd done before she'd stumbled across a murder scene and into his life. It didn't really matter what he'd done before. He didn't have to do without her now.

She looked up then, and met his eyes across the crowded club. Her smile was private and knowing and made him instantly hard as a rock. Then her gaze shifted, her eyes widening.

JD followed her line of sight, as did Thorne. It was Gwyn. She'd come out of the office and was standing along the back curtain, alone, her expression stony. But her eyes held pain, just as they had for six months. She'd slept with a monster who'd murdered so many.

'She hasn't smiled in six months,' Thorne said, his booming voice gone deep and quiet.

'Has she seen the therapist Stevie recommended?' JD asked.

'I don't think so. She keeps to herself, comes in, does the books. Keeps my calendar for court. But she doesn't perform. Doesn't socialize. I even got her new bullwhips, but she didn't care. It's like she's not in there anymore.'

'She's there,' JD said. Over the months he had come to actually like the oversized defense attorney. Thorne loved both Lucy and

Gwyn like a brother and that was a mark in his favor in JD's book. 'Gwyn's got to find her way back on her own.'

The music came to a crashing climax and then there were only cheers and whistles and chants for more. Gwyn silently disappeared behind the curtain without a smile or a word.

'She'll go back to the office until it's time to go home,' Thorne said sadly.

To the apartment with three deadbolts on the door and extra locks on every window. And a gun in her closet. JD knew because he'd put the locks on for her, hoping a feeling of safety would prompt her return to those who loved her. But it hadn't and Gwyn had withdrawn into the overlocked fortress.

'Lucy worries about her,' JD said. 'But there doesn't seem to be anything we can do.'

'I worry about them both,' Thorne confessed. 'Has Lucy been out to see her mother?'

'Yeah,' JD said. 'She went out there the first day she could walk after getting the cast off. The orthopedist gave her a cane and she got up to her mother's stoop at the same time Sonny Westcott was leaving his house. It was awkward.'

Thorne made an angry face. 'I'll bet.'

'Sonny's walking with a cane too. Evan did some real damage to his spine. Anyway, Sonny stood on his mother's stoop glaring for a minute. Lucy glared back. If it had come to a fight, I would have put my money on her.'

Sonny Westcott had, as JD had predicted, remained mute on the question of his involvement in the murder of Ricky Joyner. The only satisfaction was knowing that the entire town knew what he'd done and what he was. He'd never hold a law enforcement position again.

And Sonny Westcott now lived with his mother. That might be worse than prison.

'No question,' Thorne agreed. 'Lucy versus Sonny, Lucy every time. How was she after seeing her mother?'

JD sighed. 'I'm glad she saw Sonny on the way in. After a few hours with her mother, she was whipped. It'll take a lot of work for the two of them to have the most basic of relationships.'

Kathy Trask had been, by turns, wildly emotional and coldly withdrawn. Lucy had been right – her mother's physical and mental health was very fragile. Their conversation had been painfully mundane. 'But Lucy tried,' JD said. 'We went back again today, then we'll go out there on Thanksgiving to take her out for dinner.' After they had their main dinner at Stevie's house. 'When we left today, we went by Ron Trask's grave.'

'I'm glad I wasn't there,' Thorne said quietly. 'I might have spit on it.'

'I wanted to,' JD said. 'I think Lucy did too. She just stood there for the longest time, staring at this amazingly expensive headstone her mother had commissioned, then she walked away. I don't think she'll be going back anytime soon.'

Thorne pointed. 'Here she is.' Lucy had made her way through the guests on the floor and looked up into Thorne's face, her expression desolate.

'I want to make Gwyn better, Thorne, but she won't let me.' Lucy sighed. 'And don't tell me she needs time. I know she needs time.'

Thorne pressed a kiss to her forehead. 'Then I'll tell you that you did great out there. I'm so glad you're back.'

'I'm glad to be back.' She looked over at JD. 'Did you tell him?'

'No. I thought you'd want to.'

Thorne's dark brows went way up. 'Tell me what?'

Shyly, Lucy lifted her hand and Thorne's face lit up in a smile. In that moment JD was very glad Thorne loved the two women like a brother, because otherwise JD might have become a very jealous man. Thorne gave the ring on her hand a dramatic assessment.

'It's a frickin' rock of Gibraltar, Luce. Why didn't I see it on your hand from way over there on the stage?'

Lucy blushed. 'I didn't have it on when I was playing. I'm not used to the feel of it on my hand yet.'

'I guess not,' Thorne teased. 'Plus you could blind the customers if it reflects the wrong way. When is the day?'

'In May,' Lucy said. 'Second Saturday, hold the date. I want to tell Gwyn. Do you think it's okay?'

Thorne hesitated. 'It's fine,' he said. 'Just don't be hurt if she doesn't respond the way you want her to. She'll come around, but she'll need time.'

Lucy squared her shoulders. 'Well, I need a maid of honor, so here goes.'

She marched herself to the office and slipped in the door, knocking after she was already in the room. If she'd knocked before, Gwyn might have told her to go away. It had happened.

Gwyn looked up, her brows furrowed. Then she smoothed the frown into a placidly bland expression. 'You played well, Lucy,' she said quietly. 'We haven't had a full house in weeks. People were waiting for you to come back.'

Lucy sat next to the desk, glancing at the spreadsheets Thorne had always managed. Gwyn had been hiding back in the office for months. Ever since she'd learned she'd been played by a master. 'I went to my father's grave today.'

Gwyn's eyes narrowed. 'I would have spit on it.'

'I did,' Lucy said, then shrugged when Gwyn's brows shot up. 'I thought about it,' she amended. 'I needed to go for me. For closure, whatever the hell that is.'

Gwyn glanced at Lucy's hand. 'You have new bling,' she said carefully.

Lucy stared down at her finger. 'JD proposed. I said yes.' She looked up, met Gwyn's eyes. 'I want you to be my maid of honor. I want you to sing at my wedding.'

Gwyn let out a very quiet sigh. 'I'd be happy to be the maid. But get someone else to sing. Lucy,' she said between her teeth when Lucy started to protest. 'Get someone else to sing. I'm not going to. I can't. Not yet. Please respect that.'

Lucy nodded, relieved and dismayed at once. 'Are you angry with me?'

Gwyn's eyes filled. 'No,' she whispered. 'I'm happy for you. I need you to believe that.'

Lucy's broken leg and ribs had mended, but Gwyn's heart had not. 'I believe you.'

Gwyn grabbed Lucy's hand. 'We have a lot of planning to do.

Leave it all to me. You'll have the best wedding in the history of forever. You'll have the reception here, of course.'

Lucy sat back as Gwyn put the club's books away and began to make a list. Gwyn filled up a page with to-do items, then her pencil stilled and her shoulders sagged. 'Stop looking at me like that. I'm okay.' One side of her mouth lifted in a sad parody of her old smile. 'I will be okay. You'll see. For now, I have to plan what will be the happiest goddamn day of your entire life.' She waved her hand at the door. 'Leave me to make a list. You're on in five.'

Lucy closed the office door behind her, unsurprised to find JD waiting for her outside.

'How'd it go?' he asked and she shrugged.

'Better than I thought.'

He dipped his head to kiss her gently but thoroughly. 'Better still?'

'Yes, much better.' Once again he'd softened the edge of her worry. She lifted on her toes to kiss him again, still surprised at the instant yearning that welled up inside of her every time he touched her. 'I love you,' she whispered against his mouth and felt him smile.

'I love you too.' He ran his hands down her back, closing over her rear end. 'I keep thinking of the last time I kissed you here, in the club.'

Her body grew warm. She hadn't been cold in six months. 'If you're thinking what I think you're thinking, you can stop thinking it right now. It's November. It's too cold for an alley.'

JD grinned, his dimples appearing, making her wish it were twenty degrees warmer. 'Then I can't wait for spring.'

Keep reading for exclusive bonus material from

you belong
to me

and an extract from
the next in the Baltimore series

no one
left to tell

The story behind
you belong to me

Years ago I became a *Law & Order* addict, watching the show whenever I could. One day I was watching the opening credits, where Jack McCoy and his Assistant District Attorney du jour are walking toward the camera with Lenny Briscoe with his partner, and I thought, that's the series I want to write.

So I did. Two cops, two prosecutors, all working together, their stories intertwined. It was the first time I sat down and planned a series before starting the first book.

Where are the you belong to me characters now?

- Detective JD Fitzpatrick still works homicide. When the job gets too much to bear, he is soothed by Lucy's music and the sound of their son's laughter. He has recently joined VCET, the Baltimore PD/FBI task force led by Joseph Carter, and has been partnered with Special Agent Kate Coppola. In his spare time, he coaches a youth softball team.
- Dr Lucy Trask has returned to the morgue, her maternity leave over. But she works part-time so that she can spend time with her son, Jeremiah, named after her old teacher and mentor, Jeremiah (Jerry) Pugh.
- Gwyn Weaver is still single. She has never gotten over her involvement with a murderer and the darker side of her personality is becoming stronger. She wants to make murderers pay, but still maintains enough of her honor and humanity to keep from going vigilante. But she is ready for a huge change, senses it's just over the horizon, but she doesn't know what it will be. (I do!)
- Thomas Thorne continues to manage a thriving defense practice, but with the addition of a death scene investigator, he has expanded his practice to include private investigations. Thorne is very happy for Lucy and very worried about Gwyn. He doesn't take time to worry about himself, but despite all the women who parade in and out of his life, Thorne is lonely.

- Daphne Montgomery still works as a prosecutor in Baltimore and is the heroine of *Did You Miss Me?*
- Stevie Mazzetti continues to work in the police department and is the heroine of *Watch Your Back*.
- Cordelia Mazzetti stars alongside her mom, Stevie, in *Watch Your Back*.
- Clay Maynard continues his private investigative work as the hero in *Watch Your Back*.

Fun Facts about
you belong to me

- I hadn't planned for Lucy's alter ego to be quite so . . . animated. Her leather wearing self was inspired by a few seconds of the movie *27 Dresses*, where the main character is trying on the twenty-seven dresses she's worn as a bridesmaid over the years. One of the outfits was goth and I thought, *There. That's Lucy*.
- Lucy's music just happened as I wrote. A year after the book's release, a reader sent me a link to a Lindsay Sterling video in which she plays the electric violin in a very cool rendition of *The Phantom of the Opera*. Her costumes, the energy of her music . . . she is Lucy Trask. How very cool!
- Lucy's friend, Gwyn Weaver, is a former circus performer who ran away from the circus to sing with a rock band only to find herself working for Thomas Thorne. I thought, 'Nobody will believe this character,' and then one day as I was writing, I went for a manicure. The nail tech was new and . . . a former circus performer who'd run away with a rock band. Living in Sarasota, you occasionally meet circus performers. Sarasota, Florida was the winter home for Ringling Brothers Circus and the location for John and Mabel Ringling's Circus Museum and the Ringling Clown College. Gwyn has a fascinating story – I can't wait to tell it!
- The name of Lucy's club, Sheidalin, is taken from CL Wilson's *Tairen Soul* series (with her permission, of course). In Wilson's books, the sheidalin are mystical truthspeakers. In my books Sheidalin is the sum of certain letters from three names, each name representing someone who the three owners has loved and lost. 'Lin' is Linus, Lucy's older brother who she adored.

no one left to tell

Prologue

Six years earlier

He was near. Crystal could hear his heavy breathing, feel him watching her. If she looked to the right, past the perfectly manicured hedge, she'd see him. His eyes would be hungry, his body aroused. But she didn't look at him. Wouldn't give him the satisfaction.

Instead she glanced over her shoulder. The door to the gardener's shed was ajar, just as he had said it would be.

The gardener's shed. She lifted her chin. He could have had her meet him anywhere on the grand estate, but he'd chosen the gardener's shed. She'd make him pay for that. She'd make him pay for everything he'd done.

She quietly pushed at the door to the shed, taking a last look behind her. The party by the pool was in full swing, the music loud enough to be heard in the next county. Luckily the estate was as big as the next county or the cops would have already been here, handing out citations. She smiled bitterly, the very idea ridiculous.

The cops would never hand out citations here.

Which was a good thing for the dancers, she supposed. *And for me.* Everyone was so busy having fun that no one had seen her slip away. The partiers in the pool were having the most fun – coke and sex the party favors of choice. But not everyone was in the pool. The dance floor under the bobbing Chinese lanterns boasted its share of gyrating bodies. Every woman still clothed was dressed to the hilt, making Crystal grateful she'd had the good sense to go for the tiny, expensive dress and the even more expensive shoes. Her credit card was maxed out.

But I fit in. Well enough to get her entrée to the party of the season – and that was the important thing. She wanted – no, she *needed* – to be here. To see his face when she told him who she really was. That she had evidence that would ruin him.

That she now owned him.

He'd be shocked. Stunned. He might even beg.

Crystal smiled. She really hoped he begged.

She flicked a final glance at the big house, looming large and powerful on the hill above the partying crowd. *He could have had me there, in one of the bedrooms*. There were, after all, ten of them, each one decorated like something out of a magazine.

But here she was, stepping into the gardener's shed. No matter. *Someday all of this will belong to me.*

She closed the door behind her and frowned. This really was a gardener's shed. It was filled with tools and smelled of gasoline. Meticulously organized, the walls were covered with anything and everything a gardener would need to keep up an estate this size. Two riding mowers took up most of the concrete floor. There was no convenient cot in the corner as she'd expected. Not really any room to do anything.

Crystal rolled her eyes. *Except maybe kneel*. It figured.

The door behind her opened, closed again. 'Amber,' he said.

Crystal took a moment to still her racing heart. *Amber*. That's how she'd introduced herself. If he'd known her real name, he never would have met her here. He would have ignored her, just as he'd ignored the phone messages she'd left with the damn butler up in the big house. That was the tricky part about blackmail. You actually had to get the target's attention to lay out the terms. She had his attention now.

Showtime, girl. Make this count. Your future rides on the next five minutes.

'You came,' she murmured seductively. 'I wasn't sure you would.'

He chuckled, the sound far from friendly. 'You knew I was there,' he said, 'watching you.'

She kept her voice smooth. 'Yes. I was hoping for somewhere a

478

little more . . . comfortable. Somewhere we can . . . talk.'

He made a humming sound, considering. 'Talk? I don't think so. *Crystal*,' he added and her heart leapt to close her throat.

'You knew,' she whispered.

'Of course I knew. I had you followed. Pretty thing like you, coming on to me. I have to be careful. There are all kinds of bad people out there, Crystal. You never know who might try something stupid. Like blackmail. Are you going to blackmail me, Crystal?'

Fighting panic, she slowly lifted her arm to retrieve the lipstick-tube of pepper spray she'd slipped into her tiny handbag, glad she'd come prepared. Mentally she counted the steps to the door. Six steps. She could do six steps. She'd get by him.

She had to.

Go for the spray slowly. No sudden moves. Don't let him see your fear. He likes your fear.

He came closer and she could feel the heat of his body. 'You never should have come.' There was a mocking lilt to his voice that chilled her to the bone.

'I have pr—' Something silky brushed against her jaws a split second before it slid down to her throat and tightened. *Proof. I have proof.* But the words wouldn't come.

Can't breathe. She flailed instinctively, her nails clawing at her throat. She kicked backward, trying to hit his knees, his groin, anything she could reach, but he yanked her up until her feet no longer touched the ground.

No. Please. No. Her lungs were burning. She pawed at her purse, grabbing the pepper spray, fumbling as she pulled at the cap. *Just get away. Have to get away.*

She wrenched the cap from the tube. *I don't want to die. Please don't let me die.*

'Bitch,' he muttered. 'You come here, threatening me. My family. Did you think that would work? Did you think any of this would work?'

She aimed the spray, but his hand clamped over her wrist, twisting, forcing the tube lower. Forcing her finger to press. New pain shot through her eyes, burning, blinding her. She screamed, but her voice was trapped. She was trapped. She dropped the tube, her hands desperately rubbing her eyes.

Make it stop. Please, make it—

He stepped back, breathing hard. Her hands swung limply at her sides. He dropped her to the floor. She was dead. He'd killed her.

I did it. For a long time he'd wondered how it would feel to drain the life of another. Now he knew. He'd finally done it.

The bitch. *She thought she could come here. Control me.* She'd learned. The hard way. *Nobody controls me.* He wadded the silk scarf with which he'd choked her, shoved it in his pocket. Leaned over to scoop her purse from the floor and hid it under his coat. He opened the door a fraction.

Nobody was coming. Nobody was watching. Everyone was partying. Having a great time. The music of the band would have covered any sounds they'd made. He slipped from the shed and disappeared behind the hedge. It was done.

One

Baltimore, Maryland
Tuesday, April 5, 6.00 A.M.

Paige Holden pulled her pick-up into the last parking place in the lot, a scowl on her face. Of course it was the one farthest from her apartment. Of course it was raining.

If you were back home, you'd be pulling into your own garage right now and you'd stay warm and dry. You never should have left Minneapolis. What were you thinking?

It was the mocking voice. She hated the mocking voice. It seemed to slither into her mind when she was least prepared, usually when she was most exhausted. Like now.

'Fuck off,' she muttered, and the Rottweiler in her passenger seat gave a low growl that Paige took to be agreement. 'If we were back home, that little kid would still be with that bitch of a so-called mommy.' Her teeth clenched at the memory, only hours old. She wasn't sure she'd ever erase the sight of that child's terrified face from her mind. She didn't want to.

She'd accomplished something tonight. Someone was safe who otherwise wouldn't be. That was what she needed to hold on to when the mocking voice intruded. The faces of the victims she had kept safe were what she needed to remember when she woke from the nightmare. When the guilt rose in her throat, choking her.

Zachary Davis would be okay. Eventually. *Because I was there tonight.*

'We did good, Peabody,' she announced firmly. 'You and me.'

The dog pawed at the truck's door. He'd been cooped up with

her in the cab for hours, patiently waiting out the night. Doing his duty. *Guarding me.*

That he did so made her feel safe. That she still needed a protection dog to feel safe in the dead of night annoyed her. That she still jumped when anyone made a sudden move pissed her off. But for now, that's how it was and she was learning to live with it. Her friends back home told her to give herself more time, that it had only been nine months, that recovery from an assault could take years.

Years. Paige didn't intend to wait that long. Briskly, she pulled her hood over her head, clipped Peabody's leash to his collar. She'd walk him, then grab a coffee and a shower before her next appointment.

And then she'd catch a few hours' sleep. When she got tired enough, she didn't dream. A few hours of dream-free sleep sounded like heaven.

Peabody made a beeline for his favorite spot, the lamppost where the neighborhood dogs stopped to pee. He was sniffing when her cell jangled. Juggling the umbrella, she glanced at the display before wedging the phone between her ear and shoulder. It was her partner of three months, who until she was a licensed PI was really her boss.

'Where are you?' Clay Maynard demanded, bypassing any greeting as usual. He was brusque, maybe even a little rude, but he was very smart. And still grieving a devastating loss. Because Paige keenly understood his grief, she cut him some slack.

Under the gruffness resided a good man who, in the three months since she'd moved to Baltimore, had become more like a big brother than a boss. She'd trained with dozens of over-protective 'big brothers' just like him during the fifteen years in her old karate *dojo*, and she knew how to deal with his irritation. Keep it cool, make him laugh.

'Standing under a lamppost watching Peabody pee. If you want,' she added wryly, 'I can send a photo. Peabody won't mind an invasion of his privacy to ease your mind.'

There was a beat of silence, then a grudging chuckle. 'I'm sorry. I called your landline and you didn't answer. I figured you'd be home by now.'

Paige wanted to remind him she was thirty-four, not four, and that he was her partner and not her keeper, but she did not. He'd found his last partner brutally murdered. He didn't want to feel responsible for anyone else's death, and this Paige completely understood, maybe even better than Clay himself.

Thea's face, always hovering somewhere on the edge of her mind, now barreled front and center. Terrified, with that gun to her head. Then dead.

And no matter how many Zachary Davises you save, she'll still be dead.

'I had to give my statement to the cops.' Thea's face faded to the edge of her mind, replaced with what she'd witnessed through a window just hours before.

'Had you seen anything like that before?' he asked.

'The mom snorting coke, sure.' It was one of her earliest memories, one she rarely shared. 'The mom letting her son be groped by her strung-out boyfriend, no.'

Six-year-old Zachary Davis was the subject of a brutal custody battle. Mom had developed a cocaine addiction. Dad filed for divorce and sole custody. Mom was fighting for joint custody, claiming she'd gone clean. Worrying the court would side with Mom, John Davis hired Clay to provide proof that his wife was actively using drugs.

Which was why Paige, as the junior member of Clay's PI agency, had been sitting outside Sylvia's apartment all night, taking pictures. They'd expected Sylvia to do coke. That she'd let her boyfriend put his hands on Zachary . . . Paige hadn't expected that.

'He would have raped a little boy,' Clay said evenly. 'You stopped that from happening. Now Sylvia will have a record – for possession and for prostituting her son.'

'I was lucky. A cruiser was a minute away when I called 911. If it had been any longer, I would have gone in myself, kicked in the door if I'd needed to. I couldn't have stood there watching that child be assaulted.'

'I couldn't have either, but the boyfriend had a gun. Your black belt wouldn't have protected you from a bullet.'

Paige found herself rubbing her shoulder where an ugly puckered scar marred her skin. Clay had been kind. He easily could have added, *like it didn't last summer*.

Her palms suddenly clammy, she wiped them on her jeans, straightening her spine. 'I had my gun.' Which she hadn't that night. *I'll never make that mistake again.*

THRILLINGLY GOOD BOOKS
FROM CRIMINALLY
GOOD WRITERS

CRIME FILES BRINGS YOU THE LATEST RELEASES FROM TOP CRIME AND THRILLER AUTHORS.

SIGN UP ONLINE FOR OUR MONTHLY NEWSLETTER AND BE THE FIRST TO KNOW ABOUT OUR COMPETITIONS, NEW BOOKS AND MORE.